CRUSHED

# CRUSHED

## KATE HAMER

FABER & FABER

First published in 2019
by Faber & Faber Ltd
Bloomsbury House
74–77 Great Russell Street
London WC1B 3DA

Typeset by Typo•glyphix
Printed and bound by CPI Group (UK) Ltd, Croydon CR0 4YY

Quotation on page 63 taken from *Macbeth: York Notes for AS & A2*
(York Press, 2001); reproduced with permission.

A CIP record for this book
is available from the British Library

ISBN 978–0–571–33665–4

2 4 6 8 10 9 7 5 3 1

For 'M', my strange enchanted boy

And oftentimes, to win us to our harm,
The instruments of darkness tell us truths,
Win us with honest trifles, to betray's
In deepest consequence.

*Macbeth*, ACT 1, SCENE 3

Parents, you have been my undoing and your own.

*A Season in Hell*, ARTHUR RIMBAUD

The idea of having a knife close by without him even knowing plunges through me in a shock and wakes me up from this lank and dreadful state. The pointed carving knife is too sharp to hide in my pocket – it would slice right through. I take it out of the drawer. The curve of it has a deathly menace. In this house it's used for carving, boning, forcing deep into the flesh and twisting there. It's been here for as long as I remember, and each and every time I've glimpsed that menace it's caused me to shudder, even at the age of five, so now it seems the most fitting and best thing to take, like it's been waiting for its purpose all along. He will not see it. He will not know it's there. Only I will know that, how close it's got to him, and when he leaves, when I see his figure moving off away across the fields, only I will know that there was another scenario already played out in my mind, one where I've torn out my anger and fear on him, one where he is left ripped and bloody, his insides hanging out in ribbons. And knowing that will cause electricity to stir about me. It will make my hair stand straight up with static and the power of it will gather inside my belly. It will keep me going for days. It will show me how I'm in control, of my thoughts and everything, and if I order it all correctly they can work for me rather than against. I take one of my mother's snowy tea towels – bleached, then boiled for an hour on the stove's top until a season of mist and rain fogs the windows – and I wrap it round and round the shining blade and with precise care insert the package in the pocket of my mac.

# Act I

# THE FALL

# I

# Phoebe

It was a book full of hate. The words must have been scratched underground at the dawn of time. They should've stayed there and never come to the surface.

It set it all off again.

I've had to come to the only place that can calm me down. The corner of Pulteney Bridge. The only thing is, I've lost a shoe so people keep looking. My tights have an open gash from toe to thigh, flashing bright white flesh. I try to cover my face with my hair so I won't be recognised. Things get reported back. I don't know where my bag has gone – perhaps I dropped it on the way and didn't notice.

I'd been calm as the sea before that book. It may as well have come crawling towards me on its elbows, dragging its black and bursting body behind. I should have heeded the inkling I had straight away that it was a bomb about to explode.

I lean against the cool stone of the bridge and look over the water to the weir. Usually it soothes me, but not today. In this water are hidden many ancient things. Sometimes one pops out – a coin, a tin mask, a figure of a bull, a crown, a pin. People are always surprised. Why should they be? The river is at the end of a vast drain sluicing straight down from the Roman bathhouse.

The sun glints off the water. The ancient buildings look more friendly in this light. It turns their darkness the colour of honey. The trees are full of early summer and shake their leaves in the breeze. Yet despite the bright surroundings I cannot be contained this time and I have to lean further over the wall, sickness cramping my stomach.

I'd tried to explain to Grace.

'It's just a book,' she said. 'It's just a dusty old copy with half the pages falling out because they won't pay for new ones. What are you on about?'

Her soft blue eyes travelled from side to side as she looked behind me. Her hair is cropped close to her head. The sight of it always makes me feel tender because I know she cuts it herself. It's so short you can see the shape of her pretty little skull. I wanted to get her attention back. I cupped my hand over my mouth and whispered to her, quoting from the text.

'I've been eating on the "insane root" again. Not now. Not today. A couple of weeks ago.'

Her eyes snapped back on my face and she nodded and gave a little laugh. 'I'm partial to a few substances myself.' Then she frowned. 'You want to be careful, though, you know. Stuff like that can be dangerous.'

I turned away from her. I was bored of tellings-off. I felt light and free. Nothing bad was going to happen. It was just the warm day that had made me feel there could be a bomb, and Mr Jonasson being so close. All the pieces of me that had flown out came back and began fitting themselves together safely with hardly any gaps left in between.

That's where it should've stopped.

But, no. I had to take it further, didn't I? I had to go on testing myself, trying things out.

I've been told once, *thoughts are just that* by a woman with a face that looked like a little pussy-cat. The more I stared at her the more she seemed to resemble one.

Usually my tests are of the mundane kind. If I think *There will be a red car when I turn this corner*, perhaps there will be one. What if I wish for blackberry ice cream on the menu and there it is? If I want that plate to fall, it might and shatter on the stone floor. If, if, if, if. The results so far have been inconclusive.

Not this time.

It must've been the darkness of the story that made me do it. It was to show myself it couldn't happen, that the light and airy feeling was how things were going to be from now on. One last little time, I *thought*. TRY IT OUT.

Was it five or ten minutes later we heard the commotion? Perhaps I was the only one that went towards it. I slipped out and ran down the road until I saw. There was mangled metal. Blood ran down the walls.

I froze a good few moments before I ran again.

I reach for the front door key that I wear on a heavy chain around my neck. It's more precious to me than any piece of jewellery could ever be. Hard won. I clasp it now like a rosary. There's probably keys down there in the water too, along with the other old Roman stuff washed down from the baths. I can almost see it all, bubbling up to the top. Statues and pendants and nails surfacing at once in a thick and filthy mass, and I feel sick again and have to lean right over the wall. A car behind me beeps, once, loudly. They thought I was about to fall, or jump. Maybe I was. I need to move, but maybe I don't have a choice.

# 2

# Orla

Well, that was sickening.

I feel shaken to the pit of my stomach as I walk away. They haven't got enough tents to cover it all up because the blood goes right along the wall on Walcot Street. They were trying to do it in the chaos and then they made everyone drive or walk away and closed the road as quick as they could. Horrific. Stuff like this just doesn't happen in a place like Bath. I didn't mean to look but it's hard not to. It was mesmerising. It's unbelievable how much blood people have in them. The red was in a stripe coming out from the back of the plastic they've rigged up. I could see how it had got cemented in between the blackened old stones and I wondered how they were ever going to get it out. They'll have to scrape right into the gaps and use hoses so there'll be a wash of pink water swirling across the road.

Behind the yellow tape there's people trundling around in white plastic suits now. They look so out of place against all that dirty ancient stone, it's like flickering beings have been beamed in from the future. My heart feels like it's never going to slow down to its usual pace. I want to cry so badly. I'm only trying to hold on until I get home. I concentrate hard on looking at the normal little things I see every day to keep me going until I can wail in my bedroom. There's a shop of mirrors full of glitter. There's the giant carved head looming over the undertaker's door – Bath is full of odd things like that, carvings and statues and old buildings. When I was little I always used to whisper 'Hello' to the head as I passed because he looked like he was asking, 'Is it your turn yet? Will you be next?' And I thought starting a conversation might please him so he'd decide not to choose me. He seems to be staring extra hard and pointedly today. It must be because of what just happened. 'Hello,' I whisper in a trembling voice. 'Not me right now. I'm not ready.'

By the time I get to the fruit shop with bright green plastic grass in the window, my breathing has stopped hurting so much.

How many times and in different lights and times of day have I seen all these ordinary things? Hundreds. Thousands. I try to make them take the place of what I've just seen.

That's when I see Phoebe's bag dumped in the shop doorway. The sickness returns. What's happened to her? *What's happened to her?* I pick the bag up and stand, rubbing the striped canvas between my fingers, wondering what to do. It seems strangely violent, this familiar bag being here that I've seen a million times, swinging on Phoebe's shoulder, the hard outline of books showing through the fabric. It's not exactly her dumped body but something makes me think of it. I hug it close, shaking now. God, she frightens me sometimes. It terrifies me the way she carries on. My heart lurches: what if it's her that's been killed on Walcot Street? What if it was her blood I saw? I close my eyes and sway, the idea being so shockingly awful. No, it can't be. I won't allow myself to think that. I'll never make it back.

I hurry on, the taste of home so strong now it's almost on my tongue. I can't wait to collapse inside and feel safe, to phone Phoebe and make sure she's all right. But up ahead are Belinda and her crew, and they're walking so slowly I'll have no choice but to pass them – it'll look too odd if I slow down to their pace behind.

As I catch up with them their tense bright faces tighten towards me.

'Orla, did you see it?' Samantha's eyes are starry with the sight of the blood. The ribbon of it in the sun is still glittering her eyes.

'Yes. Horrible.'

We all nod even though I can see it's put a spring in all their steps. They'll go home and dissect it together, crouching on one of their beds with their arms around their knees and big, pointy-cornered smiles on their faces they can't wipe off they're so excited.

It's such a beautiful day. The sky is a perfect blue. I have an intense longing to be off this dusty pavement with these girls clucking and mauling over the horror like they're actually sticking their fingers into it and dabbling there. I think of our garden just down the road. It's my favourite place in the world. Walled in on three sides and with an apple tree in the middle. In the summer, green vines crawl up the brickwork and the scent of the passion flowers passes over me. Mum and Dad aren't really that into it so I can poke about in there to my heart's content. Even when it's cold I'll sit out on the bench wrapped in a blanket. In the winter the plants have their own bare beauty with all their bones and pods showing like they've been turned inside out. I need to be there now.

'Got to go.' A wave of awkwardness washes over me. What's wrong with me? I can't even make a quick getaway without breaking into a terrible sweat.

'Hey,' Belinda calls after me. 'What was it Grace was saying today?'

I shrug like I don't know but I heard perfectly well. I was sitting right next to her. Someone had just read a piece out from the supplementary notes. It was Simon, I think.

'The role of the witch is to demonstrate the female, intuitive, otherworldly power of the mind.'

And while we were all pondering it, supposedly thinking about discussion points, Grace came up with one of her own.

She said, 'Did somebody actually write this shit?'

It wasn't even under her breath. In a way it was kind of thrilling, like breaking the law must be.

Everyone heard but nothing happened about it. It never does. She gets away with anything because of her *circumstances*. Grace might be only sixteen, while Phoebe and me are seventeen, but Grace always seems by far the oldest – as if she's twice our age and she's been married and had three kids already.

Finally I see our house and the face of it seems like the sweetest thing I've ever laid eyes on. As I'm trying to get the key into the lock, the door opens and I collapse inside into Mum's arms.

'Did you see?' she asks. 'Carol from church just called and told me what's happened. She's stuck in the traffic.'

I nod and I can feel my mouth turning down so sharp at the corners it actually hurts.

'Oh Orla.' She hugs me tight. 'My darling, darling girl. I was hoping you hadn't. I was hoping you'd never have to witness something like that.'

# 3

# Phoebe

The door glides shut behind me and I stand in the hallway, sniffing the air like a hunted animal.

*She's* here.

She might be smoking upstairs but the smell gets into every last corner of the house. Left to its own devices, this place smells of its own loveliness. Hard to put your finger on it: a smidgen of dust, honey, jute rugs, good clean soap.

The cigarette smoke is an abomination; it takes forever to fade.

There's the faint sound of the television from above. The front door closed with such a small metallic click, I'm hoping against hope I'm as yet undetected. My heart beats so hard I can feel it in my jaw. I need time to deal with the dreadful chaos of my appearance before I'm seen. To deal with the hole in my tights that splits down my leg from thigh to foot, with my bare toes that are grey and dirty at the ends where they've scraped the pavement, and decide what to do about the missing shoe.

I begin softly, softly creeping up the first set of stairs that leads to the sitting room.

The fourth step creaks and I look down and my stomach twists into a terrible and painful panic. It's all I can do to not cry out because for the first time I see *the book*, the one that caused all the trouble, has been in my grasp *the whole time* like we've grown into each other. My hand is clamped so hard into it in a claw, I have to use my other hand to prise the fingers off one by one. Deep indentations are left on the soft red cover and the gold letters that spell out *Macbeth*.

How could I not have known it was there? I could've thrown it in the river, where it belongs, but now it's got into the house, infecting everything. It's brought the murder inside. It's brought in its hate.

There's a movement overhead and I have no choice but to shove the book up my jumper. I look behind me and with another lurch see that my cut toe has left a badge of blood on the golden boards of the hallway. I slither back down, fall to my knees, lick my cuff and scrabble it off.

A voice calls from upstairs.

'Phoebe?'

Oh God. Oh God. If I rush past as if I haven't heard, even with hobbling on the side of my foot, and get beyond the living room and then up the second flight of stairs, I might just make it to the bathroom. At least there's a lock on the one on the upstairs landing. As I sprint upstairs I hear her clonking across the wooden floor of the living room in her heels. The noise gets louder the closer she gets to the door and I vault up the second flight. I lunge for the bathroom, just managing to pull the skirt flaring out behind me as if I'm tucking in my tail. I push the bolt across as I hear the living room door open.

Her voice calls up the stairs. 'Phoebe? Is that you?'

I keep silent, breathing onto the mirror above the sink so my image is obliterated by condensation. It shrinks to a tiny circle, a nucleus of itself, and I huff out so the mist balloons again. My fingers pass all over my head and face, smoothing, flattening, wiping, making good any damage.

Close to my ear – 'Phoebe, what's the matter?'

My whole body jerks. How come I didn't hear her coming up the stairs? She must've taken her shoes off. She's so close the door vibrates.

'Nothing.' I stand on the tiles, balling my fists.

'I need to talk to you, Phoebe.'

'What about?' I ease off my shoe and as silently as possible lift the lid of the bin and place it inside. I put my hands under my skirt, hook my thumbs into the waistband of my tights and peel them down.

'There's been a murder down on Walcot Street. It's just been on the news. Some poor man squashed by a car against the wall. Did you see anything?'

See anything? *I caused it.* I want to scream – I thought murder, and murder happened. I thought darkness, and darkness was right there. It was supposed to mark the end of it and it's begun all over again. However many times that counsellor pussy-cat face told me my thoughts were as insubstantial as a breath of air, that they certainly didn't have the power to make things happen outside of my own self, in my heart of hearts I never did believe her.

I got there before the emergency services even. The traffic had stopped, zig-zagging this way and that, and people were climbing out of their cars to look or covering their eyes. Car alarms were going off all over the place. You could see exactly where the body had been scraped from the band of blood along the wall. The car that had done it was mounted up on the pavement, the engine still full of roaring threat. It was metallic grey with bull bars on the front. The driver was completely still. He was staring at the body on his front bumper as if he couldn't believe it was there. The body was so mashed and bloodied I hadn't even known it was a man.

I think I'm going to be sick. I clap my hand over my mouth to catch it. I sense her straining to hear on the other side of the door.

'Phoebe? Are you all right?'

I take my hand away. 'Mum. I'll be down in a minute.'

'Tell me what's the matter. You sound strange.'

'Won't be a moment.'

I flush the toilet and with some wet scrunched-up toilet paper I dab at the cut under my big toe, but it's dried to almost nothing now. I'm a quick healer. Always have been.

When I open the bathroom door I get the shock of my life. She's still there, waiting.

'Oh.' I can't help it sounding like a cry. At the bottom of the stairs her high-heeled courts lie on their side like some killing has been committed on their wearer.

'Your shoes.' I realise I'm not making much sense. 'What are they doing down there?'

As if puzzled, she follows my line of sight. 'I don't want to make marks on the new carpet. Listen, I need to talk to you. Come to the sitting room when you're done.' She pauses, frowns. 'What happened to your tights?'

I look down and realise I have them still balled up in my hand.

Inspiration strikes and I don't skip a beat this time. 'Bled through. My period started.'

This is a risky strategy. She's always asking about my periods, wanting to know the details. Sometimes I feel she'd like to weigh me before and after, and weigh all the blood too, and keep the information in some little secret notebook she'd read in bed at night with her glasses stuck on the end of her nose. If there were any discrepancies I'd have to have an explanation for them. On the other hand, this may just be the right trick to distract her, and my period is just about due so it all fits in. All these things are like coins falling into correct slots one after the other, giving me an enormous sense of relief.

She nods. It's worked. 'I'll see you in a minute.'

I go to my bedroom to put on new tights. I take out the copy of *Macbeth* from under my jumper and put it on my bed. I've held it so hard its shape is malformed. I close my eyes and try to think. I'd liked the beginning, loved it even, the witches with their beards and rags. They'd excited me. They were glamorous in a way. Then came the murders and I'd felt only uncomfortable stirrings, nothing dramatic. Then I'd gone and done the experiment. The one I'd vowed never to do again, the one that pussy-cat face tried to tell me wasn't real. I said to myself, *In the next ten minutes, make something bad happen.* Make something as bad as all the killings in *Macbeth*. If I think hard enough about it, it's possible it will come to pass. It will be a final conclusive test to see if my thoughts can make things happen. Of course, I'd done it many times before with no real consequences. I was on the point of not needing to any more. Now this. Now I know I'll have to spend hours and hours trying to control my thoughts and turn them away from bad directions. It will take all my energy.

Dear pussy-cat face, see, thoughts are *not* just that. I told you so.

I put the torn tights under my mattress. Something else to sort out later along with retrieving the shoe and perhaps burying it all in the garden.

16

When I walk down to the living room, Mum is smoking again. She lets out short sharp jets as she watches the TV screen. This living room must be one of the most beautiful in Bath. It's on the first floor and we're high up so you can see the city and the hills that circle around. It's breathtaking. It has yellow velvet sofas and a lofty Georgian ceiling patterned with paint-encrusted acorns and oak leaves from which a sturdy five-armed brass fitting hangs. Polluting this room with dirty smoke is a criminal act.

It's as beautiful as Rapunzel's tower.

When I was little I loved fairy tales and the one I read over and over was *Rapunzel*. I always felt I'd be fine if I could just live like her for a week or two. I'd have a chance to heal over and face things. What I really envied about Rapunzel is that she had to let her hair down before anyone could get in. She could decide, and her hair was her weapon that kept her safe. As far as I was concerned, Rapunzel in that high tower was living like a pig in shit.

'I had a call from the school saying you ran off.'

I freeze.

'What's going on? Do you know anything about what happened? The traffic was terrible.'

'Uh-huh.' I'm thinking, hard. 'No, I don't know anything.'

'Where did you go, then?'

I stay mute, just shrug my shoulders, and she steps closer, coming towards me.

Every time I look at her I realise I'd prefer to see her through something: a honeycomb blanket; a thick sheet of greenish glass; a grille like the one the priest hides behind in a church. When there is nothing between us I have a strong urge to bite her nose.

I let my fringe fall into my face to veil her from me.

'For God's sake, push the hair out of your eyes,' she snaps.

I do, thinking, *Well, it's your nose.*

I take a step back to create distance. 'I thought I heard a crash, so I ran out. I didn't see anything, though.' As soon as it's out of my mouth I feel my story is entirely successful. Her face straightens out and the curiosity is replaced by a look of boredom.

'Well, you shouldn't have done. You know how I hate getting calls like that. You can't just take off whenever you feel like it.' She eyes me suspiciously. 'So, you didn't see *anything*?'

'No, no, no.' I back away with my hands in the air. I sense another visit to pussy-cat face coming on and I'd rather walk over hot coals than that. Breathe. Breathe.

She shakes her head. 'They're saying it couldn't possibly be an accident, that it was murder. Poor man got spread halfway down Walcot Street by the car. Dreadful.'

I think I really am going to be sick now. I put my hands up to my mouth. I'm lying, of course. I saw it all, but I ran away from it as fast as I could.

I wasn't going to get close to that, was I?

Back in my room I review what I've got to do. Before I came up I managed to turn the knives and scissors in the house so they point towards the living room and where *she* is. Pussy-cat face is the only one who knows about this habit and we worked hard to eliminate it, although sometimes needs must. I still have to dispose of the shoe and tights. Calm down enough to face dinner. The copy of *Macbeth* is still on my bed, glinting wickedly. Now I know for sure that that book is a curse. If I try to throw it away something else terrible will happen, so I'm going to have to live with it in the same room for now and that's another burden I'll have to bear. I try to keep things under control as much as possible, keep this room drained of myself too so there is nothing for *her* to go on – no clues that she can get hold of to examine or interrogate me. But it's exhausting just thinking about what I have to do to keep everything on an even keel. There's food for a starter. I take sandwiches to school, but they can be put in the bin or flushed down the loo so that's OK. Whenever the food goes into the bin, I'm so happy because I look at it and think, that could be part of me by now, adding to my hips and thighs and molecules. Sometimes I'll warm something in a pan, then grind it down the sink in the waste disposal so there'll be the smell of cooking in the kitchen when she comes back. You have to be forensic about these things. It's the only way to make them work. If she moans about the breadboard covered in crumbs I actually want to lean over to her and say, 'Look, don't you understand? It's evidence. I'm leaving you *evidence*.'

She disconcerts me with her comings and goings. Dad is a high-flying barrister so he's out nearly all the time, but Mum's job hours as a part-time speech therapist are wholly unpredictable and I never know quite when she's going to appear. It took ages for her to give me a front-door key, but it was getting ridiculous, the amount of times she came home and I was sitting on the doorstep in the rain, waiting for her. I know she was reluctant. Sometimes I wonder about her clients and feel so sorry for them, being forced to speak and having words dragged up out of their throats by *her*. I understand how they must feel. I know for a fact she's read my diary for many years. Every day I pluck a hair from my head and insert it in the page, only to find it on the floor on my return. How many thousands of hairs have I pulled from my head over the years for this purpose? Enough to make ten headfuls. The diary has become a kind of game between us. I'll have a thought, a real thought, then I'll translate it into my diary as something either puzzling or without meaning. So, for today, my real thought is, *I made murder. It was that play that made me think to do it.* Now I suspect again that my thoughts have consequences and everyone was lying about that. But I'll translate it in my diary as something like, 'Studied *Macbeth* today. The themes of regicide and the gradual descent into madness after committing an evil act are fascinating. As is the role of the witches who predict that Macbeth will be king, which actually prompts him to kill the King in the first place so without them he may never have done it. Looking forward to hearing more.'

I mean, what's she going to do with that?

I'll even spend time injecting that girlishly naïve tone to it for a measure of authenticity.

My mobile rings and makes me jump. It buzzes across the bed towards the copy of the mangled book.

'Phoebs?'

It's Paul. I know the Cockney edge to his voice straight away. It's so different from the country burr around here.

'Yes.'

'I've got some more— Bloody hell, you don't have to shove.' He must be talking to someone over his shoulder.

'Paul?'

His voice sounds far away. He's taken the phone away from his mouth.

'Leave me out of it,' I can hear him saying. 'You can't swing a frigging cat in here, let alone *that*.'

I curl my hand over the mouthpiece. 'Paul, Paul,' I whisper urgently.

He comes back, like he's been off swimming and has just popped to the surface. 'Listen, Phoebs, I gotta go.'

The line goes dead. I go to calls logged and press delete. Two seconds later it rings again and I jab the answer button without looking at the number.

'Paul . . .?'

'No, it's Orla.'

'Oh. Hello.' I can't keep the disappointment from my voice.

'Listen,' her voice is tinny, eager. 'I've got your bag. It was dumped in a shop doorway. What were you thinking of? Phoebe, are you there?'

'Thank you, thank you.' It's warm and very, very heartfelt the way I say it. I can picture the sticky warmth of it spreading down the phone and flushing her round cheeks a deep pink and making her speckled hazel eyes shine. I lean my face against the cold wall beside the bed. 'I'd completely forgotten about it.'

After I've got rid of her I lie back. I'm exhausted to my bones. I have the sense of disasters averted, one after the other. I've had to work so very hard to keep them at bay, and now I'm battle-weary from them and from the day. I let the softness of the pillow absorb the back of my head and just for a few moments allow myself to give in to a swelling tide of absolute relief.

# 4

# Grace

'You are such a good, good girl, Grace,' Mum says.

No I'm not, I think. I'm a horrible bitch who often feels tired and resentful, but one thing I will say to my credit is that I know what needs to be done, and I usually manage to plaster a smile on whatever.

This morning it was getting Mum ready for her big day with her friends who are coming round. It was getting her up early and taking her to the bathroom and pretending not to look at strategic moments while at the same time I washed and dried her, then levered her into her white polyester dress with the matching hat that looks like a garlic bulb. A hat, despite the fact she will be entertaining her friends Rosa and Averill inside. They have hats and she doesn't want to miss out. Now, the cups and saucers are set out ready, the bread is buttered and the Battenberg cake is sliced.

I look over the table, anxious I've missed something because things get on top of me sometimes and it can make me forgetful.

'Cheer up. It may never happen,' Mum says, and we both have a hollow laugh at that.

Mum's decline was a slow and rambling one. I must've noticed it first when I was about nine. It didn't seem anything then. The eye that slipped sideways, momentarily, then righted itself. The stumble on a stone in the road that, when I looked clear-eyed to the ground, wasn't actually there. It took a long time to get over the magic of the idea that really there had been an obstacle, something to stumble over, until my nine-, ten-, twelve-year-old eyes had to finally admit that there really was no stone in the road and never had been. Yet all these things were just part of the texture of our lives, like the loosened threads in the weave of my favourite green and black Welsh blanket. We slipped slowly into it. No shocks. No alarms. So by the time her diagnosis of MS came through, it was like it had happened long ago, and they were giving us old news that had already been dealt with.

My father leaving went along the same lines. He was there, or should I say more accurately his *presence* was there – because he came and went more or less as he pleased – through my early childhood. Then the presence got gradually less, like mist thinning. I think it's because of this, that there was nothing more definite in terms of a traumatic event – a huge row, a slammed door, a suitcase by the door – that I think of him as slightly ghostlike, as if something of him still lurks behind the framed photographs and the dusty display of artificial daisies and poppies on the sideboard.

The buzzer to our flat goes and I pick up the phone on the intercom.

'Come up,' I say to Rosa and Averill.

I buzz them through the main doors downstairs, help Mum into her wheelchair and wheel her through to the living room where the table is set out. Mum starts panicking a bit as I try to help her onto the dining chair, so we tuck the wheelchair under the table instead. She fusses around with the cups and saucers.

'Don't worry. It takes an age for Averill to persuade Rosa

to get into the lift anyway. You've got loads of time.' They both dislike the lift, especially Rosa; she always says she thinks she's going to have a fit in it. Plus they both say it smells bad, which it does, but as we live on the top floor of Bath's only tower block it's a bit awkward otherwise. Mum and I both sit looking at each other over the tea things.

'What's taking them so long?' she asks eventually. I haven't said but I was beginning to wonder myself. Then the buzzer sounds in the hallway again.

'Hang on a tick,' I say and go to answer it.

'We've had to come back outside, Grace,' says Averill. 'The lift's broken.'

'OK, well, you'll have to take the stairs. I'll put the kettle on.'

'Are you kidding?' I can hear Rosa's voice behind Averill's. 'You know how I am with heights. It's bad enough going in the lift.'

I sigh. 'Wait there. I'll be down now. Mum,' I call out. 'The lift's broken. I'm going to rescue them from outside.'

I run all the way to the ground floor and they're both standing in the weak sunshine, peering through the glass for me from under the brims of their hats.

'Come on,' I say. 'She's expecting you. You know this will be the highlight of her week. You can't let her down – you'll be fine.'

'Yes. You're right, dear,' says Rosa, tucking her handbag under her arm and hitching up her dress like she's about to scale the Andes. 'I will do my very, very best.'

The first two flights go quite well, then on the third I look behind me and she has frozen, her hand gripping onto the rail and the tuft of her white hanky poking out from underneath.

'Listen, dear.' Her mouth has gone strangely rictus-like. 'I'm not sure if I'm going to be able to do this. I don't want to let you down but . . .' She looks up, her eyes wide. 'I've had a bad week. That murder really upset me. It was a jealous rage, you know. Did you hear about it? A lad had been seeing this man's missus and the man found out – I'm not sure how, they didn't tell you that bit – and he went out looking all over Bath for him in this huge car of his, and when he eventually found him he went absolutely crazy and drove into him and ended up dragging him all down the wall in Walcot Street. Killed him. It was all over the news. Oh Lord, you did hear about it, didn't you?'

'Yeah, Daniel told me.'

'Are you still on with your lad?'

I suck in my cheeks. 'It's better not to watch the news, Rosa. You know it doesn't agree with you.'

'Yes, but . . .' Her hand grips tighter. 'It's hard not to when it's on your own doorstep.'

I don't point out it's not only when it's on her doorstep. The Twin Towers was almost two years ago and it still terrifies her. She really does need to stay away from the news.

A voice floats down from above. 'Girls, what's going on?'

It's Mum. She's managed to get herself out of our front door somehow.

'For fuck's sake,' I mutter under my breath. 'You two stay there,' I say and vault up the flights of stairs.

'Mum, honestly. How did you get out here? I hope you haven't locked us out.'

'I put the door on the latch. I wanted to see why they are taking so long.'

'Rosa's having a bit of an issue with the stairs. She'll be fine.'

25

'Rosa,' Mum shouts down the stairs. 'You can do it.'

A weak, wavering voice comes back. 'I'm not sure that I can, Jenny. I will try, though.'

I dart back down, panting now. They haven't moved an inch upwards.

'Let me take your arm,' I say to Rosa. I feel myself losing patience and I take a deep breath. 'You can hang onto me on one side and Averill will take the other.'

We manage another flight before Rosa sits down abruptly on the floor.

'No. I just can't, Grace. I'm sorry to let you down but I can't. I'm so dizzy I think I'm going to faint. I can't look.' She puts her head in her hands so she doesn't have to.

There's a burst of male voices from above us. It rings the building, bouncing floor by floor.

I look up. 'Mum. What's going on up there?'

Laughter peals down. 'Mum? Look, let me see what's happening.'

I run up the stairs again, breathless now and cursing all the sneaky fags I've had out on the balcony. Nearly at the top, I stop for a breather and hear heavy footsteps. Then – I can hardly believe it – around the corner comes Mum, her wheelchair being carried between Marshall and Harry from the flat next door like they were handling nothing heavier than a shopping bag. Mum is grinning and laughing as she gets swung about. 'Careful, boys,' she says, although you can tell she doesn't really mean it.

I put my forehead onto the backs of my hands for a second and just lean there, forehead to the banister.

When I look up she's seen me. 'Look, Grace. I'll go down to them. Stuff the Battenberg. We can all go to Jolly's.'

'No worries, Mrs H. We'll have you down there before you know it.'

I follow them, my heart lurching at the way they are practically running round the corners, making her laugh as she tips from side to side.

I have to heave up the stairs one last time to lock up, then I join them all outside.

'Thanks, boys,' says Mum.

'No problem, Mrs H. Anytime. Cheers, Grace.' Marshall and Harry make off into the day, bunching their puffa jackets up against the cold as a chill has interrupted the warm weather.

'Honestly,' I mutter, grabbing onto the handles of Mum's wheelchair. 'Come on then.' I try not to contemplate the fact that we might have got her down, but fuck knows where Marshall and Harry are going and if they will be here to carry her back up.

'Don't be a spoilsport, Grace, you'll put a downer on the day and it's not often enough I get out,' Mum says. I open my mouth to snap back but before I can she points. 'Look, there's Daniel.'

The other two women's heads whip round to look at Daniel crossing the grass with a bag of shopping under his arm. I feel the tips of my ears pinking.

'Hi Grace,' he says, smiling at me. He kissed me in the lift once and I nearly exploded. We've been sort of on and sort of off since then, but it's difficult, like it feels too much. I pull up my hood and tug it across my cheeks.

'Hey there.' Today he doesn't ask me anything; he only nods at us all and goes quickly inside. Maybe he's going off me or got tired of waiting. Who could blame him?

I turn and see Mum studying my face with that shrewd look of hers like she knows it all. 'What?' I say. 'Stop it.'

She twitches her shoulders in a shrug. 'I know I'm not allowed opinions,' she says.

'Maybe you've got an opinion about how we're going to get back upstairs,' I flash back at her, but she ignores me and it occurs to me then to see if Daniel will be around later to help me with Mum, but he's already disappeared up the stairwell. I might be just about able to manage the other side. I'm stronger than I look. I'll buzz him and see when we get back. I sigh heavily and tell myself to stop mooning over him like a silly bitch. We wheel off, the three of them chirping to each other like birds about the murder. I glance back, right to the top where our flat is, with its balcony looking down over the other buildings, and contemplate the absolute fucking irony of living in the one and only tower block in the whole of this city.

# 5

# Orla

There's my Phoebe. I catch her figure striding across the square. Her long blue coat ripples around her tall figure. She's chewing on what I can see is an orange. As she gets near she slings what's left of it into a bin and stands in front of me licking her fingers.

'You look lovely.' I feel a bit breathless, like I always do when I've just said something real. It must've sounded stupid but she just stops licking and smiles, her lips shiny from the juice.

'It's my disguise.'

I screw my eyes against the brightness, looking up at her. Often, I haven't got a clue how to respond to what she says.

She shoves her hands in her pockets and hunches forward.

'What were you doing just now?' She laughs but doesn't take her eyes off my face. I know I won't get away without answering. Sure enough: 'I saw you before you saw me. You looked moonstruck, craning your neck *up there*.' She cranks her head back so her dark hair falls away from her face as she looks up. It's the same spot that I was fixating on but she doesn't see what I see. The fall.

She sits next to me on the bench and puts her arms around me and gives me a hug, then lays her cheek on my shoulder. 'Come on, darling. What were you looking at? Tell Phoebe.'

There are two small interconnected squares in the centre of Bath: this one, with the looming face of the Abbey;

29

and the other, just a few steps away, surrounded by shops, the side of the Abbey and the old open-air Roman Baths complex, steam from its thermal spring hovering constantly above the wall. Whenever I'm waiting in this spot I always study the Jacob's ladder carved up the front of the Abbey. The angels climbing it seem in such awful danger, clinging on for dear life like they might be flung crashing to the ground at any minute. They look in as much peril as if they were swinging on one of those ladders dangling from a helicopter. It makes me dizzy to see them holding on, desperately trying to make it to heaven, but I can't rip my eyes away. I know that feeling. It captures something that I can't put into words.

I look down and see Phoebe's face has changed. She's seen someone behind me and she's forgotten all about the cross-questioning and she pulls her arms away. The next thing a man dumps himself down next to her and the bench shakes. His parka wafts out the smell of cigarette smoke.

She turns to him. 'Paul! What happened when I was talking to you on the phone last time? Sounded like you were about to have a fight.' She giggles a ridiculous baby's giggle. I roll my eyes but so she can't see me doing it.

Paul scrunches a nostril and breathes in sharply on one side, shifting some mucous about. 'Nah. Nothing like that. Just got a bit lively. You know, tasty.'

'Ooooh. Exciting.' Phoebe moves closer to him and they begin to speak in voices too low for me to catch.

I study him over the back of Phoebe's neck. His hair is cut in that boyish way close to his head and slicked down so you can see the paleness of his scalp in between. The boys who work in the garage that Dad takes his car to all have the same haircut. It reminds me of the feathers of a newborn chick, sparse and wet-looking from gel. The style is far too young for Paul. That and the fur around his parka hood fight against the groove that runs from his nose to the corner of his mouth and the thin tidal marks of lines around his eyes. His pale eyes flick up and down and sideways.

He looks up and catches me staring. 'Hey,' he says, extending his hand across Phoebe towards me.

I don't want to touch it. It's clean but thin and white, vulnerable, with fingertips that end in feminine points. The softness of it against his flinty eyes makes him seem more hard-edged somehow than if his hand was big and square and clasped mine in a rough handshake. I graze the tips of it and that feels feminine too, like I'm supposed to kiss it. The sensation makes my stomach squirm. I wonder if all this shows in my face.

Phoebe says, 'Orla, stop staring. It's rude,' so I suppose it must do. She's laughing again and I truly hate her at this moment. She's gone over to him and away from me without a second's thought.

'I'm not.' I stand abruptly, sick of the thick intrigue swirling about them.

'Don't go,' she says. 'Honestly, what's wrong with you? You can't take a joke or what?'

I look down. How I would love to be like her, all clean lines and pale skin against dark hair. She sprawls all over the bench, her legs apart. She's so careless. If I had beauty like that I'd hold it carefully, polish it, not let it get kicked about and dirty like she does. Sometimes I think she doesn't deserve it.

'Come on,' she says. 'This won't take a minute and then

we'll do something nice. Go for coffee or an ice cream or something.'

*Stop it,* I think. *I'm not a little girl to be wheedled around with treats.* It's obvious I should leave but I'm rooted to the spot.

'Yeah, that's it.' Paul grins up at me. 'You can be our lookout. We're going into the church.'

I can't go now. It would be clear I'm running away like a frightened kid from whatever they're up to. Tears prick in the back of my eyes and I turn so they can't see. It's the roller-coaster of being with her. One minute it's all warmth and light and the next it's like turning round and finding someone has left, even though her body is still standing there.

'Come on then.' I start cutting towards the shadowy mouth of the Abbey while they follow, giggling, behind me.

I wait inside the arched entrance for them to catch up. Phoebe looks even more as if she were drawn with a flowing and precise pen now that she's on the outside and I'm in the gloom. They swerve past the wooden 'suggested donation' box, giving it a wide birth, and Phoebe chucks me under the chin as she passes.

'Follow us,' she says. 'It won't take long.'

I sit behind them on the plain wooden rows of chairs. The inside of the Abbey smells like gravestones. Their heads so close I feel like I'm some kind of witness or the priest at their wedding. I can't wait to get out of here and shake the sense that I'm forever superfluous to everything, to the meat of things. That it's always other people that have real relationships with each other and however much I grab for it, love will always be out of my reach. I focus furiously on the huge window ahead and the tears gather and make the colours of

32

the stained glass starburst, then shatter. I wipe at the wetness, fingers sliding over my skin.

I hadn't planned to go out until Phoebe called and suggested we meet up. I went to tell Mum. She had the *Radio Times* in one hand and a pen in the other and was circling things to watch.

'Some great old black-and-whites on this afternoon, and there's that whole box of Charbonnel and Walker in the cupboard that's hardly been touched,' she called out in a sing-song voice, but then she looked up and realised I had my coat on, and I watched as she tried to keep the crushed look off her face. I saw her rallying, adjusting to the disappointment. I know it'll be fine when Dad's back from the rigs, but that's still weeks away.

'Off out?' she said, smiling.

I nodded, then hardened myself. 'Yeah, see you later.'

Now I can't think of anything better than *Rear Window* or *Odd Man Out* flickering over me, my brothers' voices ringing out somewhere far upstairs, as I wallow on the sofa and eat expensive chocolates from the box on the floor.

Out of the corner of my eye I see Paul passing something in his thin fingers to Phoebe. It flutters white before it disappears inside her coat. His face half turns for a moment.

I'm pretty sure Paul glimpses the tears shining despite the dark and it makes me want to crack open his skull with its chick-like hair right here and now. If there was something heavy in my hands, like a crowbar, I think I would actually do it. The surge of violence through me dries up my tears. It feels good, healthy even. I wait it out until they're done and we all emerge outside, blinking in the sharp light.

Paul trots away quickly in a diagonal across the square.

Phoebe links arms with me. 'You are lovely,' she says. 'Putting up with him.'

I jerk my arm away so fast it pulls her hand out of her pocket and walk swiftly into the adjoining square, but when I turn she's followed me.

'Steady on,' she says mildly.

'No. Sometimes it feels like I don't know you.'

She pauses, like she's considering this. 'Well, it's true in a way. There's lots of things you don't know about me.'

I don't know if she means it or is deliberately being mysterious. I feel myself tense up again but I try to keep my voice light. 'Like what? Relationships I don't know about?'

She must be talking about lovers. It's true. She is so beautiful it's bound to be true.

She shrugs. 'Well, it is a fact I get a lot of attention from men. It happens all the time.'

My throat hardens. 'Like who?'

'Like loads of them. Like that teacher for one – Mr Jonasson. He can't take his eyes off me.' She laughs.

'What? For God's sake. He's way older than you.'

Her face pinches up. 'There's no reason why he shouldn't be interested in me.' She tosses her hair. 'I think that's a very limiting way to think about adult relationships.'

'I'm going home,' I say. 'I've got better things to do than listen to this.'

'No you haven't,' she says, taking my arm again and changing gear like she's always doing. 'What are you going to do there?'

And yes, the thought of the house, sweet with chocolate, a carnival of black and white from the TV screen playing over the walls, the clinging undertow of my mother's heavy powdery perfume in every room, is horribly suffocating now. The charm of home that I'd felt in the church has been quickly murdered by the bright outdoor light.

I sigh deeply. Give in. Like I always do.

'I suppose we could go in there.' I nod over to the Roman Baths. 'It might be a laugh for old time's sake. We were always being dragged around there as kids. D'you remember?'

A line of Japanese tourists walk behind a yellow umbrella like they're following the sun. They disappear round the corner to the pump house that was built on the side of the old baths for Jane Austen types to take the waters. Now, you can sit in The Pump Room and have a meal or tea accompanied by a trio of musicians on violin, cello and piano. You can taste the sulphurous water that gets pumped up from the outside into a drinking fountain and gaze out through the window onto the green waters of the old Roman Baths and imagine them all there, lounging about in their togas. My mother adores it. She puts on a best dress and runs her hands over the snowdrop-white tablecloths. Her excitement always makes me ache for her, her deference to the waiters and her sly excited glances over to me as we study the menu. She never takes the plenty at home for granted like I do. It makes me ashamed sometimes.

'Maybe,' says Phoebe. She tugs at the skin around her mouth with two fingers.

It's turning colder and the boiling sulphurous spring that feeds the baths forms an especially thick layer of steam, floating above the balustrade. You can smell it in the air, hot and wet, with a hint of deep middle-of-the-earth rottenness where it comes from. The breeze whips the steam over the wall from the baths that are open to the sky and into the square where we're standing, and I feel it against my cheek and breathe in a deep whiff of its dense wetness. There's a sadness to it that chimes with blackened stone doorways and the angels clinging and falling. It's Phoebe; I know that. She always gets me this way. With her, either I'm ecstatic or stiff with tension or just plain sad.

'Yes.' Phoebe brightens up and stops the picking at her mouth. 'Of course I remember. There's the big archway with the hole inside where all the hot water gushes up from the rock. Inside the archway it's all bright red.'

'It's the iron.'

'What?'

'The iron in the water makes it that colour. It's a natural thing.'

She frowns. 'That's not what it really is.'

'What?'

'I remember seeing it as if it was actually hell in there. That's the answer.' She comes closer to me. 'Perhaps Bath is actually built on top of hell and that's why they've built all these teashops and museums over it to try and squash it down. What d'you think?'

'I think you sound unhinged.' I never know if she's joking or not.

She grabs my arm. 'That's what those angels you always stare at are doing. They're trying to get away.'

A curl of fear unfurls down my spine. How does she do it? I can't seem to keep anything from her. 'What angels?'

She shakes her head at my feeble attempt at fakery, not bothering to contradict it.

'Think about it and you'll see.'

36

And the trouble is, I *do* think and I *do* see. I remember the archway she was talking about, deep inside the baths complex, where inside the rock is red and folded and the stinking hot waters that feed the baths to this day burst out. Then there's the angels scrambling up the front of the church and I know, without a shadow of a doubt, that I will never look at them again without seeing them frantically escaping the hell right next to them. Before the Romans even, there was worshipping here – Neolithic people rolling around in the hot mud and thinking they were being blessed by gods. The air is thick with the centuries of it. There's layer after layer. The hot spring has drawn us all here. The more you think about it, the more the chocolate shops and the tourist tat look like an evasion of the visceral truth. Those people can never know the power of this place that lies under their feet.

'Perhaps you're right.' I think of the glittering blood along the wall on the day of the murder. Now somehow, the way Phoebe has painted it, I can see the whole city running with red. 'That murder . . .'

'Stop it.' She's tapping her eyelids, over and over.

'What's the matter?' I say.

'Nothing. I can't talk about that at the moment.'

'Why?'

She holds onto my sleeve. 'Not now. We'll talk about it another time.'

'It was *gruesome*.'

'Shut up. Will you just fucking shut up about it.' A couple walking past swing round at her shouting, scan us and move on.

Phoebe turns away from me, still tapping around the

sockets of her eyes, then whirls back. Her face has changed, like she was doing something to it while I couldn't see it. She's smiling now. 'D'you reckon it looks like women's parts, the red hole in the ground where all the water gushes out?' She barks out a laugh, then studies me for a response.

'Fuck off,' I say weakly.

'Yes, yes. Can you imagine it? All those funny little Iron Age men scrabbling around worshipping like they told us. Worshipping the big hot hole. I can see it now.'

She's watching me and I can't help it; I feel the blood flooding into my face. She's doing this deliberately. I think about looking away but something in me keeps me staring straight at her so it's she that has to break the spell. 'Look at you,' she says, a slant of familiar affection in her voice. 'Let's get you away from all this. I'm going to take you for a big fat ice cream whatever you say.' Then she heads off and I follow her like a lumbering cow.

In the café the light arcs in through the window. It touches her face, highlighting it. She counts out a pile of silver and coppers to pay for her ice cream.

'You've spent all your money then?' I can't help it. I know I sound prudish and disapproving but I hate to think of whatever Paul has passed her. She seems too fragile for whatever it might be.

She makes a face. 'I hardly ever have any money. Mum's so tight, always has been. I got the shitty little jobs when I was a kid – like cleaning the whole bathroom and landing for twenty pence. When I stopped doing that she more or less stopped giving me anything. Dad does sometimes – he shoves it into my pocket when no one's looking like he's doing something wrong. That's what I just spent.'

I look at Phoebe. She always seems so stylish, but for the first time I can see – see how her height, her good looks mean she can pull off a kind of deception. Shift slightly and you notice the worn hem on her skirt, the split where the plastic has begun to come away on her shoes that aren't really Converses but some cheap approximation of them. I remember an old parka she wore for three years in a row. Maybe it's not all lies about how her mum treats her. I'd always assumed her style was her charity-shop aesthetic, a way of showing how little she cared. I have a rush of feeling for her. For the real her – or the closest I get to it that she shows in little glints.

She carries on. 'Dad's made a mistake marrying her. I can see it in his eyes, but he thinks there's nothing he can do about it.' She scrapes her teeth on a frill of dry skin on her bottom lip, tearing it off in a strip before it disappears into her mouth.

'Mum always lets me have what I want. I can give you some, if you like. She just says to me "take what you need".' I blush at the obvious warmth of my generosity.

'Steal?' It's like she's tasting the word in her mouth, seeing if she likes it.

'Yes.' I agree, though that's not how I'd meant it. I'd thought *give*, not *steal*.

'Maybe some time when I really need it,' she says, like she's the generous one. She lets ice cream drip from her spoon and she looks younger again. I reach over and free a curl that's stuck to her cheek.

'Don't do that,' she says. 'I didn't say you could do that this time.'

I sit back in my chair and fold my arms.

'Come on, don't be like that,' she says. 'I'm just not used to it yet. I know, it's a nice day – let's go to the Spinney.'

'I suppose.'

She stands abruptly, nearly knocking over the glass ice-cream bowl. She looks excited now. 'It's ages since we've been there,' she says.

We found the Spinney about nine years ago. That was the age where we were still playing hide-and-seek among the trees. Make-believe homes with leaves for plates. Strange mashes of river slime and flowers, ostensibly for making spells but really to enjoy the disgust of them, the wafts of stink they made. We'd vowed to keep the place a secret and as far as I knew all three of us – Phoebe, Grace and me – have stuck to that. We didn't even know what a spinney was. I still haven't bothered to find out, and who knows what ancient children's book the word drifted out of and stuck. We still call it the Spinney. It's so utterly quiet. The air is coloured green from being filtered through all the leaves. It's hard to know why it's even there: a stone wall cutting off the river from the rest of the field so there's an isolated, tree-filled space between. Perhaps there were once suicidal sheep who chucked themselves in the water and drowned so the farmer built it to stop them. Whatever reason, the gap between the river and the wall is our Spinney.

We set off. It's on the edge of Bath, in the countryside really. Even as the houses thin out to nothing, it's still a long lane and two fields away. As we walk, Phoebe nips off the tops of cow parsley and flicks them into the river.

'Remember the wishing bowl?' she says, as she skips along. 'Remember the stuff we made in there?'

'I guess,' I say, but of course I do.

The wishing bowl inside the Spinney is a deep pitted hole in a rock that sticks out into the river, curved at the end like a crochet hook. It's imprinted on my brain. The filthy water bright with flower heads slopping over the side of the hole, berries pearling up to the surface. The rock wreathed in our chains of wild flowers and the nip of wild garlic in the air. The plump child that was me standing in a shaft of sunlight, diligently pumping away at it with a stubby branch as thick as a cudgel. 'Please let Kirsty Rainworth's hair fall out, please let my dad buy me a dog, please let Dad not have an accident on the oil rigs, please let Miss Cosgrove's arms fall off . . .' The industriousness I applied even to incantation and enchantment. That child sickens me. *You always were a silly cow*, I think.

'We actually peed in it once because we said it would make the spell stronger. We really did. What horrible little girls we must've been.' Phoebe throws back her head and laughs, and light catches on her teeth.

I make out I don't remember because for some stupid reason it embarrasses me, but actually the memory is so clear I can nearly see it. It was a cold day and we all took turns. A plume of steam rose from the bowl like the bang and smoke of a real magic spell had flashed inside its crucible.

'You know what you'd wish for.' She glances at me slyly and sends another flower head soaring into the river.

I pretend to yawn. I need her to calm down right now. It's frazzling me, her energy.

'Come on. Name it. You know what you want.'

A horrible creeping sensation shoots up the back of my neck into my hair. She's staring at me, pouting her lips out.

'Leave it,' I say. It comes out gruff and uncomfortable.

'Yes, yes, you do.' She cups her breasts with both hands, her thumb and finger angled as if about to tweak her nipples. 'You want my body and everyone knows it.'

'Fuck off,' I say, aware of the hot gust of breath as I speak. 'Just fuck off.'

I can feel dust sticking to my top lip.

She shivers her hands at me. 'Please, bowl. Give Orla what she wants,' she incants, in a stupid play-spell voice.

'I mean it. Stop it.'

'Calm down, it's only a game.'

'You always say that.' I'm shouting now. She's been cranking me up all day and I've had enough. I feel like I'm going to explode.

'Look at you, all red in the face. Really, calm down.' Her eyes slant towards me, laughing.

We've both stopped walking now. Face each other. She's taking something out on me that I don't know about. The mystery of not knowing makes it worse, like I'm shut out and the door is bolted.

I feel huge beside her, like I could pick her up and toss her in the air, like I'm a giant and she's a tiny doll.

'You'd better stop winding me up like this,' I yell. 'It's not fair.'

She turns away, rolling one shoulder. 'You can be such a child sometimes, just look at yourself,' she says softly. 'Just go and look at yourself now and see what you see.'

And I do. It comes to me in broken pictures. The plump arm of a child pounding at the wishing bowl. A great red open gob of want. Dust and sweat. Fat little legs going back and forth to school.

She is so light, Phoebe. I can almost imagine she's a bird when I shove her. I barely know I'm doing it until I feel her thin bones beneath my hands and the surge of energy that goes through me. Just one hard shove and she seems to take flight, and for a second I blink, looking up for her, hollow-boned and laughing, swooping against the blue sky and brimming with the joy at the novelty.

But then I hear the frantic splashing. I edge forward to where there's a disturbed dent in the tall grasses and cow parsley that fringe the riverbank and peer over.

'No,' I breathe. 'No, no, no.'

The water bulges, shatters into broken light as Phoebe rises and falls and flails as the water crashes around her. Her hair flattens into a black skull and a thick snake of it winds itself into her mouth and I stand frozen, watching her.

'Bitch. Bitch,' she splutters, then shoots backwards, slipping on slimy rocks beneath. I never knew it was so deep.

'Phoebe,' I cry out.

*I can't come to you*, I think, my mind tangling. *You'll pull me under and hold me there until I choke on blackness.* She rears up again and the look on her face is like an animal trying to save itself. She gulps and water spumes out of her mouth.

'Phoebe, I'm so, so sorry,' I call over as she manages to stand with water eddying round her thighs, steadying herself.

'How could you? How could you do that, you bitch? I hate you now.' She wades over to the bank towards me and I can barely breathe because the look of her is like a monster dripping from the river, water falling from the ledges of her, not my beautiful Phoebe at all. The shock and fear have changed her into something else and she's

43

turned ugly as sin. It's the animal fighting for survival, the one that would do anything, showing through her beauty. It's so distorted the sight of it shocks me to the core, but I know because it's Phoebe that at some point I'll tell myself it wasn't like that at all. That whatever I've seen has just been a trick of the light, the shock addling my brain, the day turning in on itself.

# 6

# Grace

Get up, bitch, I tell myself.

Sometimes I wonder why I talk to myself like this, insult myself in this way. Though absolutely I do know really. It forces me to calm right down. It keeps me in line and doing what I need to do.

I roll out of bed, coughing into the pillow. How long is it since I've remembered to change my bedding? It has a fusty scent. Later perhaps. Time falls through my hands with everything that must be done and before I know it, it's night again and it takes just about all I've got to flop into bed.

Usually I have a few moments for myself in the still heat of the morning. The central heating has clicked on while we were both asleep and its heavy warmth lies over everything. Mum feels the cold even in the summer. I'll wander through the flat or I might even smoke half a joint on the balcony outside.

It usually calms me, this interlude. But this morning I'm agitated. Daniel texted me, *Hey love, how you doing? Be nice to cu soon sometime*. So I texted him back. *Not today fraid.* Now I'm agonising if it sounded so curt he'll finally have had enough of me. I think about sending another text but it'll probably make things worse. He knows the situation I'm in so he should really leave it to me to say when I can be free or not, and today is check-up day for Mum so I need to put the whole thing out of my mind.

I walk through the flat, wiping sleep from my eyes and noticing everything that's wrong. There's an off feeling about it all, as if it's conspiring against me. I notice every grimy corner. Every cobweb dancing in the breeze. The cooker with its dull glaze of grease on top. The corners of the bath where dark grime has accumulated. Red blooms around the base of the taps there. It's some kind of bacteria, I know.

This weekend I'll get up early and blitz the place. I'll buy a bucketful of cleaning products and I'll spend the whole day scrubbing, chasing every grain of dirt and capturing it between shiny bubbles and washing it down the drain. Every scabby corner. Every silted-up cupboard where pipes drip and coagulate crusty stuff around their joints. The dried-up insects that tick their way up to the tenth floor and squeeze through gaps that aren't really gaps only to curl up and die by the painted skirting. Not until then will I feel calm and free.

I start to breathe easier and the feeling of doom blows off me like a hat. I feel sparked with energy. The cleaning vision gleams bright like some beautiful shining temple on a hill. Because it's in the future, I can hold its gleam in the palm of my hand and keep it balanced there, before it has time to sink into my bones and weigh me down.

'Mum,' I call, skittering down the hallway, my socked feet sliding on the bare boards. 'Mum, wake up. It's check-up day. You're going out!'

I crack eggs into the frying pan while she sits at the table.

'You didn't have to take me, chicken,' she says, using my old name. I refuse to let it close my throat up and give in to sentiment. I absolutely refuse.

'Of course I do. How else would it happen? Who else

46

would do it?' I crack a line in another egg and split it with both thumbs into the pan. 'Who else that bothers about anything anyway. Besides, I've already told school I won't be in because of it.' I wipe the slime off each thumb on the back pockets of my jeans.

She could have gone on her own with the duty ambulance.

'Shall we arrange to have her picked up at seven?' the woman asked on the phone.

The duty ambulance fulfils all the appointments by picking them up one by one so the journey is a snail trail around Bath that can last for hours. There's the afflicted whose wheelchairs are strapped either side so they don't go careering around like loose roller skates inside: they are variously pale, drooling, gagging, some with heads bent over so far they nearly touch their knees. The journey goes on for so long Mum gets sick. She has to get up at the crack of dawn and there's no time for her to come to slowly like she needs.

'Well?' The woman was tapping at the other end of the phone. Computer keys maybe. Or perhaps her pen on the edge of her desk.

I closed my lips in a tight seam. No, damn you. Fuck you. If I have to load my mother up in a wheelbarrow and cart her down to the hospital myself, I'll do it. You counter of sick bodies. You bright-sounding lame bitch.

I undid the seam of my lips to draw in a deep breath.

'Thank you, it's fine. I'll make my own arrangements. I'll take a day off and cancel the carers for that day and I'll bring her there myself.'

The tapping stopped. 'Righto then.' A trill on the phone like she'd turned into a bird and then a click.

47

Now I walk through the flat, flicking cushions back into place while we wait for the taxi. Outside the living room window, beyond the balcony, the sky is high and pale blue. It stretches over this doll-sized city, right across to the hills beyond, where black-and-white cows move slowly in their green squares. The balcony is my personal place, my solace. It's where I can allow myself to be stirred by the world. Where I can watch the moon nailed like a bright disc to the sky. Where the sun's rise at dawn leaves bloody tracks, and when it sets I watch as the lights below open up the darkness once again. Where I can give myself permission to dream about the future and about Daniel. I can let myself be filled up by all these things – out there, in private. I can get wildness out of my system.

I wait for the toot of the taxi. I'm alert for it, and when it comes the sound rises sharply up to me through the open windows of the balcony like it's a ball being thrown up in the air. The lift has been mended so we take it down to the ground floor and I use my foot as a doorstop while I manoeuvre Mum out of the main doors. She squints up at the sky and I try to remember when she was last outside. Actually, I remember, it wasn't too long ago: we went out with Rosa and Averill last week. But all the same she looks fearful this time, like she's getting out of the habit of going out. The taxi smells of chocolate inside and as we drive away I can hear kids playing in the tiny playground, its margins wreathed with toothy dandelion leaves. We slide past it, past the few mothers numb with fatigue watching their children leap and bend until it's time for school.

At the hospital we wait lined up. A woman in blue cotton trousers and matching top approaches with a clipboard.

The trousers show up the width of her thighs that look out of proportion to the rest of her.

'I'm Maya. I'm the clinic co-ordinator.'

We both nod dutifully and Mum smiles widely at her, and only I know the effort it takes her to do this. The stress of these appointments weighs badly on her.

'You can have your chat to the social worker before Mum goes in.'

I'm instantly and completely on high alert, though no one looking at me would be able to tell a thing, I'm sure.

'I haven't got a chat with the social worker.'

The clinic co-ordinator leans back as if to let her torso take a few minutes' rest on those thick legs – legs that would see her through anything. 'Yes. Yes, it's down here. Miss Kinsella, she's called. New. Do you want me to take you through?'

'Mum?' I turn to her.

She looks vague, which is how I know she's known about this all along. *You stupid*, I think. *You stupid, stupid, stupid.* Don't you know how hard I have to work to keep things boxed up so nothing escapes? Don't you know the effort it takes? And there you are, ready to let it all be split apart to satisfy some idiotic worry you have about me. A worry that was there in your head on the day of some random phone call or chat with one of the carers but would probably be gone ten minutes later – and now I'm here having to deal with the consequences.

'Go on,' Mum says. 'It won't do any harm to talk.'

I let my face scrunch up at her to let her know I'm not happy. *Let yourself be carted into some nursing home*, I think. *Then you might learn to keep your mouth shut.*

49

I allow myself to be led like a dumb beast. I expect many things of Miss Kinsella. What I don't expect is her to be nice. When I realise that, I know I have to be even more extraordinarily careful than usual.

'Hello, Grace.' Bright smile. 'Sit down. Now, remind me, how old are you again?' Our file is in front of her. She was looking at it before I came in. She knows how old I am.

'I'm . . .' I have to clear my throat and start again. 'Sixteen,' I say. 'But not far off being seventeen.'

On the back of the door there's a sports shirt and black leggings on a hanger, trainers on the low bookshelf. Her hair is damp around the edges and there's the dry pungent scent of shower gel in the room.

'So young!' She smiles at me again.

*Careful now*, I think, *careful, careful, careful.* Don't let on how bad Mum is and how she's getting worse, yet how, somehow without ever articulating to each other, you both conspire to minimise this. Don't even give a hint of how sometimes you wake up and wonder how another day is possible. But on the other hand, don't be too bright. It'll hit a false note and they'll be alert for that.

'Tell me how you're coping, Grace. We know how brilliantly you've done so far. Your mother is extremely well cared for. But we also know there's always going to be a cost to that. A cost to you. Talking about that cost may help and, who knows, there might even be something we can do, if not to resolve it, then at least to ameliorate the impact on you, just a little.'

She folds her hands on top of each other and I notice the gleaming scab of red varnish on each nail.

'Well . . .'

She sits up, waiting.

I really don't know how true the danger of our situation is. There's no one I can ask. To me, it feels immensely vulnerable. To me, it feels like Mum could die or be taken away at any time, but how real that is I'm not sure. Sometimes I'm fine, and sometimes I'm trapped in wave after wave of anxiety about it. One thing I am sure of, though, is that none of this can be allowed to show. Miss Kinsella sitting in front of me is never, ever going to know how far I'm prepared to go for this. She has no idea that, if needs be, I will fight like a wolf from the forest whose pups are about to be eaten, like a fucking snake on its prey. I give no indication of it. It's what I've learned. Let it show and you're fucked. I breathe and attune myself to the quiet of the room. I let myself be blown on gently by the breeze coming through the window. I pause to sniff up the scent of shower gel and, under that, the smell of her scalp's warmth, cooling now after taking exercise. I ride on all of it.

'Weeell,' I start again cautiously. *Give her something*, I think. If you just give her one or two things and they appear authentic, yet they're not so bad as they can't be easily managed, then maybe that will satisfy her and she will once again fade away into the background static she was part of before you set foot into this room. 'I've been wondering, and it could be a really, really big help, if perhaps just once a week – we wouldn't need it for more than that – we could get a meals on wheels. I've heard about them from Mum's friends.'

'Well, that's a new idea. To give you a night off?'

Actually we have McDonald's on a Saturday night and that's our night-off treat. I wouldn't be able to wrestle that

Filet-O-Fish out of Mum's cold dead hands, but of course I don't mention that.

She laughs. 'I'm not sure they're exactly cordon bleu but I can look into it, certainly.'

She shuffles her papers around. 'Anything else?'

'Um, I don't think so. That would be just grand.' I smile.

She frowns. 'Listen, I'm wondering if, rather than seeing you at the hospital, it might be better if we make a regular date to catch up at your home. Where do you live?' The papers rustle and the back of my neck, the back of my head, tingles. 'Snow Hill. I think that could be really nice, don't you, Grace? I could just pop round now and again and have a cup of tea. When might be good for you? We can put it in the diary. There's so much support available – I was even talking to a charity this morning that provides respite care for people with MS – and we can run through it all properly so we can see if there's anything that fits you personally.'

I need something to distract her with. It's the memories of being twelve and all the questions that's done it. It felt like an invasion and always somehow thinking I was about to say the wrong thing and that one wrong thing would be the one that got Mum taken away.

Then it got easier. The last one – I can't remember her name – got put off so easily. I just didn't bother answering the intercom. She never took the time to talk her way in through the main front door – which is simple, there's always someone willing to let you come in behind them to take the lift to the top floor and ring our doorbell. I have a feeling this one is different. She'd climb all the flights of stairs even if the lift was broken. She'd hammer on the door if there was no answer to the bell. And then, she'd be inside.

She'd be looking at the dirty corners, the dead woodlice rolling like grey pearls on the bare boards, the rose wreaths of bacteria around the taps. The carers don't mind, and it's not their job anyway. This one's different. This one's bright eyes will flick to every corner like they're twin hundred-watt torches lighting everything up.

'It's school that's the hard thing actually,' I say in a rush. I need to act quickly, before that date in the diary. I have a plan to make her forget. It's reckless, but it might just work. *Please let it work.*

She's slightly startled. She thought our time was almost over, just the goodbyes and the shuffle out of the door to go.

'What about school, Grace?'

'I'm thinking, now I'm nearly seventeen – more wondering really – whether I should keep it up. I mean, I could leave now legally.'

Her eyes pop open. 'You've been thinking of leaving?'

I nod. 'It's something that's occurred to me recently. I'm not sure which way to go.' This is a lie of course; I have no intention of leaving. Escaping every day and sitting in a damp-smelling building while voices drone away about God knows what is what truly keeps me going. The structure of it is important too. The bells, the rules and regulations, the time for exams, lunch and study time all give me a feeling of having a framework in my life, possibilities. Often, I feel so guilty about Mum being alone it clenches my guts at the thought of it, but it doesn't stop me going. That's what a true bitch I am.

'Plus, because of when my birthday is, I'm one of the youngest in the sixth form. I think perhaps that adds to it – makes it harder.' This bit is true but I've surprised myself by telling her that.

53

'Well, Grace,' she's saying. 'This is something you need to think really carefully about. Of course we know how much you want to devote yourself to your mum, but you have to think of your own future and a time when, well, we don't have to go into that – you know the trajectory of this. Honestly, Grace, I really think it would be a mistake to abandon your studies at this point.'

I pretend to consider it for a while. 'I think you're right,' I say finally.

'Really? Would you like me to speak to the school? See if there are extra measures that can be put in place? Although I can see they're aware of everything.'

'No, no.' I say it too quickly, then steady myself. 'You're absolutely right about staying on for the second year of sixth form. Like you say, I need to think about my future.' I smile and get up to go. 'I'd better be getting back to Mum.'

She holds up one finger. 'Just one second. Let's get that date into the diary now.'

I sit back down and sigh and close my eyes and wonder if any of it really honestly matters as she leafs through her diary. Maybe no one actually cares enough to do anything anyway and she'll just come and have a cup of tea so she can tick some box somewhere that I don't even know about.

I try to remember exactly what I said to her as I make my way back to Mum. Not that it's meaningful in any way; I realise that apart from my one slip it would pretty much have been completely fake because I wouldn't have known how to make her understand how I really am about everything. That is, as long as I have the open balcony – the sudden hot smell of rubber, the stars trembling in the sky, the slap of rain against my cheek, a place I can go and feel the rush of the world – I'll be OK.

Mum wants me to go with her into the consulting room.

'Can I have the curtains drawn?' she asks when it comes to the examination. We keep up the pretence that I haven't seen every inch of her. I don't mind. It helps her keep a sense of dignity; I know that. Your own daughter shouldn't be looking after you like you are a baby.

'Of course,' the nurse says and rattles the curtains around the couch, but she's not really thinking about what she's doing, I see that; her mind is elsewhere. She leaves a big gap so I can see the top of Mum's bare thighs and buttocks on the couch. I nearly get up and draw it myself but I don't. They don't like you interfering, or making out that you know more than they do, that's what I've learned.

I sit by the desk and listen to their murmuring voices as they examine her. I can't seem to take my eyes off Mum's bit of leg. Just seeing a disjointed piece of her is so weird. It makes me feel disconnected from who she is. The skin is very, very pale with a bluish tinge and a vein snakes up it. It's an ugly sight. And as I look I think of the nurse half pulling the curtains round. I think, *You fucking bitch, not having the decency to finish closing them properly. It wouldn't have taken you a second to do it*. However, at the same time, I also make a resolution. I resolve not to let that fucking bitch see one thing on my face that shows what I think of her. I will smile, because when you are unwell I've also learned your very existence counts on people like this, and they can either make it worse or better for you, so I will smile and look grateful for every tiny misjudged thing she does.

I've already decided to walk back home with Mum. The fresh air will do us good, and besides, it's pretty much on the flat all the way, just a push up at the beginning and a hill right at the end where I need to hang on tight. As I push, and look at the back of her head, I start getting the same feeling I had looking at her piece of leg in the hospital. She has her hair cut in a bob and her head looks much smaller and frailer than I remember it being at home. Perhaps it's seeing it out in the harsh light of day that's doing it. We carry on in silence until we're at the top of Guinea Lane and nearly home.

'All right, Mum?' I say to break the silence. 'What do you fancy for tea? We could get some of those ready-made pancakes again for afters.'

She turns her head slightly. 'Grace, I need to go, quickly.'

'You'll have to hang on. We're ten minutes away yet.'

'No, really.' She sounds panicky. 'I really, really need to go now.'

We're at the top of the hill so I put the brakes on the wheelchair sharply. 'Listen—'

'Oh,' she gasps. I dodge round the front just in time to see the stream of pee waterfalling off the plastic seat, splashing over her shoes and beading in the dust on the pavement.

'Oh, Grace,' she wails. 'This is awful, awful.'

A couple of schoolboys walk past. They're not too bad really, in the scheme of things; they widen their eyes and roll them at each other. All the same, I straighten up, say 'Fuck you' and that sends them scuttling away down the hill, back to their mummies. I swear to God if they'd laughed, I would have grabbed them by their collars and knocked their heads together until their skulls cracked, so they've got off lightly.

'Mum, don't worry.' I put my hand over hers. 'We'll get you home and cleaned up in no time.'

She's twisting her hanky in her hands, writhing them under mine. 'God, this is awful, awful. I can't bear it, Grace.'

The yellow pee is tracking its progress towards the gutter, gathering the dust as it goes. Drops continue to splash from the seat, spattering the pavement, beading on her nylon tights.

'Don't worry about it. You can put my jacket over your lap if you want. You can—'

'God bloody help us. Having to put up with this.'

Then I don't know what it is – the stress of the day, or the pee gathering and rolling down the hill – but I feel a spurt of laughter in my throat.

'Mum, stop it now.' I'm choking with laughter. I feel panicky, I can't squash it. It keeps bubbling up out of me.

She looks up, her mouth twisted. 'Honestly, Grace. It's hardly funny.' She looks furious and for some reason that makes me laugh harder.

'I know, I know.' It's me wailing now.

'Come on, calm down.'

'I can't.' I cross my legs. 'I'm going to pee *myself* now.'

'What?'

'I really am.' I twist my legs together to try and stop it.

'Bloody hell, Grace.' She gives a short, unexpected bark of laughter and puts her hand to her mouth like she's just shocked herself. Then she starts. Her eyes crease up and her hands flop over the armrests and she gives herself over to hiccupping waves of laughter.

'Oh God.' I sit down with a bump on the window ledge beside us, jam my hand between my legs and force my thighs together as hard as I can. 'I really am. I'm going to wet myself.'

She lets out a snort and holds her belly in her hands and gives in to it. I squeeze tight, choking on my own laughter, and think, *If anyone passes, what the fuck will we look like? What the fuck would someone think?* Both of us hysterical, with Mum sitting in a puddle of pee, me with my legs twisted around each other like pipe cleaners and the yellow stream rolling down the hill.

# 7

# Phoebe

Every day as I watch him he appears gilded.

I arrive at school before Mr Jonasson, so, with lids curtaining three quarters of my eyeballs, I wait upstairs as he drives into the little tarmac car park on the other side of the wall beyond the scrubby patch of school lawn. He disappears for a moment as he unlocks the heavy wooden door in the wall. I draw back so I can't be seen as the door opens onto the garden and he emerges and picks his way down the cracked path towards the back of the school.

At home time I race upstairs, my feet clattering on the bare wood, to watch the same in reverse. The light is sweeter in the late afternoon. It touches the edges of all things and makes them honeyed. The Scandinavian blond of his hair is almost white in the young summer light. I have to think of him returning home to the smell of dogs and kids' puke and things boiling.

I know Orla has emerged through the shadowy door behind and is standing there looking at me. I thought she'd left for the day but I just saw the flicker of her in the window. She also has a smell of dry biscuits that she can never quite cover with the expensive perfume her mother buys her. I can't remember its name but I know the scent is marketed as upbeat, quirky, pitched perfectly for a seventeen-year-old. Something a good and concerned mother wouldn't be afraid to buy for her daughter. Something that won't give her *ideas* aside from wandering through a benevolent field of flowers, moody and alone.

Her presence is stopping me from concentrating on the dull ache in my breastbone from seeing Mr Jonasson leaving. I can't wait. In the morning I'll be in his class. I'll get there early and sit at the front.

'What is it you're looking at, Phoebe?'

I half turn my head. 'Not people skulking in the shadows, that's for sure.'

I make certain my voice is thick with menace. I haven't forgotten what happened at the river. She can make her stuttering apologies all she wants. I'll forgive her when I can no longer taste the river water in my mouth and when I stop thinking of the blackness underneath.

As he talks about *Macbeth*, Mr Jonasson walks back and forth at the front of the classroom like he's an actor on the stage.

I'm teetering. Caught like an acrobat about to fall from a high wire. On the one side is fear of the malign play. On the other, the fact of being close to Mr Jonasson. It's got me in a state of unbearable trembling. Being in the same room as him is a kind of breathless joy.

The turmoil, though. At one point Mr Jonasson quotes from the play, describing a mind that is 'full of scorpions', and for a moment I actually think he's talking about me. I was doing so well. Now I'm right back with my old behaviours – everything but the cutting – as if they never went away. The thoughts that loop out of control and all the rituals and tappings and ridiculous things I have to do to try and stop them. The play has got me at it again. It makes me want to experiment like I did on the day of the murder, but I'm also trying to catch that bad thought and stop it before it gets processed, and between it all my mind is at war with itself. *Macbeth* is the wound and a red ribbon of blood stems from it; it travels in a band across the wall in Walcot Street and ends with me, tying me up in knots so the three things are bound fast together and there is no escape.

Despite the turmoil I'm certain that none of this shows on my face.

As Mr Jonasson passes me he taps his hand, once, lightly on my desk and the gesture is so fleeting but seems so freighted with meaning I feel I'm about to fall off my chair. It's so thrillingly intimate, as if he's marking me out, choosing me as he walks past. It's almost nothing, like being touched by a moth's wings, but it gives me a tiny taste of what it must feel like to collapse against him and be held up by strong, loving arms and have that warmth light me up, quieting there, safe and blissful.

He's serious when he speaks. He holds the book open on one broad palm.

'Now your first-year sixth-form exams are over, we will look properly at the text of this play that we will be studying fully next school year. We touched on it the other day . . .'

The day of the murder. The man who did it is now in custody. The funeral of the victim has been and that bloodied body lies cold in the ground, yet the red threads of that day are here. The open wound of the book in his hand, the writing inside sticking out like tendons and veins, just like the dead man's must've done.

Mr Jonasson stops, pauses. I swear his eyes flick over to where I'm sitting. Yes! His gaze rests on me. 'Phoebe, could you read out the plot summary on page eight?'

Again I feel like I'm going to fall off my chair. For one sick, dizzying moment my eyes are locked onto his blue gaze and I truly feel I won't be able to read out a word. I scrabble through the textbook while everyone looks on, shuffling their feet restlessly.

'Macbeth, a brave warrior, is told by three cunning witches that one day he will become King of Scotland. His wife, Lady Macbeth, eaten up by greed and ambition, is complicit in encouraging him to murder King Duncan and seize the throne. Soon suspicion surrounds him and he has to commit more atrocities to protect himself. The former brave warrior becomes a tyrant and he and his wife descend into a world of murder and madness.'

I take a deep breath.

Mr Jonasson nods. 'Yes. It's one of the darkest of all Shakespeare plays. Quickly, before the end of the lesson, consider these lines: "Stars, hide your fires, Let not light see my black and deep desires." Macbeth thinks he is driving the action, but the seeds of those actions have been planted there by the witches. Yet in reality were those "black and deep desires" already in place, waiting to be ignited? More than anything it is a play about the mind. The mind, the play tells us, can do anything. It can see things that are not there. In the later stages of the story, after he has killed, Macbeth will see a dagger floating before him that he is compelled to follow. Lady Macbeth sees a spot of blood on her hand that, however much she tries to wash it away, she cannot rid herself of.'

Mr Jonasson pauses and looks towards the window and his eyes tighten against the light. He carries on.

'Lady Macbeth's suicide – as the York Notes call it – is "A final desperate act of the mind seeking to cleanse itself"—'

The bell pierces the room.

I gather my bag and linger while everybody else fights to get out of the door. It's just the two of us now. Rowdy voices and footsteps ring out from the corridor.

'Did you not bring your copy?' asks Mr Jonasson.

So that's all the palm-touching my desk was about. It was marking the gap where my copy of the play should've been, the place where nearly everyone else had their copies open on their desks. I am not chosen. My moth's-wing fantasy is in tatters.

'I'm sorry, I lost it. I must've dropped it on my way home.'

He snaps the book in his hand closed with one easy movement. 'Take mine.'

'That's OK.'

He leans forward, smiling and proffering the book. I have little choice but to take the book and drop it in my bag.

'Perhaps you could read it over the weekend?' he suggests.

'OK.'

His smile passes through me in a wave. 'Lucky you. My Saturday always sees me at the library, nine-thirty sharp, trying to finish the endless task of a PhD. Then in penance for having a few hours to myself I have to wheel a trolley around Waitrose doing the weekly shop. Oh for the days of a whole weekend to read.'

I nod enthusiastically. Is it possible? Is he purposely telling me where he'll be in the morning? My cheeks begin burning so I have to turn away abruptly with a garbled 'Bye then', cursing myself for not staying and hearing if there was anything else he was going to say.

As I walk down the corridor I am again teetering. I still bask in the warmth, the intimate exchange of his smile, but the weight of the book drags at my shoulder. As if one copy wasn't enough for me to deal with. Now they've doubled.

I lie awake all night, wondering what he meant, and as the birds start singing I've definitely decided that he told me exactly where he'd be deliberately. I will get up early to do my hair and get ready, and I will go to the library and meet him. If I leave the house early enough, I could even be back before anyone else is up, as they'll be enjoying their Saturday morning lie-in and the tray with the papers and croissants and a dish of butter that they love so much on weekend mornings. It's generally assumed that one must not leave the house without an interrogation as to the purpose, and leaving so early is bound to raise suspicion. Coming back, if I am discovered, then at least the deed will be done and it will be too late for *her* to stop me.

I must've slept for a few hours, but excitement wakes me up good and early. I sweep my hair in a top knot, arrange a few loose tendrils around my face, and take out the bits of make-up I've got and line them up on my bedside table. I don't want it to look too obvious to him that I've dolled myself up, so I just elongate my eyes with a black eye pencil and content myself with rubbing a little Vaseline into my lips.

When I'm ready I crack open my door and listen. My bedroom is on the top floor so any escape entails getting past Mum and Dad's room on the floor below. The house seems to sigh a little to itself but apart from that everything is quiet. I begin my creep along the corridor and stand, hesitating, at the top of the stairs that lead to the next floor. I wait there for so long that when the doorbell rings, the shock of it drills through me and for a moment I think I'm going to tumble down the flight of stairs and break my neck. I stand swaying, forcing my body to right itself, and down below I hear the bedroom door open and Mum emerging, grumbling sharply to herself. I can see her over the banister from above. She crosses the hallway below, tying the belt of her dusky pink velvet dressing gown tight around her waist. The skirt of it kicks out as she walks so she looks like a rose blooming then returning to bud over and over. This is terrible. The doorbell never rings on a Saturday morning. It's like this is being done to thwart me on purpose. I lean forward, listening as she opens the door. There's a muffled voice from outside and hers, rising in annoyance.

'It is precisely because we don't want to get up at the crack of dawn, because it's the weekend, that we have the newspaper' – she sounds out the next word – 'del–iv–ered. If you're going to ring the bell to ask which one we have, then we might as well make the journey to the newsagent's ourselves . . .'

I can almost see her pursed mouth spitting out the words.

'Emma. Who is it?'

Christ, Dad's up now, padding down the stairs to find out what's going on.

'It's this new child they've hired,' Mum says, then turns back to the open door. 'Surely you have a list, don't you?'

There's a fluting, garbled answer from outside and then Dad's soothing voice intervenes. 'Now then, Emma, I'm sure it won't happen again. You go and get the coffee on and I'll deal with this.'

I strain my ears to hear her marching into the kitchen and Dad being appeasing and kind on the doorstep and, when he knows Mum's out of the way, sneaking the boy a fiver, saying it's because it's his first paper round, he'll soon get the hang of things, but really I know it's compensation for Mum being so horrible. Then Dad disappears into the kitchen too. The house falls silent again. I stand and time seems to dissolve. Once they're back upstairs, wide awake, I will never summon the courage to get past their bedroom. I know I should seize my chance and slip out, but I'm paralysed.

Swiftly, before I can think about it further, I begin scurrying down the stairs. The back of the front door with its brass letterbox and thick layers of cream paint is in my sights when the kitchen door bursts open and, I can't help it this time, I do actually cry out, and Mum and Dad both look up at me – Dad with his leather slippers as shiny as conkers, holding a tray with orange juice, coffee and the paper on it.

Mum says, 'Phoebe, what on earth are you doing leaving the house at this hour in tarty make-up? Honestly, as if I haven't had enough. Get back to your room at once. What a bloody morning, people ringing bells and creeping about.'

I'm frozen.

She frowns. 'Go on. I've got my eye on you, you know. I found that powerful antiperspirant under your bed *again* and I've told you already it's not healthy for a girl your age to be using products like that. Really, Peter, you must stop giving her money – see how she spends it? Plus, I found those tights the day you came home after that murder. They were buried in the bin, and they might have been ripped but there wasn't a single period stain on them, and I will get to the bottom of what all that was about one day, so go.'

And it's not her that makes me flee but Dad's face, frowning slightly, looking puzzled, half opening his mouth and shutting it again, that makes me turn and run. I really did, I thought I'd buried those tights so deeply in the kitchen bin after I sneaked them out from under my mattress that they'd never be discovered. Upstairs I sit on the bed and cry all my make-up off in rage as I think of Mr Jonasson waiting for me. That and knowing I'll have to go to school all sweaty and stinky like before, now she's taken my Right Guard.

When Mum and Dad finally leave the house to buy some bits and pieces for their weekend trip to Oxford, I dash out behind them as soon as I think they will have cleared the street. By the time I reach the library I'm hot and uncomfortable and not at all how I wanted to be looking. Inside, I search every nook and cranny, desperate to see his blond head bent seriously over his papers, but there's only people shuffling the pages of newspapers about and kids lumped on brightly coloured chairs, flicking over pages without bothering to read them. I could scream in frustration: he's gone, and it's *her* fault, I know it is. It's almost like she arranged that paperboy deliberately.

I wander out and the sights and sounds of Bath busy with its Saturday morning strike me as the dullest thing I've ever seen. There's only one thing left to do, and I know it's not ideal but I head into Waitrose and eventually find him fitting plastic carrier bags of shopping into his trolley on the paid side of the till.

Something flashes in his eyes. 'Phoebe, what are you doing here?'

Something about the way he says it and how his eyes cast around, seeing if anyone's looking, as if this is embarrassing, gives me a crushed feeling in my chest and I try to smile but find I can only shrug and say, 'I looked for you in the library,' and then I feel even worse because even to my own ears my voice sounds flat and accusatory.

'I've got to pack the shopping in the car,' he says, and pushes the trolley round the corner. I really don't know what he intends me to do so I trot behind him, feeling like an idiot, but all the same just needing some flicker from him, some resolution to this whole business or I can't stand it. When he sees me getting in the lift with him I can't read the look on his face but I take that as a good sign, and once we're down in the underground car park he seems to calm down a bit. He finds his car and he starts unloading his trolley, with me handing him carrier bags one at a time. When he's finished he slams the boot down and dusts his hands together as people do when a job is done.

'Listen, Phoebe,' he says, and he sounds a lot nicer now he's over the shock of me appearing. 'You are a promising student and I'd like to help you but we need to be together with the book. So thank you for the help with the shopping but the supermarket isn't the place to do it, you know?'

He reaches over and squeezes my shoulder and somehow I manage to nod and say goodbye and wait until I'm stumbling out into the bright daylight for the tears to jab in the back of my eyelids, because I know now that I've been an absolute stupid child and his kind voice made it so much worse, and now my most fervent wish is that I could take this horrible morning and smash it to pieces.

By early evening, when I arrive at Bertha's front door, I'm exhausted from the fits of emotion that have been going through me all day. I've been thinking about the way he squeezed my shoulder, though, and how perhaps that is something positive for me to hold onto. The way he did it – intimate – makes me more and more sure it is. It's a relief to arrive at Bertha's cool quiet house where Mum dumps me every time she and Dad go away, even though at seventeen I know it's ridiculous they won't allow me to stay at home on my own. It mystifies me how Bertha and Mum have stayed friends all these years. They have nothing in common at all. Maybe it's because Bertha is single so Mum feels she can drop me off at a moment's notice. It's either that or Orla's for the night and I've been palmed off on her family more times than I care to remember. Right now I can't stand the thought of staying with Orla. It's not just that I haven't forgiven her by a long way for trying to drown me. It's the girlish whispered confidences that form a hot condensation in the room. The suffocating night smell of her. I can't help breathing it all in from my little truckle bed that's been wheeled out from underneath hers for the occasion.

'Hello, dear.' As Bertha answers the door, she smiles at me, showing all her great white teeth, and her little dog Paddle skitters around her feet as usual. She's ugly in a way that's completely fascinating, like Baba Yaga in a book I had as a kid. It's not only the enormous teeth but also the hair that straggles around her thin face and the flapping feet tied up into huge, flat lace-up shoes.

I love Bertha's house for all the opposite reasons that I love mine. Going into her hallway feels like entering an underground tunnel. While our house is all dry and airy like a beehive, here there's a delicious chill of ancient bricks and the cold strikes up into your shoes from the floor. It must be the place it's built, low down; you can feel the presence of a water table close by. The colours are all rich reds and dark browns in the dimness. Absolutely nothing changes here. As usual, I tap the silk orchid on the heavy sideboard as I pass, sending it nodding madly. I let all the things I love about her house set off little explosions of pleasure under my skin. The glossy plants with polished leaves that seem to thrive despite the gloom. The clock that chimes the quarter hour. There's glass panels in all the doors so nothing is closed off. It seems to go on for miles in every direction. It's like being in the safest and most beautiful underground bunker.

'I had dinner at home.' I haven't, but getting out of a meal has always been an advantage of coming here. 'I'll just take my stuff upstairs and read before bed,' I say.

I lug my bag up to my room and dump it on the floor. I put my hand between the white sheets and feel the chill there, then sit on the bed and allow myself a moment of feeling completely joyful. Bertha never asks me anything about any-thing. Her eyesight is so terrible I think she can barely see me and I love that. I feel so happy being just a blur.

I take out the York Notes. It occurred to me today that if Mr Jonasson really is going to help me with English, then I don't want to seem thick about it. Bringing the horrible play here seemed like too much, but I can at least read the notes so I will appear to know what I'm talking about.

I lie back on the hard pillow and open the book. I can hear Bertha downstairs and it makes me smile; I imagine her as a mole shuffling about all her corridors. I try and concentrate, I really do, but the beautiful summer sounds coming through the shuttered window and Bertha below, who always leaves me alone, have led me to a state of relaxation that's so rare it's approaching bliss. Then it occurs to me I could enhance that, and what an ideal place to do it – here where I'm left so totally alone – and my hand twitches towards my overnight bag, where the little plastic bag with the squares of blotting paper I bought from Paul has been tucked inside the lining ever since. I shake out my bag over the bed and the plastic bag falls on the white lace cotton duvet cover. Each piece of blotting paper has an image of a bee stamped on it. Paul is very specific about his images. The bee represents the soul, he says, and LSD sets the soul free. It's an old-fashioned choice. Paul kind of prides himself on that, like he's a curator of rare wines that only the discerning will ever know about. I've never been a very dedicated drug user like him. It's been confined to spliffs and, two or three times, ecstasy. It's not only the cost, but I've always been too worried about the effects being marked on my face, leading to interrogations of one kind or another. But the acid intrigues me because I feel it might have something to teach me, to open up places inside that exist but that I'm not yet aware of. Sometimes I feel so squeezed in this little world I have to inhabit, it's like I've been stitched into it. For the moment I'll have to be content with finding new worlds to explore inside myself. My heart squeezes as I carefully tear one piece of blotting paper down the middle with the tips of my fingers and put one half on my tongue.

I lean back, push in my ear buds and find some music with a droning chant on the shuffle, then wait.

I feel so safe here that when hammering on the bedroom door reaches through the music, it's the equivalent of a bomb going off and I nearly fall off the bed. I tear out the ear buds. I hold them dangling from one hand in mid-air, frozen.

'What is it?' I call out finally.

'Phoebe, I've made us something to eat.' Bertha's raspy voice makes the door panels vibrate. This is new, this interference. We usually leave each other completely alone. What's happened? She's chosen the worst possible time to change our habits.

I take a moment for my breathing to slow down. 'It's OK,' I shout back. 'I said, I really don't need anything.'

'Listen, your mother's been on the phone.'

So that's it. A steady drip of dread begins to gather around my heart area.

'She wanted to check you'd got here all right.'

I sit up. 'OK.'

'Listen, Phoebe. Let me see you. It's odd shouting through the door like this.'

This is starting to remind me of the day of the murder, with me locked in the bathroom and my mother's voice questioning me from the outside. I slide off the bed and open the door an inch. There's her bulging eyes, catching the reflected light from my bedroom window as it slants through the shutters. Normally I would look at them and have warm feelings and think, lovely blind eyes, but in this instance I'm on alert, sniffing danger.

'Dear, I've made us something to eat. Your mother said you didn't have a thing before you left.'

*So*, she's been after me, crawling down the telephone wires. I wonder whether she's guessed what I'm up to. When I picture my mother I see her as an insect covered in a hundred long, long feelers all reaching out and tasting the air and the vibrations, ready to pick up any tiny thing amiss. But there wasn't anything, I'm sure of it. I left it all perfect. The diary entry for today: 'Cumulus clouds gather on the eastern edge of Bath, just on the horizon.'

I can't feel any effect of the LSD yet but just the *idea* of it coursing through my bloodstream while I'm having a conversation with Bertha means I have to cling onto the door.

'OK,' I say. Not able to think of an excuse. 'I'll be down in a moment.'

We sit opposite each other at the dining table. The red cloth is chenille and feels soft on my knees. The clock tocks on the mantelpiece. She has cooked fish and a little mess of something that looks like ratatouille.

'I hope you like it.'

I nod and pick up a flake of white fish on the end of my fork. 'Thank you, Bertha.'

As I'm about to put a forkful in my mouth I have a terrible moment and have to put it back down on my plate. It's only going to be a matter of time before she starts talking about the man being ripped open on Walcot Street. People can't leave it alone. Every time it's mentioned a klaxon goes off in my head. She's bound to bring it up and I don't think I could bear it if that dreadful wash of blood and guts came slippery-sliding into the refuge of Bertha's house.

'Don't you like fish, dear?' she asks, and then I realise Bertha would regard that subject as 'not suitable for the table'. I'm safe.

'Sorry, yes. It's lovely.'

I look at her peering down at her plate, and I *really* look, like I'm seeing her anew. She's so kind. There is the most beautiful cut glass of something she calls Crémant beside each plate that she says is better than Champagne. She's got out her best napkins with birds patterned on them just for me. Paddle sleeps peacefully under the table. Guilt stirs in me at how I was thinking of her before. I wonder how many women over the centuries with faces like hers have been thought of as Baba Yaga, as hags exiled to forests or deserted moors or isolated caves, left alone to mutter and prophesy. I notice all the little things that she does to compensate for that face and it nearly splits my heart. The cardigan that sits over her flat chest is a deep berry colour and the wool is as fine and light as fleece caught on a bramble. The silk cuffs that show beneath the sleeves are immaculately laundered above her skinny hands. She wears a maroon scarf with yellow polka dots tied in a bow that is both elegant and would have taken time to get just so. I ache at the image of her doing that in the mirror.

'Bertha,' I say suddenly. 'Do you mind being single?'

She smiles, as if to herself. 'This is 2003, dear, not 1903. A woman living alone is nothing to remark on. Why do you ask?'

'It's just . . . I often think I'd like to live alone too and I was wondering what it's like.'

She wipes her mouth with her bird napkin. 'It has its compensations.'

I watch her calmly eating. Why have I never wondered about her before? I really don't know much about her. 'Bertha,' I go on. 'How long have you known my mother for?'

She puts her fork down. 'Well, let's think. We met at college so it must be going on thirty years now.' She smiles over her plate. 'I wouldn't say we were close friends and I

74

hadn't seen her for years so it was quite a surprise when she turned up on the doorstep with a baby in tow. She'd tracked me down somehow.'

Her tone of voice talking about my mother – there's something about it I recognise and I go looking for what that is. Then I remember. There was a session with pussy-cat face where the new receptionist sent me up to the consulting room when I arrived. When I slipped inside the room it was empty but I could hear voices in the adjoining room, then someone crossing towards the door. They must've been holding the door handle because it was kind of jiggling up and down my side and I heard, clear as a bell, pussy-cat face saying, 'Well, you know how it is. It feels like I can only do so much with Phoebe without treating her mother. I know one shouldn't diagnose like this, but all I can say is Mum has the most obvious case of narcissistic personality disorder *I've* ever seen.' And even though I know they're supposed to be completely neutral, there was that same tone of dislike in her voice I've just heard in Bertha's. Then the door opened and pussy-cat face swung into the room with a pile of files under her arm. Her face looked stricken, and furious. 'I didn't know you were there,' she said. 'Donna is new but I have told her that the clear procedure is for me to *come down* and *fetch* people for appointments.'

*Donna's going to get it*, I thought, but I pretended like nothing had happened and I could see pussy-cat face begin telling herself I hadn't heard.

At least the session gave me something to think about for a change. I pondered about it for weeks and looked up 'narcissistic personality disorder' in a psychological textbook in the library, and to be fair it did all sound very much like the way Mum is, but the more I thought about it the weaker I felt. It was so complicated and what could I do about it anyway? The knowledge began to fade. At home everyone carries on as normal and Mum holds down a job and Dad seems to manage with her, so I began to wonder if pussy-cat face was mistaken. It's only me that seems to feel so angry towards her, which is why the way Bertha said what she did is interesting to me. I wish I was a bit more with it so I could think about it clearly.

It makes me wonder if it's possible – and this is the very first time I've thought this – that it's actually *me* Bertha likes, and *me* she wants to keep up with. The idea is exciting and makes her seem even more endearing. I smile across the table at her and she smiles back with all her teeth.

Then I look behind her shoulder. The shadows behind the lamps and carefully dusted ornaments on the sideboard are growing knobbly. I have the sensation of time unravelling, out of control. When I look behind me the outside has grown dark at the panes of windows. 'It seems to have gone dark so suddenly,' I cry out before I can stop myself.

She wipes her mouth carefully. 'Not really, dear.'

I look down and my plate is nearly empty and I can't remember what any of it even tasted like. It's only the fish bones left, beached to one side, and the plate strikes me as a miraculous and tiny treasure island. I'm transfixed as left-over smears and bits of food become sea vegetables and a miniature tide. I tear my eyes away.

'I think it's time I went to bed.'

I hold my breath and wait for her to react. I have no idea if my voice is normal. I could be shouting or whispering. I might not have said anything at all.

'All right, dear. Let's take the plates through.'

We carry the plates out to the kitchen and stack them in the dishwasher.

'I'll just come up and get my book,' she says.

I follow behind her and as she climbs the stairs her legs stretch out like paint running down paper. Each stair twitches, just once, as I put my foot on it.

She pauses with her hand on her bedroom door. 'Good-night.'

'Yes, goodnight,' I call out, as if I hadn't a care in the world. 'Sleep tight.'

'You don't need to shout, dear.'

I close the door behind me and relish drinking in the safeness of being in my bedroom. I open the wooden shutters and the window wider to the night. I breathe in the damp night air and look upwards, and it's at that moment I nearly collapse with the beauty of it. It absolutely crushes me.

I fall to my knees.

When I first saw that tiny bee on my fingertip, I had no idea the power it held in its wings that were no bigger than grape pips. How it could show me that all along I've been half dead and what it feels like if the tombstone rolls off. How it could scratch the skin of the world right away to reveal the raw and unnatural beauty beneath. I want to feel like this forever. Great glassy tears run down my cheeks and sobs choke my throat as above me the stars cavort and whirl in a Van Gogh sky.

# 8

# Orla

Last Friday; the nature of evil.

I couldn't take my eyes off Phoebe as she listened, rapt. A shaft of golden dust triangulated behind her profile as she tilted up her chin in concentration. When I did finally drag my eyes away, I watched Mr Jonasson to see if he was stealing looks at her or if what she told me is all in her imagination. Hard to say. I felt rocked by emotions I didn't seem to have control over.

It seems we were all in a state that day. I found Grace outside smoking behind the bushes, crouched down, dripping tears onto the ground.

I asked her what the matter was and she went into a rant about what useless crap we were learning. 'No one's interested in what you really have to do to get by,' she said. 'My life has gone to shit and no one cares.' Then she hugged her stomach with both arms. 'Fuck's sake,' she said. 'I think there goes my period starting too. As if I didn't have enough on my plate without bleeding like a stuck pig once a month. I'm so disorganised. I knew it was going to start and I still didn't put anything in my bag. Have you got anything?'

A group had emerged from the back door, Phoebe among them.

'Hey,' I called out to her. 'Come over here.'

I didn't suppose she had anything. It was just an excuse to engage with her. She let slip once that her mother won't let her buy tampons. She's supposed to always use pads. Whenever she comes round I always find a couple of my tampons missing from the box. I suspect she puts one in to sit at the dining table and lord it over her mother not knowing what's inside her.

She turned and gave me a look so cold it went right down me to the soles of my feet. Was it that look that made me finally ask Eleanor for a drink? I think it might have been, and that's why I'm here in this bar on a lazy sunny Sunday ordering two Manhattans. I have a flush of worry in case I'm asked for ID. It would spoil everything to go back to the table bringing apologetic explanations and two glasses slopping Coca-Cola over the rims. But it's OK. There's a certain heaviness, a chunkiness about me that I know makes me look older than I am. I guess I should give thanks for that today.

I grip the sides of the tray. The drinks in their long-stemmed glasses feel unstable as I pick my way over to where Eleanor's sitting. She's waiting, inserting her fingers into corkscrew curls of her hair. It's almost Afro hair although it's darkly blonde. It's the only thing that stands out about her. The rest is pure pink-and-white Home Counties and screams horse riding, skiing, family holidays in Cornwall, brisk walks before a Sunday lunch. With her springing curls and her healthy skin she reminds me of a patch of fertile ground that life and growth practically jump out of.

She smiles as I approach. I wonder if this place is special enough. It's a chain that does both food and drink or just drink, faux continental, with staff keeping their eyes on the clock for the end of their shifts. It does, however, have cosy booths and red glass in the windows that gives it a muted, intimate air, which is why I chose it for this encounter.

'Lovely. Thanks, Orla,' she says as she takes one of the glasses, the drink inside gritty with ice.

'Did you want something to eat? I should've asked. I . . .'

She puts her hand over mine. It's cold from the icy glass. 'No, I'm not hungry. This is just right,' she says, and to demonstrate the rightness of it she dips down and takes a sip without taking her eyes off me, as if to say, *See, perfect.* It's a flirtatious gesture too, I'm well aware of that, and the knowledge sends jitters rippling through my diaphragm.

I nod and fumble with my own drink, letting bitter-tasting ice crystals slop into my mouth.

'So, your school . . .' she says.

'Yes, it's an odd little place.' I laugh too loud. Bath is peppered with private schools but ours is the Oliver Twist among them. You can see it on open days with all the serious parents with burning eyes – leaning on sticks, some of them, because they had their kids so old. They've come for the tiny classes, the high-minded curriculum that includes Classics. They don't care about cracked loo seats or the freezing draughts that whistle down the corridors. The contrast with where Eleanor goes makes me feel more unwieldy beside her. The privilege I've glimpsed has been astounding. It curtains them so completely that we can look in but they can't look out. Everything about our school crumbles, drips, creaks. The head teacher limps and flaps her skirts around in her down-at-heel shoes. In the basement a fat cook toils in a boiling kitchen to serve up watery stews for lunch. The canteen itself doubles up as a classroom so the wooden desks feel silty when you run your fingers over them. They can only keep this school going by paring everything down and down. It's a peculiar little institution for those with parents that want private education but can only afford a sliver of a fee, or for the delicate creatures whose parents worry they might be eaten alive in the state system. There are a few scholarships for deserving causes, like Grace. I'm sure there must be a story to each and every person who's washed up there. Me: too sensitive for the ordinary school; crying with a kind of frantic fury if I was teased. Bullies made a beeline for me, deliciously sure of the response. Phoebe says she was thrown out of her last place when she was twelve, although she could just be making that up. Grace just knocked on the door one day. She'd seen people coming in and out and got curious. She said to them she wasn't stretching her abilities where she was, though she told us afterwards she wanted to come here because it's so close if she needs to pop home. Her boldness must've impressed them because they took her in. Lessons are strange, old-fashioned. There's dictation that goes on until your hand cramps up.

I tell Eleanor where I live, wanting to serve up some normality in contrast to all that. Our home is all golden stone and climbing roses; a lovely rambling family house purchased by my dad's hard graft on oil rigs. She'll understand that.

'I know it,' she says, nibbling on a speared cherry that is nearly black.

'The best bit is the garden. I kind of keep it myself. My parents aren't interested so it's mine really.' I picture it now, waiting for me, and feel a little ache of homesickness. There's something about being able to grow things. Last year I even scattered seed and grew bitter leaves that I picked and ate on slices of white bread and unsalted butter. 'Orla's weeds,' my family teased, but I didn't care. 'I've got a few tools – I mean, a spade and some cutters – and I'm fixing it up. I can see exactly how I want it in my head.' Then I'm off, talking about the bulbs I planted last autumn, seeing them pushing up through the ground. The clump of arum lilies I've been nurturing and the sculptural head I found in a second-hand shop and lugged home.

Even as I'm talking, I'm thinking, *Is this a date?* When I called her and asked if she wanted to meet, I thought at the time it would be obvious. But really, is it? After all, how normal is it for two girls to meet for a coffee or an illicit drink, then go off to grub around in the make-up counter for an hour, returning home later with sparkling stained fingers to parents demanding to know, 'What have you done to your face?' I'd hoped that the cocktails would signal something else, but who knows? It's so complicated.

She also doesn't look like someone who would hang around make-up counters.

I peter out talking about the garden. It was a stupid subject. Why would she be interested?

'It sounds awesome.' I try not to think she says it gamely but it silences me. 'I'd like to see it,' she says, staring right at me, her eyes not flinching away for a second.

I realise in a rush that's why I went on about it so much. That that's where I was leading her all along. I clear my throat. 'Come back with me. The house is empty at the moment.'

I know my mother is out. She has a hair appointment, one of the rituals undertaken before Dad's return, alongside the manicures, the picking out of a new dress and the rubbing in of creams like she has to shore something up that has desiccated in his absence. My two brothers have been dropped off to play at friends' houses beforehand. I know all this because I carefully checked it out this morning.

I hold my breath. She stirs the slush of ice at the bottom of her glass with her straw, meddles her finger in the bubbles of condensation that have arranged themselves as neatly as polka dots on the outside.

'OK.'

Behind her, the black-and-white-suited waiters flicker past the windows, giving the impression of the end loop of a film. The reddish light pouring through lends the room a sophisticated, erotic air. But despite the fact I felt myself colour with pleasure at her assent, I feel uncomfortable. I'm fully aware that Eleanor, with her sports-mad radiancy, is a kind of stand-in for something else, something I ache for and can't have, something called Phoebe. My passions have only found a kind of ventriloquism in this other girl. Despite all that, I'm luring her back anyway and it makes me feel creepy, like a spider bringing its prey back to a web.

I'm about to change my mind, make some excuse, but already she's pulled on her green jacket with the flowery lining that she shows off by folding back the cuffs. I push my glass away and follow her out.

I let us into the house and we walk through the silence of it straight out into the back garden. Instantly I feel I've talked it up too much and now I'm seeing it through her eyes: on the small side, ringed with neglect. The efforts I've made here are neither picturesque nor beautiful. Instead, they look like the work of a daft old woman who makes knotty craftwork that nobody wants for charity sales. It stinks of loneliness. The small rose garden I started a couple of years ago was planted in the wrong place and now the scrubby roses there have been stunted by the shade. The giant clay female head that I thought would transform the space into something mystical and Eastern I failed to see the deficiencies in. The modelling seems grotesque now; the thick nose, the undefined eyes, the lips stuck on like an afterthought.

'I haven't been out here for ages,' I lie, going back on what I'd told her in the bar.

She puts her hand over mine. 'It's lovely, Orla,' she says, not taking her eyes off me. 'It's really lovely.'

Then the best of it seems to burst into life and the passion flower flopping over the wall and its sweet scent is swirled by the breeze circling around us like a fizzing sparkle of magic-wand trail in a cartoon. It turns the moment rosy. I lean forward and kiss her full on the lips.

Beneath my own mouth hers stays rigid. She doesn't move away, yet neither does she respond. I can feel the hard boniness of her teeth behind her lips and realise she must be gritting them, waiting for me to stop. Yet still she doesn't move away so I try again, try to push the tip of my tongue between her lips. We stay like that for about a minute, with me waiting for some kind of sign, a response, just something. When finally it doesn't come I stand back.

Her face is composed, not quite happy enough to look pleased, but all the same I detect a quiet satisfaction there. I see then that it's something she expected to happen, wanted to happen as well. There's something bovine about her now, a kind of calmness, and I realise in an instant that this is something that she needed to do and was now out of the way. She'd been planning too, and this, her first girl kiss, was the

84

starting pistol to the rest of her life and other far, far better kisses, and that's all she was expecting it to be.

I have a sudden longing for Phoebe's spiky weirdness so strong it nearly tilts me over. If she were here she'd be roaming around, picking at things, unable to stay still. She'd say something like, *Let's rampage, let's go outside, at least, and look at people in the street and pretend we know them, let's* . . . No, no, no. I will not think of her. I will not.

I shove my hands into my pockets. 'It's cold. Let's go inside,' I say abruptly.

She shrugs. 'OK.'

I feel the almost chemical sting of tears behind each eyeball. All I want to do is get rid of her now. Curl myself up in a ball somewhere warm and attempt to heal over the day.

She follows behind as I head towards the back door. I notice a peel of paint coming loose by the cast-iron latch as I push and my eyes adjust to the darkness inside, all the time knowing something's wrong, something's amiss, before my vision adjusts and the lumpy shape of my mother sharpens into focus.

As soon as I see her I can tell Mum has watched it all from the kitchen window, past the taps silhouetted against the light. Her jaw is stuck to one side as if she's biting the cheek inside and her eyes are blinky, darting to look at Eleanor over my shoulder. Her distorted face contrasts with the hard bell of blow-dried hair that frames it. A teapot with the lid off stands next to the kettle that plumes steam. I can see her moving to the window to pass the few minutes it took for the kettle to boil. I can see her hand going to her mouth.

'I'll be going,' says Eleanor behind me. She's assessed the situation quicker than I would have given her credit for.

When the front door clicks shut I turn to Mum and cross my arms. 'You're very early.'

'Really.' She puts her fingers to her eyelids and flutters them there. 'Really, Orla . . .'

'I've done nothing wrong.' I can't help but feel the opposite to that, though, seeing her neck mottled red from distress.

'You won't be able to have children. You know that, don't you?'

'Don't say that.' I feel a fury building inside. 'Not everyone has to be like you and Dad. That's not the only way it works.'

'Oh, you think you know the way the world works, at seventeen – you know it all, don't you?' Her fear has turned her arch, superior, and my fury tightens up another notch. 'But let me tell you, missy, you don't. Families aren't built that way.'

'Shut up. Stop talking about what you don't know about. I can have children.' I'm shouting now.

'Really, Orla, don't raise your voice to me.' She's going blinky again. She wants to make ridiculous pronouncements without them being questioned. She stands and smooths out the sheeny fabric of her full skirt. In the run-up to Dad returning she starts dressing all feminine again, like she's in training for something.

'Fucking look at you.' I'm spitty and shouting now. 'Your ridiculous clothes, all your make-up larded on. You don't need all that to have children, it's just not true. You don't even have a *job*. It's pathetic. What the hell do you think you know about the world?'

'Orla, stop this now. You don't know what you're talking about.'

'Yes I do, and I *can* have children. I've got a bloody womb same as anyone else.' I'm yelling at the top of my voice now. 'I can have hundreds of children if I want to.' There's a pining ache in the pit of my stomach where one might grow. 'I can have a child. You know what? I'm going to have a child. I'll have a baby and fuck you all.'

'That's enough. How dare you speak to me like that.' She turns back to the kettle. 'Your father is back before too long, thank God.'

'You're so fucking weak. How am I supposed to learn anything from you?' I start crying big snotty tears. I have to get away from her so I run up the stairs but my bedroom appals me. The frigid lace hanging at the window and the walls the revolting vulnerable pink of newborn mice, their skins so thin the blood shows through. I want to wreck, to wreak, to tear it all to bits. I grab a diamanté necklace dangling from my mirror. I'd hated it the moment I found it in my hands and had inexplicably gone up to the counter and bought it. I'd been thirteen. I guess it had corresponded with some vision I'd been manufacturing then, to the point of buying things I actively disliked. It comes apart surprisingly easily in my hands, crumpling as I dismember the segments and fling them across the room. Then I lower myself unsteadily on the pastel-covered bed. The breeze rocks the lace at the window and outside the sun dips down. It pierces into the room and it seems like every single bit of broken necklace winks at me, like some alien creature or an insect that can replicate itself from any tiny piece that is ripped off its body.

I think about facing my mother. It's not even that she's caught me kissing another girl that bothers me, or that we've fallen out; it's that I know – without a shadow of a doubt – that the real reason I never could have confided in her is that every time she looks at me from now on she'll be thinking, *My daughter likes vaginas. My daughter wants to touch a vagina. How awful, and it'll make Orla end up a barren old fool and it'll mean no grandchildren for me to dandle on my knee.*

I sit on the edge of the bed with the bits of necklace glinting around me. There's nothing to lose now. I feel like I've reached the very shore of desperation, that it no longer matters what I do or say, so I reach for my phone. When Phoebe answers, her cracked voice sends a vibration through me.

I push my mouth close to the phone. 'Listen, Phoebe. I know how much you've been hating me and this is the last time I'll try and communicate. I mean really, if you want to tell me to fuck off you can, and I'll leave you alone, I promise, but I have to tell you how really, truly sorry I am. It was stupid and childish pushing you into the river like that and I don't know why I did it or what comes next, but what I do know is that I'm feeling really fucking desperate right now.' I stop, a sob blocking my throat. 'Really, really desperate.'

'Orla.'

'What?' The word squeezes out painfully.

She's silent for a minute and my heart beats so hard I can feel the throb of it in my neck.

'Orla. I have something wonderful to tell you about.'

# 9

# Phoebe

No fog or filthy air. Just a June day so ripe it looks ready to burst out of itself. The sky turned into a flag by the crossed aeroplane trails against the blue. The early morning rain sucked dry from the trees still hanging in the air. *This is my witch's prediction*, I tell them, *that we won't be missed.*

Yes. It's as easy as that for three girls to vanish into the day, as if they'd been borne away on a breath of wind, not a hair left behind and with just a pocketful of walnuts filched from the bowl on the sideboard for sustenance. Take a right turn instead of a left. Cross the road instead of staying on the same old side. Slip through the wooden fence threaded through with grass and you're nearly gone. Over hill, over dale to where seeds pepper the air, then fall in a soft slurry onto the surface of the moving river.

Then the Spinney. Squeeze through the gap underneath the wall and we're there.

'This is true magic,' I say. I place the squares of blotting paper around the wishing bowl. 'It absolutely is.'

*How perfect*, I think, because the little pyramid printed on each one turns the wishing bowl into a three-cornered star.

'Now, who's first?'

Grace picks up the paper on her fingertip and puts it on her tongue and only a second later her mouth is closed. She's eager because she's had enough of her world as it is.

She's craving for escape too, it's as clear as day. Orla takes longer. She sits there cross-legged with the paper on her out-stretched tongue for ages before she flicks it back into her mouth.

Me, I slip mine into the breast pocket of my blouse.

It was a last-minute decision. I want to see what they look like. I want to see if there are any changes on the out-side. I'm curious not just for its own sake, but also for other purposes. I need to know what *she* might be able to read on my face. If my hands twitch, telling tales all on their own. If I smack my lips repeatedly with my tongue without realis-ing. If, as legend has it, my pupils turn to pinpricks.

There's quiet for a moment.

'I can't feel anything,' says Orla finally. I have the idea she was on the point of pretending to feel the effects, then gave up.

'It takes longer than that,' I say. 'You have to try and kind of float into it. Let's all lie back and look up at the trees.'

'Isn't it true you'll see something awful if it's a bad trip? Something from your life?' Orla asks.

'Don't say that,' I blurt out. 'I don't want to see anything about that awful murder on Walcot Street I made happen.'

'What the fuck are you talking about?' Grace cocks her chin at me.

'That man that was splattered down the wall.'

'Phoebe, why on earth do you think you made it hap-pen?' asks Orla curiously.

I shake my head. I hadn't wanted to get onto this subject. 'I just did, OK.'

I don't tell them about the nights I've lain awake, sick and trembling, thinking about it and what I did. Worrying that it might happen again.

'Phoebe, that's insane,' says Orla. 'You can't possibly believe that.'

I shrug. 'Not really,' I lie. 'Come on, let's lie down and concentrate.'

'I worry about you sometimes,' says Orla as she flops down.

We lie three in a row. *We could be lying like this, capped with headstones one day*, I think. Though admittedly the chances of us all being buried together, side by side, are slim, for who knows where we will all end up and where life will scatter us. All I can hope is that it's a very long way from here and from *her*. That is my heartfelt wish.

I hear Grace stir beside me and she slowly stands up, for all the world like she's getting up out of her tomb and seeing a world she thought she'd never lay eyes on again.

She looks around her. 'Christ,' she says, 'Christ alive.'

I bite my fingers in excitement and try to sneak a look at her face but she's staring in the other direction. She puts her fingers lightly to the base of her spine and kneads there. 'Christ alive,' she says again, swivelling her head to look upwards at the trees.

I have to practically stop myself choking on my fingers.

Orla lifts her head. 'What? I'm still getting nothing.' She sounds like a whiny child.

'You have to wait and not be watching for it,' I say. 'Let's do something to take our minds off it. How about doing the wishing bowl like we did when we were kids?'

'We could ask for what we want in our futures, like our hopes,' says Orla.

'Predictions,' I say, correcting her. I wipe sweaty fingers down the front of my white blouse. They leave dirty marks there like I'm leaking my own mud.

There's a moment's silence then we seem to move as one, crab-like, to the wishing bowl, and I realise doing this has been in our minds, humming away in the background, as soon as we set out for here. It's covered all over with ivy, the stems like centipedes on hundreds of fine, hairy suckers. I tear off the ivy, and its suckers protest against their murder with a quiet ripping sound.

'What now?' I'm panting with the heat and the effort.

'We need to decide what we want.' Grace is moving her fingers to her face a lot – up to her eyes, as if she's checking they're still there.

'Yes,' I breathe out in a hiss.

Orla looks embarrassed. I know she's thinking about our last conversation about the wishing bowl and how she nearly drowned me afterwards, so I take her hand to show her it's all over.

'Go on,' I say. 'You go first.'

'I know what it is that I want,' she says. 'It's never, ever to be like my pathetic mother.' She crosses her arms and looks like she's about to cry.

I take a walnut out of my pocket and smash it with a stone on the rock. 'I thought you and your mum were best of friends, like sisters. I thought you did everything together.' I root around for the sweet knobbly nuggets among the bits of shell.

'She's a bitch.' Orla tosses her head. 'She's a lame bitch that's never even had a proper job.'

This is interesting. Orla and her mother have always been as thick as thieves. It's another reason why I hate staying there. I always feel like they're going to have a good old analysis of me after I've gone, tucked up on the sofa together with their hands dipping into the biscuit tin. I can almost feel their knives digging in on the walk home as they dissect me like downmarket versions of pussy-cat face.

I pleat my fingers together. 'You know what, they're all bitches. It's because they've outgrown their usefulness and they know it. They try and pretend they haven't by organising everything so they can feel the world would fall apart if they weren't there. But it won't. It'll go on just the same whether they exist or not.' I stick my chin out. 'Our mothers are completely irrelevant. I want to go before I get like that.'

'Go where?' Orla has a sweat moustache.

'To die, of course.'

Grace's smile is loopy, lopsided. 'I don't. I'm going to live to a ripe old age. I'm going to be an old, old lady with a hat.' She stretches out her arms towards the trees.

That makes me think again. Grace always seems wise, like she has an animal instinct I just don't possess. I know I sounded convinced when I said I wanted to die before I'm old but I wonder if that's true. I think about Bertha. She doesn't meddle or organise. She just goes about as herself and that's enough. It almost makes me long not to look the way I look but to be as ugly as she is. It would make life so easy to look like that.

'You need a better prediction than that.' I go back to Orla. I'm not going to let her get away with it, not doing this properly and just moaning. 'Come on.' I snap my fingers under her nose over and over in case she's drifting away.

'Stop it.' She pushes my hand away. She gathers herself and I swear she seems to grow about a foot like she's left the ground. She cradles her stomach. 'All right. What I want, what I want is proper love. Love so strong it can turn the day into night, then back again.' Her fingers knead her stomach, then she wraps her arms around her own shoulders and holds herself. I can see she believes this is real now. That she can make things happen. 'What I want is love so strong it's like a blade that can cut me open. Love that could burn me to death. I'd sell my soul to the devil for it. I want another life to totally entwine with mine. To have somebody who is mine and mine alone.'

We stare at her, stunned, for a moment and she shrinks back down into herself.

'Well, it's not me.' The words are out of my mouth before I can help it. I examine her face to see what impact they've made but she looks closed off, like she might not even have heard.

I need to do something. Even though she was talking about love, she sounded so desperate it's like she's brought an evil presence down among us. I can feel its taint in the air. We need to banish it before it takes over our whole day.

I have an idea. A smile goes creeping all across my face. 'We should do it again.'

'What?' Orla wipes the moustache away with her fingers.

'You remember, what we talked about before, about pissing into the bowl.'

'What?'

'You know. You did it when you were nine.'

She pretend-heaves. 'Yeeuk.'

'Come on.'

She doesn't nervous-fake laugh like she normally would. She looks over to where Grace is. Grace has moved away from us. She's standing, watching the flow of the river with

94

her face screwed up in concentration and her head cocked to one side, like its babbling has something to tell her that's absolutely vital for her life. Her hair has grown a little bit; she's let it go as far as the tops of her ears. It's the colour of burnt butter and it makes her look softer now it's marginally longer. She seems almost child-like for once. She usually looks like she's about to smash your face in.

'D'you think we've upset her? Grace's mother's not a bitch,' Orla says quietly. 'We shouldn't say things like that in front of her.'

'True, but that's only because she's so sick. If she wasn't she'd be the same as all the others.'

Orla is scratching the hard-packed mud miserably with a stick. 'D'you think they hate us too?' Orla looks up, like she's surprised herself. 'Perhaps when we get as big as them, or even bigger – I'm a head taller than my mum – they start hating us too, but they have to do it in private. It's a secret because you aren't supposed to hate your own offspring.'

'Of course they do.'

I sneak the blotting paper out of my pocket and put it on my tongue. I want to look inside that pyramid now. I can't wait any longer. The time for observing others will have to wait.

'Listen,' I say, as I feel the paper turn to mulch in my mouth. 'Wouldn't you be disappointed if you had children and all they did was grow up and wish you were dead? I'm surprised you've only just realised it.'

'I don't wish my mum was dead.'

'Yes you do.'

'I think they're afraid.' Orla stops, like her scratchings have finally revealed something to her. 'I think that's what it is: they're afraid such a lot of the time. They live in fear. You can see it distorting their faces.'

With this, I must admit, she might have a point. It's a surprising thought. Maybe *she* is afraid of me and that's why things are the way they are, but before I have a chance to answer, Grace turns abruptly. 'What are you talking about?' she calls over.

'Not much,' Orla calls back. She doesn't want Grace to know we've been talking about her mother. She's as touchy as a cat about that.

Orla hugs her arms around herself again. 'I think it's starting. Fuck, fuck. Phoebe, I'm scared. I'm really, really scared.'

'Don't be,' I breathe. 'It's wonderful.'

She puts her hands up to her head. 'What if I can't control it?' Her eyes are wide, terrified.

I go up to her and wrap my arms around her. 'Sssh, you don't have to. It's better if you don't try.'

I feel the wet of tears on my neck and she whispers, panic in her voice. 'Phoebe, hold me, hold me. Fuck. Fuck. Fuck. There's something behind that tree. I can't see it but I know it's there.'

She leans back and her face is a downward mask, like the painted face of tragedy in the theatre. It plants a horrible cold seed of fear in me as well.

'Stop it.' I shake her. 'You're making me afraid too. Don't be a silly cow about it. Breathe slowly.'

'Don't shout, for fuck's sake. There's no need to shout at me. I'm frightened. Hold me again like you did just then. I feel like I'm going to fly up off the ground and spin off. Please.'

'Sssh, there, there,' I croon, as much to calm me down as her. I put my arms around her tight like I'm pulling her back down to the earth. We nuzzle, hot cheek to hot cheek, and I focus over her shoulder. A group of crows rise up together in crooked flight. They burst into a million pieces in the sky and the pieces fall down on us like soot. I put my hand out to catch a flake and it slips through my fingers. It's astonishing. I'm transfixed by the beauty of it.

She nuzzles back into my neck, hiding her eyes and whimpering.

'Just try looking,' I whisper right into her ear. 'It helps you to see everything as it really is, what everything is truly made of.' I feel her begin relaxing into my arms. We melt into each other, our flesh reaching out for the feel of flesh, and her sobs begin to change to snuffling.

'What's the matter with her?' When Grace comes over I can tell she's really far gone. Her face is hectic.

'Nothing. We were just talking about doing the spell, like we did before when we were kids.'

'Peeing in the bowl?' Grace throws her head back and laughs.

Something tilts in me at the sight of her. Her real self is shining through the dirt of the world. She's a monkey now, chattering her teeth, and I wonder why I've never seen her monkeyness before. Her dear little ears stick out from her hair. She's saying, 'I'll make the piss. I don't care. This is what happened the other day. It all spilled out of my mum and it was terrible, but this will make it all better and we can conjure an extra-strong spell. We can say exactly how we want things to be from now on and everything will be completely changed forever.'

'What are you talking about?' I ask, lifting my hair from my shoulders. But right at that moment a shaft of sunlight pierces through the trees and I have to let go of Orla to fall on my face and grovel there in the earth before it, because the light has the words of God printed inside it like a stick of rock. They are saying: *You girls are absolutely perfect in this moment.* When I lift my head back up, the words are melting, dripping down inside the tube of sunlight, and Grace is squatting on the rock with her knickers around her ankles. She must have taken off her shoes because her feet are bare and white against the moss and ferns.

Orla is smirking behind her, calm now but with tear stains on her face. 'For fuck's sake, Grace,' she calls out. 'We weren't being serious.'

'No,' I say. 'Let her. She knows exactly what she's doing.' Because I realise now with great certainty how false the words in the sunlight are and the real revelation will come from Grace, who squats there like some pale sprite on her throne of ferns and ivy. It'll come from her pee, which will be a kind of divining mirror because it's come from a place so deep within her, like the thermal spring from the centre of the earth that feeds the Roman Baths, but the fact that her knickers have a piece of grey elastic hanging loose makes me ache for her anew. What kind of prophet has to put up with that?

'Go on, Grace, do it,' I call out.

'I am,' she calls back from her throne, and I can hear gushing and splashing from underneath her. She stands up, pulls up her ragged knickers and kicks out her foot to shake off the drops, then leaps off the rock.

The three of us crow with laughter. The laughter pushes

me to the ground and doubles me up. It makes a different sort of tears stream down Orla's face. It bounces off the sky and back at us like an energy we're emitting. When we're nearly done and have exhausted it, I sidle up to the rock on my hands and knees.

'Christ, Grace. When did you last drink any fluids?'

The piss is murky dark with a scum of bubbles; the surface of it still trembles and the reflected trees part and re-form.

She waves my question away. 'What else? What else?' she screeches.

I take a couple of walnuts from my pocket and lob them. They fall into the bowl with a splash, then bob up and float on the surface.

We howl some more and Orla dips into her pocket, takes out a sticky packet of Haribo and shakes them in; jellied red hearts and lips follow bright yellow stars, rings and fried eggs.

'What will you wish for?' Grace asks, and as soon as she does I know for absolute certain what it is. The trees above us knit together to make a dark place for what I'm about to say.

'The house, the house. I want the house for my own.' I jump around in excitement at the thought and a shoe comes off. 'S'all right,' I shout. 'I'm always losing shoes.'

Grace *is* a monkey now, her white foot on the bottom branch of the tree, then up to the next. She's shed her school blouse now and underneath, her neat breasts are in a greying sateen bra with a ragged flower at the centre. Halfway up she stops.

'Yes,' she screeches. 'Phoebe will be queen, queen, queen of her house. She will reign supreme from the top floor with

99

her crown that I will weave for her out of rubbish gathered off the ground. She will look out at her subjects from above with an iron gaze but she will rule justly.'

As soon as she says it I can see it as clear as day. Me at the top window, staring over all of Bath with glassy eyes, a rough crown of woven rags and stones tipping over my forehead. I'm so excited I open out my arms and let out a piercing warrior's cry. Orla cowers and covers her ears.

As I yell I make another silent prediction. Mr Jonasson will be as one who is under my spell and because of that *she* will be as nothing any more. It will be like she doesn't exist.

When I've exhausted muttering my prophecies, I walk over and look up at Grace's bright eyes.

'Rapunzel, let down your hair,' I call up and have to double over I'm laughing so much, because even if she's grown it a little bit, hair isn't something Grace has ever had a lot of. It would never be enough for anyone to grab onto. Finally I stop laughing and straighten up. 'What about you? What do you want?' I shout. She's lobbing bits of twigs and things that look like pine cones towards the bowl, and one hits like a bomb and an arc of urine splashes up Orla's front.

'Shit,' she yells. 'That's horrible. I'm covered.' She dances about like a crazed shadow, batting herself in panic all over – her shoulders, her hair – even though the sparkling yellow stain is only up her front. But we ignore her.

Grace swings her legs from her perch. 'I want a toad,' she shouts. 'Like a proper witch. Bring me a toad.' And I pretend to look under rocks, my belly tight with laughter, not caring about scraping my hands when I heave them up.

'Not here. Not here. I'll try that one,' I call out to her. 'Hang on for a tick. I'll get something.' I find a snail under a stone, a crisped mucousy flap hanging at its little door. He bobs his head inside and the flap goes down after him. 'Look.' I hold it up for Grace to see. 'Will a snail do? It's a huge one.' I can feel the weight of it like a stone in my hand and without waiting for her answer I let him go, *plink*, into the bowl and he sinks to the bottom. I carry on looking for a while but my hands are sore now, and when we're bored of that game, Grace leans forward on her branch and nods.

'I know what it is I really want, more than anything.'

'Go on.'

'My own life. I want my own glorious life, but to have that, to want it, means Mum would have to die.' A look of panic passes over her face and she wobbles on her perch. 'No. No, I'm not wishing that. Don't think I'm wishing that, spirits.'

'What spirits are you on about?' asks Orla.

'Nothing, no one. I didn't want the bowl to think I wanted her to die. It's only that I never want to have to look at a fucking drip or a wheelchair or an adjustable medical bed again. I want the bathroom cabinet not to have a single bottle of pills in it. I want her to get better so I can walk out of the front door of our flat and not think about what's happening there all day. I want to be able to think about the future and not see a gaping black hole in front of me. I want to go out with Daniel properly, like anyone else would.' There are tears shining in her eyes.

She's never said any of this before. Usually she keeps her cards close to her chest.

'Come down,' I say.

She climbs down, her feet clinging to the branches, and we huddle around the wishing bowl in a circle, our hands touching each other's hands and heads and shoulders, winding towards the other, wanting the connection of flesh and hair. I feel the real crackle of magic go through us all and it's like the world has been changed forever. Later, I think, I'll picture this, our hair in stripes across our faces, our foreheads shining with sweat, our eyes wide open and demented, our crouching postures animal, the gritty earth lodging in our fingernails as we dig them into the mud – I'll picture this and I might reel in disgust or fear; I might hold the image away from myself as if I might be tainted by it. But right now, at this very moment, I feel a strange elixir course through my veins as if we are capable of flight and the many other impossible things that usually remain hidden from our view.

We walk home through a golden red afternoon. It's the time of year where the light stays, as if the sky is lit with lamps, right into the night. I sense the evening ahead and how, if the room is empty, I will watch out over Bath and the darkening evening like the queen that Grace saw, like the Rapunzel I always wanted to be.

We slip back into the home-going throng as if we'd never been away. Tomorrow we will have to deal with the excuses and the forged sick notes, except for Grace of course, who has a permanent excuse. Questions may be raised why the three of us all went missing at the same time, or perhaps the loosened atmosphere after exams means no one will delve too hard. That's all for tomorrow. Now, we glance at each other, looking for reassurance, for the certainty that we have got away with it and that we are nearly home and dry; but it's for pleasure too because a shared and secret delinquency is a joyful thing.

There's something more, though. We have all been changed by today. There's a feeling we've been a long way away and are now returning, and while we were away, lines have been crossed and decisions made. We have all told ourselves what we truly want deep down and we've never dared to before.

'Have we really changed the future?' Orla whispers.

'Of course,' I say, because I can still feel the hum of the elixir and the day travelling in spirals around the coils of my brain. 'Everything will be different from now on.'

Yet, and yet, and yet as soon as I peel away from the others and begin walking up the hill to home, the headiness begins to vanish into thin air. The street of the murder feels so close but even as I scurry away upwards to my house, it doesn't seem to get any further away. Dread creeps in like rats into an empty building. We've fixed on our futures too soon, I think. We shouldn't have done that. Only words, I tell myself, it was only words and thoughts, and then that fear creeps out and, like it's left a gap, another one instantly muscles in.

I wonder how I look on the outside.

I don't have the time to linger and compose myself. If I'm late I'll be questioned, and right at this moment I think that could make me crumble. The idea of being the Queen of the House seems an impossible one now, a silly fairy tale that could never come true. I stop and put on my jumper over my mud-smeared blouse, but the thought instantly arises, *Will that look even more suspicious on such a hot day?* If I leave it off, do the mud smears on my blouse create words as clear as any logo, forming the shapes of eyes: 'look, look' – telling her to examine, to pry, to prod further?

I stand, torn, stuck about whether to have my jumper on or off, and the fear grows until it's nearly enough to fling me to the ground. It makes the world swing back and forth until I'm dizzy. Surely it doesn't matter any more about the jumper because my demented face will give it all away.

I begin climbing the hill again, sweating. Because I can't figure out her timetable, I don't know if she'll be there or not now when I get home. It feels like she does it on purpose, to keep me in continual suspense.

I reach the blue painted front door and fish out my key from under my blouse, but just at the point that the tip of the key is in the lock an idea occurs to me that is so terrible I nearly cry out.

*What if* I didn't write something bland and pointless in my diary this morning? *What if*, instead, I wrote something so awful she'll be waiting for me with the diary in hand, all pretence gone that she doesn't read it every single day?

This used to happen when I handed in essays, so instead of listing causes of the First World War, or writing a creative story about travelling, I imagined that what was inside that exercise book being passed up the line and tumbling into the pile on the teacher's desk was a catalogue of blood and depraved thoughts; that it was bursting with confessions, tracer lines of mutilations, of vicious thoughts criss-crossing the page. Several times I made some ridiculous excuses, my cheeks hot as the teacher looked on while I scrabbled to find my exercise book to check on the contents.

Pussy-cat face told me how to stop this, but for the life

of me I can't remember what she said and I turn the key as fast as I can now because I can almost see what I wrote this morning, how the ink flowed out of the pen and formed the words, the handwriting sloping forwards.

*God, I can't stand that cunt of a mother. Just looking at her face makes me want to drive a knife into it. Today I'm going to take the day off and take enough drugs to sink a battleship. I might even finally give Orla what she wants. I want to scream and run through the streets half naked. I want to batter someone because I'm sure now I made that man get killed by thinking things so dark they exploded around me.*

*Oh, and also.*

*One day I'll fuck that teacher whether he likes it or not.*

I put my hand to my mouth like I'm going to be sick and fling open the door.

I sniff the air. She's not here.

Upstairs, I see by the hair that's hooked over the back of the chair this time that she has read my entry for today. I open up the plain notebook, clawing at the pages until I find the last entry, written this morning even after I'd planned the debauchery of our day. I remember smiling to myself as I wrote. I freeze. There's movement from downstairs. There's no clackety-clack of heels on wooden boards but I know it's her. Her movements are sharper, quicker than my dad's measured step; she opens curtains with a flick of a wrist, *snick, snick*, like she wants to catch something going on outside.

How did this happen? How did I not smell her? She

must've stopped wearing that perfume. Or changed her shower gel to disguise her scent. It's special stuff that she gets from the South of France – mimosa – with a dry, sweet smell but fleeting, hard to catch in the nostrils, although I'm so vigilant I always do. Maybe she's stopped using it on purpose so I can't find her about the house and trace if she's there. I think of the wishing bowl now. The snail crawling out of it with drops of piss falling from its stalk eyes, the ivy already pointing, realigning itself and growing fast towards that centre, everything speeded up like in a film. Nature stirring its own pot. I've no hope of being in control.

My insides feel liquid as I turn to the correct page, my sweaty, dirty fingers making marks as I go. There it is. I read, then close my eyes and stay like that for a long, long time.

*Another normal day ahead. Will anything ever happen?*

# 10

# Grace

One, two, buckle my shoe.

There's this rhyme I remember from when I was a kid and I use it as another way to make myself do the things I have to do when I'm tired. Five, six, pick up the bits. Seven, eight, no time to wait.

Or, at other times, seven, eight, bit of a state. Nine, ten – fuck that then.

Sometimes I look at my skinny-bitch body in the mirror. There are muscles popping out like little apples all over from the unnatural heaving and hefting. It doesn't matter, though. I don't even know why I look.

Three, four, get in that door. The door in question? The one to the concrete community centre. Through the windows that are criss-crossed inside the glass with wire are my compadres, apparently. They are wavy through the glass, like people who are time-warping. In my hand I have the referral letter from Miss Kinsella introducing me to the Young Carers' Support Group. I have never remotely thought of myself belonging to a group called something like this.

I also have absolutely no idea if I have to do this, if it's some kind of condition of being able to carry on as we are, and I didn't feel like I could ask. If I refused, it might be a signal to the Miss Kinsellas of this borough that I'm not coping, hiding myself away; 'not engaging' is a term I could imagine her using. It could be that the referral to come here is one of those complicated instructions with a meaning I can't quite stitch together and I simply have to obey so life can continue as normal. It seemed safer just to come. Have a cup of tea with them. Not say too much. Slope off home afterwards and forget about the whole thing.

I run my fingers through my hair, tidying it back. It's got much longer and it feels silken and luxurious between my fingers. It's felt like a dare to grow it like this so it tickles my ears.

I crack open the door a little to peek in, but in the room every single head arranged in a circle turns towards the noise and I have no choice but to plunge inside. Every chair is full except one. I guess that's mine.

A woman who looks only fractionally older than everyone else stands.

'You must be Grace. I'm Cherry. Help yourself to tea or coffee from that table over there and come and join us.'

She smiles and sits back down. All these young faces in charge. It confuses me. When they're old they are both easier and harder to resist. Cherry has smooth black hair that fits neatly over her skull and falls in a wave over one shoulder. The end that rests on her collarbone is curved upwards like a boat. It glistens and I'm momentarily transfixed by it. The sheer maintenance of keeping your hair in that exact state astounds me.

I am too busy marvelling at her hair to realise the moment has gone on a beat too long. I turn away to the table loaded with thick cheap white cups and saucers and an urn, and I help myself from the jug of bright-coloured orange squash there. I take the empty seat and sit, uncrossing and crossing my legs, sipping repeatedly on the squash and feeling totally exposed as the one hundred per cent useless bitch I am. A girl two down, wearing a cardigan a dirty red colour, lifts the eyelid closest to me and pierces me with a gaze that says she's seen that I'm a useless bitch too. The room is sweltering. She must be just about dying inside that thick wool cardigan that goes halfway down her hands.

Cherry says, 'Let's pause now and welcome Grace properly.'

They seem used to this because there is a round of applause and I flush bright pink and knot my legs together even more, because, even though I can fully recognise the essential lameness of it, I've never actually had a round of applause before.

'We're not normally so formal,' she explains with a tiny laugh in each word. 'But there's a lot to get through today.'

While Cherry drones on about some trip or other in a minibus, I use the time to look at everyone else over my glass: the plump boy who seems about twelve but could be older sits with his hands cupping each other in his lap, his round glasses catching the light every time he tilts his listening head; the girl with patches of rash up her bare arms that look like salt has been stuck on there; the older boy wearing an Arsenal T-shirt and staring at his own outstretched jiggling foot.

After I've carefully looked at each one, I have to go searching for a name for what I am feeling because it is surprising and so new I can't identify it. But when I do, I see that for once I am sitting in a room with a group of people that can roughly be called my peers and I am not feeling in the slightest bit jealous *or* superior – which would be the norm for me, swinging between the two – because it's clear as day that all of us, bar Cherry of course, have come crawling out of broken little shells to be in this room. We all have this in common and it's so utterly obvious that for a bright heated moment I hate them all with a burning intensity because I thought I hid it so damn well and I can see now that I've been fooling myself all along about this.

Then I have to chase up what's happening because I haven't been listening.

Cherry blows through her lips, past her shiny pink lip gloss. 'Would you like to say anything, Grace? Perhaps you could share a bit about yourself before we finish?' She's trying her absolute hardest, I can see she is, but I'm drowning. The room feels wet. I seem to have trouble understanding everything. It's what I've learned here about myself. I didn't want to be shown that. It's floored me. There's the LSD that's still swirling round my brain too, I realise. The river – I could almost feel its coolness washing over me as I watched – is here again in this room. I shake my head. The tinkling of it is in my ears.

Cherry carries on. 'Is there anything in particular that worries you that perhaps we could help you with? There may be someone here in this room who also has that specific concern and can share with you their experience of it. I'm aware that doesn't make problems go away but sometimes it can be good to know about the different angles of it.' You have to hand it to her. She is a trier.

I clear my throat. 'Ummm.'

'You don't have to.' She smiles. 'It's not compulsory.'

'Umm.'

'Honestly—'

'I often think about the homeless,' I butt in.

Cherry's smile freezes. I don't stop, though. Everything in the room has become heavy with meaning. Being with all these people has opened a little door in me that I can't seem to close. Flies swarm out of it.

'Have you seen the way they have to sleep in car parks, and all the money that's right here in this city? Have you even seen it? Sometimes I think they must be, like, invisible, and that maybe it's only me that can see them because people go past without a glance. Sometimes they look like they're about to tread on their hands, like these people don't even have three dimensions or are even really human, like they're rats or something.'

I'm fully aware that this is not the kind of concerns Cherry meant. Still, I can't seem to stop myself. There's a restless wind outside that bangs the branches of a buddleia tree against the misted glass of the window, over and over. I stretch my hands.

'And then there's the bees. Did you know that Einstein said that every mouthful of food we eat is only there because of the bees and currently, right as *we speak*, there is something happening to them? They're only just finding out – and they don't know why – that bees are abandoning their hives, and if the bees go, so do we. The more I think about it the more I worry. I mean, how will the human race survive without them?'

All the time, I'm thinking, *Will nobody – please – stop me?* Because I know that spewing out all this stuff is the only way to stop me naming the one actual and real fear that I have, that I'm guessing everyone in the room has so it's gathered together and made strong, like the holy spirit gathering above our heads: it's what can I do to keep my mum alive and how will it be if she dies.

Red-cardigan girl snorts and mutters something that sounds like 'Nutter' under her breath, and it's *this* that finally brings me to a stuttering stop.

'Well,' says Cherry. 'Phew.'

I stare miserably down. She's wearing yellow suede pumps with yarn bows that are curled at the ends like old-fashioned moustaches.

'That's a lot to get off your chest,' she says. 'Thank you.'

Then I think, *Maybe I will come back here again one day.* Maybe it's a good thing that something was set loose in me because I usually am so tight-screwed shut it hurts. Maybe it's among the girl twirling her black plait round and round her finger and the boy with the glasses who keeps pressing his damp-looking hands together that I finally get to let go just a little.

A pale fingernail of moon shows in the blue day sky as I walk home. Gusts of wind rattle rose petals to the ground. *It was that fucking day at the wishing bowl*, I think. It's gone through and through me. It made me see whole layers of things I barely knew about. Phoebe and her wishes, her predictions and the *possibilities* they're loaded with. Flinging them around like sweet papers, like it's that easy. It made me think that anything was available to me, that I actually had choices and could make them happen if I only willed it enough.

The wind dies down. Coldness begins to fall like a blanket. It pecks at the dried sweat on my face. It's happened so quickly, like the river that threads through the middle of the town has sucked all the hot air into its brown snake belly.

When I get home I take the stairs. I dawdle, pausing near our flat to catch my breath and look through the slit of window over the rooftops. A mist has begun to creep in so they look like ghost houses. The feeling of possibility is still all over me, sticky and insistent. It's not good for me; it'll seep into my bones and make them soft. I want to shower it off. Get back to the bare hardness of things. Today was the opposite. It showed me exactly who I am and where my place is. And yet – and yet my real desire is to stay with the first one, the feeling of the wishing-bowl day. I want it so much my sincere *wish* now is that it'd never happened. I realise I'll never go back to that community centre and those people. Despite everything, I'm voting with the wishing bowl and its shitty magic.

I arrive at the flat. Three, four – now get in *that* fucking door. I realise the moment I put my hand on the door handle that every single time I touch the cool metal I have a jolt of anxiety that courses through me like an electric shock. I hadn't acknowledged it before, how I linger, shuffling my feet about for a moment before I plunge inside. It's the fear of what I might find inside.

Later it gets worse. I'm restless in my legs. All over. Even my ears twitch.

I put Mum to bed and plant a kiss on her forehead as I always do, and she says, 'Night, night, Grace,' turns over and falls to sleep almost immediately as she nearly always does.

I prowl the night spaces of the flat. The moon is slim but it still exudes light so the areas near windows are lit weakly. I crack my knuckles. I pace, feeling the warm wood of the hallway under my feet turn to thin carpet and then cold concrete out on the balcony. I light my cigarette and wonder if anyone can see me from down below, if anyone notices the glowing point going up and down to my mouth from so far away.

It's Saturday night and the only time I've been out was for the carers' group. I put the radio on. They're playing music I don't recognise with a jumping beat. I do my own little dance in the kitchen even though the light's off. I screw my feet into the cold lino doing the twist. When the track stops I stop too and stand in the dark, panting. I do a stupid walk halfway down the hallway, duck-like, then ski the rest.

I hesitate by the front door, then turn and ski back down the hall, take a turn around the living room, dance back to the front door and stand panting behind it, looking up at the orifice of the spyhole, then skirt away again. I force myself to reverse into the stuffy clutches of the flat. I feel resistance, like I'm pushing myself back into a bouncy castle; the impulse for the opposite forward motion is so strong.

I spin round three times. Stop, dizzy. Unsteadily take a few steps, then spin round three more times. Is this a magic number? It must be, because I lunge, quick and sure so there's no time for mind-changing. Take the spare key we keep on the shelf by the door. Slide it into the back pocket of my jeans. Feel my hand reaching up to grasp the cool metal lozenge of the handle, then yank. Step through.

The door clicks behind me and I'm outside. My heart pulses painfully underneath my collarbones. I can feel it in my neck, going off like an alarm clock.

I start walking away and the automatic light pops on to my left. I look down. I have no shoes, just baggy socks with rounded half-empty toe boxes. They're ones Dad left behind years ago that I wear for slippers. I stand undecided and the light extinguishes itself. I hesitate, breathing hard, then walk towards the slit of window where the moonlight permeates. I think: *This feels dangerous. This feels so fucking dangerous.* Mum is sleeping upstairs and with each step I'm feeling more and more like a balloon floating away and the threads between us are snapping. Another security light pops on, spreading its beams, and I halt, bathed in its rays.

This block of flats is a modern anthill, I decide, mounded, rising above the city. All of us tucked in our little compartments. All the breathing that goes on in here, all of us, in and out. The light goes out and I grin stupidly into the darkness. I explore each floor, traversing the hallways, lights clicking on and off, the only things alert to my presence. Once I'm down to the ground floor, Mum seems like a little bug, tucked away so far above my head, her unsteady breathing the very highest and lightest breath of all. I begin climbing again. Floor two. Third floor. I stop and tap on the door. I'd known it all along. From the moment I skied down the hallway, no, before that, as I did my solitary twist in the dark kitchen, I knew this is where the night would end.

There is a long silence and I nearly turn to go but then I detect a scuffling from inside, someone against the other side of the door using the eyehole to check who's outside. The alarm hammer in my neck starts up again. I swear I feel the roots of hair at the nape of my neck stand to attention.

The door chain rattles as the door opens a crack. I see Daniel's smile flash in the dark recess of his hallway as he recognises me. He unhooks the chain and the door opens wide. It's ages since we've seen each other properly and I don't really know how things stand.

'Grace!' He's pleased to see me. 'I wasn't expecting you.'

'Oh, is it a bad time?'

'No, no—'

'I mean, is it convenient for you?' I interrupt, and my laugh sounds like a silly bitch's high-pitched whinny, even to my own ears.

'Sure. Sure. Come in,' he says, and leaves the door wide and swinging, and I plunge after him, almost dreading but also longing for the click behind me because that would mean two doors between Mum and me, and somehow with that it's so much easier to muffle the thoughts of her. *What the fuck are you doing, Grace?* I think. *What the fuck?* But all the same the door clicks and I'm on the inside.

His flat is always spare. A real boy pad. The objects ordered neatly on the sideboard that's in the same position in the living room as ours: a polished cow horn; a carved wooden box; a deck of playing cards neatly aligned with the wall. So different to our raucous jumble of false poppies, lace doilies, display cups and saucers patterned with more poppies and with improbably gold rims, all of it coated in a layer of dust. I know that his mum no longer lives here, that she met someone down on the south-east coast and moved in with him, although it is still her name on the rent book. She does this because she wants to do right by Daniel; she loves him, and would rightly lie through her teeth to ensure he keeps a roof over his head.

I resist the urge to crack my knuckles. 'Sit down,' he says, and I do, shucking off my horrible thick socks when he's not looking and balling them up into my pocket. Without them, my feet look long and thin. I tuck them under my thighs as I sit on the sofa so he can't see.

'Hey,' he says, after he's opened the wooden box and extracted a small plastic bag stuffed full and a packet of the extra-sized Rizla that all get placed on the sideboard next to the cow horn. 'Hey, it's good to see you. How are you? Do you fancy a smoke?'

He puts his hand to his chest and I try not to acknowledge how I see – no, drink in – how it makes a muscular brown starfish against the white of his T-shirt. I do not need to notice that. It will do me no good.

'Yeah, why not?' I smile up at him.

'You OK?'

'I could do with a bit of company, truth be told.'

He stands, scratching the dark curls on his head, looking at the grass and the Rizlas. 'Hey, how about starting off with a little vodka? Do you fancy one?'

I nod and he brings the bottle, icy and dripping from the freezer, and pours me a slug in a proper shot glass. The liquid is glutinous from the cold. As I sip I feel binds, wrapped around my core, breaking section by section in the wake of its passage. I'm surprised he can't hear them crack.

I look up, my smile all loopy.

He sets down the neatly rolled joint so it's precisely aligned to the deck of cards.

'Have you had anything to eat tonight?'

I shake my head. I had some beans when I came back from the meeting. I ate them cold, spooning them from the tin as I leaned against the kitchen counter. I could've made something better but often the bother seems too much.

'You look like you've got thinner. Come on, come into the kitchen and I'll make something, and the grass can be our afters.' He picks up the joint and tucks it behind his ear.

I follow him, holding my cardigan shut, my bare feet padding on the floor. I perch on a stool at the kitchen counter, prop my elbows there and watch as he prepares the meal. He chops an onion and then cloves of garlic into a translucent pile on the blue plastic chopping board. Then he takes a greaseproof-wrapped parcel of mince from the fridge. He stands a metal contraption that looks about a hundred years old next to it.

'Ever had home-made hamburgers?'

'Uh, no.'

'My mum taught me how to make them when I was a kid. She spent time out in the States when she was young and she said everyone does it out there. She said if you eat the ones you buy frozen in the supermarket you may as well be eating a dog turd.'

With one part of my mind I see him there, as a kid, kneeling up on a chair next to her as she shows him how to pack the mixture in the machine and bring down the handle to press it flat. See him wrinkling his nose when she talks about eating dog shit. See her showing him how to use a knife safely. I feel the whole weight of love that's happened in the room. I had that too, I did. I don't forget that, despite the fact it had to end and that was no one's fault. If there's ever a point where I might be a mother – though I know what would have to happen first with Mum to make that possible – I want to be like that, like one huge towering unbreakable pillar of strength for my child.

But another part of my brain is thinking, *What the fuck, Grace? What the fuck do you think you're doing down here so far away from home?* I pour myself another dose of vodka to shut that voice up.

We eat sloppy hamburgers at the kitchen counter; slices of pickle fall onto my plate and I scoop them up and eat them, and it's delicious. I had no idea how hungry I was. No idea at all. I laugh at things Daniel says, only half listening, and bathing in the sounds coming up off the street. Cars, and people calling out to each other on their way home, the sounds here so much more distinct than on our level where they arrive in whispers, tattered into threads on their journey upwards. But then I'm putting the corner of my hamburger down, the bun indented with my finger marks, and I'm gradually turning silent, although Daniel hasn't realised yet because he's in full flow and he's saying, 'Maybe you should think about yourself for once, Grace.' He lights the joint, takes a deep inhale and passes it over to me, and I shake my head and he *still* doesn't shut up. 'What's going to happen in the next five years, Grace? You look peaky, Grace. I worry about you, Grace. You look so tired sometimes.' I see that he's a bit drunk. That he was probably drinking before I arrived. I take the joint out of his fingers, take a deep draw, then stub it out in the ashtray.

'Finished?'

He blinks at me. 'What?'

'I asked if you'd quite finished or if there's more where that came from.'

I punch my fist on the counter top and the plates and cutlery rattle.

He spreads his hands. 'Now then. I didn't mean, honestly, Grace. There's no need.'

'What do you know anyway?'

'Nothing. I know nothing. I'm so sorry, Grace. I'm sorry I said all that, I really am, but, it's just, I care for you. Now I've gone and said all the wrong things and offended you.'

'You have no right.' And before I know it I'm crying great huge heaving sobs like some stupid bitch out on the street who's drunk too much and lost her phone and argued with her boyfriend. I turn to run out of the room and I realise drool is coming out of the corner of my mouth and I draw the back of my hand across to wipe it away.

'Grace, stop it.' I hear Daniel behind me and I know that maybe he did cross the line, but I'm behaving like a real fucking stupid hysterical little bitch. When he comes up behind and puts his arms around me and pins my arms to my body like he's afraid I'm going to hurt myself, I just sort of lean back into him and we move to the bedroom, which is also exactly what I knew would happen when I first looked up at the peephole of my flat door and thought about rolling myself up like a tube and threading through it.

Then I feel him resisting, pulling away. 'We don't have to,' he says softly, and I say, 'I know.'

We fall into each other and it's nothing like anything before. The few boyfriends I've had, whatever I did with them, was not something that would occur to me to miss or to want again. I hardly even remember it. Not like this, I think, as sleep descends; this is something I will never forget as long as I live.

When I wake the ceiling is pimpled like newsprint even though there's light trickling under the slats of the window blinds. My thinking flicks about, trying to identify what's happened and where I am. When I stir there's a soreness between my legs that isn't unpleasant, not unpleasant at all, because there's good memories attached to it that somehow slightly elude me. I roll heavy limbs to my side and see an arm flung across the pillow, and after a second or two I identify it as belonging to Daniel.

I sit bolt upright. 'Shitting hell.'

He stirs beside me. I swing my legs over and my feet slap on the cold floor. 'Shitting hell. What time is it? Where are my clothes?' I see them strewn over the floor and make a dive for them.

Daniel's arm shoots out and scoops his phone off the bedside cabinet. He brings it close to his face and squints. 'S'all right.' There's a clack as his tongue peels away from the roof of his mouth. His voice is porridgy with sleep. 'It's only eight-thirty.'

A bolt of dread and anxiety spirals through me. 'Eight-thirty? Christ. Christ, that's an hour after I should be . . .' I twist myself into my shirt and pull my jeans up, not bothering with underwear.

'Grace, calm down.' Daniel is sitting up now and rubbing his eyes.

'I can't,' I say over my shoulder as I run out of the flat. I pound at the button beside the lift but it's having one of its slow days. The noise coming from inside is like someone's grumbling innards.

I take to the stairs, sprinting as hard as I can. The alcohol and spliff from last night is slowing me down but I force myself, ignoring the stitch in my side, taking big gasps of air and running up flight after flight until I see our own front door and the flat blank eye in it. I think it looks blinded, like something terrible has gone on inside.

The key? I grope to recall, then remember the feel of the smooth way it tucked into my back pocket. I thrust a hand into each pocket and feel about, getting more and more desperate and practically pulling my jeans off because, with a mounting, sick realisation, I understand that it's not there.

I take the steps two at a time, nearly tumbling down the stairwell, until I arrive panting at Daniel's door. He seems to take an age to answer.

'Come on, come on.' I pound again and he opens it, barefoot in jeans and a T-shirt, and I push past him on into the bedroom and get down on my hands and knees and start using my hands like they're fucking landmine sweepers.

He appears at the doorway. 'What are you doing?'

'Key,' I gasp. 'Help me.'

'What?'

I kneel up. 'My front door key. It must've fallen out of my back pocket. Please, please help me find it.'

He drops down next to me and begins groping around the carpet and flipping up the duvet so he can get under the bed.

'Grace, is it really necessary to be so anxious? I mean—'

'Please, just help me. Please just do that. I know what she's like. She will have tried to get herself up with me not there. She thinks she can do it but she can't, and she won't accept it. Now please, please, I'm begging you, just help me find that key.' I'm crying now and he crawls to the other side of the bed to look.

'Not here.' He stands up and opens up the blind and scans the floor. 'There.' He points and I see a glint of silver and I pounce. Somehow it's got itself wedged in between the carpet and the skirting board. I prise it out with my fingers, crying out when it slips from my fingertips back into its crevice and I scrabble after it again. When I have it I palm it so hard it cuts into my skin.

'Don't follow me,' I say, terrified at the thought of someone else *seeing*. 'I need to go and sort this out on my own.'

He puts his hands out. 'It'll be fine.' And that's the last
sight of him, through the doorway, holding out his hands
and telling me everything will be all right before I trip and
fall on the staircase, then pick myself up and run so hard my
breath is a ragged ribbon being pulled through my chest.

It's hard to unlock the door because my hands are trembling and when I kick it open I stand in the hallway, panting,
and it's like the look of the front door, everything in the flat,
is angled wrong as in a nightmare because it knows something terrible has happened here.

I sprint towards Mum's bedroom saying, 'Sorry, sorry,
sorry, sorry, sorry. I'm just so, so sorry,' as I run, and when I
fling open the door I see what I knew I would see from the
moment I woke up, and that is Mum's damaged frail body
in its pink and white rose-sprigged nightie lying in a broken
heap on the floor.

The staircase is a red puzzle above and below. I have the sensation of the step as if I'm standing on a swing so I sit down abruptly. Downstairs there's a murmuring voice. I peer between the dark wood of the banister and see the top of her head from above. She's put her jumper back on and she paces back and forth, talking quietly into her phone. I steal a little further down to see if I can hear. By now I'm close enough to catch a word or two. 'Unbearable.' 'Never before.' 'Urgent.' 'The place where no one goes.' At one point she yells down the phone, 'It's too late for that.'

# Act II

# THE DEEP

# 11

# Phoebe

The Beloved has returned.

The Beloved – my sister Verity – arrives for the holidays from her university in York. She sits there on the end of the sofa with *her* and they both bare their teeth at me. It's a hundred times worse when The Beloved's here because they are like some unstoppable two-headed monster. They'll eat me alive and I'll end up in their shared stomach, being digested by their acid.

'Phoebe. Can't you try and get along with your big sister a bit better?' Dad asks.

Why can't he see it? Why can't he see how they are with me?

Because he doesn't want to. He wants everything smooth and easy and polite. He can't stand upset or trouble.

The Beloved has her feet tucked up beneath her bottom. She leans against our mother in affection, snuggling her cheek against her shoulder.

I turn to go.

'Off out?' asks The Beloved, sneeringly. For some reason, The Beloved takes it as her intrinsic right to interrogate me as much as *she* does.

I swing back. I stand, silent, deliberately on display.

I understand how the light from the window will be catching the curves of my face. I'm fully aware how my hip bone will be appearing, jutting forward, just so in my black jeans.

The effect will be spare and elegant. This one thing never fails. By doing this, I can demonstrate definitively, absolutely, that I am unequivocally the one that got all the looks, and there's nothing, short of throwing acid in my face, they can do about it. The Beloved's own face is unformed. Her colouring is muddy and her body rounded in an unpleasingly unhealthy child way. My mother is up now and messing with the TV stand in preparation for their night's entertainment. Little bowls of nuts and crisps await on the coffee table.

'Look at you,' The Beloved says softly. 'Your jeans look practically spray-painted on and that purple eye make-up makes you look like a street walker.'

*She* catches the end of the conversation and looks up.

'Verity's right.'

They copy each other by staying barefaced and make-up free. I'm sure The Beloved would love to cover up that face with cosmetics but she pretends to like being 'natural'. I think it makes them both feel morally superior. I don't care. I wet my fingers and scrabble at my eyes, wiping it off. When I'm done I catch the glance from The Beloved, the sick jealousy in it, and I realise that naked-faced I look even better than before and she regrets saying anything.

Our mother returns to the sofa and they take up their positions once more. As The Beloved looks up at me she closes her lips and pulls them tight across her teeth. She leans in closer to *her* as if for protection. Then, and only then, am I able to leave with a sense of triumph, to leave them huddled together in the living room upstairs and go down to the front door. Once I'm there I decide to take my coat because I can see mist pushing on the outside of the window.

'You didn't say where you were going, Phoebe. It's nearly twilight out there.' *She*'s come out of the living room and is standing at the top of the stairs. Her shadow grows long until her head is on the bottom stair, upside down.

I make my voice conciliatory. 'Orla's asked me to hang out,' I lie. 'She's got some new jacket she wants to show me.'

'OK.' She pauses. I can tell she's torn between refusing me and wanting to be alone with The Beloved. I taint it for them, skulking around the perimeters. I spoil their together time.

'Orla's asked me to stay, so I might even do that,' I drop in. Normally, such casualness wouldn't be allowed. I should make the most of it. I take the chance that they're too wrapped up in each other that checking phone calls won't be made.

'Mum, it's coming on.' It's The Beloved from the living room. There's the sound of the TV in the background.

*She* turns on her heel and walks away. Her shadow-head bounces up the stairs, one at a time.

Outside, as I slope down the hill, my confidence fades. I'm so scared. I'm so fucking scared all the time. I'll do anything to relieve it. I chatter to the moon through the glass of my bedroom window. I ask it to be my mother and look after me. I polish its shine in my mind so its rays can continue to protect me the next day when it has been wheeled away from me across the sky.

My wish at the wishing bowl to become Queen of the House made me feel wonderful for a time. It felt real, as if by commanding so it would come true; I believed it completely. I could feel it strengthening me inside like after a sickness when you start to become well. Then The Beloved came and the idea of being Queen of the House began being smashed up piece by piece until now I'm just a spider scuttling around in their presence. It's worse than ever.

That little show I just put on. I know how people look, how they're mesmerised by my shine. It sickens me really. Such a sham. Like I'm wearing a dress that doesn't really belong to me. There's rot inside which one day will eat away at that face and then everyone will see. I don't even long to bump into Mr Jonasson like I normally do when I'm out. I wouldn't be up to seeing him right now. The urge to ring Paul and find out where he is and whether he's got anything becomes like another sickness the longing is so great. I press his number almost hoping he doesn't answer. When he doesn't I hesitate, then ring Orla.

'Meet me,' I whisper into the phone, even though there is no one around.

'Umm. I don't know.'

'Meet me,' I say again, trying to make it sound like a command.

She sighs. 'OK. I'll see you on the square outside the Roman Baths,' and I wonder what's made her so reluctant.

Sometimes I think, Dear Pussy-cat face, look at me so radiant and well. However did the pack of you believe I needed a cure? Look how easily I swirl my hair into a top knot, glitter my eyes, eat a pastry, laugh, study complicated algorithms, sigh.

Other times, like now, my little internal letter to her can backfire. Let the thoughts pass, she said. Ha! Dear Pussy-cat face, I am so very unwell. There's an oozing feeling down the back of my head that won't go away. I have the urge to shout at strangers. Escape seems impossible yet I attempt it all the same. Food is a constant issue. I can still feel the chop from last night weighing me down like a stone. The thoughts I keep having of the day of *Macbeth* and the murder and the splattering blood are like a train with endless carriages: as soon as one leaves another shows up. They go: *Do it again, go on.*

And I plunge into mist that gets thicker and thicker the lower down the hill into town I go.

Orla doesn't look particularly pleased to see me and my stomach churns. She's the one person I can usually rely on. She's hunched in her middle-aged short camel coat against the unseasonal cold. It's been so hot you feel the contrast quickly. The fog has probably come snaking down the river; that's what usually happens, even in summer. A few tourists amble out of it and look up to the outside of the Roman Baths to where you can see the statues pointing towards the main bath inside. Tonight they are dark shapes in the fog. I suck up my breath and smile.

'What are we going to do then?' she asks snippily.

I manage to smile again. I need to win her back. 'I just wanted to get out. Come on. Let's go and have a cider in The Flute, on me. You can go to the bar, though. They'll ask me for ID and you look older than me. I'll hide around the corner.' I silently hope I have the funds to cover a pint and a half of cider.

I walk behind her, touching the sides of buildings as we go for support. They feel grainy under my fingers.

I sit at the scarred, sticky wooden table thinking yet again of *Macbeth* while she's at the bar. When I'm feeling good I feel I could be like the witches: ferocious, lording it over everybody with their second sight and how they don't need what everybody else needs – food, a house.

Bad days like today I'm Macbeth, shivering and terrified. It all turns into badness after the beginning. That play is cancer. It started all this off again, I'm sure of it. It should be banned and every copy burned on a pyre where the flames lick against the sky. It is not for the tender mind. It's not even only me that thinks so. In the theatre the actors and all the people putting on plays won't even utter its name. They call it 'The Scottish Play' instead because they think it's such bad luck. Mr Jonasson told us that. Just the thought of him popping into my head makes me woozy with want.

Orla comes back with the drinks and drops the few coins left over next to my hand. I must've done something to upset her. She most often offers to pay.

'It's great to hang out.' My voice sounds desperate even to myself. 'Have a bit of fun. We could get hold of something.' I crease my eyes at her. 'That might brighten up the evening.'

It doesn't work. 'I'm guessing that would mean seeing your friend Paul again.' She puts her hands in her pockets. 'No way.'

'All right, all right.' She's got the upper hand somehow. I'm not sure how this has happened. 'It's fine.' I lift my glass up and choke back a couple of mouthfuls. 'Let's just enjoy this. We can think of something else that's fun, I'm sure.' I stop; she's scowling at the window that is frosted on the bottom half and on the top half thick with the mist outside. Looking at it makes me feel like there's a hand against my face.

'What is it, Orla?' I ask. 'You're being really funny with me.'

She purses her lips. 'If you don't remember, I'm not going to tell you.'

I could scream. This is the last thing I need. 'Look, you know how much you mean to me. Just tell me and I'm sure it'll be fine.'

When I look up I nearly fall off my stool she's staring so hard. '"Not me," you said. That day at the wishing bowl when I made my wish about love, you said, "Not me."'

I genuinely don't remember this.

'And I tried not to think about it because I was in such a state, but honestly I can't get it out of my head now.'

'Orla, darling, we were all off our faces that day.' I'll say anything to stop her being cold. I can't bear it. 'You probably misheard. You mean such a very, very great deal to me. I can't imagine ever saying anything like that.'

I see her face soften a little and again I'm amazed at what people will tell themselves. That black is white. That night is day.

'Let's do something magic,' I say, draining down some more cider.

'Like what?' I can see that she's a bit excited despite herself.

'Give it another half an hour and I'll tell you.'

Of course I don't know what I meant by 'something fun'. I haven't got a clue. She follows me out of the pub while I rack my brains for ideas. Back in the square the mist makes everything just about impossible to pick out.

'Have you thought what to do yet?' I hear her voice close to my ear.

I think with panic about returning home. The two of them – *her* and The Beloved – curled together like a single complicated shellfish on the sofa, and the bright ceiling light blazing down so there's nowhere to hide. The least worst option would be staying with Orla but I don't want that either, not yet anyway, not while I have this energy fritzing my insides. I feel something move across my cheek and take in a mouthful of warm steam. My mind jitters for a moment, seeking to identify the taste of it. Hot, with an edge of an egg boiling in a pan.

'I know,' I say. I'm almost too excited to speak now. My throat seems to have narrowed to the size of a drinking straw. 'Look, the place is all closed up for the night. Let's get into the baths.'

She pauses. 'Break in? What's the point? What would we do if we could?'

I move closer and she becomes a little more defined through the mist, her eyes blinking rapidly at me.

'You're not listening to me. I said, let's "get in" the Roman Baths. I mean get in the water.'

'Are you serious?' She looks really alarmed now.

'Of course I am.'

'How deep is it?'

I haven't thought of that. How would I know? The sulphurous water is always deep green, like the sea – some algae that grows in there apparently.

'About waist-deep.'

I see the moon of her face look up, assessing the wall with the balustrade on top, and I have a rush of triumph. The statues beyond have almost disappeared altogether in the mist now.

'It's easy,' I whisper, although it's so quiet I'm guessing the square is empty. 'I noticed scaffolding poking up on the other side the other day. They're doing some restoration work. If I can get on your shoulders, I can get over this wall

136

and help you scramble up. Or vice versa. Then we can climb down to the baths on the scaffolding.'

'I don't know. What about cameras?'

I wave my hand in front of her face. 'See that?'

'Just.'

'Well, that was about a foot away from your face. Any cameras will be miles off. Oh please. Please, it'll be such a laugh. It'll be amazing.'

I'm seized with the longing to immerse myself in the waters I've been glimpsing my whole life. The biggest main bath is open to the sky so as the sun strikes on the shifting deep green surface of it, it's so bright it cuts into the back of your eye. Or, when it rains the drops sink in great globules, hissing and spitting into the heat of the steaming water. The hot gushing waters that feed the bath come from such a deep and secret place, anything could be down there, and the steam that rises from its surface is like messages sent from the ancient gods that reside not in the sky, like the new ones, but right inside the middle of the earth. The wishing bowl is part of it somehow, I feel sure of that, connected by a web of water and magic, the urge to make offerings and utter incantations, to throw in coins and curses. I feel it all far down in the pit of my stomach.

I have to get in. Now I've thought of it I'll do anything to make it happen.

'I don't think I'll even need to get on your shoulders. Put your arms around my waist. If you hoist me up I think I can make it, then I can pull you after.'

She encircles me with her arms, heaves and launches me upwards. I grab onto the top of the stone balustrade and clamber up.

'I can't believe it.' Her voice is hot and excited from below. 'I think we're going to manage it. Now me.'

She takes her coat off and slings it upwards. I grab onto it and drop it on the terrace, then lean over to her. 'Come on. It's best if you do it in one go without thinking too much.' I grab onto her arms and pull so hard I think they're going to come out of their sockets as she scrambles, finally teetering on her stomach for a moment like a seesaw, as if she could go either way, before slithering down to the ground on my side.

'Keep down, Orla. If this weather starts clearing, people will see us from the square. We'll have to crawl round to the scaffolding on our stomachs.'

'My coat's going to get dirty,' she mutters.

'Fuck your coat,' I say over my shoulder as I crawl along the rough stone terrace.

When we get to the top of the scaffolding I hear a sharp intake of breath. 'Oh my God,' she says. 'I don't think I can do this. That looks *terrifying*.'

'It's fine,' I say, though I have to admit, if not out loud, that it looks a lot more perilous than I imagined. Even with the mist to soften everything, the scaffolding sheers away right down so the front legs of it almost look like they're disappearing in the glinting water. A waft of sulphurous steam hits our faces and Orla starts coughing.

'Look, I'm going down first. I think the only way we can do it is by sort of swinging ourselves round at the bottom to avoid the water. You have to be confident with it.' Because I can tell she's going to protest and start changing her mind, I jump onto the wooden platform of the scaffolding and start climbing down. It seems the strangest thing when the name carved into stone, VESPA SIANVS, that you would

138

normally see from below is right in front of my face. At the bottom I manage to swing round using the steel pole to avoid getting my feet wet. But when it comes to Orla's turn and I coax her down for what seems like forever, she nearly slips and manages to get one leg of her jeans soaked through right up to the knee.

'I knew that would happen,' she says. Her voice sounds tiny and afraid in the dark, and I know I'm going to have to bolster her again before she starts crying or trying to climb out or something.

'You've done really, really well.' I bite on my lips, hoping she won't detect my false nannying tone. I'm shivering with excitement with the water lapping and steaming right next to me and Bath lying so close, oblivious, right the other side of the wall. There's the sound of a car engine and it seems so near we both move towards each other, Orla's eyes as huge as a cartoon animal's now.

'I'll go in first? Test the waters.' I chuckle at my little joke.

'What?' She grabs onto my arm. 'You're not really going to get in there,' she whispers.

'Of course.' I shake off her hand. 'That's what we've come for, isn't it?'

I look out across the water and I can see the shining mass of it. I reconstruct it in my mind. I know from school trips that the open rectangular main pool is surrounded by pillars and there are steps in between that lead to the water's edge. There are alcoves all the way round too, where rich Romans were taken to have oils rubbed into their skins and where they were scraped at with flat knives so the dirt was removed from deep inside their pores. When you come here you're not even supposed to put your hand in the waters, though it's so tempting – they're so luscious-looking I don't know how everyone resists. To my right I can just hear the hot waters hurrying through the ancient channel towards the Great Bath. We had it all pointed out to us as kids. 'Don't go near the edge,' we were warned.

I shuck off my coat and hook my T-shirt over my head, chucking them on the wet paving stones. I'm so excited now I'm fumbling at my jeans, my fingers slipping on the buttons in my eagerness.

I sit on the side, the stone warm and wet under my thighs and buttocks. The water is dark oil in this light. It sloshes slightly, turning over itself like there's something alive just under the surface. I plunge my legs in and the warmth floods through them like an energy – and how it happens, I'm not sure, but it's like the pool has the ability to suck. Perhaps it's just the side that is wet and slick but somehow the rest of me slithers in too, in one long continuous motion. My hair shoots upwards and I feel the sharp tug at the roots. I open my eyes in panic and underneath is warm and black. I take a choking mouthful and taste the bitter sulphur.

*I'm drowning*, I think. *I'm drowning, I'm drowning.*

The gods have taken hold of me for trespassing on their territory and they're shaking me to bits. They want to kill me for it. A thick black oblivion pushes through me like a dark snake and I fall further and further.

There's a flash of something in my brain, and clear and present I see ancient Rome whirling past me rather than my own life. Rome, and all her energies and what she's left behind. The toga pins and statues. Her rising triumphal arches. Her bubbling springs and pipes. The flash of a red cloak disappearing round a corner. The shining arc of a single spear held up to the sky.

*Minerva*, I think, because the tiny spark in my brain has reminded me that it's her temple, that she is the goddess of the thermal spring feeding this place and all the coins and curses and wishes are directed to her. The beautiful Roman goddess Minerva, not some ugly old men gods.

Then my foot touches the bottom, hard, slips against something with a strange texture and somehow that propels me up again and I spiral up and burst out, spraying spit and water.

I choke out water as I thrash. The mist is thinning and the crescent moon swings above and its reflection shatters in the water. I know as soon as I break the surface something profound has taken place. I feel utterly *changed* as if radiation has passed through me and altered all my cells and the way I'll be forever and even what will happen. Somehow, I begin to find my swimming stroke, and the water seems to help me do that. Minerva saved me.

I can make out Orla now, standing on the edge, wide-eyed, her hands in her pockets. The ancient columns behind frame her.

'I thought you said it wasn't deep,' she says accusingly.

'Orla,' I whisper urgently. 'Something happened in here, something extraordinary.'

'I'm not getting in there. I must've been mental to agree to this – it's dangerous.'

'Really, Orla, there's something here, in the water. You have to try it. It's so powerful.'

'Have you finally lost it?'

I lift heavy wet hair off my forehead and push it back.

'What? No, look, you've got to get in and feel it.'

'It's dangerous, and quite honestly I think we could get into terrible trouble for this. I want to go home.'

'Is that all you can worry about? Getting into trouble?'

I'm angry with her now. I've brought her to this wonderful place and all she can do is moan and be as cautious as a little old lady afraid of slipping and cracking her little old body. Her refusing feels unlucky too – like the goddess will be offended because we've disrespected her by Orla not submitting to the waters.

'Please,' I say.

'No.' She sounds like she's going to cry. 'I don't think we've thought about this properly. We haven't even planned how to get out. Perhaps we should've done that first.'

'What, like do a flipping health and safety assessment first and have every detail organised like this is a school trip? Perhaps we could go to the gift shop at the end. You're such a coward, Orla.'

I roll over and start swimming away from her, the feeling of the water warm and delicious under the soles of my feet, and let the choking feeling dispel. Then I remember how I want to keep her onside so I swim back.

'All I'm saying is that it seems a shame to go through all this and at least not see what it feels like. Come on.' I flip onto my back. My toes rise up in rows of white nobbles from the water. 'It's lovely.' I swim over to her and the moonlight strikes on the tears flowing down her cheeks.

'I really want to go home now. Come and stay with me and we'll curl up with some tea and—'

My anger – Minerva's anger – flares up again. 'I've organised this lovely treat for you and all you can do is *blub*. It's pathetic. I suppose we'll just have to go then if you're going to get all hysterical.'

I dry off with my coat as best I can and dress myself, the fabrics feeling like they might almost tear my tender boiled skin. We start climbing up again, Orla first so I can see her bum wobbling about above me under her short coat.

'I know what I felt at the bottom,' I shout up.

'Sssshh, keep your voice down.'

I switch to a loud whisper. 'It was lead. I remember now. They have to drain this sometimes and I remember reading about it in the paper and seeing photographs. It's completely lined with lead like a big lead water-filled box. It's what they lined Princess Diana's coffin with.'

She stops and looks down. 'What?'

'Don't you remember? All those men, the pall bearers, they could barely carry it because it was so heavy.'

She doesn't answer, just keeps clanging her way to the top where she waits for me and we slither back over the wall into the square. Back in the real world I retain the power of the place. I feel every cell of my body lit up and I know for certain I've been boiled inside the very cauldron of the earth.

Orla asks me to stay with her and I say I will but that I need to do something first. Of course, she wants to know what it is, but I say I can't tell her and in a way that's true because I don't know myself yet; I simply know I'm not ready to go and be suffocated in her bedroom. Once she's left I walk the streets. My hair is still wet and sulphurous. My body feels clean, every pore sucked of its dead skin and dirt. Underneath my clothes, my bra and knickers are still damp. I don't care. The shivering makes me feel alive. I long for something as extraordinary now outside of the waters.

Somehow I feel female and not female all at once. Like the waters have taken all the worst of it and left the best and most powerful bits. When The Beloved is home the smell of women in the house is enough to practically choke you. When The Beloved and *her* are menstruating, which they do at the same time, the bathroom stinks of the iron of blood so strong you can almost taste it. The Beloved once told me that her periods are like torture, the pain is so intense. That she produces clots that look like chopped liver. It was before mine had started and she was trying to frighten me, but it's true all the same: I've heard her talking to *her* about it. I don't know why men fancy us really. We're disgusting. I suppose they don't really know about all the gore.

The steaming waters I've just bathed in have stripped me of all that, though. I feel clean and hard and capable of forging destinies, as if the spear I imagined really is in my hand with its point thrust forward. I walk the streets fast but feel I'm never going to tire. The night-time gardens stir beside me. They smell of earth and roses. The croaking of a frog comes as loud and pure as the playing of a harp string. This city is so small. Nature surrounds it, seeping into its rivers and front gardens. I stop, and the sound fills me with a joy that pushes into every little bit of me.

I begin walking again, fast. I know exactly where I'm going now. I'm going to where Mr Jonasson lives in his little brick house on the hill with his wife and two children. If one of my wishes at the bowl has been derailed for the time being, there's always the other one. Minerva has shown me that it's all possible. Anything is possible now.

# 12

# Grace

'Mum, it's Gracie,' I whisper. There's no response.

I put my hand to my mouth to stifle the emerging scream. My bowels turn to jelly. Slowly my legs buckle and I sink to the floor. A pool of blood swims before my eyes.

My list at the wishing bowl pounds in my head, what I said that day – not a drip, no wheelchair, no pills or appointments. Please God I never want to see a fucking adjustable medical bed again.

'Mum, I'm so bloody sorry,' I whimper. 'I'm so, so sorry. I wished those things because I wanted you better. I think I said that too, I'm sure I did. Please, please, please be alive. Mum, please. Please. I'll give anything for my stupid-bitch wish not to be true.'

Of course I knew something bad was awaiting me. Of course I realised that, with me being late, she would have struck out on her own, cursing to herself, furious at her own inability to do that simple thing of getting out of bed unaided and in her fury become reckless. I'd seen it all before, but of course *before* I'd always been there to avert the disaster I could see arriving a few frames down the film, and this is so much more horrible than anything I could have imagined. I see it in fragments, like my brain can't take it all in at once.

Mum lies on the floor with limbs that are so muddled there appears to be too many of them, like the tangled thready legs of a dead spider. Now it's just as I knew it would be. But, no, again, the picture in my mind didn't include the press of flesh into the carpet that has left an embossed criss-cross on her cheek because she's been lying there so long, or the spitty thread of blood hanging from the corner of her mouth, or the roll of her eyes that look up at me like the real her got imprisoned inside this tangle before she died. It never included the *detail* that, when it comes to it, is the real outrage. The thickness of the blood on the floor as it congeals.

'Mum.' I'm crying so hard now, snot is coursing down my chin. I feel sick and light at the same time. I think it's possible that it's not happening but then I sit down with a thump and the pain shocks through my buttocks and I know it is. 'How could I have left you?' My words are followed by a half-keening wail that I switch off by slapping myself on the mouth with my fist.

A sound comes from her. 'Sssssssshhh.'

'Mum?' I lean in closer.

'Ssssshhh, Gracie,' she whispers.

'Mum, you're alive.' I'm laughing as well as sobbing now. 'You really are alive?'

I lean over and smooth away the grey hair that she usually keeps so neat, and that is now plastered across her mouth and chin. With my other hand I cradle her skull and the feel of it under my fingers makes me want to weep even harder. *You'll stop crying, bitch*, I say to myself. *You owe her that at least.*

'Mum. Please God, what's happened?' I gasp to this bloody mess on the floor.

She opens and closes her mouth like she is the baby bird

and I am the mother with the worm. I peel off the rest of her hair from her chin and gently push a pillow under her head.

'Now, what have we here? What's to be done?' I mutter the inanities in a kind of sing-song like a nurse. I look at the puzzle of her limbs but when I try and untangle them she gives a sharp piercing cry that resonates at the bottom of my skull.

'Oh Mum.' I bite at my knuckles, trying to choke the sobs down, but they come thick and fast and I go back on my promise not to cry, and then I feel I'm about eight years old again, crying with my mouth stretched in a stupid upside-down grin. I'm holding onto her and moaning, 'Mum, I love you. I love you so much. I'm so sorry.'

'It's OK,' she breathes. It's just a wheezy whisper but I catch it.

Slowly I ease my arms underneath her and she feels such a bag of bones, and the frailty of the *creature* she is is so obvious it almost finishes me. I lift her up and gently, gently I lay her on the familiar faded flowered cotton bedspread; it's printed with pink poppies and blue gerbera, a kind of flowery ocean, because this one place has grown to encompass everything and the outside world has shrunk to the extent that it has no meaning.

Gradually she begins to unfurl, bit by little bit, like one of those Japanese paper flowers in a cup of water.

I rub off my tears with a towel and go to make some tea. I bring it on a tray with our best china, the gold-rimmed cups with the poppies. Slowly, painfully, I manage to prop her up on some pillows and then I sit cross-legged on the floor beside her and watch, the teapot pluming steam through the spout. When I think she's ready I bring the cup to her lips and wet her mouth. I carry on with this, sip by tiny sip, so after about forty minutes she has managed to drink half a cup. There is a little colour in her cheeks. Not much but a little, and I feel it's there just because of the sheer gargantuan effort of will I've somehow exerted to make it OK.

'Grace,' she whispers. 'Grace, love. I think perhaps you should call an ambulance.'

'Mum—'

'Really, I think you should. I think this time we do need to get me checked over.'

My heart clenches. If she goes to hospital all this will come out. They'll find out she was on her own while I was with a boy downstairs, hung over, addled with grass.

'No.'

'Grace, I really think . . .' she whispers. Her eyes are closed so she doesn't see me taking the mobile phone from her bedside table and pocketing it in my grey hoody. 'We'll deal with this ourselves,' I say.

'But—'

'Mum. No. We are going to be all right and we are going to manage and we are not going to call an ambulance and we are not going to call anyone and you can stop fussing and stop worrying because I'm not going anywhere and I am going to take care of absolutely everything.'

Later, after she is asleep, I drag myself down to the bathroom and stare at myself long and hard in the mirror. *She could've died, bitch*, I tell my reflection. *Let that sink in, bitch, while you're poncing about with boys and growing your hair out all over your pretty little head.* My reflection disappears while I grub about in the cabinet and find Dad's old clippers, and I plug them in and they start first time with a harsh buzzing noise.

*From now on you're a fucking soldier*, I tell my reflection as I start to shear off hair in rows that drips in clumps into the basin. You are Travis fucking Bickle. You have something to fight for and you must fight with all your fury and all your might and there is no room for compromise on that. You are a warlord, and if you ever fucking forget it, all you have to do is to look in the mirror at your bitch-head that will from this moment on be shaved as a permanent fucking reminder of that fact.

# 13

# Phoebe

*'I'm soooooo happy.'*

I'm aware this is a risky thing to write in my diary. *What's going on?* she will think. She'll lift her head up like she's scented something on the wind. I can see her parting her lips and putting her finger thoughtfully on the page as she tries to work it out.

All the same, I couldn't help it. It has to leak out somewhere. I will work to divert her attention to a different place. I'll show joy over something small and insignificant: a silly new dress I've seen; an invitation to a party; an unexpectedly excellent essay mark that really I care nothing about. Maybe I'll even intimate that there was a burgeoning romance with a boy that had me all in an adolescent quiver but was subsequently cruelly crushed by him. That will please her greatly. *So that was the source of joy,* she'll think. Like a detective she will feel like she has cracked the case.

Although of course she won't have done.

I've done something bad, bad, bad and I don't even care.

Last night as I walked I was convinced that the hot spring waters had washed off some of my female glitter. I didn't mind, though. In fact, I was glad for it because there was something durable and hard underneath. Something that couldn't be cracked in the way I normally crack.

When I arrived at Mr Jonasson's house I could see that he wasn't home because his little red Citroën wasn't parked outside. His house is mean and shabby compared to ours. Poor Victorian rather than the Georgian glories that most of Bath is made up of, but the very good thing about where he lives is that opposite the houses is a small urban wood. It means I can stay under its canopy and watch him coming home or leaving in his funny little car that I'd recognise anywhere. It means I can watch the lights as they click on and off, marking the passage of people through the house. They are very thrifty. From the rate at which lights are switched on and off, I'm guessing a light is never left on in an empty room. Whenever I hide out there to spy on them, I get so excited I swear I can feel my hair stand on end. I'm cloaked in trees and darkness and that is the power of it. Last night I felt like that but a million times more because of the way the baths had lit up all my cells.

Their house was in darkness and I wondered if that meant they were away for the weekend on some disgusting nappy-and-breast-milk-soaked adventure. It occurred to me it could simply be that he had to park further down the road and they were on the other side of the house so were at home. Not knowing made it even more exciting somehow. I slipped into the darkness, threading myself through the trees. Above me was the *tweep, tweep* of a little bird who'd forgotten to go to sleep; my tiny familiar perhaps. Everything felt like it was turning my way. The trees were dark skeletons, surrounding me like a personal guard. Mother moon was above me in the shape of a hook as if ready to pluck Mr Jonasson up and dangle him for me. I bit at the skin on the sides of my nails. How had it been last time I saw him? I replayed it minute by minute. Hadn't I felt it, as he perched on the edge of his desk and spoke about 'character is fate', hadn't I seen his eyes constantly flicked to the side, where I was, even though because of where his desk was placed it was an unnatural place to look? I'd felt important for the rest of the week. 'We'll arrange an extra lesson very soon,' he said to me with a smile, and the smile was so intimate I lit up like a lantern. So I'd been wrong that horrible day in the underground car park. He'd wanted me all along.

*Character is fate.* I wondered about that, there in those woods, and what it meant for me and where *my* character would lead. Although truly I felt those Fates were with me last night and I was in their hands rather than my own. Fates, in the old sense of the word: beings – three women spinning out the mother thread of every mortal from birth to death. I could almost hear their movement among the trees; feel their breath on my neck, their thread tugging sharply on my belly button, yanking the crinkled skin where once the coil of an umbilical cord, dark and shiny with blood, had attached me to *her*. And was that Minerva – the goddess who presides over the thermal spring – her soft footfall in the grass behind me? Perhaps she'd silently followed me through the streets from the Roman Baths. It wouldn't surprise me.

When I'm that little spider scuttling around *her* and The Beloved, I have no character. At home it's reduced to a pin-prick. But knowing that someone like Mr Jonasson sees something in me that, in my best moments, I truly know is there changes everything. Last night the world felt aligned: the moon, the cars parked on the street opposite, the metal railings, the lilac tree that was lavender-orange in the streetlight – all in a constellation with me at its core, and my character swelled and bloomed. I became complete. It almost didn't matter if I saw him there or not. I could have swallowed up the elixir of the night and returned home pregnant with its potency. But those Fates had other things in mind for me.

I heard the hum of a little continental engine coming up the hill and I moved closer to the edge of the trees to see. The streetlights had turned the red car to grey but I felt the adrenaline rush as I recognised the number plate. I had a moment of indecision. I could stay here in my little hollow of darkness and merely watch him park, lock up his car, step to his front door. The time spent retrieving his key, his slowness in the putting-down of his bags to unlock the door I'd take as unwillingness to enter back into the family fray. Except I felt the sharp, urgent tugging on my belly button; which one of the Fates was it? I didn't know, but she was telling me I couldn't wait for our private lesson.

'Hey, Mr Jonasson.' I addressed the back of his head.

He whirled round. My passage over to this side of the road seemed to have happened in a twinkling.

'Phoebe.'

Again, he didn't seem pleased to see me, but this time I didn't take offence because I guessed his wife and children were in there at the back of the house where I couldn't see the lights. Perhaps they were already all tucked up in bed.

'What are you doing here?' he asked, as he put his bags back down.

'Just passing.' I affected nonchalance. 'I'm staying with a friend tonight, you know, Orla.'

He looked down at my hands, which were in the pockets of my raincoat. It's an ancient man's Burberry. I like the style of it.

'Where are your things?'

'Things?'

'Yes.' He smiled tiredly. 'Your toothbrush and your night things.'

'Oh, we just use each other's.' I bit my lip. This happens to be true, but he's Swedish, so he might find that sort of thing disgusting.

'It's quite late,' he said, glancing towards his own front door. Was she really in there or not? I was burning to know. I've glimpsed her in the distance. Tawny blonde hair done up in a ponytail. She wears that sprigged vintage style of clothing, infantilised and nursery-ish, that so many young mothers seem to adopt. That, or the head-to-toe boating theme, with stripes and anchors. Both looks seem designed to turn women into cheerful puppets for their own children.

He looked at me silently for a moment. Suddenly he seemed more awake; I could see the shine of his eyes in the darkness. He said, 'You shouldn't be walking the streets after dark.'

He cares! I didn't point out that this was sleepy Bath, not a big city like Stockholm where I know he is from.

'I'll be all right.' *Better to seem brave and foolhardy than snivelling and scared*, I thought. *It makes people more likely to want to rescue you.*

'Come on.' He leaned over and retrieved his bags. 'Tell me where she lives and I'll take you. You shouldn't be wandering around alone in the dark. It can be quite lonely around here. It might not be safe.'

As we walked to the car I had a spurt of anxiety at the thought of him realising I was out of my way. Why should I be in his street that doesn't lead from my house to Orla's?

154

It's ages away from both. I puzzled this as we reached the car that was still warm and ticking from being driven. *He doesn't know where I live*, I told myself. *It won't even occur to him.*

Predictably the car was given over to the transport of infants. There was a complicated baby seat in the back, alongside a booster seat with a flowered cushion on top. All that hard plastic and metal for protection, like exoskeletons for their soft tender flesh. I'd expected it to smell like baby food or baby sick but it didn't. It smelt clean and rubbery, and it made me wonder if Mr Jonasson himself is sickened by these things and keeps his car, his own little domain, as spick and span and without odour as possible. I know I would if I were him.

I thought about living in the car, crawling underneath the wheel arch and weaving myself into its workings. Every time the car started up (the wife has her own car) I would vibrate in his presence. How much better to be in the house, though. If I could follow him through the open door and whoosh up to the attics or live among his shirts and jackets in the wardrobe, breathing in his smell. It might be enough. I could feed my obsession silently. I'd even prefer it to this, and thinking that made me I realise how scared I was as I climbed into his car.

My hands trembled badly as I did up my seat belt. I could hardly believe I was on the inside. He was nervous too, I realised, by the way his thumb tapped a rat-a-tat-tat on the steering wheel, over and over. Neither of us spoke as he started up the engine and manoeuvred the car out of its parking space, and again I panicked that it might be that finally, finally we were alone together and I might find that

I couldn't muster a single word in his presence. Because of that I plunged in, stupidly, awkwardly, enough to make me grimace ahead out of the windscreen.

'That was such an interesting lesson we had last week,' I gushed.

To my surprise he didn't appear disconcerted. I could see him grinning out of the corner of my eye. I couldn't believe it. It had worked. He was flattered.

'You like *Macbeth*?'

How could I answer that? *No*, I wanted to say. *That* thing *is anthrax; it's doom and violence. It's blood falling down the walls.*

'Of course,' I said brightly. If we were going to talk about this, we'd have to stick to the parts that didn't scare me. 'I love the witches.'

I saw him frowning in the light of the dashboard. 'Hmmm. But it worries me the attention they receive within the play. It's disproportionate. Of course they are quite peripheral to the core.'

'Really?' That's not how it struck me.

'Yes, just some hocus-pocus that Shakespeare dreamt up to please the crowds. They loved that sort of nonsense. Plus it was politic as they were a sop to James, the king on the throne at the time, who was obsessed by the subject.' He sounded vehement in his opinion and it brought out his accent, the Swedish up-and-down of it as if his voice were on springs. 'It's a diversion, an entertainment. The real content is that Macbeth has the seeds of his own destruction within himself. He is a tragic hero.'

I wondered at the vehemence. He clearly wanted to be right, and even though I didn't agree I didn't say anything, just stroked my little patch of beard in the darkness, the pale fluff on my Adam's apple, secret hair kept in plain sight.

This conversation was so stilted and seemed to be leading so far down the wrong path, I changed my mind about keeping quiet.

'Yes, you're right about that. I completely agree.' There was a short silence that felt like it urgently needed filling. 'Do they have Shakespeare in Sweden?' I asked to fill the gap.

'Of course.'

He turned to smile at me and not for the first time it struck me how female his eyes were. The long lashes that fringed them were those of a Hollywood starlet. It gave him a sleepy, almost shy, look.

There was a terrible aching silence in the car, worse this time. Even our awful conversation was better than this. At least it covered up the sense that this was dangerous, dangerous, dangerous. I imagined how it would be if someone we both knew spotted us.

We drove through Walcot Street and I tried not to, but I couldn't help looking up at the wall where the man's body had been dragged like a butcher's carcass. In this light I could almost see the sticky dark blood again. I closed my eyes and tried to breathe normally. My mind swooped precariously. *Make something bad happen again*, it said. *No, no, no – I cancel that. I cancel it now!*

'Are you all right?' His voice next to me made me jump.

'Yes, I'm fine. We're nearly there.'

Before the journey's end I needed to get onto something more profound, more soulful, where a connection would be made but I'd run out of time. My mission seemed to have failed. I considered taking him around the block, or on a diversion, but guessed he would smell a rat.

I cleared my throat. 'Just down there.'

'I'll drop you on the corner,' he said, and only afterwards I realised that meant he'd planned it all already and saying he was worried about me walking in the dark was just an excuse because he didn't mind not seeing me to the door.

The engine idled and stopped as he parked behind Orla's mum's car. The familiarity of her boxy Volvo looked strange in this situation.

'Thank you,' I said without moving.

He stayed, impassive, in the driving seat and I felt a sick disappointment in my guts. The streetlights lit up the edges of his fine blond hair and his cheekbone was framed in the car window.

'Here we are,' I said. Then with mounting excitement I realised neither of us was moving. I could hear his rushed breathing in the car. I felt such a churning terror at what I knew was about to happen that a cold sweat covered the back of my neck like dew. But I didn't budge. I remembered my wish at the wishing bowl and it all seemed fixed already. I felt I couldn't move even if I tried. The Fates were practically sitting on me, pinning me down.

'Phoebe,' he said.

And after all I found I didn't *want* to move. The fear teetered into excitement and I felt alive and so powerful, as if I could take flight if I wanted to. For the second time that day I leaned forward to let the light fall on my face. I let it illuminate me as if I were on stage. I'd been charged by the baths inside and out and now my witch light was a-shining; that's how much he really knew about the subject: he was under the influence of it himself without even realising.

The next moment he moved forward too and his lips were on mine and his fingers were in my hair. The feeling of his mouth surprised me. It was soft and unexpectedly female too. I wondered how I always expected men to feel tough and hard but realised then that they have their many softnesses, just like us. Their delicacies, like Paul's little fragile hand I touched by accident once. The kiss went on for longer than felt comfortable, as if he was choosing how to face me when it stopped, then something changed again, an abandonment, and I felt his wet tongue urgently in my mouth. When he finally withdrew I smiled at him to show him he'd done the right thing.

'You are lovely,' I said, and somehow it seemed to be just the right thing to say.

He looked down, almost bashfully, and said, 'Well, thank you. You are very lovely too. You know, I worry about you sometimes. You look so drawn and pale.'

'Really?'

It surprised me that anything showed on the outside.

He nods. 'Yes, but very lovely all the same.' He brushed my cheek and smiled.

I touched his arm as I let myself out of the car. I needed to be alone with this, to turn it over and examine it, because I was so scared and wired by this point I'd do something stupid and give myself away if I didn't escape. I loitered by Orla's gate until his tail lights were out of sight, then walked up and down the darkened street, my footsteps tapping in the dark like Blind Pew's stick. What I was beginning to realise was that the waters had washed none of my female glitter away. The feeling of being clean and new, almost masculine, dry as seaweed blown by the wind, was in part false. I saw that reflected in his face when I put my own into the light. The glitter had remained intact through the boiling but I was wearing it differently. Now it was like an external skin, a wetsuit-like thing that skimmed over the surface. The waters had reached further than that. Bone-deep. They'd gone underneath that skin and cleaned out my marrow, lit a primitive fire in the hollows there that smouldered hotly while on the top everything appeared unchanged.

It was a kind of marvellous trick.

Once I'd crept into Orla's bed the feeling stayed with me. I couldn't help but hint at what had occurred she kept on at me so much. When I told her I'd seen Mr Jonasson and sworn her to secrecy she became very strange. She grabbed onto me in bed and held me so hard I thought I was going to break. It was almost like sex, I think, though I didn't mind. I was just glad she'd gone back to loving me.

# 14

# Orla

This is the first time I do it and because of that I know it will also be the hardest.

That thought is very precise as I stand over Mum's handbag.

The bag's decorated, fussy – a little like her – with clinky beads and a gold charm in the shape of V for Veronica clipped on to the hinge. The clasp is not even shut properly and this gives me a moment's guilty thud to the heart; that the level of trust is so high she leaves it around with the mouth slitted open. All the same, the moment passes and I discover the true meaning of the term 'light-fingered' as my hand does enter so very lightly there, barely touching the contents until I feel the bulk of her purse and I ease open the top of the handbag with the knuckle of my thumb, only to discover that the purse is lying casually open too. There are sounds of running water and banging saucepans from the kitchen on the other side of the wall, and it's those everyday noises that bring a sudden flash of sweat to my back and temples.

If I asked, she would give me the money, no question. No, that's not right: there would be caveats, hundreds of them. *Do you need anything? Take it, take it, get yourself a manicure, a new blouse, do you need any skin stuff? I've seen the sweetest tops in that shop we went to last week. Have you ever thought about a kitten heel? Have you ever thought about having a perm?*

'A perm?' Phoebe shrieked when I told her. 'Who the flip has a perm in this day and age? Go on, you should do it. I can't imagine you all curly. That's hilarious. You'd have to go to some weird old people's hairdresser to have it done.' Then she shook out her own beautiful dark natural curls around her shoulders.

I know the seam of what lies beneath all this generosity of my mother's, even if she doesn't. She's been grooming me – literally – for my future attraction to a mate as far back as I can remember. It's so medieval it makes me feel sick. Deep down I know she doesn't even realise she's doing it. Her own mother did it to her. But if I asked for the money under these pretences, she'd want to see the badges of it being spent. Smoothed-out skin plump with artificial hydration. High-smelling bath bombs studded with real rose petals in paper bags. A new hair colour, hint of auburn perhaps, her own much lamented natural colour from when she was my age which she has never been able to properly reproduce in later life.

I skin a twenty and then a ten off the roll that is pushed haphazardly in the change section, pocket the notes, skirt past my mother and go into the garden before she can say anything or try to read my face. I need the coolness. The summer has barely started but already there's a fist of green and red blackberries hanging over the wall, waiting for the sun to turn them a deep autumn purple. It's all so relentless. It's like I need everything to stop just for a little while so I can just rest and think clearly. Sometimes I long to live by the sea. I crave the salt sting in the air, the lash of hair whipped around the face. The air here is so often sultry, brewed in a valley as it is. It begins to rain, just a few drops, and I lean my face towards the wetness, and the feel of it on my face is something that is only a tiny taster, a shadow of what I need. Mum's head bobs into view inside the house. She's at the sink, washing dishes. The sight of her should make me feel guilty but it doesn't. I simply feel disconnected from her behind her window.

I can still feel Phoebe's arms where she held me through the night. God, she's so fucking beautiful. She has something about her that means you can't stop looking. It's almost biblical. Sometimes she stands with her square palms outstretched and she could be John the Baptist or one of the Three Wise Men or even Jesus. That's the power of her. I can't take my eyes off her. It was my other wish at the wishing bowl, to possess her, the silent second part of the wish to have someone only for myself, except I know when I'm thinking clearly that it will never be her, and that's so painful it nearly kills me. I said it that day under my breath and it's hard to think that something so powerful barely stirred the air as I whispered the words.

Last night I was woken by a sharp patter on my window that took me a while to realise was a rain of stones. When I pushed up the sash, Phoebe was standing there below on the pavement just like that, with her palms turned upwards, and my heart started knocking so hard I could hear it in my ears.

'Come down and let me in.' It was a whisper but it drifted up to me like smoke because the night was so still. I think as long as I live I will remember that moment. Seeing her in the pool of streetlight, her face upturned. I put my hand to my mouth to stifle a laugh because it seemed such a comedy-sweet re-enaction of Romeo and Juliet's balcony scene.

I opened the front door with trembling fingers and she

sauntered in. 'Sssh, everyone's asleep,' I whispered. 'Where have you been?' I couldn't bear for the moment to be broken by one of my family barging into it. It would destroy the atmosphere that seemed so perfect to my bleary senses.

I was glad my bedroom was submerged in darkness so I couldn't see it properly and be reminded of its revoltingness. Again, I resolved to rip it all apart as soon as I could. It was a dusty fairy tale; a story that had been told all wrong and threaded through with phoney facts all along. The remnants of years ago when I was trying so hard, everything in the room a staged diversion – the loops of lights in the shape of sunflowers wrapped around the cream iron bedhead. The pink striped rag rug. The glass vase of artificial sunflowers, now coated in a layer of dust in the corner. I remembered how, at about the age of twelve, my mother and I had decided that sunflowers would be my 'theme'. It seems such a strange and pointless exercise in hindsight. It appears like childish vanity now – or worse, an attempt to pin me down before I'd had a chance properly to *become* so I'd be forever stuck inside a sunny whorl.

We curled round each other in bed. She felt freezing, even in my borrowed pyjamas. Something had happened, I could tell.

'Where were you?' I asked. 'What's happened?'

She wouldn't tell me for a long time. She even pretended to be asleep for a while, but I knew it was fake stillness and I shook her out of it.

'Tell me,' I whispered fiercely into her ear. I even turned the light on to wake her up.

'All right,' she said. 'But first you have to promise me not to freak out or tell anyone.'

'Of course,' I said, although everyone knows these promises are meaningless.

She bit her beautiful bottom lip. 'I've seen him.'

'Who?'

'Him.'

'Paul?'

'No, our English teacher, of course.'

I tried not to let the rising fury show in my face.

'What happened?'

'Well, I was out walking the streets and he pulled up in his car.' Her eyes went round. 'Do you think he might've been driving about looking for me? D'you think he's that crazy over me?'

'It does seem rather a coincidence,' I said, though she didn't seem to hear the coolness.

'Well, after we drove around for a bit—'

'You got in his car?' I couldn't keep the anger out of my voice now.

'Look, if you're going to interrupt all the time I'm not going to tell you. We drove around for a bit. It was wonderful. We talked and talked for ages like we've known each other forever, and Orla . . .' She sat up. 'He kissed me.'

I wanted to strangle her. How could she? How could she?

'What sort of kiss?' Hoping it might be a peck-on-the-cheek-goodnight kind.

'It was a proper full kiss. Passionate, like we were tasting each other.'

I switched off the light and grabbed onto her so hard our bodies felt almost painful against each other.

'Promise me you won't see him again,' I said into her hair.

She didn't respond and she lay in my arms, still and silent, for the rest of the night.

I couldn't sleep. The memory of *our* year-old kiss flared up and plagued me. It had happened in the little park down from her house, shrouded in trees and full of dinky little Victorian touches that makes it slightly dreamlike and wonky like an illustration in a children's book. It's on a hill with the paths cut into it and we used to call it 'the slanting park' in the way we had of naming everything like that. We were sheltering from the rain – carrying an umbrella wouldn't have occurred to us – and there was something so stirring about the sheets of rain, the rumble of approaching thunder, as if the world was being realigned in a new and exciting way, that sent shivers down my arms. The dish-sized leaves caught the rain above us and funnelled it down in a complicated pattern so it sprayed over the edges of the tree and left us dry. Phoebe felt the excitement too; I know she did. She hooked her little finger inside my curled palm and drew me close. I didn't need any more encouragement. I held her chin with my other hand and kissed her. It felt perfect. Wet but not slobbery, and soft and hard at the same time. Her mouth even seemed to have a tang of the salt that I craved. That's what I've held onto since Eleanor. *That wasn't my first kiss*, I want to tell that bovine face each time I see her. *I've kissed somebody who is truly astoundingly beautiful and special, and that specialness has touched even the stupid uncouth person I am.*

The moment was like an exquisite perfect musical note hanging in the air before dissolving.

Though even as our faces were moving apart I heard

something to my right and turned just in time to see a young mother dragging a child away and pushing a pram with her other hand. She was huffing her disapproval. Her back was stiff with it.

I turned back to Phoebe. 'I've got to go,' she said.

And my heart twisted painfully. I could tell by the evenness in her voice that she was neutralising what had just happened. Not a hint of excited breathiness, whereas I could *barely* breathe. She was preparing the way for ignoring this – or worse, pretending it had never happened. She left me there alone under the trees and I watched her getting drenched as she walked away, the rain darkening the back of her blue coat in a triangle.

The kiss has stayed unacknowledged, although she comes to me when she needs to be held, like last night. I watched her impassive face in the semi-darkness. She seemed unnaturally still. I must've fallen asleep myself at some point. Perhaps when the dawn was creeping through the layers of lace curtains with tiny shells stitched onto their hems, so they tinkle on the painted boards when drawn aside with a sound like shingle being dragged along by the sea. When I woke she'd gone. I wrapped myself in my dressing gown and froze as I opened the bedroom door. I could hear her downstairs talking to my mother. I tied my dressing gown tightly and went to join them.

'Glad you had a good time last night,' my mother said, brightly gesturing with her coffee cup in the shape of an owl, its little nubbed ceramic beak standing out in a vaguely obscene manner. I startled at the weirdness of her statement, until she added, 'Makes me less guilty about going out with the girls,' and I realised Phoebe must've somehow extracted that information, then persuaded her we'd had the evening in together, watching movies or trying on make-up or some other thing that we're supposed to do.

In the background my two brothers raucously foraged breakfast, knocking over cereal packets and cramming juice back in the fridge without looking to see if there was space in the door shelf. Phoebe smiled at me through the steam of her own cup, rabbit-shaped.

'You just wait till your father's home.' My mother addressed the boys' backs grimly. 'Then you'll see what's what.'

'Thanks, Veronica,' Phoebe bobbed her head in the direction of my mum. 'Better go now.' Mum never minds that Phoebe calls her by her first name. I think it makes her feel like 'one of the girls'.

My mouth rounded in a childish O of disappointment. 'But if you wait we can walk together.' I knew I sounded petulant and needy.

'No, I must go. I need to get some things for school.'

'I could come with you.'

'No time to wait. Got to go.'

She had that hunted look in her eye, the need to flee stamped there, like she's about to be suffocated. She's always flitting like that at a moment's notice. She's like water. She grabbed her coat. 'Bye then,' she said awkwardly before ducking out of the room, leaving the little family tableau behind, my mother chewing ruminatively on a corner of toast as she watched her go.

The garden feels like a relief.


It's my last day of school before term ends because Mum has got rid of the boys and booked us both into some awful spa break and then Dad will be back. Everything changes, I tell myself.

Already school has that carnival feeling of the end of days. The noticeboards have been ripped clean. Builders are there, sizing up the back windows for repair over the summer. Somehow it makes the building seem like there's more light flooding in, the parquet showing up pale and honeyed, because all the old familiar patterns have been peeled away.

I stand very close to Phoebe. 'I have something for you.'

I crunch the notes in my hand and deliver them in her palm squashed up into a ball, like they don't matter, like I was stealing something that has no meaning to the likes of Phoebe and me.

The glint in her eye tells me the fundamental untruth of this. 'Well, we can have some fun now. What do you say?'

I nod.

'Good girl,' she says and mock-pats me on the shoulder and swings off. I know it should infuriate me. She's patronising me and she's using me but I don't care. It feels painful now, the idea of not seeing her automatically every day; I can't even think about it. Her existence is like sharp bright berries that I feast upon greedily. I want to stain my mouth with them.

Any guilt about stealing the money has faded in the light of the importance of the project. I'll do it again, soon. I'll give her anything she wants.

I wander off, feeling so lonely it's like it's got me by the throat. Teachers wait in their doorways and make people line up so they will enter classrooms in an orderly fashion. I see Grace in the corridor. I think about approaching her but I change my mind. You never know what reaction you'll get and today she looks so white her lips stand out the colour of a bruise, her eyes large and startled in her thin face.

She's cut off all the hair that's grown out; actually, it looks more like she's shaved it off. It's so short you can clearly see the scalp beneath, so pale, the colour of a pearl.

# 15

# Grace

I shouldn't be here.

I'm sure I look weird. I feel like I've gone into some sort of shock or something, and the noises in the school corridor are muffled like I'm walking underwater. I had to get away, though. I couldn't think in that flat. I could only creep around Mum as she lay on the bed, dried blood under her nose, and then go out of her room and silently scream on the balcony. Eventually I plucked up the courage to clean the blood away with a damp flannel. All night I kept peeking around Mum's door, terrified at what I might see. Then I checked again this morning before I left.

She's alive, just.

What a bitch-coward I am coming into *school* of all things, I tell myself. I must be crazy leaving her like that, but on the other hand being away means I have to start calming down because if I break down blubbing here, then everything will be lost.

'Are you all right, dear? You look terribly pale.' The head, Mrs Reid, stops me in front of the lockers. She's always asking me that; it's a pain really and especially so today when somebody being kind could just about tip me over the edge.

I swallow, nod.

'Well, the door to my office is always open, you know that, dear.' Then she's off, squeezing my arm lightly, because she's distracted by some commotion around the corner that she swiftly moves to take charge of, while I stand there dry-swallowing over and over again.

Around me my fellow pupils look so strange as they surge to their classes. Shovelling crisps into their faces, braying out honking laughs, wallowing along in massive pillowy trainers. Actually I know it's me that's the strange one, the alien, the ghost among them.

Three, four, cross that fucking floor. The parquet floor to the school office to tell the secretary I won't be staying for the rest of the day, which is our system.

Then I'm outside, blinking in the bright sunshine, ready to face anything I have to face.

# 16

# Phoebe

What is a witch?

I go looking for them to distract me from thinking about *him*. I believe they might give me clues too on how to feel better and stronger than I do.

I find them inside the Internet. There are thousands of them flying around in there.

I wait until lunchtime when it's quiet. The school library's old dial-up connection takes an age to get going. It beeps and clicks and I wait as it creaks along like some ancient contraption being fired up.

I start to get excited.

I can feel them all gathering in there, massing darkly and then feeding their way down the tubes to find me.

Then the old screen lights up with a crackle. It doesn't take long to find them. I feel my blood rising when I do.

I realise that I will never forget what I'm learning. That the facts of it will carve new pathways in my brain and these creatures appearing on the screen will all be huddling inside my head forever.

I stand up. Shake myself down and go on looking.

They do not just feature in silly children's stories. I learn that they perform 'unnatural acts'. They fly. Not always on broomsticks either. They use anything to hand – branches or cooking forks or a goat with horns. Sometimes they fly in hordes, sometimes alone. They congregate. A witches' sabbath. I can almost hear a crystal ping inside the computer like they're landing inside the screen, battering against it with their forks, trying to escape into the room.

They make flying ointment. It's almost sweet, like little girls mashing up plants and thinking they're making magic. It reminds me of our wishing bowl and the messes we've made in it, mud slopping over the side and splattering our ankles. Though their ointment has hemlock in it, other herbs too. Sometimes creatures caught for the purpose. They use the blood of animals; moles caught at midnight. Witches know all the charms and tricks. They have all the philtres and poisons. They like to make stinks. They like everything to be backwards. Sometimes I too have a longing to invert, for everything to be made upside down or inside out. If I could fly, I'd swoop up to the top of a tree and hang off a branch by my toes. Smile at passers-by, which would appear to them as a grimace.

They kiss the devil's arse.

Sometimes these women are old and ugly. I see the words hag and crone. Harpy, harridan, scold, targe, drab, Fury, weird sister, necromancer. An old woman so envious of others she eats her own heart in fury. Munches and sucks on it.

Sometimes they are young and beautiful. Siren. Succubus. Harlot. Bitch.

I hear my breath in the room as I read on.

They have the ability to start fires; flames crack open from the ground where they've just walked. They chew glass. They are penis snatchers.

Their feet point backwards.

There's the three weird sisters from *Macbeth* of course. How scared Macbeth is of them. How drawn to them he is. They'll do anything to carry out revenge. 'In a sieve I'll thither sail,' they say; they can do that, across the seas using their brooms for oars. They whisper things to Macbeth that are the end of him. They are the thoughts you should never listen to but do, and I know what that's like.

It's not fair. Macbeth wants their power even though he's disgusted by them. He wants to take their visions of what's to come and use them for his own ends, and not give them anything in return. He should leave them alone and not try and take what's theirs and get on with his own life. He's not a tragic hero; he's a thief. *That's* what makes him so evil.

Of course I won't tell Mr Jonasson I think that. I know he likes being the expert in these matters and I don't mind him thinking he is, I really don't. Every time I remember our beautiful kiss it shudders right through me.

He was right about one thing, though. The witches were hated and rounded up. Murdered in droves. No wonder they keep everything that makes them safe around them like I do with the pointing knives and scissors at home. They need these things, these creatures. There are favoured animals, friends almost: little scurrying creatures that do their bidding, carrying out wicked deeds under cover of rustling leaves and night. Hares, pigs, cats, weasels, dogs. A favourite is a yellow bird that hops from tree to tree and is a friend and lookout. Toads too, the bigger the better. Skinwalkers, they take the form of animals and walk in their fur on all fours.

There's always something that gives witches away, though. Some mark or token on their bodies. A bruise or teat or fold of skin. They go looking for these, the accusers. They poke around the women's bodies like they were putty, searching out what they are determined to find. Then it's the trials. That's when all hope is lost. That's the point where there's nothing you can do about it any more. All the ointments and witch sabbaths disappear like mist in the glare of it. The questions are overwhelming; they surge over you like a tidal wave and flatten all the ramparts you've spent years and years building.

I get up and pace around the empty room, feeling upset.

The trials remind me of being with that counsellor woman that Mum made me see – pussy-cat face. How she ran after me; even though she was on her leather chair and I was on the red sofa the whole time, I knew I was being chased by the slimy smiling witch finder. Tick-tock went the clock, sometimes fast and sometimes slow. When she caught up with me, which happened more and more as time went on, she conducted a thorough search. Having your mind searched is the very worst sort of intrusion. Sometimes I managed to shut the proceedings down: I'd put up a roadblock and feel pleased with myself that I'd somehow managed to outwit her. More often than not my roadblock didn't work. I'd turn to flee, giddy with escape, and there she was. She'd got round it somehow and was simply waiting as the clock ticked out. Tick-tock. By the end of the session I was nearly always skewered, a beetle pegged out on pins for view. I'd go home. 'How did it go?' my mother would ask. 'What did you say?'

I drink deeply from a bottle of water and sit down to read more about the trials.

Many didn't realise they were witches. Is it possible to be a witch and not know? Yes. It can be driven out of you. Also, we cannot drown. However hard they try to drown a witch, she keeps getting right up out of the water, like getting up out of bed. If she drowns and her prone body floats up, lifeless, to the surface, that's the only way you tell she was innocent.

A real witch will keep getting up.

Then, all that can be done is to burn or hang her.

I touch my own throat delicately.

The youngest I find that was hanged was five years old.

Mr Jonasson doesn't arrive at school till after lunch. I hear his voice murmuring in the staffroom. What excuse is he giving them, I wonder? Does his absence mean he's trying to avoid me? Perhaps he'll skirt around me the next few days and then disappear off into the summer like nothing ever happened. Or, is it because he's in such a ferment he's had to take the morning to become steady? I linger in the corridor and try to hear but his voice is too low for me to pick out the words. I bite at my fingers. I'm tempestuous with not knowing, my feelings roiling and churning inside me. Looking for witches was supposed to be a distraction but I think it might've just made things worse. I'm so het up I want to scream out loud. At the end of the dark corridor is a window and the day glitters outside. A group of boys come round the corner and I can no longer stand there listening because all their eyes are on me as they approach. I make off before they pass me with their loud voices and their eyes, always querying, seeking out, looking for vulnerabilities, inching towards what stays hidden. I run towards the day, the bright window and clatter downstairs, and stand in the sun, the light breaking around me into shards.

As I'm taking my coat off the peg at the end of the day Mr Jonasson slides up to me. Even though this is what I've been waiting for, imagining all day, somehow I feel disappointed when I see him. I'm exhausted from all the time spent trying to catch a glimpse of him, trying to hear what he's saying, trying to guess what's happening and what he's thinking. It might be just tiredness but he's not as gilded as he appeared last night. Somehow the Swedishness of him looks awkward and plodding in the sharp light from the row of windows above the coat pegs. Yesterday it was strange and fascinating in princely white and blue, his blond lashes like feathers. Today his eyes are shot through with red like he's been drinking and the collar of his blue shirt cuts into his neck and his pockets sag.

Out of one of his saggy pockets he takes a cheap mobile phone. 'Here,' he says.

I turn it over on my palm. 'What's this for?'

'So we can talk over the summer. I might not get another chance before we break up. See, I have one too.' He slips another identical phone out of his pocket to show me, then drops it back. 'So we'll both have an extra phone that we use only to talk to each other. Quick, put it in your bag.' He looks over his shoulder, uncertain and nervy. 'You want that, don't you?'

His saggy pockets and red eyes fade and what I saw last night hoves into view again. His eyes lower and I want to kiss the lids and feel the delicate skin on my lips. I nod so fast I think my head'll drop off. 'Yes, yes, of course.' I let the phone drop into my bag among the books and orange peelings. My stomach turns over at what we are doing.

'Can you keep it hidden?' he asks. 'I won't ring – let's text to make it easier.'

He's clearly never met my mother but I'll have to worry

178

about that later. I'll have to find a hiding place she'd never think of. Even as he's standing there I spin through the possibilities: under the floorboards in the shed; high up in a tree; burial in a glass jar.

'Easily,' I say quickly. I don't want to let onto him how scared I am by all of this. How it sets my heart off ticking frantically with the fear and excitement. I need to be as adult as he's being about it all.

At the sound of approaching footsteps he turns on his heel and strides away. I stay where I am, calming down, for an age. Now he's not actually in front of me, now he's just an *idea*, the summer opens before me like a golden flower. I smile into the coats and close my eyes and rest my face among them and breathe in their fetid smell.

Outside, Orla is waiting for me.

'Hey, she says. 'I thought we could make some plans for the summer before I go. D'you fancy going to see a movie next week?'

'Only Americans say "movies", Orla.' I know I sound harsh but I can't stand it, the way she's trying to cling onto me. Especially now I have this golden flower.

'It's just . . .'

I wave my arms about in what seems like an unnecessary fashion but it serves to make her back away. 'Look, I might ring you sometime,' I say. I want her to go away so I can gloat over what's just happened.

Her face looks so hurt and broken I nearly retract but she walks off before I have a chance. The feeling of having been nasty stays in my chest like there's some poison there. I take the phone out of my bag and hold it in my pocket all the way home. Concentrating on that makes the feeling go away.

# 17

# Grace

I do not think and I will not think. I will simply act.

If I can order everything in this flat it will be as a citadel against the outside world.

I can put everything into place bit by bit and ignore the tightly knotted tangles inside; if I pretend they don't exist they will cease to be eventually. I shouldn't have gone back to school today. That was pure selfishness, wanting to take my miserable-little-bitch hide out of the situation for a few hours, but I hardly stayed and I do feel clearer for it. I know what needs to be done now.

First off, I have to think about who might come here and discover what's happened.

It begins with the carers. I caught them this morning and managed to talk my way out of them coming up. I look up the number in our phone book, the lettered indexes grimy with handling. Certain letters are dirtier than others, the C for Carers for instance.

I feel almost faint with nerves as I wait for the agency to pick up.

'Hey, is that Debbie?' Does my voice sound high and tight? I think it does.

'Speaking.'

Relief blooms in my chest. Debbie is extremely vague. I always double-check that she's written everything down or put it into her computer when I call. I don't trust her to do it otherwise.

'Just to let you know we won't be needing anyone for the next fortnight.'

'No?'

'No. Mum's going away, I mean we're both going away. We're staying with her sister, which is so great because she's brilliant at doing everything. Bed-washing, turning, everything. And they've got a massive house – a bungalow, in fact – so it makes everything brilliantly easy, and there's loads of people there – relatives I mean, all relatives – and they cook lovely meals all the time and everyone helps out.'

My mother doesn't have a sister.

'Sounds good.' Debbie yawns at the other end of the phone.

'OK, bye then.'

'Bye.'

'Debbie?' I panic as I'm about to ring off. 'Have you put that into the computer?'

'I will do.'

I hang onto the telephone receiver like I'm drowning and it's a fucking life-saving device. 'Can you do it now? I mean while I'm on the line. Sorry. Then I know it's done, that's all.'

She sighs. 'Yeah, yeah.' There's the clicking of computer keys and she comes back onto the line. 'Satisfied?'

I lean against the wall and close my eyes. 'Thank you. Thank you so much for that, Debbie.'

The line goes dead with a blip and I take a minute before I put it back onto the cradle. I hold it tight against my cheek and jam the earpiece into the bone.

'Shitting hell.' I wipe my forehead. 'Shit me to hell,' I whisper. 'Mum?' I yell down the hallway. 'Mum?' The walls bounce my voice back to me but there's no reply.

181

She's asleep, I tell myself. That's all it is. Now stop being a shithead and get on with doing what you have to do.

I put on a load of laundry. The pee-stained stuff that is starting to infiltrate the flat with its smell. I hesitate, then add an extra dose of conditioner after the wash has started. I take out the tins and packets from the cupboard and assess what we have, stacking them into groups for meals. Tins of sausages and beans that will go with instant mash. No, this is no good. I know it's no good yet it's hard to know what is. We've been living on this stuff for years. No, no – think, you know what is good. You are not an unintelligent person. You just need to focus and start to think in a different way. I begin a list: oranges; almond oil for massaging feet; nettle tea because Mum talks about having that as a kid and how good it is for you, if you can even buy it; vitamins; vegetables; chicken breast; cotton wool; Radox.

I knock softly on Mum's door and call out. 'Mum, are you awake yet?' There's no reply. She must still be sleeping. I take out the wash and put the sheets into the dryer and start another wash of towels and pillowcases. I make a bucket of soapy water and scour out the bathroom. In the living room the air is dry and fusty so I open the windows. No balcony moment for me yet, I decide. No distractions or one second of misguided pondering. Not even a cigarette; that can be much later when I finally feel satisfied that everything is done that can be done and Mum is comfortably tucked up with a cup of tea. I bash dust out of the sofa cushions; it billows in clouds that set me sneezing. I push the big square pouf thing close to it and fetch spare pillows and blankets to make a makeshift bed, a place where someone can lie and breathe in fresh air and glimpse the sky. I get the Hoover and vacuum every inch of carpet and the tops of the skirting boards that have accumulated a tube of felty dust along the ridge. In the hallway I hoover up all the little curled dried-out grey bodies of woodlice and they fly through the air into the mouth of the Hoover like they're being called up to heaven by a higher force. I can't help smiling at remembering how my friends and me called them 'chuggy pigs' when we were little and loved to dab at them with our fingers for the pleasure of seeing them roll into a ball, tight and hard as a bullet. Wipe the smile off your face, you silly bitch, I tell myself, you can smile later when this is all done. You can sit and grin stupidly to yourself for hours about insects if you like, but in the meantime get on with it. Just get the fuck on with it.

I coil the flex of the Hoover around the drum and stow it back in the cupboard. I give the cushions a final pat and check the room. Just a moment, I think, just one little moment of weakness before it all has to begin. I push through the doors onto the balcony, and down below it seems almost blurred with my vision being out of whack, with the feeling of a tide breaking over my head. I hold onto the rail, then fold helplessly until I'm sitting and the cold of the concrete strikes through my jeans. And before I know it I'm putting my hands together and I'm praying. I can't believe it, I'm actually praying to the big wide blue sky. I'm asking for everything to be all right and for my mum not to have died in that room while I took my miserable-little-bitch hide to school for a few hours, too scared and too pathetic to face things. I vow that I will not waver again and that I will do whatever is necessary to protect what I love. There are no lengths to which I will not go.

*Remember, Grace*, I tell myself. *You are a soldier now and you cannot shirk these things.*

Then I stand and hitch up my jeans and go down the hall to Mum's room and knock on the door once more. I'm terrified every time I do this, thinking she could be lying dead in there. Now the relief of seeing her with her eyes open surges through me.

'Right, Mum?' I ask.

She nods. She's still angry with me for not calling the doctor, but she'll have to get over that. She's realised I took her mobile phone away and she's angry about that too, but she'll come to see it's all for the best.

My own phone rings and I sigh when I see it's Daniel. He came up yesterday after I'd left his flat and I wouldn't let him in, and now he thinks it's something he's done, that I didn't like the sex or I'm angry with him or something. I told him Mum was fine. I couldn't let him in in case she started yelling like some kidnap victim or something.

I have to get rid of him so I answer.

'Grace, I'm coming up to see you whether you like it or not. I know you're there because I saw you coming in earlier on.'

The line goes dead and I run to our front door, sliding I'm going so fast. No way can I let him in. Absolutely no way. I put the chain on the door and stand behind it and wait.

He rings the bell in short sharp bursts, and when I open the door a crack his hand is raised as if he was about to start knocking too.

'Grace, tell me what I've done and why you won't let me in the flat. I'm frantic. Did you really have that bad a time?'

My heart turns over. *No, no, no, no,* I want to cry out. *It was wonderful. I felt like I was dissolving and re-forming, over and over.* But I think of Mum just down the hallway and how, if she hears his voice, everything could be lost.

'It was all right,' I hiss over the chain. 'But you just have to leave me alone for a bit. Stop bothering me.'

And his face looks such a picture of misery I nearly fling off the chain and run into his arms.

He looks down and shoves his hands in his pockets. 'Well, if that's what you really want.'

'It is,' I say and close the door in his face.

# 18

# Orla

I'm taken aback at how utterly glorious it is to see my father.

He breaks the tension in the house, like he's slicing through those awkward plastic parcel bonds that need scissors, then, once cut, the contents that have been so tightly pressed together are finally given the relief of falling apart.

I can't even worry about Mum telling him about my kiss with Eleanor. I'd been dreading the idea, thinking he'd reel away from me, horrified at his own daughter. But when he hugs me and I feel the warm rough texture of the wool of his jumper, I know that'll never happen. He'll sweep Mum's concerns aside like raking glasses and cups from a table with his arm, and say, 'So what?' She'll be soothed, say something like, 'Oh well, you know how I worry when you're away, Martin. I eat myself up with it. It'll probably all blow over.' Then she'll giggle and smooth her hands over her new tight hairdo and give in to the relief of not having to take responsibility for anything any more.

Before dinner they have a couple of sherries, honey-coloured in tiny glasses with a splashy red rose printed on each one. Mum wears a big bouffanty skirt even though she's cooking. She's nervous about it; I can tell by the way she holds the tea towel in front of her, but she doesn't want to spoil the look by wearing an apron. After she's checked the contents of the oven Dad pulls her towards him. They stand like that for a few moments, then start swaying gently to a tune on the radio. I'm itchy with envy, even though the scene is a cheesy fifties movie. That word 'movie' triggers something in me and I remember Phoebe mocking me for saying it. 'Only Americans say "movies", Orla,' she said, as if I was trying to be something other than she allowed me to be and I needed slapping down for it.

'I'm off out,' I announce to their entwined figures, and I'm out of the kitchen before they even have time to separate.

'What about your dinner?' I hear Mum calling, then Dad saying, 'Leave her. Let her go,' as I open the front door.

Outside, I let the tears spill off my face without even trying to hide them. *They've got each other*, I think. *What have I got? Nothing. The girl I'm madly in love with simply sees me as amusing; she actually enjoys cutting into me and making me feel worthless. I have nobody and never will have. My desire at the wishing bowl will stay just that and will never be fulfilled.* The swell of my self-pity feels almost pleasurable in its intensity, in the way I can give myself into it, the way it grows so it touches every part of me inside and there's no room for everything else.

I skirt the town, past Brown's Hotel where people stand outside in the sun, studying the menu, and down towards the Abbey square past the shops selling expensive chocolates and pottery for tourists. In the square, pigeons nod up and down, pecking at the crumbs people aren't supposed to feed them, and a layer of steam hovers over the Roman Baths. People are dressed in summer colours; tourists wander with ice creams, some with more than one camera around their necks, which always puzzles me. Sun splashes across the climbing angels carved up the front of the Abbey, all fleeing upwards away from the hell of the boiling waters so close. I look at the dark mouth of the Abbey and shudder, remembering the time with Phoebe in there. God, she's twisted me so hard I feel I'll never untangle. I need something rapid and violent to happen to unwind me. If there was an earthquake now I swear I'd feel better. I crave a battle or a stabbing. Instead, it's people moving around like they're on wheels, docilely licking ice creams or queuing up to have a cream tea in The Pump Room while a mime artist cavorts in front of them for coins.

'Wotcha.'

I turn. 'Oh hi.' It's Kai from school, his long leather coat pointing outwards like a skirt and nearly reaching the ground. He must be baking in it but somehow his skin remains pale and cool-looking, in contrast to his black eyebrows. I know I don't sound enthusiastic to see him, but then I remember there was some bullying at school targeting him, and with everything that's going on, I feel a blooming of sympathy. Besides, who else have I got to talk to?

I give what I hope is a warm smile and I feel my recent crying jag sting the creases under my eyes. 'Where are you off to?'

He shrugs. 'I thought I'd go and see if the pet cemetery in Parade Gardens is still there. I used to go there all the time as a kid and for some reason I woke up thinking about it.'

He is clearly even more bored than me, but I try to look enthusiastic at the prospect of studying a dog's grave. The alternative would be to slink back home and be a bit player in the cinematic garishness of my parents' romance.

'Oh yeah? A pet cemetery? I don't remember that.'

'Want to come?'

'Why the hell not.'

Unless you have proof that you're a Bath resident, you have to pay at a funny little booth at the entrance of the gardens. Kai has brought his and gallantly digs into his pocket and pays for me. It feels like the nicest thing that anyone's done for me as far back as I can remember.

The Parade Gardens have always struck me as sterile. The grass is cut tight so in the summer you can see the soil beneath turning to dust. The planted-out displays are a sea of acid bright annuals – busy Lizzies or petunias. Strangely, it seems archaic and of a different era in a way that the Roman Baths don't. A buttoned-up time when women in long skirts would take the air, leaning on their husbands' arms, a troupe of white-clad children playing at their feet. Though maybe it was never like that. Perhaps people looked as dishevelled and generally confused about life as they do right now. There's something about this place that makes me long for my little garden with its corners thick with spiders' webs and the fruits of everything ripening and then falling rotten into the over-long grass. The sudden whiffs of sharp greenery or dry mouldering.

We range past picnicking kids pushing sandwiches into their mouths before going back to their football and head to the small stand of trees in the middle where Kai reckons the pet cemetery of his childhood was. All these familiar things; it seems odd to be here with Kai, walking the grey pathways by his side, his coat dipping to the ground on the inclines so that it scrapes on the floor. What am I doing? It's like I've got a plan that I'm not aware of yet.

The scrub of trees looks impenetrable. Across the grass I notice a man with his wife and a clutch of kids watching us suspiciously.

'Let's go round the other side,' I say.

We skirt around, looking for a way in.

'Are you sure this is where you remember?' I ask. The place looks like a knot that's been tied up too tight to unpick.

'I'm positive. There was a little pathway through it when I was a kid and all these cute little cat and doggy graves – Pal and Fido and shit like that. My sister used to pinch the flowers and lay them on the stones and work herself up into tears thinking of them. Look, that branch will bend back.'

His hand on the whip-like branch is surprisingly strong. He levers it back and an entrance into the knot opens up so quickly it feels like a fairy-tale moment, an 'open sesame' to a different world. I duck under his arm and he follows me, the branch whipping us tight shut inside behind him.

'This is quite creepy, being in here and no one can see us.' I feel hectic and giggly with the notion, the smell of dusty dead soil working into my eyes and up my nose. I can hear all the sounds of the park outside. The thwack of balls being kicked, parents calling for their kids, the buzz of cars from the road beyond. The bark is peeling off the slim trunks of the trees and I nervously begin stripping it off and crumbling the bits between my fingers.

'What now?' I ask.

'I'm going to look for the graves. They might still be here as it's all grown over like this. When things get forgotten about, people leave them alone.'

He drops down on his haunches and begins sweeping aside dead leaves with his hands.

'Fuck me,' he crows. 'They're still here. Look – I've found one.'

I lean over the tablet of stone he's uncovered. 'What does it say?'

'"Our mate Chum."'

'Really?' I feel stupidly excited at the discovery. 'When did he die?'

'I can't see. That bit's stuck in the ground. I don't want to start digging it out in case Chum decides to bite me. I'm guessing a ghost dog is more vicious than a live one.' He crawls underneath the tangle of branches. 'I'm going to look for more.'

I hesitate for a moment and then drop to the ground and crawl after him. I feel like a kid again, like we're playing a brilliant game that'll go on and on until we're exhausted.

'This one's like those bed-style graves,' he calls over his shoulder. 'Nooksie . . . Dooksie – something like that. I can't quite see, it's in a dark patch.'

His black leather coat looks like a giant insect case as he crawls in front of me. In the middle of the trees a space opens and he kneels up and looks back. His face is splashed with shadows but I can see the childlike glow in his eyes. The wide grin. I feel the same. The slights and minor and major humiliations and hurts of daily life seem a million miles away in this enchanted garden, which feels like a great dry nest that's just for us, keeping us safe and apart from the world.

He sighs, then sits and then lies back and looks up into the dappled light above. Everything is silent for a long moment, until he breaks it. 'I love it here.'

It's so simple what he says, so heartfelt, my heart tips towards him. I remember his closed-up face at school. His boots, his long hair and black clothes, all like plates of an armour he has to construct every morning. Each day the configuration of T-shirts or jacket might differ but it's all formed for the same purpose and has to be constantly remade and maintained. I crawl next to him and put my arms around him and pull him towards me. He doesn't resist, nor does he move towards me. When I open my eyes there's a tear trickling down the side of his nose.

'Sad really, isn't it? This is the first time I've been happy in about a year. Finding some crappy stuff I remember from being a kid. Dead animals. Pathetic.'

'Sssh, it's OK,' I whisper and I pull him closer, brushing the black hair away from the whorl of his ear so I can whisper into it. 'I love it too. I'm so glad you've shown me. Thank you – it's magical like a storybook. It's wonderful.' *Phoebe would love this place*, I think, before resolving never to show it to her.

Kai smells of citrus shower gel and creamy shaving foam, and the shock of him being so near that I can catch his secret smells floods through me. Up close I can see the pinpoints of hair on his chin where he's shaved them off this morning. Just the fact of his nearness moves me to an almost unbearable pitch. I kiss the side of his face, his eyelids; his brows are soft under my lips. I crave the closeness so much it's hard to stop. He lies there letting me until I finally come to a halt. I open my eyes slowly and the greenish light has a quality to it that's almost church-like. Cool and strangely coloured. The smell's like that too, a damp mustiness that penetrates right to the back of the throat. It makes me feel almost stoned with its sense of thickened air, every stalk and leaf delineated. I prop myself on my elbows and everything gradually returns to its usual state. My eyes begin to be able to pick out what's in the dense dark spots, branches tangling overhead. I start laughing, an hysterical choking sort of laugh.

'What? What is it?'

I can barely talk because of it so I just nod to past his head and he turns and sees the inscription and the tiny gravestone.

'"Dec.30.1908,"' he reads solemnly. '"Dear Little Fritz."'

I roll over towards him, warm from the kisses. Something is coalescing in me. The wish at the wishing bowl and me yelling at Mum that I'd have a bloody baby if I wanted to, see if I couldn't. That was the germ of it all, the wishing bowl day, that's when it all started. It made me think about things that had been unsaid until that point. I'm reckless from the aridity of the day and of my life. If nothing counters it soon I'm going to die. *To have somebody who is mine and mine alone.* I can have a baby. Who's to say I can't? I won't have anyone telling me I can't. I can have Kai's baby, and the want and need opens up in a raging ragged welter of pent-up feeling.

# 19

# Phoebe

*Hahahahahahaha.*

The Beloved has gone.

Travelling, apparently, with a clutch of her friends from university. They intend to eschew the hedonistic delights of resorts – vulgar – and instead will be heading to the lesser travelled, and therefore better, parts of Italy, then Croatia, where they will absorb local cultures like a cluster of voracious amoebas as they move from town to town. According to The Beloved, these plans were half-hatched already when she came home from York and she simply neglected to confide them to anyone because she didn't want to jinx the whole adventure by talking it out of existence. Both The Beloved and I know that to be untrue. We may be on opposite sides of the fence but we both know the value of needing to make a quick getaway. We've had a long and detailed training in it.

*She* is bereft. Her eyes have been moist for nearly two whole days now. Her mouth downturned. Sometimes, she looks so sad the hardness in my stomach dissolves and I long to make her better. I feel about eight years old again, looking up into her face and thinking what I can do to make her smile, or to gain a glorious flicker of attention. Then it passes.

At first I felt relief that term had ended. Groups of girls or boys in packs unnerve me. I had plenty to look forward to.

While *she* was distracted by The Beloved I would lounge in my pyjamas. I would take a fat book off to my room – like a cat dragging a dead bird – and feast on it until my eyes were blurry and the light was beginning to fade. I even felt I might become interested in real food once more and make myself something spare and light, delicious in its coolness and simplicity. While the house was empty, Dad at work and the others on some excursion, I would run baths and scent them with the gorgeous bath fragrance that Bertha gave me, Quelques Fleurs, for doing well in exams. She handed the parcel over to me with the solemnity of a religious cere-mony, informing me at the same time that the fragrance was made up of over three hundred different floral essences. I eke it out and leave the cask in plain sight, standing guard over my diary. Every day I come home and expect it to have vanished. The mobile phone I had from Mr Jonasson is yet to ping, and although still pleasurable to think of and have because it was something meant just for me, the thought of it was fading in comparison to all these solitary delights. I really started to feel I liked the idea of an affair more than the reality. Healing, I felt, was just around the corner.

All these fantasies were swept away by The Beloved going. Now, once again I am picked over, watched and meddled with. The mobile phone has again become my one interest and focus. Did I really want him so badly? I do now. I keep the phone jammed up behind the ivy that grabs onto the back wall in the back garden. When I was younger I used to think the ivy looked like a determined child clambering over the wall. I used to have all sorts of ideas like that, but no more. I don't know why. It's like there's no room for whims and fanciful imaginings such as those while my mind is taken up by so much bigger and more dangerous things.

It's a risky mission but four or five times a day I go and check the phone, occasionally bringing it to the house to feed it with electricity. So far the screen has remained resolutely blank. It only occurred to me later on the day he gave it to me that he had my number but I don't know his.

So that's all that's left to me, the *hahahahaha* delight in someone else's displeasure and an empty phone. Both our summer dreams have rattled down into a few disappointing coins at the bottom of the tin. We weave around each other, baring teeth. Her part-time job seems more unpredictable than ever so I never know when she's going to pop up. It means I am constantly on my guard and can't get on with anything.

She brushes her short hair as she paces the kitchen so little strands drop all around her onto the floor and the kitchen counters. The brush makes a scraping sound on her wiry grey hair. There's something on her mind. I sip my tea fast even though it's hot and scalding. Finally she comes to a stop in front of me.

'What's so funny?'

'What d'you mean?'

'Your diary was open when I went into your room to dust this morning.'

Lie. Lie. Lie. Lie.

The hairs stand up on the back of my neck. My hands are shaking on my mug. I know I closed it. I put the hair across the page perfectly. Today's entry read simply: 'Hahahahaha.'

I also know there is no point contradicting her. I breathe slowly in and out. What's she up to, bringing down our fourth wall?

'Something seems to have tickled you pink.'

'Not really.'

'Something must've.'

She's angry, I realise in a rush. We are so in tune she knows what I was laughing at. Laughing at her and her misery. She's so furious now she can't hold back from saying anything.

'Maybe I was thinking of a joke. I can't remember now.'

Her eyes slit towards me.

While she's on the computer in the study next to the kitchen I slip outside. I'm beginning to lose faith in the phone and its blank screen but I'm so rattled it's sent me scurrying for it. I put my hand up beneath the ivy and feel about, then once I've grasped it I hide behind the plants to look. There's a little envelope in the window. I squeeze myself flat against the wall and open it.

*Can't stop thinking about you*, the text reads. He signs it off with his first name, Lucas, and the intimacy of that plunges me into a warm bath of pleasure. I lean against the wall, embraced by ivy, and allow myself ten glorious minutes wallowing in *Lucas*.

With shaking fingers I text back, *Me neither x*.

I cage the phone again in the tangle of ivy branches, but as I'm walking away I hear the text button ping. I hadn't thought to turn that off. That was dangerous. I switch off the volume, then look again.

*Meet me tonight?* it says.

I send mine winging back. *Of course. I know a place where no one goes. I'll show it to you. I'll wait at the bottom of your street at 7?*

I don't know how I'll get away but I'll have to think of

something. I look up at the back of the house. The long narrow sash windows remind me of eyes. Any minute I expect one to lower in a sudden blink. I shudder.

The garden looks dry and dusty today. I struggle to remember spending time in it when I was little. Were there ball games, den building, impromptu picnics? The refreshing slap of water on the legs from a hosepipe on a hot day? I can't remember anything like that. Perhaps I've just forgotten about them. My mind is so unreliable sometimes. I don't trust it. No, it's always been a desolate space out here, I'm sure – little used. The presence of swings or paddling pools in other people's gardens always surprised me, their blown-up, plastic multicoloured shapes incongruous against the grass.

I squint up at the windows again and wonder how long I can wait around for his reply before suspicions are raised. It's never been a place I've spent time in so it will look odd. I wonder about keeping the phone in my room and quickly discount the idea. I check the phone again and it's blank. I realise, like me, he must have to find a secret time and space to text. I like the idea. It makes me feel a lovely private bond with him that's delicious. After ten minutes' waiting I'm nearly giving up and thinking I'll have to get back inside when the reply comes in the form of a single X.

Back inside she's still on the computer and I try not to let any excitement show on my face, though I'm paranoid my cheeks are flushed. I worry that she's looked out into the back garden and seen me but she shows no signs of it. Instead she sniffs. 'We have the dentist today,' she says.

'Have we?'

'Yes. I told you.'

She didn't but I'm used to this. I no longer query it. These days I simply agree.

'What time is the appointment?'

'Two o'clock. What's the matter? You look like your cat's just gone missing. Have you got anything better to do?'

It's OK because I'll be back in time to meet Lucas, but the dentist means a ride in the car with her, not something I look forward to. No, that's an understatement. Something I dread.

'No, I haven't got anything better to do.'

She nods. 'You need to be ready in an hour.'

The air in the car is fraught with meaning. The way her bracelets jangle sets me on edge every time she changes gear. The stuff she used to clean the leather interior inflames my throat into a spasm, a sickness. We take the Bristol road and Bath thins out and disappears. Why we have to travel so far to the dentist I don't know. Yes, I do. Everything like that – clothes, husbands, dentists, electricians, watch repairers – have to be some sort of 'find', a gem to be gloated over. I sink down into the seat, wanting to disappear.

'Sit up straight.'

'OK.'

We drive further, green and brown countryside blurring through the window. I study her out of the corner of my eye and a part of my heart caves in. The grooves below her eyes look a little more crinkled than yesterday. Unhappiness has aged her overnight. Suddenly, I'm hot with the idea of making her happy. It floods me. It's a regressive position, I know that, the child in me, but when it arises I never seem able to resist arcing upwards and trying to grab onto the bait.

'Mum?'

'Mmmm?' Her rings click against the wheel as she steers.

'Shall we do something this summer?'

'Like what?'

'Well, what were you planning to do with Verity?'

She's silent for a very long time. The silence makes the car feel as if all the air has been sucked out of it. I crack the window down a tiny bit.

'I hadn't made any plans with Verity,' she hisses. 'We didn't have time before she went. Why, what is it *you* want to do?'

'Nothing, I just thought—'

'You're glad she's gone. You should have tried harder with her. You've driven her away.'

'No, no. I do try sometimes.' I can feel silly baby tears welling up behind my eyes and threatening to spill. 'I do try but she doesn't seem to want me to.' There's a squeak in my voice because my throat has closed up so much.

'Maybe', her hands have crossed each other to steer, 'that's because she doesn't find you particularly *fascinating*.'

A tide of misery bows my head down and I look at my fingers plaiting with each other. I pick hard at a tiny spot on my wrist bone, pinching as hard as possible between fingernails. I try to offset it by thinking about meeting Lucas tonight but somehow that all seems difficult and remote now.

'For God's sake, buck up,' she says. 'I can't stand it when you sink down like that, like you want to wallow in a pit of despair. It's so depressing.' We slow to a stop at a junction and she sighs deeply, which tells me she has come completely to the end of her tether with me. 'I can't see properly this side with those low branches blocking the view,' she says. 'Tell me if we're clear to go.'

I crane my neck and see the four-by-four barrelling towards us.

'Yes,' I say. 'Drive.'

The trees all clap their leaves together like they're an audience applauding and I feel the roots beneath us and how they weave into each other and make a basket to hold us, and the insects whizz in and out of the bark, flashing their iridescent colours, and the bacteria in the soil moves it about. And I can see the movement, in fast frame – on some kind of loop of a film that's spooling through me – and the branches thrash into my face. Leaves stuff in my open mouth and poke into my eyes. I stumble forward blindly. And I see my hands and they are shiny with blood and there's a knife in one of them and it's smeared red nearly to the hilt. And I look to the others, questioning, trying to understand what I'm doing there, what's happening.

# Act III

# THE CUT

# 20

# Grace

How does evil come into our lives? Do we invite it in? Does it sit in our cells, waiting for some trigger?

It did with Mum. It was in her DNA, all those years waiting to hatch. It's inevitable, they say, it was always going to happen. There's nothing that made it happen and there's nothing you could've done. I know it's a disease and it has no will and no feelings, but I can't help think of it as an evil that's stolen in. Or, more, that every single cell in our bodies is a tiny trap ready to be sprung.

Wrong-headed. Focus on the here and now. What's to be done? What's to be done? A list. That's what's to be done. I live for lists these days. This one is for the first portion of the day:

*6 a.m. Get up, bitch.*
*Scrub kitchen including fridge. Anything even slightly old must be thrown away immediately.*
*Put a wash on. Whites this time.*
*Prepare breakfast. Yogurt and lightly stewed apples. A dash of brown sugar for a sweet tooth.*
*Begin.*

Currently, I'm on the last item. I peel an apple, trying to keep the peel in one piece like we used to do at Halloween; when it's thrown over your shoulder it will form the first letter of your future husband's name. I don't throw the peel over my shoulder now, though. I can't look that far ahead into the future, and besides, I don't have the time and if the peel formed a D I think I'd lose it. The idea of ever having a husband is an impossible dream. I chop the apple finely, my silver ring flashing alongside the knife. I set the pan on the hob with a cupful of water and soon the little kitchen is full of apple smells. It takes me back to something. To the ground and what is real and what is not. It helps.

The stewed apple and yogurt has come from a book I bought from a discount bookshop, *Eating for Health*. At night I study nutritional groups and how the body transitions food. I read about theories that perhaps you should eat according to your blood type. I read about theories on fats and grains until the words swim in front of my eyes and I'm woken by the book falling onto the floor. I don't know how much of all this is true, yet I resolve to discover Mum's blood type when I can. One thing the book is very firm on is to only eat things that are organically produced. This is very expensive; I've looked, so I'm replacing things gradually.

When the apple is cooked to a pulp I let it cool before ladling it into a tiny glass bowl, a fancy one meant for holding dinky cocktail snacks like nuts. I found it in a cupboard when I was clearing out, flotsam left over from when Mum and Dad were together. All the things from that era seem to have a slightly jaunty aspect. It makes me believe they had fun before it all turned sour. I put the kettle on to boil, then top the apple with a spoon of yogurt and dash a little extra sugar over it today. When the kettle boils I pour the water over fresh tea leaves and let it brew for exactly three minutes, timed on the kitchen timer in the shape of a cockerel. It makes a crowing noise when it's ready and it's also my cue to awake properly. With a spoon and a napkin I take it all on a tray down the hall. Mum is a hunched shape in the bed and I set down the tray on the floor and gently put my hand on her shoulder; the bony flimsiness of it goes through me.

'Mum,' I whisper. 'Time to wake up.'

Does she stir a little? I think so. 'Come on, love,' I say. 'Come on now.'

Slowly her eyelids unfurl from their tight scrunched buds. She licks her lips.

'Grace, my chicken,' she says shakily.

'It's OK.' I dive down the bottom of the bed and flip the covers up. I take a pale bony foot and cradle the heel in the palm of my hand.

'I'll give you a massage and then you can have breakfast. The tea'll be cool enough to drink by then.'

Her face looks a little pinker today; well, the top of her cheeks anyway – there's a patch of pink right by the cheek-bone that stands out against the fresh white pillow.

This week – I find it hard to gauge time. Each day seems to be running on something, clockwork perhaps. It whistles and chugs past me round and round like a toy train. The sun rises, the cows move across the green hill opposite, right to left. As the sun comes up it lights up the city roof by roof. Clouds form, gather, disperse or grow heavy enough to break open in shower storms that cleanse the balcony of my cigarette ash. Then the day darkens. The sun plummets to the earth and the sunlit roofs go off one by one, and street lights wink on and take their place.

I shop for groceries, weighing vegetables in my hand, testing them for freshness. I seek out organic milk because

I once heard that is also extra nutritious; has more fats or calcium or something – I can't remember. Maybe I read it in that book. I mix sweet-smelling oils into the bottle of almond base oil and slick it across my hands to massage her feet, her back, her temples. I do not miss a thing. I am onto every tiny detail because that is the only way to survive, the only way to banish the filth and wreck of this world. If I take my attention away for a millisecond it will fall away into destruction and those evil traps will spring all at once.

Mum sips the tea that I hold up for her awkwardly.

When she's finished, her head falls back onto the pillow and she opens her eyes wide. 'I love you so much, Grace,' she says.

'I love you too,' I whisper, even though she's fallen right back to sleep, then the blood practically freezes in my veins because the buzzer to our flat rings in the hallway. I pad out of her room and stand by it, agitated. I'll ignore it and wait until they go away, but still I'm on high alert. It rings three times more before falling silent. I pace and potter for a while, trying to repair myself from the disturbance in the atmosphere that takes time to heal over itself. I scrape out the pan of scrambled egg left over from yesterday. I curse myself for leaving it forgotten and scrub it with a metal scourer until it's shinily new again. I'm just admiring the gleam of it when the air seems to break in half and I have to put my hand up to punch at my racing heart because some-one is battering at the front door.

For a minute, I can't move. Then, as silently as possible, I lower the saucepan onto the work surface, reach down, take off my red plastic flip flops and tiptoe to the door. When I put my eye to the spyhole I let out a gasp so loud I'm sure it can be heard on the other side. It's Miss Kinsella for her appointment. The one I've only remembered now. My prediction was right. She's one that will never go away, that will talk herself in and not take no for an answer. My whole being is on alert. I'm torn. If I open the door she'll have to come in and it's not mess or dirt around the taps I have to worry about. Those things seem completely inconsequential now. But if I don't answer she'll go away and come back even more curious, perhaps with others . . .

My hand reaches up and twists the lock and there we are staring at each other.

I bring my finger to my lips. 'Ssssh, Mum's asleep,' I whisper. 'We have to be very, very quiet.'

She hitches her handbag up her shoulder. 'OK,' she whispers back, and leans over to take off her wooden clogs, then comes in and lines them neatly by the front door in the hallway. *You'll know*, I tell myself, *when those clogs are gone whether you are safe or not.*

We pad into the living room and I sit her down and offer to make her tea; when I go out of the room I pull the door behind me. When I make the tea I splash some cold water in it so she doesn't have to let it cool for an age before she drinks it.

She takes the cup, sips, and all the while every cell in my body is lit up, my ears straining for any tiny sound.

'So, Grace, tell me how you're doing.'

I put my finger to my lips again, and then worry I'm starting to look a bit odd so I sit next to her.

'Very good,' I whisper. 'I'm very, very good at the moment.'

'Any specific concerns or worries, and of course I want to hear *all* about how it went with the group.'

'The group went very well. Cherry seems very nice. Everyone does.'

'That's great, Grace.' She looks genuinely happy. 'It's fantastic that you've got the opportunity to do a bit of mixing and try something new.'

I realise then, as she chats in a whisper, it's not simply her professionalism that's showing through. She actually genuinely likes me and, despite myself and everything that's happened, it feels quite nice. Then I come to with a jerk. *What are you thinking of, you silly bitch?* I tell myself, as I watch her pink-lipsticked mouth move. *Stop wallowing in feelings about being liked by somebody who is* paid *to like you.*

'Anything you'd like to talk about?' she asks, so as a diversion I begin telling her about *Eating for Health* and how interesting it is.

*Christ,* I think. *How the hell am I going to get through this? How on earth?* But somehow I do and she's putting those clogs back on, her movements slow and exaggerated like people are when they're demonstrating they're being quiet, and I'm leaning on the door as I hear her footsteps leading away outside, and I'm putting my hands over my head as if to soothe myself, too overwhelmed and too exhausted even to cry.

# 21

# Phoebe

There is something about hospitals that makes them like nothing else. They are hives, cut off from the world with everything humming inside.

I keep my eyes on the feet that pass as I sit on the hard plastic chair in the corridor. It's easier like that. If I raise my eyes it all becomes hallucinatory. The feet keep my interest in a safe way. I can pick out the nurses' feet because they are in white clogs or plasticky lace-ups. Slippers shuffle past accompanied by a rubber-tipped walking stick. The odd pair of high heels clip along on an important journey.

'Phoebe?'

With great difficulty I raise my eyes. Everything above shoe level seems misty like I'm looking through a veil. Dad swims before me.

'Dad.' My hands are balled into fists. I feel sick. He perches on the chair next to me.

'Phoebe, are you OK?'

I nod.

'I've just spoken to the doctor. Not a scratch on you. It's a miracle.' He squeezes my hand. I long for him to put his arms around me but he doesn't and I don't ask.

'You look so white.'

I nod. 'I feel sick. I really hope I'm not going to be sick.'

He looks helpless, like there's nothing to be done.

'Perhaps we'd better move.'

'OK.'

He pulls me to standing. 'Come on, let's go and see Mum.' He tugs on my hand to go and I lean back, resisting.

'What?'

'I said, let's go and see Mum.'

I start heaving in gasps of air. I feel light-headed. Any moment I'm going to fall on that pink and green floor and crack my skull wide open.

'No, no, no. I can't.'

'Why not? Come on . . .'

'See her body?'

'What?'

I put my hands to my head and clutch my hair. 'See her body in the morgue?'

Dad turns and faces me. His eyes are bright and intelligent. His grey hair is clipped neatly. 'No, silly. She's not dead. Did you think she was dead? What made you think that?'

I put my fingers in my mouth and bite on them. What do I remember? Opening the car door and nearly falling out. Walking around in circles on a country road, feeling dazed. Seeing her head through the windscreen. It's at a strange angle. There is blood on the glass inside. I'm dizzy and afraid. I look at the grass verge, finding a place to be sick should I need to. There's a roaring in my ears.

Dad is gently shaking my shoulders. 'Phoebe, come back to me. Come back to me, love. Everything's fine. She's got a nasty bump on her forehead and she's in a neck brace and she's going to have to stay in for a bit, but she was really, really lucky – you both were. God knows what made her drive out into the road like that. Next time I'm going to insist on a proper modern car with airbags, not a retro deathtrap.'

'The other car.' It comes out in a wail.

'Sssh. Sssssh.' He's still got his hands on my shoulders and he's squeezing there. 'Just a dint on their car. Those four-by-fours are so high up it's possible he didn't even see our car at first. It's fine, it's all fine.' He smiles at me.

I nod and take my fingers out of my mouth.

'So let's go and see Mum – it's just upstairs. You'll feel better when you see her. She's asking for you.'

I bunch my hands. I'm stiff as a tree. I just bet she's been asking for me.

I trail after his straight back. Sounds of footsteps and trolleys being pushed and medics' conversations filter through the mottled light of the hospital and seem to propel me forward. My feet drag. The walk takes an age. Along the corridor. Into a huge lift where we have to wait to let in a nurse pushing a man in a wheelchair; he's wearing a surgical gown and his leg is bandaged up. It's not fair. They should have separate lifts for the patients. Does he know that all eyes on him are glad that it's not them in that wheelchair, like he is something completely separate and has somehow put himself beyond the pale by being there? I think he does because he keeps his own eyes averted. The lift doors slip open and we're the last out because we were squashed right against the back. Two floors up, the light is brighter and I tumble out, blinking in the sharpness of it pouring through the windows.

'Come on, this way.'

I have no choice but to limp after Dad. Why am I limping? I don't even know. My knee feels bashed. I must've hurt it in the accident.

He's being gobbled up by the light as he strides far ahead and I have to squint and use my good leg to follow as best I can.

The thick feeling of dread intensifies with every step. Will she know? What will she know? As we enter the ward and pass the nurses' station crammed with cards and flowers and charts, I'm wishing just one thing. That I'd managed to do away with the both of us and none of this was happening.

In the ward I can see *her* straight away. I know the shape of her, even though now she is mummified by blankets. The light is worse again in here. It burns out the edges of everything. I hobble after Dad to the side of her bed and he sits on the plastic chair and reaches out his hand for her, patting on top of the blankets to find hers. She's as stiff and straight as a stuffed snake. As I get closer I can see that she can't move her head because it's clamped in some sort of neck brace. There's a dressing taped to her forehead.

I lean over and stuff my fingers in my mouth.

'Phoebe!' Dad sounds outraged but I can't help it. It's the nerves. It's the sight of her lying there with her chin resting on the front of the brace, her grey wiry hair standing up on end. I don't want to laugh but it bubbles out of me and my midriff aches with the pain of trying to stop it.

'For God's sake.' Dad turns away disgusted, and I nearly choke on my fingers.

Then a cold dread descends and I stop in a second. I take my fingers out of my mouth, dripping drool onto my T-shirt because I see her eyes switching from side to side. And I can see by the way the furious light in them sparks as they flick about, yet without ever leaving my face, that she knows exactly what happened and she remembers every little bit of what I did.

At home again it's so quiet. With Dad gone – he left almost straight away for some charity do or other – *her* in hospital and The Beloved far away on her travels, I am finally, miraculously, alone. It's been such a long day, the beginning of it seems far off and misty like it was a year ago rather than a few hours. I open the living room window and the cool air floats in. I light a candle and put it on the sill as if to lure the dark inside. The house creaks to me, friendly. The time I was supposed to meet Lucas was an age ago. I'm so tired I'm not sure I can be bothered even to go and look at the phone outside, although it does make me feel a little sad at the thought of him waiting all alone at the end of his street and me not turning up.

Tension runs out of me. *She* seems so very far away. I prod around in my fear, testing it like I do to see if it will ignite, but something's happened; I can't provoke it now even if I try. It's the exhaustion, but something else too. I think about it: this will be the first night spent in this house without *her*. Can that be true? I feel it is, I feel it in my calmness, a calmness that still holds an excitement at its core like a glittering jewel. The colours of the living room, the mustard velvet of the sofa, the bird's-egg green of the walls (that's one thing I can say about *her, she* does know how to put a room together) have a sweet sharpness to them that practically makes my throat close up in awe of their beauty.

What will happen when she comes home? How will I explain myself? What revenge will she exact? I go and help myself to the brandy bottle on the sideboard. I pour a glass and sit cross-legged on the sofa, taking tiny sips of the rich umber liquid. Amazingly, I find I don't even care what she will try to do. I will pass it off as a mistake. A glitch in perception. I'm so warm and lazy. I'm cool and light-headed too. I'm all of those things. Bats begin flitting around outside the window. I imagine them as tiny little witches. They swoop in celebration with me. Harpies, necromancers, shape-shifters – their brooms tucked up tight to their openings. I have such warm thoughts towards the witches. They show me the way forward and how I can be; when I'm young, old, if I am in pain. They show me that to be a scuttling beetle is not the only way to be. They plant their calloused bare feet upon the bare earth and walk through the world not being ashamed or afraid of anything. They don't even care that people find them ugly. In fact, they probably like it.

I think again about looking at the phone outside, tucked behind the ivy, but I find I don't care about that either. I remember the saggy pockets and his bloodshot eyes. He's probably in bed now anyway, exhausted from being awoken at the crack of dawn by children. Perhaps his wife will be jumping up and down on him like some tin toy soldier on strings.

Soon, I will wander downstairs and I will actually prepare myself something to eat. I'll make a beautiful arrangement on the plate. A cube of salty cheese, bright green leaves shiny with dressing, Parma ham with its delicate folds. I will sit here eating, happily sipping brandy and welcoming in the beautiful soft lonely night and watching the flitting shapes, because I realise the predictions at the wishing bowl were real and I am now truly Queen of the House.

# 22

# Grace

I wake up on the sofa and I don't know how long I've been there. There's a duster in my hand. I must've gripped onto it all the way through my sleep.

'Mum?' I call out. My voice is croaky and exhausted.

I drag myself up and walk towards her room. At the door I realise the duster is still in my hand and I let it drop to the floor before pushing the door open. What I see makes me stopper my mouth with both hands so I don't scream.

My mother, who has at times barely been able to stand let alone walk, who has been so weak in the last couple of days she has had trouble speaking and eating, who not so long ago I worried wasn't going to make it through the night, has got herself right to the window where she's standing in her cheap white lacy nightie and she's grinning her head off at me. For a moment I wonder if this is a strange dream. I pinch myself hard on the wrist and I realise it's no dream. The pinch seems to wake up my vocal cords.

'Mum, what the fuck are you doing? How did you get there?' I manage to stutter.

She grins even wider at me and holds onto the window frame for support. 'Don't swear. Grace, I had the most lovely sleep. Hours and hours and hours. And I woke up, I can't tell you, feeling so much better.' Her smile wavers a little and she sways. 'And I thought, I'll try. What's the harm in trying?'

Now I smile too. I can't help it. She looks so delighted with herself, like a little girl who's discovered she's got a special talent like being able to fly or to make herself invisible.

'OK, Mum. That's amazing, but maybe we should get you back into bed now and then we can talk about it.'

She nods. 'Yes, it may be best. Give me your arm, will you?'

Together we walk her over to the bed and I fuss around remaking it while she stands next to me still swaying. When's she's safely tucked in and I feel like I can breathe again, I pull up a chair and we both sit grinning at each other like idiots.

'Maybe it's all the massages and fresh vegetables,' she says, laughing and patting the cover with her palms.

'Really? Could it be that?'

'I don't know. I don't think so but I really don't know. But I feel better than I've done for ages after that fall – I felt like I was going to die it was that bad.'

'Mum, don't do that again without me, will you.' I reach out and put my hand on her lacy nylon sleeve. 'You nearly gave me a heart attack just then.'

'Now, Grace, don't spoil it by worrying.'

'No, I'm not. Really I'm not, but just make sure I'm here. I can be on the other side of the room perhaps, but it's better to be safe than sorry.'

'They're going to be so pleased with me in the hospital next week.' She's grinning again.

I start because I didn't know she'd remembered that. She cottons on to a lot more than I give her credit for. I had, in fact, planned to phone up in the morning and repeat the same lie I told the caring agency – that we were away having a marvellous time being looked after by a mythical sister, and sorry I'd simply forgotten to cancel the routine appointment.

'Right, yes.' I'm actually intrigued now to see what they make of this – excited even – and I want to tell her, to let her know I think this is incredible too, but her eyelids have closed again and she is gently snoring into her pillow, worn out by the effort and the exhilaration.

# 23

# Orla

The joy I feel when I open my front door and Phoebe is there is the joy of feeling that this is a Saturday morning as Saturday mornings should really, truly be. The drift of coffee aroma in the house. The sound of the shower running upstairs. Dad shuffling through a newspaper at the kitchen table. But here too, within the weave of that safety net, my own burgeoning beautiful life. My Phoebe standing in the brightness of the open door, saying, 'Want to do something today?' And *Saturday* opening up into glorious branching possibilities.

'Of course I do.' Even my eagerness feels fine. Warm and companionable instead of grabbing or needy.

Kai and our weird trysts turn to ash in an instant, aged on fast forward until they are curled grey dusty tableaux that can stay that way forever like a scene from Pompeii. Despite the skin to skin and the slick of saliva, the memory of them is a visit to the dead zone. What the hell was I thinking? Now I'm back with the living. My mind pushes away the gnawing worry.

I'm still in my pyjamas so I dart up to change, leaving Phoebe, hands in pockets, standing by the kettle and talking to Dad. She's always good with other people's parents. It's odd. They think she's polite and interested with her questions but I know the avaricious curiosity in her eye. She's probing their lives, like she's an alien and she must interrogate any normality she finds so she can learn from it. I don't blame her. I've only been to hers a couple of times but the chill is enough to send icicles up your back. I couldn't wait to get out and back to the noise and life of here. My brothers scuffling. Mum with her pink flushed cheeks and her shiny lipstick put on all wonky. I feel a flush of affection for it now in comparison.

Today outside, it's the sweetest day. In the front garden the wild rose climbs up the wall and is alive with bees. The sun toasts the wall so there's a smell like nothing else, the smell of baked stone. We saunter out together. Two girls, with a bit of money in our purses. Our lace-up canvas shoes patterning the dust on the pavement. I try not to think that Phoebe's money has most likely come from my own mother's purse; my flush of affection for my family has provoked guilt about that, but I know already it won't stop me doing it again. The need to give Phoebe what she wants is too strong, and I shove the feeling aside and concentrate on the day that is hazy above us. When I'm with her, the world can take on the exquisite quality of a Japanese print, delicate as cherry blossom, the joy of the fleeting moment.

Once we've reached town we're unsure what to do. It's always the same, like we've reached our objective. The day is long, as unknown and ready to be filled as our lives that hollow out before us. We perch next to some railings.

'Shall we go for a coffee?'

We stand up but don't move.

'What's the matter?' I ask.

'I don't know.' She's wired and twitchy now. 'It's this place. It's getting to me.'

She begins cutting through the narrow arcaded street, the

shop windows glinting on either side. The huge ancient paving stones cool in the shade.

I hurry after her.

'Getting to you in what way? How?'

'I don't know.' We're out by the Roman Baths now. Pockets of steam drift by. 'Do you remember my swim there?'

'That was a crazy thing to do. Nutter.' I manage to make it sound affectionate. We walk for a bit in silence.

'Do you want to know why I really took off just then?' she asks.

'Go on then.'

'I saw them, Lucas and his wife with a pushchair. I saw them inside one of the shops. She was trying on an ugly pair of sandals.'

'Lucas?'

'Mr Jonasson.'

Instantly, my jaw clenches so I have to push the words from behind my teeth. 'Oh, that's what you call him now? You haven't seen him again, have you?' It feels like a fruit stone stuck in my throat. Somehow we've found ourselves down a side alley and she's leaning up against the ancient stone wall. It's dark in here. I feel like pressing into her, squashing her against the wall.

'Lucas wanted to . . .', she pauses and bites her lip '. . . meet me.'

'What?' I'm trying to keep my voice down. 'You can't be serious, you really fucking can't. You're not going?'

She blinks at me. 'No, I don't expect I will. My mother's in hospital.'

'What?' It's all coming too thick and fast for me. I don't know what to believe and what not to believe.

224

'She had an accident. A car accident. I made it happen. It was all my fault.'

'Phoebs. I'm sure it wasn't. That's what you said about that awful murder and it's nonsense. I'm sure—'

'No. It was. Things are leaking out.'

'Is she going to be all right?'

'Yes. I think so but not for a week or two. It means I've practically got the whole house now, like Rapunzel. It's wonderful.' Her face lights up.

I don't answer. I guess my response must be in my face, though.

'No, don't tell me off. She's fine. It's all going to be fine. It's just I'm enjoying being by myself for a while. That's all.'

'Phoebe, don't meet Mr Jonasson.' I don't trust her at all.

'I won't.' She shrugs and balls her fists into her coat pocket and looks over to the baths. 'D'you remember what we talked about before, about this place actually being hell?'

'Yes.' I don't tell her how it's infected my mind and made me see everything differently – the angels frantically scurrying away from it. How people must've felt when they first found that hot spring bubbling from the ground, like it was a portal into another world. The red ruptured rock around it. Only an hour ago everything seemed so crystalline and perfect. A study in beauty. And now I'm seeing hell again.

'Bath is definitely hell,' she says airily. 'But since I've had time to spend on my own I think I'll be able to escape. Especially as everything's working out.'

'How do you mean?'

'With our wishing bowl things coming true. I am Queen of the House now, just like I wished for.'

'Phoebe . . .'

But she's started moving away and I can't help it; I look up to the dangling angels and I feel sick and dizzy.

'Phoebe,' I call. 'I think I need to sit down.' The nausea is the background to my days now, like ever-present static, and I block my mind to why I think that is. The consequences are too awful. I need all this to go away. For a moment I have an overwhelming and pointless urge to flee my own body.

She turns back. 'OK. Let's go to one of those stupid little tea rooms where the waitresses hate us for being so young.'

We find one, the black-and-white building so old the beams on the front slant to one side and the walls inside are at higgledy-piggledy heights. The tables are all full so we wait in the hallway, peeking through the serving hatch with its boxes of tourist leaflets and dried flower display to see if anyone is near to finishing. The waitresses are all elderly – I'd never have noticed that without Phoebe saying – with formal black-and-white uniforms and curled grey hair.

'Let's have an expensive cream tea,' Phoebe whispers. 'Then we'll just eat some of it and leave the jam spoon in the cream so it's all stained red, and crumble the scones over the tablecloth.'

'What's the point of that?'

'They'll hate it that we're so spoiled. They were made to eat everything when they were young. At school dinners they had to eat fish pie that stank, even if it meant staying after the bell rang and having to hold their noses. I've heard.'

Her eyes are shiny and she looks so naughty I can't help smiling. Soon, though, we begin to get restless. Even though quite a few people have finished they stay put, chattering at their tables, despite Phoebe peering pointedly at them through the stalks of the dried flower display.

We find an American diner-style place further down towards the railway station and Phoebe orders an ice-cream concoction full of strange colours – blues and purples. Amazingly she digs her spoon in and begins eating. Normally she pushes everything away. I watch as she lifts the long-handled spoon and lets the melting crystals fall on her tongue, the unnatural colours staining there.

'I could live this way forever,' she says. 'I don't even feel any need to enhance it. You know, with substances.'

'Have you done it again?'

'Oh yes. I did an experiment in our house when Mum and Dad were there. I put it on my tongue and just left it there.'

'What for?'

'I don't know. I was going to whip it out. It was just for the danger of it – knowing what could happen and then stopping it – but it went wrong. It melted really, really quickly and then there was nothing I could do.'

I put my hand over my mouth. 'Oh no, Phoebe. That's crazy.'

'Yes.' Her eyes are snapping at the memory. 'I was terrified. Mum can tell if I've just been to the toilet, let alone *that*.'

'What did you do?'

'I sneaked out. I knew I'd get a bollocking for leaving the house without telling anybody but what choice did I have? I couldn't let her see me like that. I walked around town *all day*.' She reaches over and lifts my coffee cup to her lips and takes a sip. 'All day. At one point I was mooching along and I looked over the other side of the road where, where—' she's finding it hard to say, 'the thing where there was, you know, blood on the walls, and there were all these faces in the wall staring at me. It was horrible.'

I shake my head. 'I don't know. Sometimes, I wonder what's the point in doing it if it's not going to be nice?'

She loops her hair back over her ears and carries on as if she hasn't heard me. 'But you know the really freaky thing? I walked the same way about a week later and there really *were* faces in the wall. Sort of gargoyly things.'

'Where?'

'Walcot Street where, you know, *it* happened.'

'Oh God, yes. I know.'

'And I thought, only in Bath. Only in Bath are there *really* faces in the wall.' She sits back.

'So what happened when you got home?'

'Nothing. She wasn't there. Her and The B . . . Verity, they'd gone out to the theatre or something so I just went to bed and tried not to think about the faces, although I wasn't very successful because I kept seeing them again all night.' Her face crumples around the edges.

A group of boys we know come and sit at the table right next to us even though the place is empty. They are a couple of years younger but I can feel how emboldened they are by being in a group and the emptiness of the place. I sip my coffee, trying to ignore their eyes roving over us while Phoebe sits licking her spoon.

'What shall we do now?' she says, wiping her mouth. 'We could go back to mine and drink brandy.'

'What about your dad?'

'He works on Saturdays too. The house is empty.' She pats her mouth with a napkin with a delicacy that's opposite to the way she ate the ice cream.

I hesitate. The chill her house gives me is deep. It takes a couple of hours to defrost back in my own house. I don't think I can face it. Besides, the brandy would make me feel even sicker.

The boys next to us have increased in volume. They want our attention but there's a bullying aspect to it too, as if they want to compete, to crush us. A balled-up paper napkin bounces onto Phoebe's bare arm and rolls across the red Formica of the table top. There's crowing, as if a bullseye has been hit; comments, just on the point of being too low to hear but which judging from the reaction of the crowd – the stoppered laughter from the others – are sexual in some way. How easily I feel overwhelmed by it; my cheeks blooming red, I try to turn my face away so they won't see. But when I glance at Phoebe she looks on fire. She's staring at them full on and something has happened to her face: it's transformed, pulled about so I barely recognise her as the girl that was sitting opposite me a few moments ago.

Then she says this thing that makes me gasp, that makes me sure that if I'm ever seen alone by them they will have their hunted wolf revenge on me.

She hisses it so loudly even the man behind the counter spins round to look.

'If you don't shut up right this minute I'm going to make sure your cocks drop off.'

# 24

# Grace

Today at the hospital it is not like before. Today is joyful. Instead of the usual hurt and painfulness of the routine examinations, where everything gradually seems to get a little bit worse, this day Mum laughs and jokes with the nurses. She smiles at the doctors. They look on in amazement.

I smile calmly as she describes how all the numbness has gone. How she is back on her feet, slowly at first but with increased confidence. She beams as she talks. When the time comes to examine her and she turns to me and says, 'Grace, why don't you go downstairs and get yourself some chocolate and a magazine.'

'I'm fine,' I say. I'm always here for her examinations.

'Go on. I'm perfectly all right to be left, chicken. It'll be nice to think of you eating chocolate and reading *Hello* for once.'

So I smile and say, 'OK,' and she takes a tenner out of her purse and gives it to me. And I can see how she enjoys this, this giving me money out of her purse like we're a normal mother and daughter, and she enjoys all the doctors and nurses seeing her do it.

I practically float down the corridor.

I leaf through the magazines in the shop and I am, I'm having a good time. This simple act seems so decadent, so wasteful in terms of both time and money there's a delight in it, even though I don't recognise even half of the characters on the covers who have either put on, or lost, great amounts of weight; have cheated on or been cheated on by their boyfriends; or been on a holiday that turned out to be disastrous or the 'holiday of a lifetime' or the holiday where husband and wife were finally reconciled and managed to fall in love again after their marriage was on the brink. I wonder what my life would look like plastered across the cover of one of these magazines and I smile at the thought, even though I could barely imagine what it *would* look like, and at the same time I sense someone next to me and seem to recognise their smell.

'Hey.' Phoebe leans in.

'Oh. What are you doing here?' It's flustered me seeing her here and I'm reluctant to have my little enjoyable bubble burst.

'My mum's upstairs. She's had an accident.' She flips a piece of gum from a packet towards me. 'Want one?'

'Oh, no thanks.' I shove the magazine back on the shelf. 'Oh my God. Is she OK? What happened?'

Phoebe shrugs and pockets the gum. 'Want to go for a walk?'

'Um, I suppose so.' I don't really want to but I'm pulled by convention because something bad has happened to her.

She's wearing an old man's raincoat that reaches her ankles and it billows behind her as we walk through the main doors.

There are little eddies of rubbish in the corners of the building as we take the concrete path; cigarette ends squashed flat and crisp packets, their colours faded and bleached. Phoebe is striding ahead and I'm reluctant to follow. The line that attaches me to Mum is getting thinner being so far apart.

She might be nearing the end of her examination now.

'Phoebe, hang on a minute.'

She stops and twirls round. 'What?'

'I haven't got long. I need to get back upstairs. Look, let's sit on this bench.'

I'm tired. I wonder if I'm unfit. She seemed to race ahead with so little effort yet I feel almost breathless. I suppose I'm stuck in so much and I need to stop smoking.

'So, what happened?'

She takes a band out of her pocket and sweeps her hair up and snaps it into a ponytail.

She shrugs. 'A bump in the car. She's going to be fine.' Her face stiffens, then loosens up again. 'What are you doing here?'

I can't help myself. 'It's Mum, she's doing brilliantly.' I lean forward. 'Brilliantly. I mean *walking* and *standing* and *holding*.'

'Wow. That's incredible.' Her eyes widen. 'Really, really incredible.'

'I know. The doctors are looking at her now. I don't think they can believe it. I mean really.'

'Amazing. Amazing.' She's muttering to herself.

'Yes, and after . . .' I can't help it – tears clog up behind my eyes. It's a release of tension I suppose. '. . . after everything, when I thought she could *die*. I've never seen anyone look so broken.' I dash a few tears away with the back of my hand, angry with myself for giving in like this, especially in front of Phoebe. Weirdly for someone who is usually all eyes she seems to have barely noticed. She's nodding and leaning towards me. I remember about her mum. 'Sorry, I should be asking about you. What happened?'

She sweeps her arm. 'Like I said, just a bump in the car. Not much harm done really. Mum's in a neck brace but, you know, she'll be all right in the end. But d'you know what the really interesting thing is?'

'What?' I hunt around in my pocket for a tissue, find one and blow my nose.

She puts the tips of her fingers together and props her chin on the point.

'Really, really interesting.'

'Yes?' I'm getting fed up with this now. I'm getting that feeling again of Mum being a minuscule bug with tiny, tiny insect breath she's so far away, even though I know that's not right and insects breathe out of their backs or something.

'Remember the wishing bowl day? Remember us making our predictions, saying what we wanted?'

'Sort of.'

'No, I mean think about it.'

I really don't want to go into that – not with my stupid paranoia after Mum's accident, where I practically convinced myself I'd caused it by wishing our situation at home was all over and done with. It's all ridiculous, garbled nonsense. I was in such a state. I believed it was all my fault in ways I couldn't even start to count.

'What's that got to do with anything? And I really am pressed for time, I'm afraid.'

'Everything.'

'Look, I've got to get back.' I half rise and she puts her hand on my arm and pushes me down again. God, I am weak.

'No, don't go. Think about it. We made predictions – you wanted your mum to get better and she is. I wanted to be Queen of the House and now I am. We made it happen.'

'So I really did ask for her to get better? You remember that?'

'Yes. Look, and now she is.'

'Phoebe, hang on a minute. We were off our faces that day. It's got nothing to do with anything.'

I want to get up again but I look at her with her eyes flashing and think of her pushing me down again. I need to get away from her.

'Hold on.' She screws her face up. 'What did Orla predict for herself? I don't remember.'

'Neither do I.' I use her preoccupation to stand up. 'I'm going now.'

'It's true.' She waves her arms about. 'It really is.'

'OK, perhaps it is. We'll have to talk about it another time, though.' I turn and walk away as fast as I can because I get the horrible feeling she's going to run after me and jump on my back like a giant spider or something. By the time I get to the main door I'm panting. I dare to look back for the first time and she's still on the bench. From what I can see from this distance she's immobile, staring at the ground.

Upstairs I still feel jittery from what's just happened. If only she hadn't seen me in the shop I'd still be cruising in my serene little bubble. I make the effort to shake her off like a coat and it partly works. There's the impression left on my arm from when she grabbed it, so I brush it away and that falls off too like a skein of old cobwebs falling to dust on the floor.

I'm just heading back to the clinic when I see Miss Kinsella hanging around by the nurses' station. I try to turn round but it's too late.

'Hey,' she says. 'Hey, I've been waiting for you.'

There's sheaves of papers and files shoved under her arm, like she's got a busy day and she's squeezed me in between meetings and other appointments. I instantly wonder how I can take advantage of this and hurry her on her way.

'Hi there,' I say, slowing right down and ambling towards her.

She shifts the files about under her arm in a bid to make them more comfortable. 'Grace. I was hoping to catch you.'

'I think I'm needed back now. Mum must be nearly ready.'

She puts her hand on my arm exactly where Phoebe had hers and I have to fight the urge to shrug it off. 'It won't take a minute, honestly, and I have come down here specially and waited.'

I halt, wondering if she's been jogging this morning. There's a healthy glow from her again that shines out in the sickly hospital atmosphere. I wonder if she jogs to counteract this place and I store up the idea, that there's stuff like that you can do to help things, for future reference.

'The thing is, Grace, this is why I wanted to talk to you. I've been making enquiries—'

'What?' I snap it out too quickly and a flush marks her cheeks. 'Sorry. I'm a bit tired.'

'No. That's fine, fine. Of course you're tired. You have a lot on your plate.' She bites her lip. 'It's about what I mentioned before, the respite charity . . .'

*Keep still and quiet, bitch*, I tell myself. *Quiet and still.*

Oh no. What if she's been speaking to vague Debbie at the agency? Fear tightens my throat. It wouldn't take much for all my little lies to come unravelling on the ground for them to pick over and examine. When the carers came back I told

235

them she'd had a dreadful time at her sister's, fallen out with her in a big way and please not to mention it because Mum would get upset. I have to hope that that holds up.

'And of course it's something you must want . . .'

'What is?' I've missed part of the conversation. *Focus*, I tell myself. *This is how they get you, by sliding things past when you're not focusing.*

'The respite, of course.' She seems surprised I haven't cottoned on to what's she's saying. 'A respite break where your mother will go into a well-equipped residential home for a short while to be cared for, leaving you free – although it would probably be best to stay with someone, relatives perhaps, so *you* get spoiled for a change. They can be difficult to organise but in my experience really benefit both parties, I mean benefit you both.' She stops, a little breathless. She's trying so hard but I'm also aware she's putting me on the spot by doing this, by coming and finding me like this. I've been on her mind.

'I'll think about it.'

She relaxes. 'Great. I'll put my thinking cap on too and I'll write or call you when something's more definite. It's a new scheme. Often it's the carer taken away but not with this one. All the same, it's worth a try?'

It's always a step further with her, I think; now it's not just me considering it but enquiries being made. Instead of being angry, suddenly I'm pleased – even though I know I'll make sure this respite will never happen – that someone is thinking about us. Being on someone's mind – outside the two of us in our tight little world, despite everything – there is a relief in it too. There is a bit of me that feels good about it.

'Mum's ever so much better,' I say. I can hear the excitement in my own voice.

'That's great.' She hitches the files up into her armpit.

'No, really, really better.'

'That's wonderful, Grace.' She smiles. 'I really must run now, and I'll be in touch.' Then she's gone, taking her glow with her, and the hospital atmosphere wraps itself back inside the place she's left empty.

A doctor that I recognise – Dr Adams – pokes his head out of his office.

'Ah, Grace. Just the girl.' Today is beginning to feel like Hunting Grace Day. 'Come in. Come in.'

I tilt my head to one side, puzzled. This is unusual. 'OK.'

I sit on the plastic chair next to his desk and he looks at the screen of his computer and clicks his mouse for a bit.

'Where's Mum?'

'Weighing and bloods. She'll be back in a jiffy. Thing is, she asked me to have a chat with you.'

He swings his head round very suddenly and looks at me over his glasses. I've got into such a habit of feeling I have to hide everything, the direct gaze makes my cheeks flush.

I squirm on the hard chair. 'Oh yes?' It's a day not only of hunting, but hunting and chats. So that's what the tenner and the magazines and chocolate were all about, I realise. Sneaky bitch wanted to get me out of the way.

'She knows you're very excited about developments.'

His voice is too kind. He's going to set me off again and I hate that. I hate that swelling choking feeling in my throat and the swimming-pool sensation of tears welling. I try to keep the shimmer of them dammed behind my eyes.

'I am. I'm really pleased. It's been . . .' I have to stop.

237

'Yes, I can imagine. You do an awful lot, Grace, for such a young girl.'

'She had a fall.' I say this suddenly, blurt it out, and don't know why. There's some urgent need to unburden myself because of the strain of it all. Those days when the world seemed to have shrunk to a pinpoint and all there was was just me, trying to keep her alive. The nights spent awake. It's made me weak. A blabber. Stupid blabbing bitch. I vow not to give in to it again.

He nods. 'There were a few old bruises. You should've brought her in, or at least got her checked over by your GP.' His tone has changed now. There's a note of censure in it I don't like and I wish to God I hadn't said anything, even though it sounds like he would have worked it out for himself anyway, and I know I can't rely on Mum to keep her mouth shut either. *Careful, careful, Grace, remember how on the back foot you need to be*, and obediently I bow my head as if in apology. *See me*, I want to say, *see how humble I am.*

'Sorry,' I say. 'If it ever happens again, that's what I'll do.' I leave the silence to dangle for a moment. I'm used to counting out these beats, making them seem just right. 'Why did Mum want you to talk to me?'

'It's about this recovery.'

I blink. 'Yes.'

'Listen. It's not uncommon, you know.'

'What isn't?'

'For periods . . . periods of remission. Remission by its nature means it's a temporary state. That's why this kind of MS is actually called relapsing-remitting.'

I'm feeling fuzzy. 'I see.' I knew that. I've heard that all before. Why didn't I put two and two together? Because this time the remitting bit was better than ever before? Or because I didn't want to put two and two together? Because it let me off the stupid-bitch hook I was dangling from.

He looks relieved. 'Good. I knew you would. You're a sensible girl, but your mother was worried.'

'Worried about what?' I'm questioning like a robot but he doesn't seem to notice.

'That you might've thought some miraculous recovery had occurred. You know, walking on water, that sort of thing.'

The ringing in my ears is like the echoes from the tiled walls of a swimming pool now. I'm drowning. I don't know why he's going on about walking on water. They're both right. I think I was hoping that.

I shake my head. 'It's fine.' It's the thing I say when I'm lost for words and it always seems to work, even if only in a partial way like now.

'Good, and you have understood?'

I nod.

He rubs his hands together and they make a dry sound, like old leaves. 'Well, let's find your mother then. Nurse will probably have her done and dusted and back in her chariot by now.'

As I'm wheeling Mum out of the hospital I lean down and hiss, 'You didn't have to say anything, you know. You didn't have to get them to talk to me. It's better if they don't.'

An arm shoots out and she grabs onto a doorway. If I carried on I'd wrench her arm off so I don't have any choice but to stop pushing. She eases round so she can look up and into my face.

'Grace, you have to realise that it *is* better. You don't listen to me, so I think if you hear things from a doctor you might sit up and take notice.'

I fold my arms. 'Being taken into rooms for little chats. I can do without all that, you know.'

'Yes, but you need to be told.' She sounds angry now and this takes me aback. 'You need to know what the facts are and not go round making up fairy tales about what's happening. I know it's because you care but in the long run it won't do either of us any good. We need to be realistic.'

She folds her hands on her lap to show that she's said her piece and I use the opportunity to grab the handles on the wheelchair and continue pushing, a bit hard and fast if truth be told, so she just about manages to pick up her feet before they get squashed underneath.

We take off down the pavement outside. The breeze flutters over me and the last weeks with their animal fear, the stifling intimacy, finally begin to fall away. I trundle Mum past offices and flats and gardens, and I can't quite wipe the smile off my face at the relief of it, that we've got away with it.

We are free again. I think of Phoebe and what she was talking about in the hospital grounds. Why not? I allow myself for one tiny moment to believe that she was right. That our drug-addled muttered incantations – me dressed only in raggy knickers and bra, mud-smeared legs – have worked and that, despite what Dr Adams had to say, Mum is forever and completely cured. The feeling is so good I don't want to let go of it. I want to believe it so much. I tell myself that doctors don't know everything anyway. It's something I've heard about, the blind seeing, the lame walking. All the way home I just let myself give in to the idea and it swells inside me like some beautiful soft healing cloud that I can float on and takes all the worry and pain right away.

# 25

# Phoebe

It's all over.

*She*'s back. Nearly two whole glorious weeks on my own and now it's all over. She is marooned upstairs in her bedroom but her presence still permeates the whole house. My diary goes unread. There seems little point in making entries in it when it's without an audience. She can barely make it to the bathroom two steps down from her room, let alone to here. My glasslike serenity, my cool-hearted witchiness, my Queenly nature, my appetite and my sanity have fled.

'Phoebe.' Her voice calls down the stairs and I have no choice but to attend.

I hover by her bedroom door, then by the dressing table.

'Come closer,' she snaps. 'It's irritating when you don't stay in one place. I can't see you properly.'

It's the neck brace. She can't turn her head. I bite into the meat on the side of my palm and approach, willing for the horrid treacherous nervous laughter to stay at bay when I lay eyes on her face.

I manage to restrict it to almost silent snorts down the nose like the soft whinnying of a pony. With luck she won't notice. I come a little closer again.

'Do you want anything to eat?' I ask.

'No. I don't.'

'Coffee? Water? Juice?' I feel dizzy. 'Herb tea?' I want

to go on forever naming drinks like this to offset what's to come.

'Phoebe, stop it.' Her eyes spark out from the pillow. She knows. She knows. She knows what I did. She thinks I tried to kill her. Did I? I can't even stand by the bed properly and get near those flashing eyes.

'Come closer.'

I inch forward.

'For God's sake. I want to be able to see you.'

I stretch my leg out and take a giant step as if avoiding a chasm beneath me. Now I am right by her and she is looking up but the flashing is gone. It's unexpected and I don't know quite what to make of it. She is looking thoughtful.

'Phoebe, there is something I want you to do for me.'

'OK. Do you want something from the shops?'

'No, not that.'

'Tissues?'

'Stop it. I want you to find Verity.'

'What?'

'You heard.' She props herself on her elbows and uses them to manoeuvre her body in a swinging action a little further up towards the pillows. The movement is almost athletic. She's becoming well horribly quickly. Soon she will be all recovered and I feel absolutely miserable. My reign over the house has been pitifully short and incomplete. It was just a delicious taste of it, a lick.

'But I don't even know what country she's in. Where do I start?'

'It may be Italy now . . . Ring round her friends and see if anyone can tell you anything. I did ask her to leave me details of exactly where she'd be but she managed to take

243

off without it *and* without getting a new phone which she faithfully promised to do after she lost her old one. I only realised she hadn't an hour before she left and I should've stopped her from going then. She needs to know what's happened. I need her here now, not gallivanting across Europe. It's up to you to find her. I'm relying on you. Everything is so difficult with this neck brace and I'm tired in two minutes every time I try to do anything.'

I'm seized with panic. 'I don't know if I'll be able to manage it.'

She falls silent again, watching me for a moment. 'I haven't forgotten what happened, you know,' she says.

The panic is so bad now I can't even speak. We just look at each other until she sighs and closes her eyes, and after a minute or two I manage to creep away.

I stand in the kitchen wringing my hands. So she does know what I did and the only way I can make it up to her is to get The Beloved to return. If not, there will be the rage, the terrible rage, and I'll do absolutely anything to avoid that.

I look around at my ruined refuge. There are bread-crumbs all over the counter. There are butter smears on the breadboard. Dad must've come and gone. How quickly my territory has been encroached and messed on, and I am left once again stateless and adrift. And now The Beloved is to return, if I am able to track her down, although the chances of that are slim. My character is once again reduced to nothing. When I opened the window of the living room last night to let in the soft night air and I called, even my flying bat friends made of leather skins seem to have deserted me.

I find the address book in a kitchen drawer and leaf through it. Mum has always insisted that we note down all our friends and their addresses and telephone numbers. I try to remember who Verity hangs around with these days but it's hard because we don't have much to do with each other. The girls I've glimpsed her with all seem the same – glossy, with flowing hair, who look you right in the face without flinching. I seem to recognise the name Betty even though I can't attach it to any of the faces I remember, but the phone number next to her name just rings and rings and I begin to panic. I want Verity here now more than anything in the world so she can head off this awful state that feels like being constantly circled by a shark so there can be no rest ever. I look frantically through the pages again. Stacey. I seem to recognise that. The phone is picked up almost instantly.

'Is Stacey there?' I wonder if my voice sounds tight and weird.

'Stacey's abroad.'

'Oh, oh – d'you know exactly where? See—'

'Who is this? Have you heard something about Stacey? This is her mother.' She sounds panicky now.

'No. No.' I take a breath and start again. 'It's Verity's sister here. Phoebe. I'm trying to track Verity down because Mum's had an accident.'

'Oh dear. Is she OK?'

'Yes, yes. All fine but Mum wants her back and the thing is we don't really know where she is.'

She breathes out heavily at the other end. 'Well, that got me worried. I thought something had happened. I can't quite relax with her gone. Hang on a minute, I'll get the itinerary.'

'Itinerary?' I ask, but the question is to empty air because she's gone off to find it.

'Right.' I can hear paper crinkling. 'I have it here. Don't you have one of these?'

'No. I don't think so. What is it?'

'One of the boys who likes making spreadsheets did it because we weren't sure if their mobile phones would work abroad or if we'd get charged the earth for ringing them, so he typed up a list of all the hostels and hotels they've booked, with their phone numbers. Didn't you get one? He made copies for all the parents.'

*One of the boys?* I want to scream down the phone. *Do you know how nuts my mother would go if she heard this? The Beloved gave her firm assurances it was strictly a girls' trip.*

Instead I work hard to keep my voice even. 'Verity must've forgot.'

'OK – right. They're in Spain at the moment.'

'Spain?' I don't think Mum or I even knew she was going to Spain.

'Yes. They're staying at the Hotel Miramar in Barcelona and here's the number. Got a pen?'

I write the number down and hang up and ring the Spanish number straight away. It's all so easy, I can't believe it. I just say her name and the line is ringing to her room and it gets picked up and it's Verity's voice at the other end. I feel overjoyed. This is actually, actually going to work. I'll be able to go up and tell Mum that Verity's on her way home and she'll lie back, tired but happy and satisfied. And that's what her mind will be on from now on – The Beloved returning – and I'll finally, finally be able to get some peace.

'Verity,' I blurt. 'You have to come home. Mum's been in an accident.'

She goes quiet at the other end of the line. 'How did you find this number?'

'What? I got it off one of the mums. Aren't you going to ask how she is?'

Silence for a moment. 'Of course. It was just a shock to hear your voice. How is she? What happened?'

'We crashed into another car but she's going to be all right and she's home now. She's quite battered up, though, and in a neck brace so she's getting really tired and bored and she says you have to come home.'

'What?'

'She says you have to come home straight away.'

'I can't do that. She's not going to die or anything, is she?'

'No, but . . .' The panic's welling up again. The last thing I expected was for Verity to *refuse*.

'Well then. I don't see what I can do by being there any-way.'

'Verity. She really, really wants you home. Please. Please come.' I know how desperate I sound. 'You have to. I'm begging you.'

'Stop it. Stop trying to make me feel guilty. I'm having a lovely time and you've got to go and ruin it. There's nothing I can do that you can't and you happen to be *there*.'

'But it's *you* she wants. You know that.'

'I'll be back in a few weeks anyway. Just tell her you couldn't get hold of me.'

She sounds like she's trying to end the conversation and it tips me over the edge. I hold the receiver away and yell into it like I'm screaming at a face. 'You have to come back. You

247

can't do this. She's going to be absolutely fucking furious with me and all this will just go on and on and on. It's not fair. It's not fair.'

Her voice at the other end sounds tiny and electric. It reminds me of an insect buzz. It opens its little tin wings and flies out of the receiver. 'Oh fuck off, you little weirdo,' it buzzes at me and then the line goes dead.

I don't bother calling her back. She won't answer. She'll be outside already with a drink in her hand and flicking her hair as she tells everyone her peculiar sister just got hold of her. Actually, no, she won't want anyone to know that she's ignoring the fact her mother has had a car accident and wants her back. She'll pretend the call never happened. Instead I stand shaking, trying to calm myself down before dragging my feet all the way up to Mum and Dad's bedroom. At the bottom of the flight that leads to their room I get the shock of my life. She's sitting on the top stair and glaring down at me. I startle so much I have to hang onto the banister. I even let out a little scream. I calculate quickly. I don't think she could have overheard what I said from the kitchen. It doesn't stop me quaking, though. Her mouth is so pursed up it looks as if it's been stitched and the thread pulled into a pleated gather.

'Well? What happened?'

I can't tell her. I can't.

I can't stand the sight of her pain. I never have been able to. It's too dreadful to witness. When it happens the look of it is like a nerve or muscle that has been severed but still lives, coloured electric blue and blood red with agony, dragging itself across the floor. It has no control over itself. It is without thought. When I was a child the house was set up permanently with tricks to deflect its might that sometimes I revisit. I'd angle the bread knife in the drawer so it was pointing at her. The thought of its point staring straight at her through the wood was an ally. I'd open up the blades of all the scissors in the house and the sight of their open pointed beaks, sharp and ready, was as if I'd armed myself. Now is just the same. I'll do pretty much anything to deflect or run away from it. I must make her believe I haven't spoken to Verity. It'll send her over the edge.

'I . . . I couldn't get hold of her. I did try. I rang round her friends.'

'You are such a dreadful little liar.'

I hang onto the banister for dear life. 'What?'

'I heard you on the phone. Talking and screaming. Honestly, you sound quite off your head sometimes.'

For a moment I think she's managed to hear me from all the way up here, like she has superhuman powers. I shake my head. 'How did you hear that?'

'Because I was down there. I thought I'd better come and do it with you so you wouldn't mess it up.'

'But how did you walk?'

'I didn't. I came down on my bottom like some child. I made it to halfway down the bottom staircase so I could hear every word.'

'Oh no.'

'What did *she* say, exactly?' There are bright red spots on both her cheeks and she's digging her nails into her palm. The sight of it makes me feel there is something screwing through my insides. The rage. The rage. It's going to happen and there'll be nothing she can do about it.

I want to collapse but somehow I manage to stay upright.

My voice squeezes out. 'Mum. Look, I can be here all the time for you. I'll do whatever you need. I promise. Really.'

'Tell me what she said.' Her face contorts into a shape that is both dreadful and familiar. It makes my heart tilt.

'Mum, you don't need to know. Everything will be all right, it really will. I promise.' My voice is just a squeak now.

'Tell me.' She grates it out.

'She said . . .' I heave a breath in and start again. 'She said it would be really difficult to come home. She sends her love and she's told me to do anything I can—'

'Oh, stop it.'

The rage doesn't come as I expected it. It stays inside this time. I wonder at the way she is managing to hold it. It must be eating at her flesh there. Very slowly she drags herself up. I know I am supposed to watch, to be a witness to it. With a series of sharp gasps she raises herself to standing, then, bent over and with baby steps, she turns to the direction of her room. It takes an age for her to reach the door and all the while we are both spangled with silence, her harsh breath the only sound that flows through the hollow of it so it presses at my ears. She opens the door and slides inside; and there's a click as it swings shut behind her.

My knees buckle. No, no, no. I will not. I will not let myself be destroyed. I heave myself up and crash down the stairs. The familiar sights of the house whizz past as I pick up speed. Outside, the light is burning bright again, eating at the edges of everything. The long grass whips at my knees as I run through it. It is as if I am pulled by a thread. It's the only escape I can cling onto right at this very minute. It's so acute. I need to act straight away. I need to make myself feel better now.

I scrabble at the back of the ivy but my hand grasps only at the tough branches or at thin air. Have I been caught? Does she right now have the phone locked inside her bedside cabinet? Is she monitoring the texts as they come in? I move closer into the heart of the plant and the sharp green winter smell fills my nostrils and the edges of the hard shiny leaves jab into my face. I feel around and my hand touches cold plastic. It's fallen down a branch or two and become wedged in. I pick it out with two fingers and switch it on. It seems to take an age, the screen brightening, then dimming and then brightening again.

Finally it lights up and stays that way. In the little glass window there's an envelope that tells me there are twenty-four messages waiting, one tucked tight inside the other like Russian dolls. Twenty-four. I want to scream again.

# 26

# Phoebe

It all got so much better when I remembered about Rapunzel's plait.

At first I wasn't going to answer the messages from Lucas. They sounded desperate and intense. I wanted to and didn't want to. It felt like there'd be no going back. Then I thought about the plait and how Rapunzel could dangle it into the world but at the same time stay completely safe even though it was poking out. She could bring stuff in, then push it out again.

I can meet him – I realised – then return. There will be no outward change that could be distinguished. I'll return to my contaminated eyrie and it will be like nothing happened, except it will have done because the spell will be broken and I'll have something for myself, something outside this crushed little world, that I can think of all the time and that will keep me healthy. It began to feel like my only chance. I needed that smile, that masculine ease, that strength and power to sweep all of this away.

The fruits are already beginning to ripen on the trees when I go to meet him. I wonder at that. It's been summer for such a short time and already everything is speeding towards ripeness. Winter and the dark will arrive before we know it. The sun will plummet towards the earth and bury itself there.

I leave Mum sleeping and take the shopping basket. I

stick my empty hand in my pocket and swing my skirt as I walk. I smile in what I imagine is a mischievous way.

*I know a place where no one goes.*

Nobody knows where I'm going or who I'm meeting except for him. It's treasure to me and I like to lay this secret treasure around me in a circle, where I can look at it over and over again.

He's waiting for me near the Spinney already. I can see him in the distance watching me approach, the tall girl in the swingy blue skirt brushing through the long grass. He puts his hand up to wave, then puts it down again.

When I reach him there's so much pollen clinging to the hem of my skirt, I am ringed with gold.

'It's very open here,' is the first thing he says. There are blobs of sweat on his forehead. He looks so awkward and jittery I have the idea that he was about to leave at the precise moment he caught sight of me across the field. One of his texts said that he was becoming obsessed with me. I know all too well how obsessions can click over onto something else at a moment's notice. Perhaps the sight of me is a disappointment and he's changing his mind. It makes me want him to stay even more. There's something about the wanting of something more powerfully when it's about to slither fish-like from your grasp.

'Follow me.' I throw the basket over the tumbledown wall and go to squeeze through the hole. I'm sick to the pit of my stomach at what I'm doing but I do it anyway. I don't even really know why.

'Really?' His jacket is hooked over his shoulder by one finger and the stripes on his shirt betray quite a plumpness on his belly.

He doesn't look the same as I imagined or remembered him. He's sweaty and nervous. There's a heaviness to his brow, a thickness to his skin that I would like replaced with more girlish features. Something more romantic. Does that make me gay? I remember the kiss with Orla, the one I don't usually think about. When I'm with her it's like we're two girl/boys together.

'You can climb over if you like. It might be better for you.'

I see he likes this, the idea of climbing rather than slithering through holes.

'OK, hold my jacket then.' He slips about on the stones because of his hard leather soles and I think he's going to give up, but he manages to scramble over in the end. I pass over his jacket, then squeeze through the hole beneath.

'So.' He grins at me, sickly. His face is greenish from being under the canopy. I turn. Walk away, expecting him to follow. He does. I can hear the crashing in the undergrowth. We're close to the river now. The wishing bowl has started to dry out around the edges, with a thick cakey sludge at the bottom where our offerings must've sunk. All that's visible now are a few walnuts, a pine cone and the jellied remains of a red Haribo ring. He lays out his jacket on the ground and I notice the finicky way he checks for mud and scrutinises the ground, removing bits of sharp twig and leaf. I swish my skirt about and watch.

'There,' he says finally and sits down, patting the space next to him. I sit on the satiny lining and he lies back and puts his hands behind his head and looks up at the trees. The gravity of lying down does something to his face. The male heaviness of it smooths away and the shadows of the leaves play across his skin. Even his belly flattens, sinking down back inside his body, and his shirt stops trying to gape apart at the bottom. I realise then, it's not manliness I was wishing away but how old he is. It's a considerable relief knowing this. I crave the maleness to counteract everything about home. The relief makes me feel fonder of him and I stroke his cheek, which still feels sweaty.

He closes his eyes. Looks almost in pain. 'I can't stop thinking about you.'

This delights me! Charmer. Spell-binder. Weaver of dreams and desires. The power goes through me like an electric charge right into my fingertips.

He opens his eyes so I can see the blueness of them and for a moment I almost wish my mother could see us both lying here. I lean over him so my hair hangs down in a waterfall and I kiss his face, his forehead, his eyelids. Delicately I kiss his mouth and then he surges forward; he takes me by the shoulders and then I'm the one lying on the ground and he's kissing me using his tongue. I could go on forever like this. The day is so soft and warm, and the feeling of his tongue is like discovering a new taste of drink that I didn't know existed before. It reminds me of the Turkish delight that the Queen of Narnia dispenses from her sledge.

He sits up. 'We shouldn't be doing this.'

'I'm fine,' I say. 'I'm enjoying it.'

He hiccups a laugh, like I've said something funny, and sits back. 'You're just a young girl, Phoebe. I don't know anything about you.'

I smile and instead of an answer I pluck the square package from the pocket of his shirt that I spotted as soon as I saw him. Like I could tell he was about to leave before, now I can tell that he'd decided not to use the condom that he's brought with him, that he was going to leave it at kisses. He looks embarrassed.

I tear it open.

'Have you . . . before?'

I nod. It's true, but the memory of the ten-minute losing of my virginity at a birthday in one of the bathrooms of the party girl's house is something I'd rather forget.

And then we do it and it's not as bad as the time before. I wonder if perhaps I'm getting used to it and that's part of what sex is all about – just getting used to it, and in doing that it'll get better and better as time goes on. I'm hoping so. In fact, it just starts feeling nice when he jerks around on top of me and I know it's all over. *That was disappointing – again*, I think, but I smile at him like it was OK because I can't bear for him to go. After he's rolled off me I get the sense he wants to leave as soon as possible but doesn't have the guts to say so.

'Don't go. Let's chat for a bit,' I say. 'I'm desperate for someone to talk to.'

'Of course. Of course. Tell me anything you want.'

He lies back down and we curl our hands together and I tell him everything I can think off. I tell him about The Beloved and my house. I tell him I knew something would happen the day I first clapped eyes on him as I watched from the window as he hurried out of his car, his arms full of books, late already on his first day. I tell him about Bertha and how she is my only respite from home because I know that everything will stay where I've put it and what a relief that is because Mum sometimes comes into my room and takes things away.

He frowns. 'What kind of things?'

'Oh, anything that she disapproves of or thinks might draw attention to me, like a nice evening dress I got in a jumble sale once. It was midnight blue and fitted me like a glove, like it had been made for me, but I came home from school one day and it was gone, just like I always knew it would be when she first saw me in it.'

I can't help it. I cry a bit then, because I loved that dress so much and I really was so sad to think of it being taken away with the rubbish and covered in eggshells and old gravy.

He sits up. 'Really, that's a very strange thing to do.'

'What is?'

'Taking things without your permission like that.'

'Oh, she does it quite often.'

'Really?'

'Yes, and reads my diary too. Though I make sure there's nothing of interest in there.' I bite my lip, thinking of the day I'd convinced myself I'd written out bloody and ludicrous fantasies.

He's looking at me, frowning. 'Very strange.'

I wish I hadn't said anything now. Even *I* don't understand what happens in our house. The hundreds of criss-crossing wires that can be plucked at any moment, sending vibrations to any corner, even to places that have been undisturbed as yet. I wouldn't *want* to.

'It doesn't bother me, really.'

He won't leave it, though. 'I can't believe anyone could disrespect boundaries in that way. Does she do anything else like that?'

I try and force my face to look blank, but it makes me think of what pussy-cat face said that time about Mum having a personality disorder and how I kind of forgot about it in the end because no one else seemed to think so. Now Lucas says he thinks she's strange too but we weren't supposed to be going into all this. I don't know why I brought it up. I wanted it all to be separate.

'No, it's fine,' I cut him off.

'What?'

'No, I wasn't upset about the dress at all. I think I might've told her I didn't want it any more so it was all a mix-up.'

That's not true at all. I really did want it and she knew exactly how much, but somehow I'm seized with feeling protective of her. Talking about her like this feels wrong, as if we're putting her in a laboratory and hurting her by taking her to pieces. I don't want to do it any more. It's private.

He's looking nervous, uncertain now, though. I think maybe I'm scaring him a bit by saying contradictory things like that. It probably sounds a bit crazy so I smile widely. 'It's all just nonsense that goes on in families,' I say reassuringly. 'I expect the same happens in yours.' Turns out that's an even worse thing to say as I've reminded him about all his responsibilities.

'I should be getting back.'

'No, don't. We're having a lovely time, aren't we?'

'It's not right. I'm so sorry. I really am.'

He actually has tears in his eyes.

'What are you crying about?'

He dashes them away. 'Nothing. Look, I'm sorry I have to go.'

'Will you meet me again?'

'I don't know. I need to think.'

'Stop bloody crying,' I say, because he's frightening me now, crying like that, a grown man crying like a stupid big baby.

He rubs his eyes on his shirt sleeve.

'You deserve better than this, Phoebe.'

I sit up. The condom is on some leaves, leaking semen. He begins clearing away like it's a messy kitchen. He does up his trousers, then folds the condom up into a tight neat square inside a tissue and drops it in his pocket. His face is blotched and tired-looking. I watch him silently, trying to guess what he's thinking.

'Come on,' he says. 'I'll walk you back as far as the road.'

'I'm fine.' I deliberately make my voice as cold as possible because I can see he can't wait to go. 'I'm going to stay here for a bit.'

'Honestly, I would be so much happier to see you safely on your way.' He looks around at the silent trees, the tangled undergrowth, the single bird hopping through the ivy that chokes the ground. 'It's very lonely here.'

I shrug. 'I like it.'

He stands, shifting his feet uncertainly with his jacket once again hooked by one finger over his shoulder.

I lie back. 'I think I'm going to take a nap.'

'Jesus, Phoebe.'

'Go on, you go. Go on, I just want to be on my own now.' I screw my eyes shut in the effort not to cry, and all the lumps and bumps and roots of the earth dig into my back. Eventually I hear some scuffling and when I open my eyes he's gone. I roll over, then sit up. It looks yawningly empty in the place where he was standing. A band of fury tightens around my middle. So he ran away from me as if I'm nothing. Perhaps I'm a pinprick to people outside the cage of our house as well as on the inside.

I stand up. There's an ache between my legs and at the top of my thighs. I flex my knee up and down so I can feel it more strongly, testing out the pull of it. I seek the knowledge that something has been kindled in me, something changed, but for now that's all there seems to be, the ache and the gap where he was beneath the trees.

I spot the wishing bowl. It's like a dead star with its magic used up and gone. I lean over and, using my hands as shovels, begin ladling out the mud and flinging it into the river along with Grace's pine cone, which plops into the water and sinks. My fingers dig deeper into the muck and unearth other treasures we put there: a Haribo fried egg and a pair of red lips, dirt clinging to the sticky gap of them. I scrape diligently until the hole is clean, expectant, yawning out for some new magic to take place. The emptiness of it looks like it could suck in anything.

# 27

# Phoebe

I go to the one I always go to when I am reduced to nothingness and fear. The one who is coloured pink and white. Who is plump and serious-faced. Who always welcomes me with open arms and loves me whatever I do. Orla loves me unequivocally. She never, ever runs away from me.

I felt like I was drowning at home. There was no respite, and nowhere to go with *her* being there the whole time and never even leaving to go to her part-time job. The house was getting filled up with steaming hot waters and they were closing over my head and gushing up my nose. When I think of Lucas I have a twist of hatred in my guts because for a tiny moment he made me feel whole. Now, because of him and the way he couldn't wait to run off and the texts he never answers, I am more smashed apart than ever. Little pieces of me are hidden around the house. In my dreams I go looking for them. I want to put them all back together but I can never find them all, and the ones I do discover – in corners, behind sofas, in the bin – have grown into odd shapes that won't fit together.

*She* is almost completely well again. She seems better than ever, in fact. Three weeks in bed, then time spent with her feet up have made her the picture of health. She plans trips and excursions for herself; the soonest is to Edinburgh, where Dad's chambers is holding a ball in a cathedral-like hotel. She's excited by this, sees herself at home in Edinburgh, in her rightful place, with its grand scale and its serious culture. She leafs through catalogues of dresses. 'What do you think?' she asks, and remembering my midnight blue dress I pick the ugliest, the ones sprouting crenulations on the sleeves and with sea-slug skirts. The ones that would make her look like a gargoyle. She stops asking me after a while and decides to make it herself. I touch the swathes of midnight blue silk that fan out over the sewing machine, the table, the floor, and weep. My tears make brief crystal buttons on the silk, then melt into it.

I meet Orla in our halfway slanted park and she links arms with me and we don't even have to talk. The relief I feel is medicinal, the edge of pain accompanying it: the touch of gauze upon a wound; antiseptic cream on a cut. Her shoulder-length dull brown hair is coiled on top of her head in a bun. She wears a plain white shirt tucked into grey wool trousers. She looks older, heavier, more responsible, like a teacher or an office worker, since I last saw her. There's two mauve smudges under her eyes like she hasn't been sleeping well, but they actually serve to set the hazel colour off and make her more striking than before and lift up her ordinariness. She takes my arm and I lean on it like I'm a little old lady as we walk into town.

'Look, there's those sick faces,' I whisper to her and we pass the ancient wall grimed with soot. The faces gurn out at the traffic from the blackened stones. I rub at my eyes because just thinking about the man being slimed and scraped across the wall still makes it feel that blood is running down inside of them, colouring everything on the outside.

'Ignore them,' she says so briskly it makes me snuggle into her side even more closely. 'They're not even old. They're something hippies stuck up there in the 1970s. My dad told me. He remembers them being put up when he was a kid.'

'Really?' I look at them again and see how this is true. They don't have the closed-off medieval faces that are as impenetrable as carp gliding under water. They have jokey bubble cheeks. There's one with glasses.

'Yes,' she says. 'Let's do something organised today. Something stupid and touristy. Let's do a proper tour of the Baths again.'

I acquiesce by resting my head on her shoulder briefly. I need to start treating Orla better. She loves me so much.

'Let's go on holiday together first,' I say, stopping outside the travel agent's, playing an old game of ours.

'All right.' And we go inside and scoop up brochures with suns wheeling across the covers.

'How about Corsica?' I ask, opening the pages onto an expanse of blue sea.

'Lovely,' she says, closing her eyes as if she could really put herself there. 'That sounds lovely.'

I put that brochure back and pick up another one and study the cover. 'Or maybe Crete?'

We gather up shiny brochures until we catch the attention of the woman behind the desk and when she makes her move, toddling across to us in her high heels and her tight blue uniform, we shove all the brochures into our bags and escape, giggling. In the old days we'd pore over them, deciding where to go in our fantasies and luxuriating in the details of hotels with whirlpools and all-you-can-eat buffets.

At the top of Milsom Street we pause to look in shop windows. I pick out a coat that would suit her and she chooses a pair of boots for me – another old game of ours.

I stop dead in the middle of the pavement. 'Oh no.'

She turns. 'What is it?'

'It's them again. I can't believe it.' I'm stiff with panic.

'Who?'

I nod in the direction of Lucas on the other side of the road. This time they're all there, his wife and the baby in the pushchair and a girl toddler with petal-shaped party skirts and angel wings dripping off her.

'Why do I keep seeing them?' I hiss. 'What's making it happen?' I back into a doorway of a shop selling lamps and silk flowers, and candles as thick as an arm.

'What do you mean? Nothing's making it happen.'

'Then why do I keep seeing them?'

'It's Saturday. Everyone goes shopping on Saturday. Bath has got, like, three streets – it would be surprising *not* to bump into someone you know.' She comes closer. 'Christ, you look terrible.'

'I feel it. I feel sick.' Over her shoulder I see them threading away from us down the street, him pushing and his wife holding the girl's hand. His wife's wearing a yellow sou'wester that reminds me of the child from *Winnie-the-Pooh*.

Her face hardens. 'You did it, you went and saw him again, didn't you?'

'Don't. I really am going to be sick if you carry on.' I put my hand up to my mouth to catch it in case it comes.

'Honestly, you're so stupid.' She's turned white. Jealousy is eating her brain. I can see it in the way her eyes deaden to me as it devours the cells behind them. 'How could you do such a thing? He's married, for God's sake. He's a *teacher*.'

264

'I know. It was a stupid thing. Don't be angry with me, Orla. I'm relying on you. Please be nice to me. I can't stand it if you aren't.'

She shoves her hands in her pockets and stares at me with her mouth open.

'Please. It was just a stupid mistake that I won't make again.'

'What happened?'

We have to stand aside for two women who want to get into the shop. They give us looks because we're in the way; the usual middle-aged-women looks that say teenage girls shouldn't be getting in anyone's way, that they should part like the Red Sea in front of the overwhelming force of their regal age and authority.

'Nothing. Nothing happened. We just kissed a bit. I thought it'd be fun but it wasn't. It was quite gross, actually. I never want to see him again.'

I look at her and my heart turns over. She looks utterly cold. 'Really, you once said I was childish but I think it's you that's such a child, Phoebe.'

'Don't say that. We're having fun again, aren't we? I absolutely promise from the bottom of my heart I won't do it again. Don't look at me that way. You know I'm oversensitive to things like that.'

She doesn't reply for a long time and I practically can't breathe. 'Does it ever occur to you that I might have troubles of my own?' she says finally.

I shake my head. It really hasn't. I grab her arm. 'Come on, us girls need to stick together, don't we?' And I mean it, I really do at that moment. Girls mean more to each other than anyone. All those conversations whispered into sticky night air. Huddled together under one blanket and watching the dawn, camping in Orla's garden. I want more than anything now for Orla to melt and for us to be carefree again, in the old way, our hair in streamers behind us, arms linked and both putting our foot forward at the same time.

'What troubles do you mean?' I ask, burning with curiosity now.

'Nothing. Nothing I want to talk about. Come on, let's get this tour over with.'

'Go on.'

'I don't have to tell you everything, you know,' she flashes at me. '*You* don't.' Then she sees how hurt I am by that and she takes my arm. 'Never mind. Let's get in there.'

In the Roman Baths most people are oblivious. They wear headphones that tell them in a dozen different languages what they're looking at. We don't need that. It's part of our normal landscape, seeing monuments that were built for ancient gods and devils, though we don't even know what they looked like, what rituals or foods were eaten in their presence, what sacrifices were made for them and what demands they enacted. I've heard a theory that the stone circles at Avebury would have been covered in the chalk that lies just under the surface all over this area, that the ground was scratched at to expose it and covered all the stones too so it looked like a space ship, and I can imagine that. Sometimes I get the feeling the old spirits haven't gone away at all; it's just that we can't name or give shape to them. They love that, being unknowable. It means they can move faster around the world.

In the Great Bath the sun sparking off the water cuts into

266

my eyes. In daylight the water has the green lusciousness of the inside of a grape. Luminous green. The reflection of fast-moving clouds fans out across the golden pillars. The sound of footsteps and voices hollow out with the acoustics. We walk on the ancient uneven tiles on the covered terrace, then emerge into the open air by the brink of the Great Bath. I remember my swim and the arc of stars swinging above, the sulphur sting of the water on my tongue, and Orla, a hunched figure like one of the minor harmless spirits still hanging about here who has been forgotten and neglected and spends an eternity feeling forlorn.

'That was so funny, wasn't it? Swimming here. Look at all these people. They don't have a clue.'

'It scared the shit out of me.' There's tears in her eyes.

I've upset her now, but I want to make it better and I think about saying something that might mollify her, but the sky darkens and there's a gust of wind across the water and a sharp rainfall; great drops fall from the sky through the open ceiling and I watch, transfixed, from under the shelter of the terrace. It's so beautiful, the sight of stormy raindrops as they plummet, hissing as they hit the steaming green water and are then swallowed up. There's a rumble of thunder and the sudden electricity makes me practically shiver in ecstasy, but when I turn round, Orla has gone.

I'm alone with the blank-eyed tourists listening to their commentaries and I'm plunged into a dreadful, dreadful panic now the plaster of Orla's company has been torn off. An unnamed paranoia grips me. Something dreadful will happen, I'm sure of it. I start thinking what it may be, the dreadful thing that will occur, and then something happens that's never happened before. The myriad different dooms cluster together like frogspawn, and I know I would only need to look inside each pod to find the black spot of that particular fear with all its own individualities and nuances huddling inside, and the power of them all bubbling together is so overwhelming I want to tip myself head first into the waters. Minerva seems to have deserted me and I wonder if she's still in the little urban woodland opposite Lucas's house; if she got stuck there. I turn and nearly trip on the lead-lined sluice that feeds the bath with the hot waters and I stumble into the darkness of the museum, looking for Orla's reassuring plump figure.

The atmosphere is much more moist inside because there's nowhere for the coiling steam from the boiling waters to evaporate. These are all the things I remember from before, from being led around, breathing in the fetid heat, pushing and shoving, on school trips, plastic mac tickling behind my bare knees and my lunch in a backpack. I stumble past the covered circular bath, the water as green as the sea, where Romans finished their bathing regime with a freezing plunge into its waters. Past the glass cabinets of jewellery, of coins and necklaces and totems, the masks used by priests; and then it's the beautiful gilded face of Sulis Minerva herself – the half-Celtic, half-Roman goddess, cracked apart from her body at some point but the head found and mounted so she can look out on us all.

I whizz by the glass cabinets containing the figures of the three mother goddesses that were made before the Romans even came here. Then there's the lead curse tablets retrieved from the sacred spring with lists of suspects of a crime scratched on their surface. 'But where is God?' I remember one little boy asking nervously, a product of our church primary school. 'He hasn't been invented yet,' I told him.

Where is Orla? Where is she? A terrible thought occurs, that she has left, abandoned me here and is this minute striding home, muttering to herself under her breath about how stupid I am, what a liar. I can see it, I can see her leaving, and I stand still and close my eyes and wave after wave of panic washes through me.

When I open them again there's Orla.

The coil of her little mouse-brown bun from behind is the best sight in the world; it's so cute I give in to trembly laughter, a wide crazy smile that I wipe off with my own hand. She's standing, leaning on the bars that protect people from falling into the open sluice running through the room. Right in front of her is a stone arch in the wall that, deep within, houses the opening – the gushing source of the spring. The stone inside is bright red, glistening with the ever-spouting boiling water. Its hard surfaces appear folded they are so worn over centuries. I stand next to her, close, and reach out for her hand to hold. I lower my head as if in supplication to her. Her hand, which at first is unresponsive, begins to twitch and curl around mine. I put my head on her shoulder and we stand staring into the crimson-hot depths of the bubbling chasm.

# 28

# Grace

When Daniel comes out shopping with us, everything is different. We take turns pushing the wheelchair. We giggle over displays of oranges in the supermarket, picking out the most plump and juicy-looking. He wraps his arm around me and kisses the side of my neck in front of everyone. 'Stop it, you lovebirds,' Mum says, looking down to hide her grin. I told Daniel everything, about the fall, about what happened and why I was the way I was. 'Christ, Grace,' he said, but he hugged me all the same and then we were back the way we were before.

We stop in a café and park Mum up and go together to load our tray with coffees and Danish pastries. I can't remember feeling like this. I have been so worn, frayed to nothing almost. When we return, Daniel holding the tray up high and gripping the sides with his strong hands, somehow Mum has managed to get herself out of the wheelchair and onto the proper café chair. She loves surprising us like this and sits smiling her head off as if she's just done a magic trick.

Sometimes he stays over. Rosa and Averill almost burst with curiosity on their visit when he surprises them by emerging from my room and leaving the flat in a blur of blue jeans and dark hair. They're disappointed they don't have a chance to pounce and only manage to sit with their mouths open while he whirls past them.

He cooks for me and I put on a little weight and he teases me about it. 'Surely it's not true,' he says in bed one night. 'I can feel a hip. And what's this?' He cups my buttock.

'It's my big fat arse.' I giggle as he squeezes away.

Soon he will have to go away for a training course but I'm trying not to think about that. It will only be for a fortnight and I console myself by washing the oil out of his overalls myself and ironing them neatly.

He laughs when I take the ironed pile down to his flat. 'They'll tease me for being the posh boy with pressed overalls,' he says, but I don't care. I want to do it, to press every wrinkle away and make neat grey walls with the perfectly folded clothes in the same way he loves to cook for me. We are careful. He doesn't stay every night, just at the weekend. I don't want my life with Mum completely taken over by our coupledom. He doesn't want the neighbours telling the authorities that his flat appears to be empty and unoccupied. It's hard enough keeping the myth going of his mother still living there with her sparse visits, even though she makes the most of it when she does come, announcing her presence by clattering her high heels up and down the stairs and ringing on neighbours' doors to ask for a cup of sugar.

I've tried to forget about that terrible time after Mum fell, that morning when I fled from his flat and holed myself up in ours, not answering the door even, and spent the next fortnight saving Mum's life. Those dark days seem an age ago now. Daniel has never pressed me for more details about it either. I sense he has seen enough in his life to know to tread carefully when he has to, even though he too is *just* still in his teens. He's worked since he was fourteen, in backstreet garages at weekends or days bunked off school. He tells me he could never miss a day now, even if he was really ill. He saves everything he can to start his own business one day, he tells me. He understands my responsibilities in a way that many boys his age normally wouldn't, the ones at school who talk of college places and their football practice on Saturdays. The ones whose mums and dads bankroll their futures studying at distant universities and their present entertainments by buying them tickets to weekend festivals where they will take drugs and slosh around in mud. And the parents will close their minds to all that and tell themselves this is a phase that has to be gone through, that their offspring must have their fun.

On a weekday I might sit with Daniel on the balcony and we'll have a cigarette and he'll say, 'Night then, early start,' before kissing me on the cheek and disappearing downstairs. What other nineteen-year-old boy would understand the need for this? How Mum and I need our lives to carry on together separately because we know, despite how good it is right now, despite remission or whatever we choose to call it, that this time is limited. It won't go on forever.

Mum and I both receive crisp white envelopes on the same morning. She opens it with stiff fingers and I realise with a chill that her symptoms are returning. I've been noticing it for several days now, the glass sliding from the hand and breaking on the kitchen floor, the speech where the slightly thickened tongue is noticeable, the slowness. I've been closing my mind to it up until now and I realise this time has been all about waiting for them to return. The miracle, the walking on water, Phoebe's insane belief in wishes and predictions were all a beautiful glass bauble that captivated me for a time but that I always knew would shatter one day. The strange thing is, it's almost a relief now it has. Fake beliefs are exhausting.

Mum holds the letter to the light so she can read it properly.

'She's done it. Well, I'll be blowed.'

'What? What?' I ask, digging my thumb under the flap of the envelope and tearing it open any old how.

'That woman at the hospital, what's her name? The social worker?'

I scan my letter.

*We are pleased to inform you that due to your circumstances at the present time, Mrs Jennifer Healy has been considered a suitable candidate for a respite break. There is considerable competition for these charitable places so we would be grateful if you could let us know as soon as possible if she is available to attend. We have written to you, as the primary carer, but have also let your mother know by letter. We have found from experience that these respite breaks have a considerable beneficial effect on everyone involved and would urge you to consider the offer very seriously.*

It's like Miss Kinsella got them to put that last bit in just for me. I can almost hear her reading the words out over my shoulder.

I shake out the sheet of paper properly, as if I could loosen the words there and send them scattering to the floor, and with a dry tearing sound rip it completely in half. There's a brochure in the envelope too that I don't even bother taking out. Mum was looking at hers as I read the letter.

'There. That doesn't need to worry us again. It's a voluntary thing. They're trying to make out in the letter that it isn't but they can't, so you don't have to go.'

Mum sits completely still on her big flowered cushion that she likes when she's on one of the hard kitchen chairs. Her clear blue eyes look over the top of the letter.

'What?' I ask.

'Grace, it could be a good idea, you know. You could have a week alone with Daniel. Wouldn't that be a good thing?'

I pick up the bits of paper and jab my finger at them. 'Those dates. He won't be here anyway. I'll be on my own. Forget about it. It's not happening. We don't have to worry.'

I notice she has not put the letter aside; she has simply lowered it slightly and her steady gaze doesn't leave my face. An unexpected anxiety tingles at the back of my neck.

'Listen, Grace.' She finally puts down the letter and takes off her glasses and clicks them shut. 'I don't think we should miss this opportunity. Like they say, it might not come round again. They've obviously gone to a lot of trouble to try and organise this.'

'No.' I clasp my arms tight to my chest. 'It's not a good idea.'

'Who says?'

'I do. It'll be the start of more interference. They won't want to leave us alone after this, I guarantee.'

She sticks out her chin and her neck mottles red. 'What if I want to go?' I want her to stop. Strong emotion is not good for her condition. 'It's my decision too, not just yours. There's a lovely garden there, and they've got a hairdresser

274

that comes round to you. What chance do I have to be in a garden, stuck up here away from the bloody ground even? This was Dad's choice and I got lumbered with it. I would've lived out in the country like my mum did. I can't tell you how much I long to have the breeze on my face and see green grass and hear birds.'

'I'll take you to the park.' My voice chokes. 'We'll go tomorrow, I promise.'

'It's not enough. I want to do this. It will do us both the world of good.'

'No, don't leave me.' I startle both of us. 'I mean, what's the point? It's just another hospital, another institution.'

'Honestly, just calm yourself. It's a good thing—'

'I don't need respite, and we don't need respite from each other, we're fine,' I say, wiping the snot on my sleeve.

And I can tell it's out of her mouth before she had time to think. That she didn't mean to say it, but that's not the same as not meaning it. 'Maybe you don't,' she snaps. 'But I bloody well do.'

# 29

# Orla

I am ripening.

I really am. I wasn't sure before but every day a little more, a little more, like a pumpkin in a field. I do a test anyway but really I don't need to bother. The sickness, the missed period, the tender breasts, it's all so obvious it practically screams 'pregnant'. I can't believe it – how stupid I was to actually wish for this to happen. I even went back to Kai's house two days in a row to triple my chances before he got freaked out and told me he didn't want to see me any more. He sensed that something was up and it wasn't his unique charms I was after. What a shitty way for me to behave. It's like I was in some sort of trance. Well, I've woken up now and the reality of it is like having cold water chucked in my face.

As if to test it out, despite the sickness, and the tenderness, despite the bloody pregnancy test itself, my fingers seek out my belly under the covers at night, checking over and over, and I feel the indisputable swelling there. I look around my room and I'm grateful I never got round to dismantling it. I need all those childish things now. I'd live inside that sunflower if I could. The glittery lace is a remnant of a magical land I want to revisit and stay in forever. My days and nights are tortures of indecision and worry.

On the one hand I'm greedy for this little life. I love it already. At other times I'm washed with doom and shame.

How on earth could I even think of giving birth to this child, a child possibly conceived in a disgusting dirty pet cemetery with a sad-eyed boy in a leather coat and wearing mascara? It's so revolting I can't bear it.

Scenarios open up in my head like a succession of rooms. There's me swaddling a baby in a blanket and nuzzling its cheek, the skin as healthy as rubber. Dad's smiling at me, Mum's come round now and he's persuaded her to let him help me buy a flat. We're happy, just the two of us there. Then a door opens on another room. Phoebe's come to see me. I'm living with Mum and Dad. There's sick down my front and my bedroom stinks of nappies. She wrinkles up her elegant nose. She shoves her hands into the pockets of her man's raincoat and makes an excuse to leave. The baby starts crying and I'm alone with it, sobbing on the bed.

I shake my head as if this could loosen all the scenarios that constantly march through my head. I can't think clearly. Mum comes into my room with an armful of clean washing and sits next to me on the bed. I'm overtaken by her warm comforting presence and I'm so tempted to tell her. I'm on a knife-edge about it. She puts her arm around me and I breathe in the lovely familiar scent of her Elnett hairspray, the one she's been using ever since I can remember.

'What is it, honey pie?' she asks, using her childhood name for me.

I bury my head in her neck. 'Nothing, I mean just being a teenager probably,' I mumble.

'Come on.' She rubs my back. 'If it's about what happened before. Don't worry about it. I just take things far too seriously and get het up and anxious about everything when Dad's away. You're a lovely girl. You'll always be my lovely, lovely girl.'

I really, really want to cry then, but I won't because I know if I do it'll all come spilling out and they'll take over, Mum and Dad, thinking they are doing their best but nothing will be in my hands any more. They will decide the outcome and I will have no say. I am utterly on my own. I've never felt it so much before; I'm stumbling through the days and every minute stretches into an hour as I try and decide what to do.

# 30

# Phoebe

So the wheels have come off her Edinburgh trip.

I am the trouble. As always.

The problem does provoke a sort of hysterical glee in me despite the solace that a few days away from her would provide. The dress remains sheathed and hanging from her wardrobe door, haunting the house like a dark blue ghost.

Bertha speaks very loudly on the phone so I heard both sides of the conversation from where I was hiding outside the kitchen door. It did pass my mind how much time *she* and I spend listening to each other in this house. An unhealthy habit, but this conversation was proving so interesting not one I wanted to break at that moment. At the other end of the line Bertha sounded slightly agitated but determined to stay calm.

'Much as I like Phoebe . . .'

Does she? Does she?

'Much as I like Phoebe, those two nights just aren't convenient. Paddle . . .'

. . . her little pedigree dog.

'Paddle is to have a little op and he will need absolute rest and silence for a couple of days to recuperate.'

'What?' My mother was incredulous. 'It's just a bloody dog, Bertha.'

I stuffed my fingers in my mouth. Wrong thing to say! Wrong thing to say!

Bertha, however, remained unruffled. 'Maybe to you, dear. But I'm not going to budge on this. Phoebe is perfectly capable of being on her own for a couple of days. Big grown-up girl like her.'

'That's what *you* think.' I can tell by the sound of her voice that *her* mouth is set into a grim line. 'Really, I was rather relying on you.'

'You always do, Emma. I'm not quite sure why.'

There it was, that tone of dislike that I wondered about before. Clear as a bell this time.

'I would've thought it's been enriching for you, having Phoebe over the years. I mean, since you have no children of your own.'

A pang of fear penetrated my heart. Mum's tone was cool and light but I could discern only too well the underlying menace there. *She's about to wound*, I thought, *she's about to hurt*. I felt terrible for Bertha, with her huge teeth and her kindness, and who didn't deserve in any way what she was about to get.

'Yes, over the years, Emma. I've been happy to do it because I like the girl. I think she has a lot of potential, given the right circumstances.'

Potential!

'But honestly,' I could tell Bertha was getting heated now and she began talking even louder, 'I think you've traded on our rather slim college friendship a little too much. I have no children, it's true, and although some women are happy with that situation, of course you know that it's a source of regret that when I was married . . .'

She had a husband!?

'. . . and we were never able to have any children despite

trying fervently and for a long time. You know that but you don't neglect to mention it.'

'Oh, I can't say anything now, can I?' She's taken aback. She is not used to people pinning her down on her lightly delivered veiled barbs.

'It's not a question of not being able to say anything. It's a question of being deliberately hurtful when you don't get your own way, like just now. You've done it too many times. No, it's true. I don't have children of my own. But looking after yours whenever it's convenient for you isn't really a substitute for that.'

There was a silence, dense and pulsating in my ears.

'Never mind.' My mother was hissing between her teeth now. 'You'll always have *Paddle*.'

There was the sound of the phone crashing back into its cradle.

My longing to be alone is so overwhelming I feel crucified by it. I want to pull up my plait, wrap myself in a soft woollen blanket, drink warm creamy drinks and rest deeply. I need to knit myself back together. Too much has happened that needs unravelling slowly and in silence. Lucas becomes more like a wound in my side day by day.

However, *she* is determined I am not left to be.

'Can't you stay with Orla?'

'She has her family there, her grandparents. There's no room.'

I don't let on that we sleep curled up together in her three-quarter bed or in the truckle bed beneath. The thought of being there among the throng of her family is almost unbearable. Besides, I can't imagine her mother would want yet another one at the dinner table.

'What about the other one? What's her name? Grace.'

'Grace's mother is very, very *poorly*. I told you that.'

'Oh yes.' She chews her lip.

'Orla could stay here,' I venture.

'Mmmm.'

I can see her thinking about it. Looking at the idea and not liking it.

Finally she says, 'Is that it? Don't you have any other friends?'

There's a sound of music from the street, tinkling through the open window, floating in on the warmth of the day. There's voices, a man and children getting out of the car. That's where the music's coming from, from inside the car. A child's tune to keep them from whining on a journey. The words of the song mention a mouse, then bedtime. I close my eyes and think about Lucas, fantasise it's him arriving outside my front door. I try to forget about the sound of his leather soles sliding on stones as he made his escape. I try to remember his blue eyes, his strong shoulders and his warm loving masculine presence. If it truly was him outside, I'd lean out right now. I'd let down my hair and let him climb up it.

# 31
# Orla

I wait until Mum and Dad are out of the house and look the number up in the Yellow Pages. I sit looking at the phone for a long time and when it rings it's like an electric shock. I cry out and clasp my hands to my heart. I pick it up cautiously as if it's intercepted my thoughts and is about to recount them to me.

'Why aren't you answering your mobile?' Phoebe's voice sounds breathy at the other end.

'Oh, it's you.'

'Who did you want it to be and why aren't you answering your mobile?'

I'm aware I'm not sounding puppy-dog bright at the sound of her voice – my usual response.

'You can talk! You never answer yours.'

She's silent for a moment. 'There's something the matter.'

Phoebe is the last, the *very* last person I would confide in. She'd probably suggest keeping the baby locked up and secret in the garden shed or something.

'I'm fine. Absolutely fine. What d'you want?'

'Listen, will you come and stay the week after next? You'd be doing me a big favour. She won't let me be on my own. I'd prefer to be, of course . . .'

'Thanks.'

'No, don't be like that. You know how I mean. It's like I'm not safe to be on my own or something. It's ridiculous.

I'm nearly eighteen. Say you will, please.'

'All right.' I want to get rid of her quickly now. She's so curious. She'll prod and pry further and further like a sharp worm until she's found the core where the growing life inside me is tucked like a pip.

When she's gone I sit looking at the phone again. My heart is so heavy it hurts. Almost like it doesn't belong to me, I see my arm and the sleeve of my red jumper reaching out to pick it up. Something worries at my consciousness; the way she sounded, wasn't right either but it's just a tiny gnat of a thought that zooms away as soon as it's arrived. I put all my efforts into dialling the number and each time I press a single button it seems to take all my will and energy.

Later, it's at the point of no return that I remember again what I wished for that day in the Spinney. Already, I can feel the tugging inside as if there's puppet strings inside my womb that are being pulled. I remember it clearly: my prediction that day flashes through me just as the very thing I wished for is being scraped out of my body.

# 32

# Phoebe

I am quite collapsed by everything.

Things have grown worse since I saw the vision of doom in the Roman Baths that day. It has bubbled into my being and now it follows me everywhere and I cannot shake off its sinister presence.

Symptoms abound.

Try as I might to pinch them out or keep them hidden, they heap up and grow. I have to sit on my hands when thoughts of cutting come in. Now I'm completely convinced I caused that man to be crushed that day, his blood and insides spread over the front bumper and the wall. It obsesses me. I turn the idea away only for it to return, multiplied in strength by ten, twenty, fifty, to haunt me again. The blood runs down the walls in streamers every night.

*Her* power increases.

The house is once more turned into a hidden arsenal. Knives aligned, scissors pointing; even the hammers in the shed have been placed with care to protect me.

In despair I turn to the witches. It gives me a glimmer, a little bit of strength to carry on. It's so strange, both my downfall and my redemption coming from the same source, the same bloody and dreadful story. I get armfuls of books from the library. The woman there is intrigued by my witch quest and helps me off her own bat, tracking things down for me by interlibrary loan. I don't even have to ask any more: there is a new pile of books when I return the old ones. I fall on them and read furiously. It's the one obsession that doesn't feel like pain; all the others hold me to dreadful account. The witches lift me up and urge me to keep going. They say there is an unseen power that I can tap into and that will make me stronger. They say they have my back.

I find out more. There is both good and evil in them. Venefica. Poisoner. Some are cannibals and cook heads. They silently converse with the dead. Yes, fiends who gobble anything, any root or poison that they think might give them power.

They can heal too, though. Plant people. Cunning folk. Hedgewitch. They make love potions that when ingested make the victim giddy and swooning. At night they venture out to gather the herbs they have planted secretly in remote places. To have such suspicious plants growing in the garden would attract attention. Result in arrest.

They are the definition of unnatural as far as women are supposed to be. Toads are nursed in laps instead of children. After ingesting certain herbs they will fall upon any man they see and tear him to pieces.

Then there's the Book of Shadows.

At first, each coven just had one book each to share around.

Now every witch has their own personal Book of Shadows, their grimoire, that must be destroyed upon their death. Intentions. Recipes. Incantations. A cookbook of magic, of the cunning craft. Formulas for the flying ointment they make to rub on their bodies so they can attend their sabbat, their gathering.

I think of my diary, each entry a shadow form of my real intention and only I can interpret what I actually meant. It is my upside-down book, everything a reflection of the truth, my true meaning written in the invisible ink of thought.

Flying ointment. Paul's pieces of paper come with a rosy print of luscious lips this time, each miniature pair pursed in the centre. I remember the wishing bowl and the jelly lips emerging from the rubble of the bowl, ruby red, swollen and dissolving and flecked with grains of soil, and I feel that everything is aligning. It's dangerous to do this but I arrange things in my room, ready for Grace and Orla coming to stay. I can't wait. I'm too excited. It seems a miracle that this has been arranged but it all came together – Mum not finding anyone to have me although I had to lie about Grace. Her mum's not there; she's on some sort of holiday but I didn't let on about that. If she'd known that she would have tried to shovel me off to stay there, which would have been horrible as Grace would never invite me of her own accord. She always dives straight off at the end of the day like she wants to keep everything at home to herself.

I nearly hit the roof when I hear a movement outside and I peep round the door. It's *her*. She's pausing on the landing near my door. I slide out of my room, hoping she won't notice the subterfuge of me pulling the door too nonchalantly behind me.

'Aren't they here yet?' she asks impatiently. 'The car is loaded up. We're ready to go.'

I check my watch. 'They're not due for half an hour.'

We wait silently at the breakfast bar, perched on high stools. She won't countenance going before she's had sight of them. She keeps pulling back her sleeve to check her watch with an exaggerated flick of her elbow.

This is the first time I've ever had friends over to stay the night and my nervousness is showing.

'What's the matter with you?' she asks. 'Stop tapping your foot like that. It's irritating.'

Finally, the doorbell rings and I hop off my stool and run down the hallway. I stop, take a moment before I answer it. Bite on my fingers. Compose my face. Try to calm my breathing down. I unlatch the heavy front door and swing it open.

'You're here, you're here.' I hop up and down.

They are both standing on the doorstep. Grace has a backpack and Orla, a flowered holdall with her night things. The light behind them cuts into my eyes. Grace has her hands buried deep in her jeans pockets. She's been buzz-cutting her hair again so the bone almost shows through. She's got wristbands and plaited thread wreathed around her wrists. Orla's dark smudges under her eyes have grown deeper so they are almost dints in her skin.

'You're here,' I say again, and flap my arms about a bit because nothing seems to be happening.

'Yeah,' says Grace at last and she swings her backpack off and puts it down. 'We are.'

Mum's voice comes from the darkness of the hallway. 'Well, don't just leave them standing around there. Invite them in.'

Orla automatically steps over the threshold and Grace squints in the darkness and hesitates, then follows after.

'Quick, take off your shoes and come upstairs,' I whisper.

As if understanding the need to move fast, Grace shucks off her trainers and starts up the stairs behind me, but we don't make it.

'Come back down,' Mum says, and we do, although I can see how reluctant Grace is as she moves at about half the speed she went on the way up.

Orla is peering into the darkness of the hallway. They both stand with their bags at their feet, looking awkward and sullen, as if this is the last place they want to be in the whole world. This is not how I imagined it at all. Mum approaches and my hands start tingling with the nervousness. I almost feel like telling them to go away again. All at once I don't want them here.

'I'll be off shortly.' She examines them suspiciously. 'I do hope you're going to behave yourselves while I'm away.' Her lips stretch tight across her teeth. 'I'm not going to stand for any nonsense – drinking or anything. I'll know if you have. And I've told Phoebe absolutely no going out.'

Grace opens her mouth to say something, then closes it again. I had the feeling that she was about to say she didn't want to be there anyway and she was buggering off. I want to cry I'm so embarrassed. It's hard to push Mum away when I'm seeing her through other people's eyes. That's partly why I hardly ever have anyone back here. It's too stressful. I can't maintain the story to myself that everything's all right. Seen through other people's eyes, that story starts unravelling dangerously as soon as *she* hisses at me, or calls me an idiot or simply watches us, unsmiling and with pursed lips as we creep past her. I became used to girls making excuses to leave early a long time ago and it was easier to stop asking them. I'm beginning to feel like this was a dreadfully wrong thing to do. Them being here is breaking a skin that is delicate and impossible to rupture without terrible consequences. They haven't got a clue how difficult it is or what it is they need to do. We all need to be as light as insect pond skaters so the surface doesn't break.

After she's burned them with her gaze for a few moments, she sighs. 'All right, well, Peter's waiting in the car. Give me a kiss, Phoebe.'

I start. 'What?'

'Give your mother a kiss before she goes. What's the matter? We're going all the way to Scotland – don't you want to say goodbye properly?'

What's she up to? What's she up to? She never kisses or touches me, only The Beloved. Everyone is looking at me and I have a horrible crawling sensation over my skin because I realise I am actually expected to go up and kiss her. She has her arms open and ready.

I take baby steps towards her and as I get closer I see the familiar tiny changes on her face. It's the start, the very first sign of the rage. Grace and Orla won't see it, they won't know what it is, but I do, even though right now it's barely a tightening of the cheekbones, a slight narrowing of the eyes, the forehead paling by a single shade. Sometimes it can be made to go away at this early stage, by soothing. Other times it's unstoppable. I wonder what's caused it now. I glance over my shoulder to Orla and Grace and I know in a flash. It's them standing there, Grace chewing gum, arms crossed, watching us curiously, and Orla looking as if she wants to be a million miles away. They are too other, they are not subjects in this kingdom and they don't understand it or know its rules. They are interlopers and she resents them being here, being in her space, breathing her air while she won't be here to regulate everything. I need things to go well so much I lurch into my mother's arms and hug her. The unfamiliar touch of her, the softness of her Liberty print blouse, the close-up smell of mimosa perfume that she has now restocked, causes a physical sickness in me and the moment seems to go on forever. I feel huge and awkward in her arms. I feel as delicate as a tiny white flower that is about to be crushed. I feel lank and poisoned and as if she's the only thing that's holding me up. I cycle through all these things.

Finally, she takes me firmly by the shoulders and holds me away from her. She takes my face in her hands and her fingers press hard in there, hurting me. I stay silent; I don't whimper or anything because I don't want to let on to the others what's happening.

'Good girl,' she says, looking me right in the eyes, and the unfamiliar closeness of them makes my own widen. 'You behave now, Phoebe.'

She puts me aside and picks up her bag. 'We don't allow shoes upstairs,' she says as she passes Orla, who immediately bends down to remove them, the product of an ultra-polite home, where she's been taught nice manners for so long and with such persistence they are tattooed onto her heart. The no-shoes rule doesn't apply to *her*. *She* struts around this house in shoes to her heart's content. It's funny how it makes everyone else seem softer and more vulnerable than her. Even The Beloved has brought that up. 'They're my high heels,' she was told, 'they always need wearing in.' Nobody else in the house has high heels – except for a party pair owned by The Beloved – so it seemed to fit, though *she* being the only wearer of them seems to add to her special status somehow. It's probably just as well: there's nothing quite like the sight of a yellowing middle-aged toenail poking through a hole in tights to get your guts churning.

The door clicks shut and Grace stands there with her hand on her rucksack. 'Christ,' she says, looking at the door. 'What was all that about?'

'Nothing.' I want to dispel the sharp crackle in the air, to make it disappear in a puff of wind. 'Nothing. What? I mean, bring your things up. Come and see my room,' I mumble, and Grace slowly, very slowly like she's making a big mistake, lifts her rucksack and holds it in front of her like it's a baby and puts her socked foot back on the stair. I see that she's wearing mismatched socks. I see how old and worn her rucksack is.

When I open the door to my room it surprises me. I'm seeing it like them and I see how devoid of personality it is, how I've managed to drain out of it anything of myself. It's so plain. Grace glances down at what I've arranged on the floor.

'Jesus, Phoebe,' she says. 'What the fuck's that all about?'

# 33

# Grace

I've got to be honest; my first instinct was to run.

The house was like an absolute fucking cathedral. I looked up, astounded. The staircase alone was monumental. Above me, it double backed onto itself. The carpet was a dramatic slash of red through the heart of the house. A heavy brass light fitting hung in the hall space and reflected the light from the windows on its golden surfaces. Through the open door to my right there was some kind of study and in there a dark wooden cabinet with glass doors that was a sort of treasure house. I've never seen such astonishing objects inside a house. It was more like a museum. I wanted to get close to that glass dome and look at the flowers inside; I wanted to cup the glass bubble in my hand, run my finger over the complicated spiky brass instrument and send the globe spinning. I have never set foot in a home like this and that's partly what drew me up the stairs – the sheer curiosity of seeing the rest of it.

It was only then, with my socked foot on that silk-like carpet, that it occurred to me how strange it was that I'd never been here before. I hesitated. I had a bad feeling. I drew back.

It's warm in here. It's beautifully clean and shined up so why did I have that sense of cold rottenness? It was underlying, like it came from the ground. I was confused. I realised when I met Phoebe's mother, though. I could see at once where it came from. I've never taken any notice when Phoebe complained about her. Stop whining, I thought, at least you've got one that's healthy, that's not short of a few quid. But as soon as I met her mother I felt the hackles rise on my neck, one by single one. *I'm not yours*, I thought, *stop trying to make me*. That's when I really considered taking off. I could easily have stuffed my shoes back on, come up with an excuse and darted away before any of them had time to think. Later, I asked Orla about it. She said she knew what I meant and that's how she felt when she first came here – although she's only been twice and a long time ago – but somehow the effect wears off a bit after a while. Is that how it works? I wondered. You just get used to shit so it becomes normal. I could see her mother hurting Phoebe's face with her hands and afterwards there were red fingermarks around Phoebe's eyes. I didn't go, though. I was tired and it seemed easier to stay, the effort of escape taking energy. Besides, Phoebe's mum would be gone soon and then I'd get to see the rest of the house.

Phoebe took us into her room like an excited child who's having a birthday party.

'What the fuck?' I asked as she opened the door and beckoned us inside. 'I mean, what the fuck?'

'Don't you remember?' she said. 'Don't you remember at the wishing bowl? We had a dolls' tea set sometimes. This is the very one.'

'Phoebe, that's really, really weird.'

She'd laid out the little rose-sprigged cups and saucers along with the teapot and sugar bowl on a white tablecloth on the floor.

'Really? What d'you mean, it looks weird in a good way?' She scrunched up her eyes.

'No. I mean it's a really weird thing to do. What's all the greenery for?' There were piles of berries in formations across the snow white of the tablecloth, like they were tracing the constellations of the sky. There were bunches of leaves in a jug and wilting flower heads.

'Henbane, deadly nightshade, witch's berry, monkshood – well, various noxious herbs and plants. I admit I've had to compromise and make substitutions.'

'No kidding. That one looks like coriander.'

I looked over to Orla and to my surprise she was nodding at Phoebe, like she knew what it all meant. 'Is this what you were talking about, having a witch's sabbath?'

Phoebe smiled back at her like, *At last somebody gets it.*

'So are some of these actually poisonous plants?' I asked. 'Is that really a good idea?'

Phoebe pursed her lips at me as you would at a child. God, she really was irritating me now. 'No. It's supposed to be *representative*,' she said slowly, speaking as if to a child. 'This is the real flying ointment.' She picked up one of the tiny cups and waved it at me.

'What?'

'Look inside.'

At the bottom was a tab of acid with a pair of red lips stamped on it.

'Why didn't you just say? Why go to all this trouble?' It made me uncomfortable, all this manic mess, this house, her.

She shrugged. 'I felt like it,' she said tersely. 'Think of it like an art installation. Let's go and get something to eat.'

Now in the kitchen she gets nervous again and she reminds me of a nine-year-old having a birthday party and who has become so fractious and overexcited that all the other children pine to leave. I long for Daniel, for the feel of his arms around me. I miss him. I miss Mum too. When I spoke to her on the phone for the first time she sounded a little uncertain, disoriented, then by the next day she'd relaxed; she'd been out in the garden and had tea on the patio with wasps buzzing around the jam. The hairdresser was coming later. It was the wasps that had really delighted her. She'd forgotten, she said, how they did that. How they clustered around sweetness. It was a forgotten thing from when life was normal.

Phoebe takes pizzas out of the freezer. 'Look. I persuaded Mum to buy us some of these. Ice cream too. And this,' she pulls out a bottle of vodka, cloudy with cold, 'is what I hid earlier.'

Christ. LSD and cookie-dough ice cream. Dolls' tea sets and alcohol. This really is fucked up. Her tension is giving me a headache. I have no idea how she affords all the drugs and alcohol – she's always complaining her parents never give her any money. She hasn't got a weekend job.

'But your mum says we mustn't drink or anything. That she'll find out if we do,' says Orla.

'Huh,' says Phoebe, sloshing some vodka smoking with the cold into a tumbler, 'you're not afraid of *her*, are you?' Her face tightens up and she looks suddenly old, like a wrinkly plum, then it relaxes again and goes smooth. 'Besides, I am the most brilliant housekeeper. It's the attention to detail that counts. You have to get rid of every molecule so there's not even a smell left behind, not even a hint of a smell.

Look.' She brandishes the pizzas, stiff discs of frozen dough still in their plastic. 'Do you want pesto and rosemary or mushroom and black pepper?'

They're the fancy kind of pizzas with bits of sundried tomato stuck on them. I can imagine her standing in the supermarket in the freezer aisle, wheedling her mum into buying them and her conceding like she's giving her daughter gold.

My mum would give me absolutely anything. She'd give me the teeth out of her head if she thought I could make use of them. God, I miss her. I'm so lucky. I'm just so bloody lucky. How awful would it be to have been dealt a rank bitch like Phoebe's mum? Mum and me may have our problems but love has always oozed out of every pore of her body, even when she's been at her very worst. It's entered my skin and I feel it inside of me, around my heart, in my stomach, like it's a life-giving chemical that pumps through my veins. So I let Phoebe pour me some more vodka. I take a slice of the pizza dripping with runny cheese. Later, I guess we'll take the acid and that will fill the evening up and before I know it it'll be morning. I'll put up with this for a night because I know the people who I love most, the ones I'd kill or die for, the ones on whose behalf I'd battle demons, will be back with me in such a short while that this turns everything else into nonsense that can be endured; it's just time to kill.

# 34

# Orla

Phoebe is like a mirage tonight. I have the sense of her fragmenting, falling apart and then re-forming into a myriad different shapes. She's like a chimera. I get used to one form and then she falls apart like snowflakes.

The vodka burns on the way down my throat into my stomach and it begins to make everything clear for the very first time. It's like I'm seeing things through the prism of its ice-cold fluid and it shows me the truth like a crystal ball would.

And the truth is – while I was battling about what to do about the baby, Phoebe was off seeing that fucking teacher, getting manipulated by him like some stupid little kid. She wouldn't have even cared if I'd told her about the baby, about everything. She doesn't care about me. It would've been an inconvenience, another creature that might have the gall to take precedence over her.

Phoebe puts the radio on and starts dancing.

I could've been loved a million times more by my own flesh and blood – a true love – than this girl who whirls about me now with her long hands pulling nervously on her clothes, her eyes lit up and giddy.

'Come on,' she says. 'Let's all dance. Let's party.'

Grace snorts and peels off another slice of pizza that's started to congeal on the breadboard. She doesn't make a move to join Phoebe and neither do I. It's pathetic and embarrassing. It's like this is the most exciting thing that's ever happened to Phoebe, us being here and having our horrible girls' night. Outside, the summer night is still warm and light. *It feels absolutely interminable*, I think, as I watch her dance, twisting her hips this way and that, her hair flinging over each shoulder as she flips her head, *like it's truly never going to end.*

'Don't you love me any more?' she asks me over her shoulder. My reply is silence and tipping another measure of vodka down my throat. Have I wounded her? I can't see. She's turned her face away from me, looking at the wall as she dances. I hope I have. I want to see her face hollowed out and pinched with hurt. She turns, looks over her shoulder again with the question still in her eyes.

'Not really. Not now.' I don't want to sound bitter but I know I do. 'Not since you started seeing that teacher, having your little fling.'

'What?' Grace's ears have pricked up. 'What teacher? What have you been up to, Phoebe?'

She stops moving and the radio tinkles on in the background. 'Nothing. Don't listen to her.'

'It's that English teacher,' I say. 'You know, the one with a wife and *two* children.'

'What, that creepy Swedish guy?'

I nod.

Phoebe is looking bright with tension. 'Shut up,' she says. 'It's nobody's business. That was supposed to be a secret, Orla.'

'Wow.' Grace downs another shot of vodka and clasps her chest as it goes down. 'Did you fuck him?'

Phoebe appears to go stiff for a moment. 'Yes,' she says

quietly. 'I did and it was wonderful.' She's looking at me, trying to rile me up.

'So you lied then. You think I care? I just think it's sordid and sad. His family would be devastated if they knew. You can't go around doing stuff like that. You've let yourself be used . . . Horrible old guy covered with chalk dust who carries a stupid briefcase like it's the nineteen-seventies. Grim,' I say, and I refill mine and Grace's glasses and we chink them together and then drink.

Phoebe grinds her hands together, then shrugs. 'Whatever you say. It was actually extremely romantic, but what would you know? Come on, let's go upstairs.'

She bounds off, leaving us.

'For God's sake,' Grace mutters, but all the same she stands up unsteadily and follows after, knocking over Phoebe's glass on the way without realising. Vodka crawls thickly across the table top, dribbling into the gaps between the planks of timber. Phoebe's mother would go crazy if she saw it gathering up crumbs as it spreads across the beautiful golden grain of the wood, probably leaving its track marks etched into the wax. I stand up too, without even attempting to clear it up. Phoebe can deal with it. It's her house.

Phoebe is waiting impatiently on the stairs. Bang! I can see she's changed again. She folds her arms along the banister and rests her pointed chin on the backs of her hands, staring down at us, catlike now.

'Come on. Time for the rest of the night now. Time to fly.' She turns and starts up the stairs and I see her differently again. From behind she is a tiny figure in her oversized blue fisherman's jumper, her red skirt gathering around the backs of her knees. She's like a thin, lonely princess rattling around in her vast palace full of echoes, with doors that are barred and chained. I get the sense she'll never escape this place. That she's doomed to stay the same forever.

Grace stumbles on the step on her way up.

'Wait,' she calls up. 'I don't remember the way. I don't want to be on my own here.'

I know what she means. It makes me scurry after them. When I get to Phoebe's room, the breath stinging in my chest from the effort, she's already cross-legged on the floor next to the tablecloth, her knees pointing sharply outwards and her ankles crossed neatly over each other. She reminds me of a chipmunk now, chattering and giggling in secret behind her hands, and my hate ratchets up another notch. Grace goes to sit but her foot whooshes away under her body and she ends up on her back with her knees up to her chest on the perfectly sanded and varnished floorboards, laughing lopsidedly at the ceiling.

It's been years since I've been here and I take a moment to look about. The walls of Phoebe's room are painted plain cream. There's not a single poster of a band with curling corners on the walls or even one of the more sugary Victorian artworks anywhere. The open door of the wardrobe shows clothes hanging with great gaps between them. I think of my own stuffed wardrobe at home, clothes belching out of it so that they pool on the floor below; the plenty of it all. Where's all the girlhood glitter here? The mess of feathers and scarves and adolescence? On the windowsill is a bottle of bath stuff and underneath an exercise book with orange covers, the kind we used as kids in primary school. The arrangement strikes me as sparse and altar-like.

Grace is still on her back. 'This is such *fun*, Phoebe,' she says. 'Who'd have thought it, that we could have such a *fun* wild time at yours.'

Phoebe's hands fly to around her eyes; she's not laughing any more and part of me can't bear the dimple of pain that appears at the corner of her mouth that she tries to iron out straight away, because Grace's mockery might be loose and drunken – not something she'd say sober – but it's still plainly there. Phoebe hunkers down in herself and the coiled knitting of her collar comes up over her chin so it looks like a blue snake circling.

That brief dimple causes an unexpected correlating hole in my heart. *I've missed her so much*, I think, despite myself, my puppy-dog familiar self bounding out of the toughness I felt downstairs. I hope desperately that this is a mere glow of the embers before the fire goes out. I need to expunge it straight away. I pick up my own little dainty rose-sprigged cup of poison and peer inside, fish the tab out and put it on my tongue.

Grace jackknifes up to sitting and picks up a teacup, licks her index finger, then dabbles with her finger inside until the tab sticks to its tip. Phoebe's head bobs out of the coil and her long hands splay into forks each side of her as she whoops encouragement. 'Go on, do it,' Phoebe caws as Grace sticks her finger into her mouth and sucks the tab in. Then Grace rolls onto her back again and lifts her behind so she can extract the pouch of tobacco from her back pocket. She throws it, twisted and moulded from her body heat, in among the leaves that are wilting in their jug, their tips touching the ground.

'Why not?' asks Grace, slurring. 'We're all off the leash tonight.'

'We'll have to stick our heads out of the window.'

Phoebe's voice has a high taint of anxiety. 'And we'll have to lean really, really far out. That stuff stinks for days. It gets into everything.'

'Don't worry.' Grace lunges for the green and gold plastic pouch. I've never seen her like this, so off guard. 'You're a brilliant housekeeper. Remember?'

'Don't you love me any more?' Phoebe asks again quickly, saying it so lightly I hardly hear and glancing over the tangle between us. It's beginning to worry her, beginning to sink in something's amiss now; her giddy nervousness is changing. She needs to reel me back in and know I'm secure, my teeth biting firmly on the same pointed hook that's going to kill me in a slow and painful death.

I shrug, relishing the idea that I'm capable of giving her pain. Something tilts in my brain. I don't know what it is, the acid, the vodka or seeing her like this, so trapped and needy. Then she flips again. She's a scorpion. She'd do any-thing to protect herself. She has no feelings for anyone else, not even that teacher.

I did it for her, I realise. I went to that clinic and I got rid of that baby, and it was all for her because I thought she wouldn't want me any more if I had it. I nurse the thought and it begins to bloom and grow so there isn't room for anything else. Knowing this gets stronger and stronger the more I drink. How did I not see all this before?

I gave you my baby, I see it now. I took it out of me because I imagined it would disgust you – me becoming a mother and baby like that. I thought it would stop you wanting me. But you don't want me anyway, not really, and I could've had something that I loved more than all the world and that loved me. I'm overwhelmed with longing

303

for my wishing bowl desire that arrived as that scrap, that flesh that was my flesh too. I'm hopeless with the unbearable ache for it.

The acid seems to kick in to yet another level. Everything goes a little slant. Phoebe's teeth grow sharper in her mouth.

Grace's hands are deft at rolling the joint, despite her slurred speech. She proffers a perfectly rolled joint at us. 'There,' she says. 'Don't ever tell me I don't have artistic talents.'

Quickly, as if acting on a stray impulse, Phoebe strips off the fisherman's jumper, leans over to pluck the joint from Grace's fingers and sticks it in her mouth.

'For God's sake, Phoebe. Put your clothes back on.' My cheeks are burning. What's she up to? She knows she's lost the advantage. She began sensing it downstairs, that my love is fraying and becoming undone. This is a demonstration of her power – the fan of ribs like two open wings either side of her, her neat white breasts in the white bra. I'm supposed to quake before it.

'It's hot,' she says.

'Put your fucking jumper back on,' I say. Christ, this place with its eternal summer evening outside. I'm hating it more and more by the minute.

She grimaces at me so the joint sticks up in the air and she quickly palms the lighter from where it lies in a fold of cloth.

'I'm warning you . . .'

What am I warning her? She springs up, trailing her jumper after her, and makes for the door. And at that very moment I realise, the stripping off, the diversion, the grabbing of the joint was nothing to do with me. It was so Grace couldn't get to light it in the bedroom and leave the accusing smell to seep into the curtains. It was *this* that was troubling her more than anything. She couldn't forget about it.

The tiny cup is still in my hand. I want to shatter. I want to destroy. I try to prise it apart with my hands but it seems unbreakable, like some little potent haunting object of a dream that can never be made to go away and that appears over many nights and in a hundred different scenarios. I bear down on it with both thumbs straining on either side but it stays stubbornly intact.

'What you doing?' One of Grace's eyes is half closed.

I fling the cup down and it bounces. 'Nothing. I want to break this cup.'

'Stamp on it,' she says, nodding.

The pain goes through the arch of my foot when I jump on it. I want to scream out loud. Ignoring the pain that leaps up my calf now, I use my heel over and over until finally there is a crack and the cup lies there in three pieces.

Grace scoots over on her hands and knees. 'Fuck, you've left a right dint in these floorboards. Mama's not going to be a happy bunny. She's going to go mental.' She laughs suddenly at the idea, her eyes springing wide open.

I need to get out. I need to breathe normal air. This house is suffocating me. I limp out of the bedroom. It's dark on the landing outside. It feels like there are spiders' webs above me, just out of reach, and they're growing down and threaten any minute to grow all over and engulf me. I shudder and try to get a grip. The rosy lips on the tab have opened but inside there seems only a black maw waiting. I wonder if it's the same for Grace. I need to change that, to change the track of this trip before it's too late. I startle.

There's a cough in the darkness. The light slits through a crack in the door of the next bedroom down the corridor. In it is a scrim of luminous skin.

I reach for the wall. 'Who is it? Who is it?'

A delicate cough again. Phoebe steps forward. Her bare shoulders shine. 'Is it true?' she whispers. 'Is it really true you don't love me any more?'

The joint is slack in her fingers. In her other hand the jumper still trails to the floor. Her eyes are dark hollows. Her hair pools on her neck either side. 'Because,' she goes on, 'I don't think I could bear it if that was true.'

I pull my lips back. They're sticking so gummily to my teeth I have to tear them away. My tongue is heavy.

'It's more than that.' I'd like to smash her delicate white bones up like I did the teacup. 'I hate you.' My words fill up the dark space like hot gas. 'I really, really hate you. You are . . .' I search for the word I want to use, '. . . abhorrent to me.'

She crumples in front of me.

'What?'

'I said I hate you, Phoebe.'

I hear a stifled sob in the darkness, then a scuffle and the place where she once stood is a pulsing cavern of darkness. Something pierces my heart. What have I done? What have I done? Remorse strikes through me. She didn't know, I tell myself. She didn't even know about the baby. Why are you blaming her? And there she was not just a minute ago standing in front of you, white and shimmering. 'Phoebe,' I call, using my fingers to feel along the corridor. 'Come back. I didn't mean it. I'm sorry.'

I'm tumbled into this new old feeling, of loving her, and

it's pain and it's relief too – because it's so familiar. I've not escaped from it. I've bumped around full circle and it's still there. It is her I love. I would give anything for her. I gave her my baby and I wanted to. I'm a ball on a board that's been careering around but I've fallen back into the hollow meant for me; struggle as much as I like, I'll never be able to pop out of it.

So I carry on inching and inching down this corridor that feels eternal. At the end of it are a few bands of light but they are curved and it's impossible to make out where it might be coming from. I cry out to myself but no one hears. I cry, 'Mum,' and 'Dad,' as if they could hear, and swoop in and rescue me from this never-ending place. Under my fingers the wall takes on the texture of jelly and I cry out again and recoil and run, stumbling towards the bands of light, knocking into a wall and swinging round it to find myself blinking, whimpering, my eyes stinging in the brightness, and I run – down endless stairs, following Phoebe, until I'm at the top of the very last bit that leads to the ground floor.

Golden dust motes fall in a shower in the shaft of light from the window. The staircase is a red puzzle above and below. I have the sensation of the step as if I'm standing on a swing so I sit down abruptly. Downstairs there's a murmuring voice. I peer between the dark wood of the banister and see the top of her head from above. She's put her jumper back on and she paces back and forth, talking quietly into her phone. I steal a little further down to see if I can hear. By now I'm close enough to hear a word or two. 'Unbearable.' 'Never before.' 'Urgent.' 'The place where no one goes.' At one point she yells down the phone, 'It's too late for that.'

Phoebe has told me more than once that her mother spies on her. That she suspects her of coming into her room at night to look at her sleeping. That she takes things away and without asking. That she examines in detail the dirty clothes Phoebe leaves in the washing basket, and when Phoebe tries to do her own laundry will point-blank refuse to let her. That Phoebe, in turn, listens to her mother, her sister, her father talking on the phone or mumbling to himself as he makes a sandwich. I didn't take much notice, if truth be told, but now, being here, I know she wasn't lying. This is a house of spies. Everybody spies on everybody. There are so many mirrors, so many hidden corners and polished surfaces. Conversations are monitored. I'm doing it myself now. I can sense how it's normal here – it's like they've grown into each other to form one big interweaving web. That even your thoughts wouldn't be your own. That being captured by the mirror is enough to make you shudder because the image in there would get stuck, waiting to be retrieved and then interrogated at any moment.

Phoebe stops, glances upwards as if she's sensed someone there, and I draw back. She hesitates, then carries on pacing and talking. I strain to listen even as I hear Grace's footsteps coming down the landing behind me.

'Meet me now,' Phoebe says downstairs. 'I can't bear it if you don't. If you don't meet me now I'll have to come over to your house and hammer on your fucking front door until you let me in.'

# 35

# Phoebe

My heart is knifed.

Can I keep up the pretence that he still passionately wants me? I want to convince myself so much that someone still does I had to speak to him. He sounded so, so cold on the phone. He sounded like my call was the very last thing he wanted. 'Phoebe, what we did was wrong,' he kept saying – 'I realise that now.' 'It's too late for that,' I shouted and he went quiet.

Oh, but I can't bear it. Three times I asked Orla and three times she said no, once by a mere shrug of her shoulders. She is the mother and the sister and the husband and the wife to me, and if I don't have love then I am marooned on an icy rock where nothing grows or will ever grow. Thank God I didn't take my tab like the others did. I'm bleeding out, just like that man against the wall. The pain is unbearable. I will tear at anybody or anything to make it go away. I am completely and utterly unloved. I don't even possess a beetle's soul, just a piece of slime – something that people want to wipe away.

I think of the bloody story. How Macbeth thinks of death, of killing, and just the image of it suffices for a time. For a while he doesn't need to do the act anywhere except for in his brain, because he can go and look at it there safely any time he wants; and the sight of it in his head makes the electricity he craves, the want and the wish and the desire go through him again and again. I understand. That's how I feel. If I think of the knife being just next to Lucas, in his radius by ten metres, it makes me feel *so much better*. It is the same relief I feel when I used to do the other thing with the knife that I don't like to think about.

The idea of having a knife close by without him even knowing plunges through me in a shock and wakes me up from this lank and dreadful state. The pointed carving knife is too sharp to hide in my pocket – it would slice right through. I take it out of the drawer. The curve of it has a deathly menace. In this house it's used for carving, boning, forcing deep into the flesh and twisting there. It's been here for as long as I remember, and each and every time I've glimpsed that menace it's caused me to shudder, even at the age of five, so now, it seems the most fitting and best thing to take, like it's been waiting for its purpose all along. He will not see it. He will not know it's there. Only I will know that, how close it's got to him, and when he leaves, when I see his figure moving off away across the fields, only I will know that there was another scenario already played out in my mind, one where I've torn out my anger and fear on him, one where he is left ripped and bloody, his insides hanging out in ribbons. And knowing that will cause electricity to stir about me. It will make my hair stand straight up with static and the power of it will gather inside my belly. It will keep me going for days. It will show me how I'm in control, of my thoughts and everything, and if I order it all correctly they can work for me rather than against. I take one of my mother's snowy tea towels – bleached then boiled for an hour on the stove's top until a season of mist and rain fogs the windows – and I wrap it round and round the shining blade, and with precise care insert the package in the pocket of my mac.

I take a moment, and into this, into the silence of the house, there's a sudden and terrible shattering noise from the other room. The sound goes through me like a scream, like pain does. It makes me gasp then stop breathing. I find for a moment I cannot move. Then, floating almost, the breath only in my throat now and in small gasps, I move towards it.

'No, no, no, no.' My voice sounds breathy and small in the vast cavern of the study.

I put my hands to my eyes as if I could block the sight out, but then I take them away and it's the same. Grace is standing, swaying slightly; the doors to the cabinet are open. Across the carpet is glinting broken glass. Bone-like ceramic flowers stud the floor around her feet.

'Fuck, so sorry,' she garbles and picks up one of the biggest shards, which bites into her hand. 'Fuck, ouch.' She drops it and blood begins to drip steadily down onto the mess.

What's to be done? What's to be done? It's like rats are here. They've invaded and they are everywhere and I'll have no chance at all of expelling them before *she* gets home. They are gnawing on the rugs and furniture, leaving great holes that even I can't fill in. I'm sick, nauseous, cold. I thank the Lord again I took no LSD. What would I do with this vision if I had? Walk across the broken glass in bloody feet until bones stuck out? Force a jagged shard into my vein?

'Grace,' I manage to say with a thick tongue, 'your hand is bleeding.'

She looks at the dripping blood in bewilderment and then at the glistening mess. Then she takes off her sweatshirt and wraps it round her arm. Our eyes meet above the glass and her face turns into a whinny of suppressed laughter.

'Oh God,' she says. 'I'm sorry. I'm so sorry. It's not funny.' But all the same she can't stop hacking out coughs of laughter and it does something to me.

It is as if something has been breached and the world has just exploded. The skin of it has been irreparably ruptured and I must slip beneath and choke in the drowning waters. There is no surviving this, no soothing or downcast averted eyes or 'Sorry, sorry, sorry' or promises for the future or explanations can avert this disaster.

'I'm going,' I say.

'Where? You can't. We have to clear this up. I'm not in a fit state. Don't leave me here either – this place freaks me out.'

She looks over my shoulder and I turn to see Orla there, open-mouthed in the doorway. 'You mustn't go on your own,' she says. 'We'll come too. He might be dangerous.' She looks white and strange. Her lips pinched. It's the jealousy again – I've got her back! My heart swells. There's triumph and relief. I shrug.

'You don't know where I'm going,' I say.

'Yes I do. I heard.'

'Look, don't worry about it. You both go home if you don't want to stay here. Don't worry about the mess and all the broken stuff. None of it matters any more. I'll clear it all up before they get home and I'll just have to apologise for the breakages and, I don't know, do some chores or something to make up for them. If anyone asks I'll say it was all my fault, I did it all and you both got frightened and ran away. Don't worry, Orla, I just need to meet him one more time to let him know what he's done. You're both right, he's a terrible man. He's awful but he won't stop pestering me. I'm going to let him know that I never want to see him again and that he needs to stay away from me. I'm going to leave him in absolutely no doubt.'

# 36

# Phoebe

Of course that was all lies, lies, lies.

I had a strange moment looking over the glittering mess, Orla and Grace standing there with their mouths open. It felt like I'd left my body. I'd entered some new state and it was approaching calm. I touched a void inside that was past panic, past fear. It made me see things utterly clearly. It was as clear as seeing ancient Rome that day, or the bubbling frogspawn, something that goes through and through the soul.

I realised I can never come back here.

I know exactly what has to happen. I know how I'm going to do it. I'll pull up my plait for the last time. I'll pack it up neatly and take it with me. It's the only thing I want. *She* can have everything else – diary, clothes, even all the spell-making instruments strewn across her best tablecloth. They will be relics falling into the empty hole of my presence. This glass can stay on the floor with the blood dripped in bright rubies on it. I won't even bother sweeping it to one side. *She* needs to know this world has shattered and cannot be mended. It doesn't exist any longer. My presence will be mere shadow, something belonging to the past, and the skin of reality will finally be broken.

When I see Lucas I'm going to ask him to take me off somewhere. The power of my need will brook no disagreement. I'll make him do it. All the power of hell will be unleashed if he doesn't, because I will tell absolutely everyone what happened and what he did. I'll leave it to the coven of mothers at the school to deal with him. I'll tell him exactly how his wife will exact my revenge for me if he doesn't do as I ask. He'll have no option.

As I put on my coat, it weighs heavily to one side with the knife, and I feel almost bright and breezy! Inside the study I hear Grace crunching over glass in her socked feet and both of them whimpering and talking in hushed urgent voices, and the sound of it all almost makes me smile. How glorious to destroy a world. What sublime relief it is. The thought of walking out of here and leaving the blood and the mess and the awfulness behind, of never seeing my family again, has made me feel a dizzying freedom I don't ever remember having before. I'm not about to let Orla know that, though. She'll hold onto my sleeve until she rips my arm off. She'll never let me go.

Outside, the normal everyday sounds overwhelm me. I tremble to their beauty. The evening birdsong is as brilliant as diamonds in my ear. *I don't even need drugs*, I think. *I don't need witchcraft. I just need to dwell in this state I've entered forever.* Sometimes I stop, struck by the crystal flow of the river or the sway of the whiskery tops of the wild wheat that fringes it. Sometimes I remember what's happened with a jolt and it brings me back inside myself. I feel sick then and have to squint in the Technicolor of my surroundings until I remember what it is I must do and hurry along. It's hard when there seems such strange beauty in the pink and gold evening, when I am so struck down with everything. It's the shock, I think.

I crawl through the gap in the wall. I half expect him to

be there already, but no. I have to wait patiently. He won't have found it easy to get away. He'll have to come up with all sorts of subterfuge and excuses. I know exactly what that's like so I'm prepared to give him some leeway for being late. I lean against a tree and pretend to examine my nails.

If they think I don't know they're there, then they must think I'm stupid.

There's the flash of Orla's pink cardigan sleeve. There's Grace's stifled giggle.

I walk up and down next to the cluster of branches they're hiding under.

'I know you're there.' I say. I hang my coat by its loop on the branch of a hawthorn tree.

There's silence; even Grace stops laughing. I walk up and down again, addressing the air. 'Just to let you know, you two don't bother me one bit. You can eavesdrop all you want. I think it's pathetic you've followed me here, but as long as you keep your mouths tight shut I really don't care, and you better had or I'll tell my mum you smashed the place up deliberately.'

I bite my lip and clamber up the base of the wall to scan the horizon. I'll just have to put up with the possibility of them overhearing what I've got to say. I'll lead him away from them anyway, so they'll have trouble catching it. I'm aware that if I scream at them now to leave he'll see their figures fleeing across the field and he'll run the other way. 'He'll be here any minute,' I call out. 'And if you mess anything up for me or make a single noise I'll go crazy.' I know I'm about to start crying now so I stop talking and wait.

# 37

# Grace

It was Orla's idea.

'Granny's footsteps,' she said.

As we crept behind Phoebe, keeping hidden, I kept exploding with giggles. It was the relief of getting out of that house. I can't imagine what her mum's going to do when she sees that carnage. She's going to go absolutely nuts. I don't understand why Phoebe isn't hysterical. It must be the drugs making her not take in the implications of it all, the same drugs that for me are colouring the sky a precise and extremely beautiful shade of mauve. Earlier, sparkles of silver stars slid down it and exploded in a shower on the ground that looked like very fine shattering glass and I laughed wildly because shattering glass seemed to be the theme of the evening. As we followed her it looked like Phoebe was well off on one too; she'd got changed and was wearing a white dress that practically came down to her ankles and made her look like one of those women on a nineteen-seventies album cover, holding a guitar and sitting in a rocking chair. She carried her old trench coat over her arm because the evening had turned hot and she didn't need it. She kept stopping like she'd got stuck to the ground. It looked absolutely hilarious.

Now the curve of Orla's cheek is only inches away as we hide out. She lets off a smell, hot and animal-like. I lean forward to sniff and she turns and nearly bangs into me and raises her finger to her lips.

I'm flying now. The woodland explodes with life, the leaves shimmering and twirling, and I get stuck too, examining a teardrop-shaped green leaf and following all its veins that take its leaf blood all around it. How happy is this leaf? It doesn't have to worry about eating or dying. It doesn't have to worry about anything. It almost makes me cry thinking about it. How I envy its simple little life. I'm so intent on it that I don't notice Mr Jonasson has arrived until I see Orla craning forward.

I can see them both through the criss-crossing of the branches. Phoebe takes him off in the direction of the wishing bowl; as she passes she sticks her middle finger up at us behind her back and I have to take the sweatshirt off my cut hand and stuff it inside my mouth to stop the laughter. The cut has closed up, the two sides of the slit touching together now and turning a bluish purple.

'Stop it,' I hiss to Orla as she stretches out her neck even further. 'What are you doing? He'll see you.'

Orla looks back and her eyes have gone buggy and huge. 'Sssh, I'm trying to hear what they're saying. She's taken him over to the wishing bowl. They're having some sort of argument.' The skin around her hairline is sweaty and she's trembling in excitement.

A hoot of male laughter floats over but it's not a happy sort of laughter – it's the kind when you are taking the piss out of something and calling it ridiculous.

Orla gets on her hands and knees, and her big arse bobbing around in the air means I have to stuff the sweatshirt back in my mouth. Outside our nest I see them both still, Phoebe with her dark shock of hair, him with his jacket off, standing with it hooked over one finger and draped over his shoulder. His jaw is thrust out and he looks tired and scared.

'Orla, leave them,' I say. It feels sordid spying on them now, not a childish game, and I'm wishing to God we'd never followed her here, wishing I'd never agreed to ever staying with Phoebe, wishing I was at home and putting on tea for Mum and me, and stopping to have a sneaky fag with Daniel on the balcony. And in that moment I feel all the delicious ordinariness of them both so acutely. I realise how it's the way they do things – how Daniel scratches behind his left ear if he's thinking, how Mum puts far too much butter on her teacake, how she whistles sometimes under her breath and says it's the same tunes her father used to whistle. All this and the soft loving looks from them – those up to now and those to come – have altered the warp and weft of me so much it's like we are all knitted together in places as one.

'Orla, hold me,' I say, but so softly she doesn't hear and I turn my head and somehow the movement of that is a trigger for everything to go wild. The woodland springs up, alive. The trees all clap their leaves together like they're an audience applauding and I feel the roots beneath us and how they weave into each other and make a basket to hold us and the insects whizz in and out of the bark, flashing their iridescent colours, and the bacteria in the soil moves it about. And I can see the movement, in fast frame – on some kind of loop of a film that's spooling through me – and the branches thrash into my face. Leaves stuff in my open mouth and poke into my eyes. I stumble forward blindly. And I see my hands and they are shiny with blood and there's a knife in one of them and it's smeared red nearly to the hilt. And I look to the others, questioning, trying to understand what I'm doing there, what's happening, why we three are standing in a circle around Mr Jonasson with Orla and Phoebe's mouths hanging open and great splatters of blood like ribbons across Phoebe's white dress. And I don't want to but I do. I turn my head and there's blood leaping out of Mr Jonasson's neck like there's a hosepipe stuck inside, and tentatively Phoebe reaches out and pushes him, just with two fingers, so that he stumbles a step backwards and at first I shake my head in confusion until I realise what she is doing and the reason she's pushed him back like that is so that he's standing on his own jacket to catch the blood that's pouring out of him. And we all stand there watching silently with our eyes as big as rabbits in the headlights as he dies in front of us.

# 38

# Phoebe

The cold shock of the water causes me to whisk back into myself for I really had left my body this time. I saw it all from above, how he bled out onto his coat. How finally he could not stand any more. Someone, and it could've been me, steadied him with her arms and gently helped him down so he could curl up on the floor.

I looked at my hands and they were bright-painted, gloved with the blood from fingertip to wrist that shone in a shaft of sun through the trees so my hands almost looked golden. I wiped them down my front and made two huge red runners down my dress.

Then the plunge and the deep shocking chill of the river.

Four of us are in the water. We three circle around him, almost protective now. Six hands all reaching out and holding him in place. We stripped him naked first. I can't remember anyone suggesting it, but then I was high up and perhaps couldn't hear – sounds were a mere whisper in the leaves by the time they reached me. It seemed somehow the right thing to do, I'm sure. Grace led us in that, I think. First we uncurled him and then undid his shirt, stripped him of that, his trousers, shoes, socks, underpants until there was a bloody mound made of them. We looked like nurses, almost.

'He's gone so pale,' I heard Grace murmur. 'It must be with so much blood gone.' And when I look down I see that to be true. He is indeed pale and his flesh looks white and moistly sheened like a bone does when it's newly stripped.

The current in the river is faster than I expected but we three can stand easily enough, all of us being young and strong.

Grace says something and I see her lips move but I can barely hear. There's a ringing in my ears as if I've been deafened by a gunshot going off next to my head, or an explosion by my shoulder. I shake my head to dislodge the ringing.

'What was that?' I ask. 'What was it you just said?'

From our ring-o'-roses circle blood flows steadily and winds its way downstream.

'We need to wedge him underneath the rock,' she says, 'the rock that the wishing bowl is on,' although I'm not sure if I'm hearing her or lip-reading. Then, 'We can hide him there but we'll have to push with all our weight,' comes in shockingly clear because the ringing has abruptly stopped. We gather around him and float him over to our rock that sticks out into the water like a giant crochet hook. He rolls in the water. His skin is slippery like an octopus. At one point Orla stumbles and lets go and my hands slide over his naked body, and it's only Grace, holding onto his foot, that stops him from sailing down the river.

Grace's face is wet, dripping. The water beads on the ends of her hair that's sticking up in points. She looks like a young soldier; with her cropped hair and wet vest, like one of those kids in Vietnam engaged in jungle warfare and stealing along the river to avoid the enemy.

'Concentrate,' she yells at me, because I got distracted staring at her and thinking these things about her being like a soldier. 'For fuck's sake,' she says. 'I can't do this on my own. The three of us need to gather round.' She takes a hand away and wipes water out of her eyes with the back of her arm. 'And we need to put *all* of our weight down to get him under the lip of that rock. That's what will keep him in place and hide him.' She wipes again, rubbing her face into the crook of her elbow. 'But it needs a lot of force and for you two to fucking concentrate.'

Orla and I nod dumbly. We do as we're told and press down on him with the flats of our hands. I want to scream. I want to cry out at the feeling of his naked wet dead flesh sliding under the palms of my hands and the only thing that's stopping me is the sight of Grace's face, all hard bone and paleness and determination. We put all our weight on him but the rock is so deep into the water we can't push him far enough to get him beneath and under the huge stone hook, and he surges back up almost straight away, mighty and white in the water, his penis flopping to one side and his balls bobbing like two apples.

'Try harder,' says Grace. 'Dear God, fuck, fuck, try harder.'

I flex my muscles and heave and push into him with my elbows and use every ounce of strength I have, and he does, he slips underneath the rock. Not having his weight to lean on makes Orla stumble face forward into the water and she has to jump right up, coughing and spluttering. I take her hand and we both stand, buffeted by the heavy flow, watching Grace as she plunges her arm into the water and feels about at his body. I don't know how she can do this. I want to scream again.

'It feels secure,' she says eventually. 'We can all get out now, but we have to see what it looks like from the bank.'

One by one we clamber out, pouring water from our clothes and hair. Grace stands right on the tip of the wishing bowl rock.

'Hmmmm,' she says, 'hmmm.'

'What is it?' I ask. I want to scream again.

'Come and look.'

I really, really don't want to but the expression on her face is so savage I don't argue. I lean over the bank and that's when I nearly puke because there's a white foot, long and lean, ghosting up out of the water. It sways lazily from side to side in the current like a fish.

'I think it will be all right,' says Grace. She crouches down and uses her fingertips to steady herself as she gets as close to the edge as she can, assessing, deciding. 'I think it will be OK. You have to get right to the edge of the bank to see anything and this place is so isolated as well.' She nods to herself. 'Yes, I think it will be all right. Besides, what can we do about it?'

'We could cut it off,' I suggest, and she stares at me and gives a short barking laugh. Her pupils are black chips. I see how the battle between what needs to be done and the effects of the LSD are raging inside her. I quail before it because I don't think I've ever seen someone be so focused or so powerful in my whole life.

I look down and I have to clap my hand over my mouth to stop myself screaming. I truly think Grace will hit me if I do.

'Fuck's sake. What is it?' she snaps.

I point silently to the wishing bowl where a huge drop of blood is pooled at the bottom, gleaming wetly like a jewel.

'Clean it up,' she says. 'Clean it up and we'll move on to his clothes. I need a minute.'

324

I use my hands to scoop up water and every time I lean in I have to look at that horrible floating foot. It's unbearable. I use a dock leaf to scrub out the blood and it makes me think of all the times we three made our spells here. Our little wishes and dreams. And now this awful dark one seems to have come about and I'm completely lost as to what can be done about it. How it can be reversed. If there is a form of words, some incantation or some special herb or poison that will bring his body back to life again. I cling onto the idea that somewhere in all those library books it might be there. I'll have to take them all out again and go through them one by one. But then I look down at my fingers and the crushed and now bloody dock leaf, and I fling it away from me with a little scream into the river because it's brought me back down to earth.

'Shut up,' says Grace from where she is, standing by his pile of clothes.

So silently, pinching my lips together in case anything escapes, I pick more dock leaves and scoop more water and keep scrubbing and scrubbing, although I can't seem to convince myself that I'm getting every speck of it.

Grace comes over to look. 'That'll do,' she says. 'Just get rid of all those leaves.' She nods at the pile I've made. 'Orla, come here.' Orla has drifted off and is standing by a tree with her hands on the trunk like she's feeling for a pulse. She doesn't hear at first. 'Orla, wake up,' Grace barks. 'Bundle those clothes up so the blood doesn't show and use the jacket arms to tie it up while I have a look at the area.' Grace rubs her finger over and over again at the spot between her eyebrows. 'Then we'll have to figure out what to do with our clothes. Somehow we have to get back looking ordinary.'

When Orla has tied the clothes into a tight bundle and Grace has inspected it to see if it passes muster, we take one last, long look around. The blood is mainly gone. It was caught by his jacket. There are a few drops clinging to the tips of stalks of grass and we carefully harvest those and fling them in the river. Now there's just a patch of flattened grass where he lay. Grace drops to her hands and knees and runs her fingertips through it, combing the grass to check nothing has been missed.

One by one we crawl through the hole in the wall and Orla passes the bundle of clothes over to me before she comes out last. Her cheeks are wet and red and I realise she's taken the chance to sob, coming through that wall, while Grace isn't watching.

We stand under the girdle of trees and look out across the fields. It's a perfect evening. Ribbons of pink dangle at the horizon. The heat has intensified to a point that all the warmth from the day seems to have gathered, as if in a bowl that is now being poured out.

Orla lifts her face. 'It's only because it's summer – that's why it's so light still. It could be really late already.'

'Shut up,' says Grace. 'Don't say things like you're a normal person. You're not a normal person any more so don't ever go thinking you are.' The pad of her finger works back and forth between her eyebrows again. 'Stay under the trees,' she warns. 'We'll take off our things and hang them on the branches to dry. It won't take a minute in this heat. Then we'll work out what looks OK to wear. We should've done it back there but I'm not going back through the wall into that place now. We'll just have to stay well behind the trees in case anyone comes along.'

So we do, and as I stand in my bra and pants and peep through the branches to check no one is coming I shiver violently despite the heat. The blood on my dress has mostly come out in the river but the whole thing has been left a horrible shade of pink. Mine's the worst because I was the one standing downstream from him, and thinking how I've come off the worst makes me feel sorry for myself. I cover my face with my hands so I can't see the clothes spread across the trees like hospital bandages.

Grace feels the clothes every now and again. 'That will have to do,' she says eventually. 'As we walk along they'll dry out more anyway. Damn.' She's unrolled her sweatshirt and is staring at it. 'I'd forgotten that I'd cut myself and used this. Oh well.' She shrugs it on. 'My vest is too stained, so if I roll the arms up hopefully nothing will show. That's mainly where it is. Now you two, get dressed.'

We do, quietly, meekly, then she makes us line up while she inspects us.

I see that I was wrong now, about coming off the worst. Orla has the biggest problem. The blood must've splashed in great gouts across her blouse, which is a soft green material and doesn't seem to have washed out so much in the river as my dress. They've stayed there and turned into black welts. Her pink cardigan is a soggy bloody mess.

'Fuck,' says Grace, 'we have a problem. You can't go back like that.'

'I can't walk home in my bra,' says Orla in a meek voice.

'No. Of course you can't. Phoebe, give her your mac.'

I clutch it tighter around me. 'No, no. My dress has gone a horrible colour.'

'Yes, but it might look like it's meant to be like that. Take

327

off your mac and let me see.'

I stare at her, holding my coat tightly around me.

'Fuck's sake.' She starts pulling roughly at my lapels so I'm almost spinning around. 'Take it off, you silly bitch. No way can Orla go home like that.'

'Just do it,' Orla roars and then begins to sob. 'For God's sake, just take the damn coat off.'

So, I take it off. Underneath, my dress is a nasty salmon pink and Grace twirls me around, inspecting. Her eyes twitch from the LSD.

'You'll do. Now let's get out of here.'

Orla picks up Lucas's bundle of clothes and we walk out into the golden heat of the evening, the three of us weaving one behind the other down the path, bordered by spreading trees on one side and a swatch of glittering corn on the other, gently undulating away into the horizon.

I start crying then because this is not the dress I want. *She's* wearing that, the beautiful blue to her ball, while I have to put up with this garish pink. It's unbearable. I can't help thinking too, if only I'd been able to keep my own beautiful midnight blue dress, if it had never been spirited away and left the house buried at the bottom of a bin, none of this would ever have happened and everything would still be safe and all right.

# 39

# Orla

I wake.

Twin beds. Rich cranberry covers against crisp white sheets. A delicate silvery voile blowing at the window. The high ceiling with its delicate mouldings of vines running in graceful swooping tracks gradually focuses. Silence. Someone in the room clears their throat.

I sit bolt up. Phoebe is on a hard upright chair at the bottom of the beds. She's been watching us both sleeping. Grace is stretched out naked on the other bed, a sheet barely covering her body. Her nipple is a pale rose in the flatness of her chest and her hip bones press upwards towards the ceiling. I can't see her face; her arm is thrown across it like she doesn't want to look even when asleep.

Phoebe blinks. 'I've been waiting for you both to wake up. I haven't had *any* sleep at all.'

In the thin morning light her eyes are huge. I'm eaten up by them. I notice the filthy mound of mine and Grace's clothes tangled together on the exquisite red and blue Persian rug between the beds. They are matted and disgusting. My green shirt is plastered with blackened blood and the fabric of Grace's vest is silty with thin mud, dried out, and patches of watery-looking red. They look like the rags worn in a zombie movie.

I unglue my mouth. 'Jesus,' I say. 'Jesus.'

Next to me, with a gasp, Grace sits straight up, her

consciousness lit up all at once. 'What time is it?' she asks.

'It's very early,' Phoebe says, her hands folded in her lap in the style of a prim teacher in an old film. 'And while you two have been sleeping I have done just about everything.'

Grace paddles about on the floor until she finds her vest, but when she lifts it up to examine it and sees the red and brown stains, the seamy dirt, she flings it aside and falls back onto the bed and bellows into the pillow. Her skinny back lurches in and out as she yells.

'Tell me what happened.' I'm aware my voice sounds very small in the high-ceilinged room.

'Orla, you know what happened.' Again, the weird tone of voice, as if I'm being reprimanded in the classroom. 'You both know. Grace stabbed Lucas and he died right in front of us.'

I look at Phoebe again. It's the shock. It's done something to her.

Grace twists and moans on the bed, banging the pillow with her fists.

Patiently, Phoebe waits until the noise subsides and carries on. 'Then we hid him under the rock. We came home and I put you two to bed because there was still a lot to be done, and I could see that neither of you were going to be any help.'

I nod. Bits coming back to me in jagged flashes. 'You put us in the shower.'

The hiss of hot water in my eyes. The acid still making everything unreliable around me, even the cubicle walls that reached up in a tower of white gleaming tiles to a dark point high above. Phoebe rubbing shampoo in my hair, rinsing and then repeating the operation all over again. Phoebe taking over from Grace as if she'd been handed a baton.

Telling us what to do, and Grace useless and flopping over now, being dumbly fed into the shower by Phoebe as I stood shivering in a towel, watching the pink stream of water head towards the plughole.

'Yes. I had to. These sheets would be covered in mess now if I hadn't and think what work that would have created. My mother has them ironed perfectly and I'd need a week to try and make them look like that. I had to blow-dry your hair as well so it wouldn't leave marks.'

There's a moment of yawning silence. A car starts up in the street far below us and the sound sets Grace off again, keening into the pillow.

'Grace . . .' Phoebe begins but Grace sits up. Her face is white and hard. She points a thin trembling finger at Phoebe.

'No. Shut up. Just fucking don't. Please can you tell me what the fuck . . . I mean, *what the fuck* you were doing taking a knife with you to see that man? What in the name of God were you thinking of? I mean, it was you who took it, wasn't it?'

Grace looks at me questioningly and I nod. 'I don't think it was either of us,' I whisper.

'Why? Why did you take that knife?'

Phoebe looks pinched. 'It's for reasons that I can't explain in a way that I think you'd understand.'

'*I* can explain it all right. It's because you are a fucking crazy, crazy bitch, that's why.' Grace clutches her head in both hands. 'And now this. Now this. Christ . . .' she whispers. 'Mum. I can't have this. I just can't.'

She stands up, the sheet falling away from her pale slim body. Her pubic hair is a dark blonde ruff. I understand it, the gesture. It's saying that the usual niceties are meaningless now between us. That we have gone beyond that boundary and to stand exposed like that is nothing any more.

She starts snatching at her clothes, holding them up.

'No.' Phoebe bounds forward. 'These need to go – you can't wear them home.'

'Fuck off,' says Grace, jabbing her legs into her jeans.

Phoebe scrabbles around on her hands and knees and grabs at what's left on the floor. 'No, I must make absolutely sure these are destroyed. You'll have to borrow something and bring it back.'

She holds our stinking little pile to her chest.

Grace shrugs. 'All right. Whatever.'

I wrap myself in a sheet and follow after them, padding down the landing. There's a smell of Dettol in the air. Flashes of yesterday come back to me, stumbling through the dark here, the pale outspread fan of Phoebe's ribs catching the light. Crying out and feeling the walls cave in under my fingertips like jelly.

Grace turns. 'Let's get some coffee first. I might be able to think better if I've had some coffee.' So I wordlessly turn and follow them downstairs. Through the open kitchen doorway there's the cool marble worktop with a food processor on it that has the shine and colour of a vampish red nail varnish. Another memory: Phoebe talking on the phone, pacing back and forth in the hallway. Me creeping down stair by stair, peeping round the corner. Seeing her holding a knife up to the light, standing immobile, seemingly transfixed by its point. Then wrapping it in a cloth as if it were a baby and putting it in her pocket. I shake my head, trying to clear the image out, hitch up my sheet and pad in after them both.

# 40

# Phoebe

Will I ever sleep again?

I'm alone in the house finally and every tiny thing that can be done has been done and checked and rechecked over and over again, but still I cannot sleep. Imps pinch at my eyelids, urging me to check once more. Demons cluster in the corners and shout every time I'm dropping off. Hooves rattle across the floorboards of my bedroom. My sorcery has turned upside down and back to front in a way that is now against me. Even though *her* dress is not here, its blue ghost walks the house and haunts me. I long even for the crowded sleep I used to have.

I lie with eyes wide open, looking at the ceiling.

When we returned last night I opened the front door on a house I'd hoped never to return to. I heard the phone ringing as I crossed the threshold and, even though I ran, nearly tripping, to the kitchen, when I placed my hand on the receiver I felt only the last dying ghostly ring vibrating through my hand. When I picked it up there was the buzz of a dead line.

'Who was it?' Grace asked and I said I didn't know, even though I feared I did.

We toured the house. At first it was with the lights off because somehow we couldn't bear the glare on us. We saw our way by the remains of the endless summer twilight falling through the windows. In this blueness I kept glimpsing the other two's eyes as big and round as saucers and I wondered if mine looked the same. I'm sure they did. I saw how that world was smashed and how now the fact of that wasn't sublime at all. I despaired of ever being able to reconstruct it. All those shards of glass; if I was given a millennium could I ever piece them together? What about cleaning the blood out of my dress? Getting rid of his clothes somewhere where no one could ever find them? It was as impossible as spinning flax into gold. It was all so much *work* I wanted to lie right down on the spot and never get up. Although even then I knew I would not be able to sleep, because I grasped that, even though sleep had now become something I craved perhaps more than anything, it would elude me until the end of my days.

Nevertheless, a start had to be made. I fetched some newspaper from the kitchen and began to pick up glass in the study. I saw now that it was not only the precious objects inside that were spoiled and smashed but the glass door on the cabinet was broken on one side too. A great jagged hole gaped. Grace crunched over glass, swearing and weeping. Getting back to the house seemed to collapse her. She weaved around, shouting. The drugs had intensified in her system so that she barely seemed to know where she was. Orla was no more use. My lovely Orla. She looked like a stranger, like someone who didn't matter to me any more. She kept looking at us both in turn and asking, 'What shall we do? What shall we do?'

'Clear this glass up,' I said.

She knotted her hands together like writhing snakes. 'But that won't bring him back,' she said.

Then like an avalanche, like an invasion, there was an

echoing down the hallway, a flooding of sound, a caco-
phony of bells. The other two froze.

'It's the phone again,' breathed Orla.

I dropped the glass so it smashed on top of the rest and I
ran to the kitchen. This time I made it.

'Hello.' I wondered how my voice sounded.

There was a silence on the other end so of course I knew
who it was straight away.

'Mum?' I whispered, and yes, I'll admit, even then, even
now, there was longing in my voice.

'Where the hell have you been?' Her own voice, ice cold,
dripped down the back of my neck.

'Umm. I didn't make it to the phone in time. I—'

'Phoebe. I have been ringing *all* evening.'

I held the receiver tight to my ear. 'What for?' I managed,
finally.

'To check on you, of course. I told you specifically and
categorically you were not to leave the house so I want to
know exactly what's going on and where you've been.'

'Mum.' Never had my longing for her felt greater.

'What?'

'Mum, please.'

'For God's sake, Phoebe. You're not making any sense.'
That's when I detected it, the slipping slur in her voice. It
made me realise not everything was on her side. It was a
tiny unpicking at the seam.

'Mum. Are you all right?'

'Yes. Of course I am. Why would you say that?' There it
was again. She's drunk. She's drunk! I realised.

'It's just that your voice sounds all strange and slurry. Are
you ill or something?'

There was silence for a moment. Her slurring didn't actually sound that bad but I could tell she didn't want to test it out again. She needed a moment to collect herself.

'I'm absolutely fine . . .'

'You really don't sound it, Mum. You sound really funny. Where's Dad?'

'I don't know.' There was a break in her voice and that's when I realised it. She was drunk and she'd had a row with Dad and she'd wandered off, and that's why she was ringing all night to take it out on me. She was on some cobbled Edinburgh street in the midnight blue dress with my ghost tears sprayed across it in an invisible corsage, and she was standing with her phone clamped to her ear, desperate and fuming. 'You still haven't told me where you've been.'

'We were upstairs and we turned the CD player right up and we were dancing so I didn't hear. Sorry, Mum. D'you think you ought to go and find Dad?'

Pause. 'I suppose so. I hope you didn't disturb the neighbours with your music. Is it turned down now?'

This house is like a castle. I don't know who the neighbours are, except for on one side I've seen a man scurrying to his car occasionally. They wouldn't hear even a faint echo of any music we play.

I needed to get rid of her now. I had too much to do. 'Yes, Mum. It's switched off now. You go and find Dad. He's probably worrying about you.'

'Yes, I think I'll do that.' Her voice drifted off, like she'd taken the phone away from her head, and then the line went dead.

Back in the study Orla had her arm around Grace, who was crouched next to all the broken glass with her hands on her head. Drools of spit were running out of her mouth and dry sobs racking over her body. They hadn't done a thing while I'd been gone. The newspaper lay exactly where I'd left it. I could see I'd have to get rid of them too and do everything myself.

'Come on,' I said. 'You'll need to shower before you get into bed. My mother will go crazy if she finds mud on the sheets.'

I showered them and tucked them up in the guest room. Grace fell asleep almost immediately but Orla lay there with her eyes wide open, looking petrified.

'Don't get up,' I warned her. 'I need you to stay exactly where you are.' I couldn't take her blundering around, having to look after her. She looked in such a panic I wouldn't have put it past her to wander outside wrapped in nothing but a sheet and stand screaming about what we'd done in the middle of the street. As a precaution I took the key from inside the door and locked them both inside. I slipped the key into my pocket and went to work.

It was strange. It was as if all my years of checking the hairs on my diary, the crumbs, the total and one hundred per cent attention to detail in the forensic rubbing-out of myself was all training for this one night.

After the glass was all in the bin I turned my attention to his clothes. Oh, I felt so sad looking at them. They didn't even seem like clothes any more they were so stiff with blood, misshapen and deformed. In the pockets I found his wallet, his keys and the mobile phone I recognised as being 'ours'. When we were arguing he told me he'd only brought it with him so he could throw it in the river in front of me as a demonstration that this silly little charade of a relationship must end.

337

I frowned down at the screen. It was a hurtful gesture, but one he never did get to perform before he got stabbed. I think the phone was in his hand when it happened. Grace – cleverly – must have put it back in his pocket. I pick through his wallet. A twenty pound note and a five. A debit card in joint names with his wife – Mr L and Mrs K Jonasson. A receipt for toothpaste and shampoo from Boots. Some blue and yellow slips of paper with numbers printed on them like the ones used in raffles. It seemed respectful to put everything back where it was. I felt tears forming in my eyes. It was so dreadful that a whole life could end with just this dirty mound of stuff: the shoes that he was probably proud of because they were nice leather oxblood brogues, compensating for the cheapness of the jacket; the black underpants boasting Pierre Cardin on the waistband that were probably chosen for him; the shirt with the jaunty stripes of pink and orange, distinctive colours that I'm sure I'd seen in a 'buy one, get one half price' deal in the window of a shop in town. The whole lot spoke so much of *striving* and *staying relevant* alongside *making do*, it nearly broke my heart. And that's before you even began to think about all the blood and mess. You'll feel better when it's out of sight, I told myself, and carried it all into the garden.

Outside, the night was still warm. I had no idea what time it was. I checked up at our neighbours' windows but they were all in darkness. It made me shudder, though, the idea that someone could be watching behind them in the darkness. I hunched up as close to the garden wall as I could as I made my way down towards the shed with the bundle in my arms. Even though Mum and Dad aren't exactly keen gardeners I was sure there must be something in there – a spade or fork or something. Burning the clothes out here could have all those eyes turning towards the back windows, pressing their faces up against the glass. I might as well put out an announcement on a loud speaker. They would have to be buried. I stumbled around the shed, starting to panic, but eventually my heart soared when I found a long-handled spade behind the other tools.

I'd brought the phone that he'd given me to bury with everything else. I chose the spot near the ivy where I used to hide the phone. I began to dig, the only sounds the chopping into the soil and my own breath. I found it difficult to know how deep to make it or even how deep I'd got because of the darkness, but eventually I judged it big enough and shoved everything in the bottom and covered it all back up with soil, which took an age.

I was closing the back door behind me, thinking about what else had to be done, when a wave of the most crippling panic fell right through me. It was so bad this time it felt like radiation – not the wonderful kind I felt in the Roman Baths, but a poisonous sort – and I was a mere object for it to get through and it was going to kill me.

What if, and I could hardly bear to think about it, what if not everything went into that hole?

What if I'd dropped something on my way? Or if something fell out of his wallet and was fluttering around in the breeze in the garden right now? What if a button had fallen off his jacket and was lying on the garden path like an accusing eye? Or it could be one of his green socks or even his underpants that slipped away from me.

I went back out into the night, nearly crying with fear and exhaustion. I took a torch with me this time, despite the neighbours, and looked all over, searching over the lawn and the tatty borders and down at the bottom around the shed, but even when I couldn't find anything I couldn't rest, so convinced was I that there was some piece of incriminating material somewhere. It was like the day I thought I'd written all those terrible things in my diary for *her* to read, only this was a thousand times worse.

I had no choice, I decided. I'd have to dig it all up again. God knows what time it was, but that's what I did. I really was crying by the time I got to the bottom, I was so tired. Before reburying it I laid everything out, piece by piece on the ground, to convince myself each thing was really there – the socks neatly side by side and the shoes. I went through his wallet, placing each item on the ground – the notes, the raffle tickets, the loose change, the debit card and receipt. Stand up and look at it all, I told myself, commit it to memory like you would with that game when you have to remember objects on the tray after they've been covered up with a cloth. So that's what I did, the torch flickering over the horrible bloodied stuff. Then I dropped everything in the hole and shovelled earth back over it.

But as I was walking away the what-ifs started again. I looked all around the filled-in hole to see if I'd accidentally left anything out, and part of me knew it was nuts but the bigger part of me was panicking and panicking and wishing I'd made a drawing of everything on the ground with labels and then ticked it off piece by piece as I lowered it into the earth. It took a huge effort of will to break away – stronger than anything I thought I was capable of – but I did it in the end by promising myself I could do this again soon, when everyone was out one day, and it would be easier in the daylight. Nobody but me ever came out here anyway, except Dad once in a blue moon to cut the grass after it reached over a foot long, but he'd only just done it and the grass is really short so that won't be for ages. Besides, I had to get inside as there was still so much to be done in there. I had to put the knife through the dishwasher, although after I had, I thought of how Lucas's corpuscles had been spread in a fine mist over the entire inside of the dishwasher, and the idea of having to eat off plates and with cutlery that had been in there nearly made me puke and I wished I'd done it in the sink. I ran the dishwasher again and again, empty, to try and make it clean again. I had to wash my white dress because surely she would notice if I got rid of it, and that took an age. I washed it first in the sink with bubbles up to my elbows and then in the washing machine with the special brightening powder she uses on Dad's white shirts and it actually came up really well. I spent over half an hour examining every seam, every inch of fabric before I put it on the line to twirl away through the night. I was beyond exhaustion by this point and dawn was beginning to creep in through the windows. I practically crawled into the shower and scrubbed and scrubbed until my skin hurt.

It was fully light before I allowed myself to rest. I lay on top of my unslept-in bed and ran everything through my mind over and over. *I'm going to have to be so fucking careful; the care I've had to take up till this point is nothing compared to how I'll have to be from now on.* I let myself rest a little before going to unlock Orla and Grace. I'd already decided what to do with them.

When Orla came screaming out of the bushes with the knife in her hand, Lucas and I were too shocked to move.

How she knew it was in my pocket I don't know. Even after she'd plunged the knife into his neck the expression on his face was one of complete surprise. An awful choking sound came out of his mouth. Then Grace, stumbling after, reached up and pulled the knife out and that was when the blood really started pumping. She was trying to save him, although I don't think she did him any favours by doing that. That's when he really started dying, I think. On the way back I realised that Grace really thought she'd done it, that she was the one who'd stabbed him. She'd got the image of the knife in her hand all covered in blood stuck in her head. I need to keep her thinking that. There's no way Orla could take it, the idea that she'd murdered someone, but Grace just might. She's the toughest by far out of the three of us. She's the only one who has the slight possibility of surviving that.

I think about beforehand, by the riverbank when we were arguing. 'What, you think I'd leave my wife to go off with a child like you,' he practically screamed at me. When I think of that, how horrible and hurtful he was, there's a moment when I'm actually glad he's dead. He lifted up his hand as if he was going to hit me and that's when Orla came raging out of the trees. But . . . somehow I don't think he was going to hit me. I think he put his hand up to push me out of the way so he could get past; that's what I thought at the time anyway. It's immaterial now, all of it. I just have to make sure that Grace goes on thinking she did it and Orla stays believing she didn't. It will be impossible otherwise.

My body feels as cold and stiff as marble as I lie and wait for Mum and Dad to get back. The other two have left. They were in their own clothes again, like last night. I started to protest about them taking my mac, but I couldn't be bothered to argue in the end and I can't go through what I had to do last night again. They'll have to deal with it themselves.

Did I actually sleep for a few minutes? I'm not sure. The angles of the light tell me it must be afternoon by the time I hear their car pulling up outside and the front door opening. I listen to them moving around downstairs and wait, strangely indifferent. Finally I hear her calling up.

'Phoebe, you'd better come downstairs.'

As I make my way down I have a sensation. It's like I'm floating, but not in the horrible sick way I did in the Spinney. This time I'm still in my body and it's almost . . . *pleasant*. I muse on the strangeness of this so much I almost forget to be afraid and think about what I've got coming to me. For a moment I wonder if perhaps that's because it won't be as bad as I imagine, but I soon have to change my mind about that when I see her face.

The rage is already there.

It's not even at the early stage. It's full-blown. It's naked. I put my arms up as if to defend myself.

'Don't you even move,' she screams. 'Don't you even cover your shitty little face.'

I lower my hands and dare to look.

The screaming continues. 'You absolute little shit. I knew you couldn't be trusted – look at this.'

I look her straight in the face. It's the first time I've witnessed the rage completely because normally I'm flailing away from it or cowering or covering my face and I only catch it in little glimpses. Now I stand and fully take in the white around the mouth and the way the lips are stretched right back and how her face is practically elongated from the power of it. I almost feel sorry for her then, because I know how much she can't help it and how it must hurt her to have something going through her that turns her face almost unrecognisable.

I don't slump or cry and I can't seem to take my eyes off her. It's like the rage is bouncing right off me.

'You're worthless,' she goes on, her screaming vibrating the room. 'You're a useless, self-centred, disrespectful, nasty piece of work.' She grabs onto her throat. 'What are you staring at?'

I don't speak, just gently shake my head from side to side, feeling the same way as when I floated down the stairs – detached and strange.

She lunges forward. 'How dare you look at me like that.' She grabs onto my wrist and presses her nails deep into the veins running up the inside. A sharp diamond on her ring has got twisted round the wrong way and it pierces me there, ripping into the skin. She grabs my face with her other hand, digging her fingers into my cheekbone and into the softness of the socket so it feels like my eye will be gouged out.

And for a moment it's almost as if we're dancing together, with her grinding my wrist and face and us looking right into each other's eyes. It's a strange dance and in a way I know it's one we've been doing for years in a hundred different ways. Close up, I notice her eyes have tiny flecks of green in them and I think how odd it is that I've never seen that before.

Finally, she lets go and stumbles backwards and stands there, incoherent now, screams grating up from her throat

344

one after the other, and the rage eating up her face, and *still* it somehow bounces off me. And I think it's that, that I'm still just staring, that makes her do it. She picks up a glass vase from the coffee table and throws it at full force into the open door of the cabinet where it shatters the remaining glass door. The noise seems deafening. It stays ringing in my ears even after everything has finished breaking.

'Emma.' I'd almost forgotten Dad was in the room, so far in the background he's stayed. He steps forward now. It punctures the room. She stops screaming and turns to him as if some spell has been broken. He puts his hand on her shoulder.

'You're very tired. I'll ring some glaziers and organise repairing the damage and see exactly what's missing.' He runs his hand over his hair. 'We'll make it good somehow. You go and rest. It's been a long journey home.'

She holds her throat and nods, and amazingly she does what he says. She walks past me without even looking and I hear her tread on the stairs.

I turn to Dad. His eyes flick down to the red welts blooming on my arm, up to my eye that is so swollen now I can barely see out of it, back down to my arm where a trickle of blood runs from the cut of her diamond ring, and then he looks away.

'She's very tired,' he says.

I long for him to hug me with his strong arms or even simply murmur some steady, reassuring words, but then he's got his back to me and he's looking inside the cabinet to see what's missing.

# 41

# Orla

How the season has changed.

The summer swelled and died in a blink. The Himalayan balsam that lines the riverbanks flowered, then suddenly all the seed heads popped within a week. When I cupped my hand around them, the plant mechanism that's as strong as steel and activated by warmth sprang forcefully inside my palm in a contained explosion – and left me with a handful of seeds that I scattered as I walked. By mid-August dried-out nut cases already littered the ground. The blackberries began to purple. How could it all be so soon, I thought, and then wondered if this happened every year and I've only started seeing properly because now I look out into the world with a kind of dumb frozen wonder.

Everything I see as *before* and *after*. In the world of *before*, even my grim encounter in the pet cemetery and the visit to the clinic I see in lush golden colours. It's always summer there and the stalks on all the flowers are tight with sap, the hues are warm and subtle and the air is a pinky gold. In *after* land the world is completely changed. It is drained of proper sounds and colours. It's not the simple change of a season. The world has transformed.

The leaves have curled and wilted on the trees, and before I know it they begin to fall and perform their death rattle on the pavement. The grass looks shabby, its nap going this way and that. There are litters of brown twigs and pods beneath the bushes in the garden. I've left the bindweed growing in the beds and the open throats of their flowers are a startling white. Each day it moves on. The elderberries ripen and fall in a squashy mess to the ground. I watch it all for hours and it seems to speed along before my very eyes. Spiders weave their webs among the decay. They pop in and out of the crevices in the stone wall. The hard-packed soil grows cold as night falls.

It's nearly dark when Mum calls me in. She hugs me close. 'What's the matter with you these days, darling?'

I nestle in as close as I can possibly get.

I see Dad over her shoulder. 'You looked like a statue out there,' he says, smiling at me. At least I think that's what he says. Sometimes I have to concentrate hard to hear what people are saying, like I'm underwater and seeing them speak above the surface down to where I'm submerged. Although he's smiling I can tell he's worried.

Why did I never see the simple love shining out of them? Why wasn't it ever enough? It could've sustained me, easily, for the next few years, nourishing me until I found new soil to grow in. If I could have just a fraction of it now, I'd bask forever in its warmth and be content. Those bright-lit days seem like an unreachable heaven.

We sit down at the table and I pick at the chicken curry Mum's made. The boys are told not to chew with their mouths full. The bowl of rice steams.

'Come on, eat up,' says Mum, looking at me anxiously. At first she wasn't bothered about me going off my food. I knew she silently approved of the fact that I'd shed those extra pounds by the way she patted my newly slim waist and said how lovely I was looking these days. Now they're

347

worried. Dad jokes about sending me packing to his relatives in Ireland who'll feed me up on stew and dumplings, followed by a greasy lardy cake and a Guinness chaser, and they won't take no for an answer. I joke weakly about 'no stereotypes then' to divert his attention.

I poke at the chicken and my stomach turns over. 'I think perhaps I need to turn vegetarian,' I say.

I look up. Both their faces are perplexed but there's relief on Mum's too. She's thinking she's found the reason for the pickiness and the weight loss. It's the obvious answer – teenage girl turns vegetarian. I can't bear to think about if she ever knew the real answer.

'Oh well, good.' She blows out of her mouth. 'I'll go shopping tomorrow. What's that stuff they eat? Quorn or something? I'll stock up. I can do you a separate dish to go with the vegetables we have.' She looks pleased, even glows a bit. This is my mother who can't abide picky eating, who always made us empty our plates before we left the dinner table. That's how much she cares about me; she'll go against the grain of a lifetime. It makes me want to weep.

I nod as if she's found the solution and help her clear the table, scraping my almost untouched meal into the food scraps bin. She hums as she loads up the dishwasher, the tight-set curls on her head bobbing up and down as she works.

'They still haven't found that poor man,' she says.

Instantly every nerve in my body is electric. I swear the cat backs away from me. I concentrate on wiping the salt and pepper grinders. I do it minutely, getting into every single gap with the damp cloth.

She straightens up and rubs her forehead with the back

of her hand. 'His poor family. He had young children too. Just think, they could grow up never knowing what happened to their father.'

In stories people turn and see the stricken looks on others' faces when something like this happens. They can read everything there. I've found the opposite. All I have to do is turn my head slightly to one side and the moment passes without comment. If I do look terrible she doesn't even see. It took an age for Raskolnikov to be uncovered as a murderer, despite his torment, despite his wandering St Petersburg in a state of fever. It takes him almost being split in two before anyone really notices.

'Orla? You OK, love?'

I realise I haven't answered. I suck breath in. 'I'm tired, that's all. I think I'll have an early night.'

'Good idea. First day back tomorrow so get a good night, then I'll prepare a lovely vegetarian dinner for when you get home. How about that?' Her cheeks are pink from exertion and cooking, from the fuggy warmth of the kitchen.

I nod and call goodnight into Dad on my way up the stairs.

'Goodnight, lovely girl,' he calls back, and I know just from the sound of his voice – angled downwards and slightly distracted – that he's doing the crossword.

I lie in bed, thinking about tomorrow. I never did find out what Phoebe did with all his clothes. I borrowed her coat again to come home. She didn't want to give it to me, became hysterical and said her mum would notice it was gone, but Grace slapped her round the face and made her do it. I was supposed to take it back and never did. That day was the last time I saw them both. Grace and I emerged from the house, blinking under a flat white sky. We looked at each other and I got the sense we were trying to trace something in the other's face that might give some clue about ourselves. It was a deep look that cut so far beneath the usual I couldn't breathe. We didn't talk or even say goodbye. We just looked at each other like that and left.

# 42

# Grace

On the first day of term I wake to an unfamiliar sound.

It's a hiss, like the noise of the static on a TV. My mind turns over until I identify it, then it grabs onto what it is. It's rain. Hard driving rain falling in waves all over the city.

The summer has been dry and warm. Cracks have been noted in the baked earth. Gardens across Bath have wilted in the heat and at night there's the tinkle of hoses as people try to resurrect them. Although it got cooler very briefly, the heat returned with a vengeance and it stayed dry as a bone. In some strange way it was like it was telling me something, that the fact of him being buried in water was causing a drought across the land and there would be no rain again ever because what I'd done had ended the world, which was doomed to die slowly by drying out. Fevered thinking, I know, and I've pushed it aside resolutely. I've made myself concentrate on what's in hand. Look to what needs to be done, bitch, I tell myself. Look to what it is on a daily basis and think only about that.

Yet I have so often wondered about the watery grave, the worry gnawing and gnawing away at me, that the level of the river has become dangerously low and left his body high and dry, exposed to the air and stinking like high heaven. Once, I contemplated going back to check but changed my mind. The idea of it was unbearable and what could I do anyway? Best left alone. So I spent my time looking to Mum. I cared for her as if my own life depended on it. The care I'd lavished before, after her fall, seemed nothing compared to this. I put the rest of my summer into it. I encouraged her appetite by reading the recipes in magazines and concocting treats. I saved up and bought some expensive soft satiny sheets. I took her out in her wheelchair any time I got the opportunity, planning out routes that took in flowers and greenery and ended in an afternoon tea in a sunny courtyard café, where I always made sure there was jam on the table to encourage wasps to come and feed on the sweetness.

On the day I returned from Phoebe's to the empty flat I sat shaking on the sofa for hours and when the intercom buzzed in the hall I nearly hit the roof. My heart pounded as I went to answer. I pressed the intercom button cautiously.

'Hello?' I whispered.

'It's your meals on wheels,' said a voice from far below.

I couldn't stop laughing all the way down. A horrible hiccupping nervous laugh. I'd completely forgotten that besides the respite care and the visit to our place – that had turned out to be surprisingly brief and manageable – Miss Kinsella actually said she'd try and sort this out. She trusted me more each time she saw me, I could tell; could see how capable I truly was. So she'd finally pulled this off as well, except the two organisations – the one that provided breaks and the meals-on-wheels one – were clearly oblivious to each other because they didn't know Mum was away in respite. Downstairs, a kind-faced old lady waited with cloth-covered stainless steel rings that steamed gently.

'Here you are, dear,' she said. 'Same time next week – just wash these up and give them back to me then.'

Did she see the dumb incredulity on my face? It was the

idea that people were still running about as normal, delivering dinners, arguing over what to watch on TV, fucking, walking their dogs. I shook my head. I needed to enter that real world again some day. I stood with the tray in my hands and decided there and then that's exactly what I would have to strain every fibre to do. There would be no letting up in that mission, no drift.

'Enjoy your dinners, dear,' she said, before zipping off back to her little blue van. I watched as she drove away.

Upstairs, I scraped all the food into the bin. I still do, every Saturday when it's delivered. It's our McDonald's night of course. Why would we be eating grey beef stew and sponge pudding on a Saturday night? Mum worries that it's a waste and we should tell them we don't want it any more. It makes them feel like they're doing something, I tell her. Best leave it like that. In reality I want to cause the least ripple in the outside world as possible. I need to lie low until that real world can be entered properly again.

That's why I've gone back to school for the final year.

I look out. The rain rolls in waves across the rooftops. It gurgles in rivulets down the windows. The balcony is awash. The building has become a giant waterfall as the rain lands on the roof, then cascades down the sides.

'You can't go out in this, chicken,' Mum says.

I reassure her and wrestle a huge old golfing umbrella from the back of the cupboard. It keeps my head dry on the walk to school. I look up and see the water streaming down the different-coloured plastic segments above. Soon, my trainers are soaked through. I can feel the water soaking up the back of my jeans, reaching upwards to my thighs. The traffic swirls through the flooded gutters so I walk as far as possible on the other side of the pavement. My heart is hammering. It will be the first time I've seen them both. What will they look like? I imagine our faces will startle at the sight of each other in the gloom of the corridor and our hearts will give a horrible lurch in tune. They'd better handle themselves all right. They'd better not break down. I'll crack their skulls if they do, I swear I will. I wonder if we'll have a silent pact not to speak or communicate in any way, almost like we'd never known each other. The closer I get to school the more sure I am that this would be best; it would be the safest thing to do.

Seeing them both ends up being exactly like I thought at first. The corridor is damp from the rain being walked in and from the coats gently steaming on the pegs above the radiator. Because of the day being so dark, Phoebe and Orla's faces rise up out of the shadows like bone moons. They float, uncertain, for a second and then we all move together and walk silently beside each other, falling into step. This is the opposite of what I'd planned and is against my better judgement, but we've cleaved each other like we're made of the same stuff now. In this moment I feel we don't need to say anything, that our dialogue will be in silence from now on.

Because the school is a huge old house our assemblies are held in a tin church hall opposite. Usually when the weather is so bad they are cancelled so we're not left soaked through in the morning to dry out for the rest of the day. Not this morning. We have to dart across the flooded road with hoods up, feet sloshing in puddles, and umbrellas in the tortoise formation of Roman soldiers with their shields over their heads. I sit between Phoebe and Orla, and the head, Mrs Reid, makes her shuffling way to the stage. There's something wrong with her leg that makes her drag one foot behind her. The contrast with her deputy, who clops through the hallways like a pony, has always struck me as funny before, but today I can hardly bear to look at them both. The sadness of her dragging foot overwhelms me. It grows in my gut so it feels like it's about to burst out of my mouth. I gag a little and Orla reaches out and puts her hand inside mine.

Mrs Reid waits for everyone to fall silent, casting her looks about the room until there's a hush. Her high forehead, clean of a fringe or anything to conceal it, gleams in the grey watery light from the windows. The room smells of the parquet floor that has been polished during the holidays. It smells of chewing gum and the acrid shower gel on bodies. Beneath all that, the bottom layer, it smells of dust.

'We begin term on such a terribly sad note,' Mrs Reid begins and my throat closes up. I push Orla's hand away and grip the seat of my chair with both hands. 'Of course, many of you will know already, from the newspaper reports, or from being told by your parents and guardians, that the member of staff who has taught English here for nearly a year now – Mr Jonasson – has gone missing.'

She looks down and rubs her hand over the plain wooden lectern.

'It's very distressing for us as staff and I know it must be for you also. All that I can say is that we must never lose the light of hope in our hearts. I know how popular he has proved among the students. We must pray every day that he will be found soon, safe and well, and be reunited with both his family and with us here in the school.'

I wonder what our three faces look like and if Mrs Reid can spot us from the stage, looking stricken and pale. Stop it, bitch, I tell myself. Mrs Reid is as blind as a bat. She's not wearing her glasses; she can't see anything. We'll be blurs to her, but all the same my heart won't stop pounding. She pauses as if it's a struggle for her to continue, as if she's about to burst into tears. Just as she collects herself and opens her mouth to carry on, a low murmuring sets up at the back of the hall. It sounds like wind moving through cornfields. Mrs Reid frowns; she can't hear it as well as us because of being further away. I see her deciding to ignore it and plunging on.

'We owe it to him to stay steadfast in that belief and to continue with our studies in the diligent and thoughtful way that he always did his very best to impart to his students.'

The murmuring grows louder. Someone cries out and there's a high-pitched laugh, gratingly nervous and stifled immediately. I turn around and crane my neck. In the back two rows people have mobile phones in their hands. They are ignoring the strict no-phone policy in class and assembly and they're reading off their lit-up screens. 'Oh my God,' someone gasps.

'What on earth is going on?' demands Mrs Reid from the stage. 'Stop it at once. It's most disrespectful.'

But she can't quieten it; it's unstoppable, the roll of information sweeping across the assembled people, jumping from one to another like lightning. Soon it reaches our row in trembling whispers. In shocked and horrified reports. In giddy excitement, with people turning their heads this way and that to either hear what's being said or to pass it on to their neighbour. Soon I piece together what it is.

Mr Jonasson's decomposed and whitely bloated body has been found. It floated down the River Avon and right under Pulteney Bridge before anyone could stop it. People gathered on the bridge and stared with their hands over their mouths. Children were hustled away quickly. The sight of it was like a white whale floating past. Police boats came out of who knows where and surrounded it like it was a monster drifted in from the sea. They fished it out of the water and took it away.

# 43

# Phoebe

I'm foggy with nightmares.

Before his body sailed down the river I hung onto the idea something could be done and that tending to my witch light could save me.

I went back to them. The soothsayers. The contrivers. To Hecate, the old goddess of the crossroads. To the three Fates that can smell the future on the wind like people sticking their heads out of the window and reading the weather. But when I looked to my own future I saw only blasted landscapes or swirling mists so I retreated back into myself and thought again.

I saw how I was too easily sidetracked and how quickly I descended into the pit, into the fear – days and nights spent in it. Every time I tried to order my jumbled thoughts and decided to take some positive steps, I became distracted and time would spin out too fast. Despite my plans, when I came to out of my trembling fugue, the library had shut again and there was no chance to go and retrieve all the books and go through them line by line like I'd been intending. Plus, I couldn't remember properly the things that pussy-cat face taught me about controlling thoughts. How could she be believed anyway? Thought; that winged thing; that wind; that spirit; that *snake* that winds itself through the coils of the brain. Simple tricks would never be enough to control it. I realise that now. It almost makes me want to see pussy-cat face again to tell her how she was wrong.

Remember, I tell myself. You read about the thing called necromancy; the raising of the dead. You don't need the books because you've studied it already; you know what to do. Trace a circle on the ground with *the* knife; there will be a special sort of potency in that. This should have been done in a cavern underground but I didn't have time for that. The bare boards in my room that still showed the scars where Orla smashed the doll's teacup had to suffice. I placed the ritual objects inside the circle: the shaving mirror from the bathroom, some perfumed oil and of course . . . the two copies of *Macbeth*. It was with trembling hands I retrieved them from the drawer, where they had lain buried under old jumpers, and placed them in the centre of the circle, where their battered bodies glimmered in the weak afternoon light. I sat cross-legged and called for Mr Jonasson to be raised up from the dead, from the watery depths where he lay, stirring all the lost Roman coins washed down from the baths with his fingers.

He came back all right.

First, in my sleep. Every night he stood over my bed and used his index finger to push back his lolling tongue inside his mouth so he could speak. Then I experienced being burned by speech as if engulfed in flames but on waking I could barely remember a single word he spoke. One thing I definitely predicted correctly, I think to myself bitterly, is that sleep is no longer sleep. I don't even know what to call it any more.

This surely is the descent into hell that, looking back, I believe I started to glimpse weeks ago. I remember seeing it in the boiling water writhing its way out of the centre of the earth, in the poisonous frogspawn, in the jokey faces staring out of the wall.

He didn't stop coming back, though. That was just the first phase. The second was when he stepped out of my dreams and truly returned.

I've imagined his face emerging from the water so many times I'm nearly convinced I witnessed it myself. It's like one of the ancient masks that have been found there in that place, but pale and bloated. It emerges in the same way as the coins, the statues, the brooches and the clasps of sandals that pop out of the river like figments from a dream.

He's come to get us. His rotten tongue wants to tell everything.


Now they want to talk to us all. Mrs Reid has organised it and presides, her eyes misting over continuously. She's dressing it up as a chat, as if their main concern is our welfare and they simply want to check out that we are all right after the trauma we've been through. I am not so easily fooled, though. She's as nosy as hell and enjoying playing amateur sleuth.

Before it was my turn to go into the classroom where they are having their interviews that they are not calling interviews, I actually thought the electric circuitry of my brain was so charged it would surely kill me. I expected any moment to fall down dead on the red and black tiles just outside the classroom. I considered taking off home but I'm frozen to the spot. I know I can't draw attention to myself like that anyway.

When it's my turn Mrs Reid says, 'Now, don't be nervous, dear. Miss Atkinson and I simply want to know how you are feeling about what happened. Anything you want to tell us at all?'

Things flash through my brain. His sweating face heaving above mine. The knife stuck into his throat. The white foot waving about in the water. I put curtains around the pictures and look over at Miss Atkinson. She's new and I notice the fine gold chain around her neck and how she's writing down what I say; I think it could be a form she's filling in. Her green eyes look up and, bam! I see it.

There's pussy-cat face. There's *her*.

There's the one that can see deep into your dreams. I know the type from long experience. I think I actually grab onto the collar of my cardigan. Then the interested look comes into her eyes.

'I'm so sorry,' I manage to squeeze out. 'I don't think I know anything.'

'Mmm,' says Miss Atkinson. 'Anything that occurs to you, it could help. For example, did you ever see him outside of school?' she asks.

For a minute I think my heart is actually going to leap out of my chest and flop around in its own blood on the desk between us, but she continues, 'For example, at any of the pubs or nightspots you go to – and yes, I'm fully aware you're underage but I want to reassure you in this instance it really doesn't matter. It's more important that you tell us if you've seen him with someone.'

I shake my head. 'I saw him in town once, no, maybe twice, but it was daytime and he was with his family. I think his wife was buying sandals.'

She smiles and I see she's not really a pussy-cat face. It was my panic making me think that. She actually looks quite bland and just sort of tired, like she has to grind through her day and when she gets home there's children or elderly parents or something else she has to look after and she's sick to the back teeth of it all. I feel a spark of my witch light returning. It's such a relief, like a warm fire after being frozen to the bone for days on end. I pray it doesn't get extinguished again.

'He was a nice teacher,' I say. 'We're all sorry he's gone. I had the same favourite play as him – *Macbeth* – and we were going to carry on studying it this term.'

Favourite play! That cancer, that holocaust, that time bomb, that warhead, that curse, that Book of Hate. I was doing so well and now I've uttered its name. I don't know why I did. It was *that* that probably made him come back in the first place, when I placed it in the circle and tried to raise the dead. It was just that right now I couldn't think of anything else to say, and I know any minute, very, very soon, I am going to crumble and say something stupid. I can feel myself unravelling and the moment hangs suspended and doesn't seem to want to move, however long it goes on for.

Just as I really am unravelling, the door to the classroom opens and my dad pops his head around.

'Sorry, sorry, sorry,' he says, putting his hands out and smiling. 'Didn't mean to interrupt but I've been looking for this one here. Bit of a thing at home and she's needed, I'm afraid. So sorry – are you done?'

I have never, ever been so pleased to see anyone in my whole life.

His grey hair, the patches on the elbows of his jacket. He wears his QC's air of authority lightly but it's there and they know it too. They sense it straight away and draw back into their seats.

The new teacher looks back over at me, her final tentacle withdrawing, its eye forgetting what it saw, moving onto the next thing, perhaps going home and looking at what needs to be done there, already feeling weary about it.

Dad leads me out to the car. 'What's happened?' I ask him. 'Is it Mum? Is she ill or something?'

'No, Phoebe. I just heard on the grapevine this was happening and I thought I'd come and rescue you. They really shouldn't be doing it. It should be done formally as it could mess up any investigation if information comes out like that. Don't do it again, will you? If anybody asks you to, call me straight away. You promise?'

I nod and he does too, like something has been explained and settled.

'Now, let's get you home,' he says. 'Look, you're soaking. Get in quick.'

But I stay put and we stare at each other over the roof of the silver car, the rain streaming down on us and running down my neck. His hair is soaked through and flattened to his head, water drips from the keys in his hand and his blue-eyed stare appraises me. It is not without kindness but it is nevertheless a lawyer's stare. His lawyer's brain suspects something. I don't know how. Maybe the smashed house that night, or something else or maybe just an instinct. He's always said that using his instinct is how he's got so far.

At home, water twirls from my coat onto the golden boards of the hallway. Each window is sheeted outside with a curtain of running water. I take off my coat and hang it in the utility room and put my shoes underneath the radiator to dry. I bring the mop and bucket and wipe away the water from behind the front door.

I look up at the staircase twisting away above me.

If it's true they know, or at least suspect, that means I am bound to them as tightly as if I was locked in chains to them. This house with all its polished surfaces, its mirrors and its sweet waxy smell may as well be my prison. There never will be any escape into a gilded future of my own making and far away, ever.

As I ascend the stairs I feel I have a disease I once read about and must have stored in my mind ever since, a disease where you bleed from every cell of your body. I bleed invisible blood into the dark corners and into the very fibres of the stair carpet. I can't seem to get away from blood. In my room I take out the first copy of *Macbeth* and sit on the bed and stare at it. Of course, I realise now, the awful book foretold it all. How many times have I thought about our wishing bowl and lain in bed in an agony of fear, thinking I didn't clean it properly and the rust-coloured tell-tale traces still remain? Or I examine the kitchen knife, turning it over and over in my hands, holding it up to the light, fetching the magnifying glass from the study (one of the few objects that remains intact after Grace smashed them that night) and examine the joint between the blade and the hilt to see if a speck has been trapped there.

I put *Macbeth* to one side and take out my diary and write in it a single word:

*Save.*

What? *she* might puzzle. Save money, save time, save buttons in a tin?

Of course, only I know this means I have to save myself. I will talk to Orla and convince her to come forward and tell everyone that Grace stabbed Mr Jonasson and swore us both to secrecy. I know I can make Orla do this because she loves me still, and if I don't I will be trapped with *her* forever like a beetle she's caught inside a bottle so all I'll ever see are *her* eyes, magnified by the glass and staring at me caught inside. I don't need to divine the future to know that.

# 44

# Orla

We have to go. Everybody was told they had a choice if they wished to attend the funeral or not, but they all said yes, so for us three to be the only absences would look horribly suspicious. We might as well announce what we did in the paper.

The funeral is in church; we all troop in out of the fine, misting rain outside and umbrellas hooked over the ends of pews drip onto the floor. The instructions were not to wear black but instead our favourite fun-loving clothes as a celebration of his life, and for some reason this seems to make it all sadder, more pathetic than if we wore black lace veils that came down to our waists. The sight of his wife with her pale strained face in a purple tulip-sprigged dress and bright red shoes with straps and buckles, which look like they should belong to an elf, nearly finishes me off. The older child has clearly been allowed to choose her own clothes and wears the same party dress with pink skirts of gauzy downward-pointing petals that we saw her wearing on the street. The boy is in a tiger romper suit.

I sit down heavily and look around, trying to stem the rising panic. The church is a thickly gilded one lit by a red lamp and with stained glass the garish colours of sweet papers held up to the light. It surprises me, all the ornament, for some reason. Since he was Swedish, I thought he'd have a simple funeral in a church with clean lines and clear glass. The lilies are ferocious. They guard the chancel with their open mouths and saffron-coloured tongues. The smell is fleshy sweet and when the coffin is borne inside on the shoulders of six men – tall relatives who've all flown in from Sweden – I cannot help but convince myself that's where the smell is coming from, from the coffin at the front that's there throughout the service, and not from the mouths of the creamy white flowers framing it on either side.

I try to keep the sickness down but the smell is in my throat. I know for certain the solace of my garden is a dead zone for me now. I'll never venture out there again. I won't be able to bear the rottenness inherent in its cycle. The smell of flowers will be like a poison to me. Nature will be something I can never stomach again.

Phoebe, who up till today has been cool and distant, keeps squeezing my hand and turning to me, her face full of concern as if she's checking out I'm all right. Maybe it's obvious that I'm not; I'm probably white as a ghost because I felt the blood drain away from my face as soon as the coffin darkened the doorway and its shadow passed over me as it was carried to the front. I keep my eyes averted from his family who all sit in the front row. Seeing them look so broken, so absolutely finished and the thought of the two children growing up fatherless nearly capsizes me.

And, I know it's selfish, but even though I'm crushed flat by seeing his family I can't help but give in to a little moment of mourning for myself. I have such a longing for the awkward plump loving girl I was that tears well up in my eyes.

I used to have this game. If I saw an old lady – and being in Bath I had my pick – who looked like she'd had a good life, someone I felt I wanted to be like, I'd follow her. I'd note her clothes, her walk, the way her little claw held her handbag, and wondered how I could learn from her. Often they were like birds hopping along, like they had hollow bones, their skinny legs stuck inside great boat-like shoes. I knew that following old ladies in the street was not a normal occupation so I kept it to myself, but now the thought that I'll never have that done to me by some gauche and slightly lost girl fills me with such grief and rage that tears spill off my chin. By that age I'll be so bent and twisted, staying in the shadows as I scuttle along, not even able to gaze on the beauty of nature unfurling in the spring, that anyone who looks will cross to the other side of the road to avoid me. The thought chokes me up and to my horror I hear a howl and realise it's escaping from my own throat. Phoebe grabs my hand and digs her nails hard into my palm in an effort to shut me up, but she can't. It's getting louder and people in the row in front of us begin to turn to look.

'Shut up,' she hisses. 'Or I'm going to have to take you out of here.' I clap my hand over my mouth and nearly gag on the effort to control my sobs.

'That's it,' she says. 'Come on. Outside.' She makes to stand but I elbow her in the stomach and it forces her to sit back down, winded. It feels like we're on the point of really fighting, standing up and grabbing each other's hair and clawing each other's eyes out.

'No,' I whisper fiercely. 'I'm not going anywhere. Leave me alone.'

Her nails dig so hard into my palm it feels like she's cutting the skin. She leans so her lips are very close to my ear. 'Well, shut the fuck up then. I've got a plan to save us both so just sit tight until the end and don't draw any attention to yourself and everything will be all right.'

I close my eyes. I didn't think things could get any worse, but the news that Phoebe has a plan is like the final straw. It even stops me crying and the fight goes out of me. Christ alone knows what awful thing she's cooking up. Any hope, any spark of anything in me dies and I slump back into the pew until it's all over and people are filing out.

The church empties quickly, like people can't wait to get away and go home, until there's only us two and the priest ambling about at the front, tidying up the altar. Grace took off with hardly a backward glance. The coffin is still there, waiting to be taken away, and Phoebe grabs me by the elbow.

'Come on, you can't sit there all day, looking like the end of the world is about to come.'

She drags me outside but I flop down on the cold stone seat in the vestibule underneath all the notices for Mother's Union meetings and choir practice.

'I can't go on like this,' I moan. 'I've been thinking, I could run away, start a new life. I don't know, go abroad, anything. This is unbearable.'

'Shut up now. You haven't heard my plan. Running away would be the worst thing to do because it will draw attention to us, and then it will just be me and Grace, and quite frankly I don't trust she has our best interests at heart.'

Her eyes have gone all hard and starey.

'Come on,' she says, pulling me up by one arm. 'Let's get out of here.'

We take the winding path between the graves towards the gate.

'Do you remember us talking about all being buried side by side when we're dead?'

'What?' I turn to face her. Rain glosses her face. 'Are you thinking we should all kill ourselves?' The idea goes through me like a jolt, but I have to admit there's an edge of relief too. For a moment it almost feels like a plan.

'No, we haven't come to that yet.' She stops and looks at the sky. 'Look, it was Grace, wasn't it, really? If we let everyone know that, and that we hardly had anything to do with it at all, everything could be all right.' She holds onto the iron gate with the flaking blue paint and creaks it back and forth on its hinges.

'For God's sake, we can't do that.'

'Why not? It was her, wasn't it?'

'Think about her mother, Phoebe. Who would look after her mother if anything happened to Grace? Besides . . .'

'Besides what?'

I bite my lip. 'I keep thinking. It could have been any of us really, couldn't it? I keep remembering seeing you in the kitchen, holding that knife up to the light. They could say it was all premeditated. That makes it so much worse, I expect. Sometimes, I even think the knife was in *my* hand. No, no, no, Phoebe. There's got to be something else.'

But she's out of the gate, banging it closed so I'm shut into the graveyard.

'I'll be stuck with them forever,' she yells over the gate. 'Is that what you want?'

For the first time I notice she's gone against the 'no black' rule. Her slender form is sheathed in some thick woollen black tunic and she wears tight black leggings underneath. Cheap knobs of faux pearls hang off her lobes.

I put my hand on the gate and it's wet and freezing. Crisps of rusted paint stick to my palm.

'I don't know what you mean,' I say. 'Stuck with who? Phoebe, I know I've got to get a grip but I can't. Every time I think of you holding up that knife—'

'It was you.'

'What?'

'It was you all along and I was protecting you and now you say we have to look after Grace.'

'Phoebe, don't lie.'

'I'm not. I'm not. It's all your fault and now because of it I'm going to be stuck with them forever.'

Her black form, dense as a crow, peels away from me and starts running down the hill as a wash of blue spreads over the sky and the raindrops on the gate shiver and start to dry up.

# 45

# Grace

Listen, bitch.

You know the time has come when you are going to have to fight like a fucking soldier in hand-to-hand combat. Like you have a baby and someone is holding a fucking knife to its delicate little throat. Like everything and everyone you love is about to be blown to pieces. That's how hard.

I used to think I was tough. Looking back, I see I was deluded. I was just a stupid soft bitch.

At the funeral I saw Phoebe and Orla bending their heads together, so close they were touching from the shoulder to the hip, their hair tangling into the other's. Phoebe glanced up and the look only lasted a second but I could see it all written as plain as day. They intend to turn me in. Three's become two and they are going to stick together and save themselves. Phoebe turned away to hide her face but it was too late. I took off without even saying goodbye and ran all the way home. I went and stood on the balcony and smoked and smoked to help me think.

Now I picture myself gradually putting on armour piece by piece. It's like the armour I saw in town one day, on men dressed up as Roman soldiers for some tourist thing. The sun that glinted off the metal pierced right into the back of my eyes. The red feathers waving on top of the helmets were the colour of newly spilt rich blood.

What I would really like to do is cover this old tower

block with armour like that, the pieces overlapping so there are no soft vulnerable spots. What a sight that would be when the sun hit. It would strike such fear and awe in the hearts of anyone who saw it, glittering and sparking against all the old crumbling stone, that no one would dare to approach and we would be kept safe inside. It would be the emperor of buildings here instead of some poor relation.

That's impossible of course, but I do something similar with my mind. My mind is like a wall and I check it nightly as I lie awake, looking for weak spaces or parts that need mending, looking to see where a new plate of armour might be needed. The thing is with those two, they don't know about fighting like a demon. They've never had anything else to look after except their own miserable arses and that gives me an advantage, a strength, that they don't even know about.

At school the teachers think I don't pay attention. They know all about what's happening at home, but I suspect some teachers also think I'm simply thick and that I have excuses made for me that aren't warranted. Actually, what I really am is *tired*. The constant wash of information is too much. I have nowhere to put it. I'm all full up. Occasionally my ears do prick up, though, because I might not be the most studious pupil in the world but I have an inbuilt radar for something that might prove useful.

One such moment was when Mr Jonasson talked about *Macbeth*. Phoebe was always drivelling on about it, about the three witches and how that was like us and how you could predict the future and all her stupid little rituals and childish spell making. But the bit that really made me sit up had nothing magical in it at all. It was both simpler and more complicated than that. It was how the three witches managed to put a thought into Macbeth's head and that thought became a picture and the picture became a plan and the plan became an action. It made me realise the power we hold: that by making something concrete for someone, painting a picture of it and holding it up and saying, 'Look, look at this,' it can plant a seed that wasn't there before. But also, these same things can destroy us: if we allow ourselves to become prey to thoughts, weak and sick with them, it can finish us.

I've been checking on Orla because I could see this happening to her. She hides her weight loss under chunky jumpers but I can see it all right. I've made a point of keeping a close eye on her, wandering down to her house as the sun sets – the nights are growing cooler and darker – and saying hello or watching from a distance as she leaves the house with a violin tucked under her arm, being ushered to her mother's car. I've tried to see from her body language what the state of her mind is.

Things have become more urgent, though.

Since I saw her bend towards Phoebe's words at the funeral yesterday I know that keeping an eye out is not enough.

Tonight I wait, sitting on the wall opposite her house until she sees me and comes out. Her head is down and her feet shuffle in their worn ballet pumps. She sits down next to me.

'Hey,' I say. 'How are you?'

She casts me a look that's almost contemptuous. 'I know what you're doing,' she says. 'Don't think I don't.'

'What d'you mean?'

'You're checking up on me. You think I'm the weakest link.'

The truth of what she says shocks through me. Obviously, I haven't been subtle.

'Think of that,' she carries on, 'the weakest link before Phoebe. That's sinking pretty low. I think about finishing it all sometimes, you know.'

'Really? God, Orla.'

'Yes, really.'

'How?'

'I don't know. Cutting my wrists. Jumping under a train. What difference does it make?'

'Come for a walk,' I say. Something about her is making the fine hairs on the back of my neck stand up on end. She looks thinner than ever. Her eyes have lost any gloss at all and are like scratched marbles. She's reaching the end of her endurance. It makes me sick with anxiety.

She shrugs. 'All right then.'

We start walking. Sunday night in Bath and the streets are nearly empty. The day trippers and the shoppers have gone home and people have yet to turn out on the streets for dinners or the theatre or trips to bars. There's a chill to the air too that adds to the melancholy of empty windows. We pass the undertaker's with the huge sculpted head above its doorway and Orla looks up at it and shivers.

'If only I could go somewhere, I'd feel all right,' she says, quickening her step.

'Go where?'

'Anywhere.'

We pass through the square; the Roman Baths are dark and hushed behind the wall. The statues of Roman rulers gaze down at the Great Bath. They weren't actually built in Roman times, though, these statues, not part of the old site like the baths are; I learned that years ago. They were put up by the Victorians to try and make it look more authentic. Orla looks up at the Abbey, which looms impassively against the sky that has just the very first tinges of dusk and the promise of turning that deep and particular shade of blue that is nightfall when the sky is clear.

'I can't bear it any more.' She rubs at her mouth.

I lean in closer. 'What do you mean?'

'I just can't bear living like this. If I don't go away I'm going to go mad. It's true what I told you, that I think about killing myself all the time. Either that or walking into a police station.'

My heart starts pounding. 'Let's buy some cider.'

'What, now?'

'Why not?'

I think of Mum watching television at home. I'll just have to try and forget about her for the moment, block my mind.

I buy a huge bottle of the cheapest strongest cider at the mini-market and we cart it to the Abbey square and take turns swigging straight from the bottle. Her voice turns slurry almost straight away as if she's been longing to get drunk.

'What are we going to do, Grace? I'm at the end of my tether, I really am. Phoebe wanted us to turn you in.'

So, my instincts were correct, but still the news jangles through my nerve endings.

I try to stay calm. 'Let's go to the station and get on a train. Anywhere, the first one that comes along.'

She looks at me. 'Sometimes I think it was me. I saw Phoebe at the house, wrapping up a knife and putting it in her pocket. When I think about it I seem to remember pulling it out of her coat and running with it. It's hard to know what's real.'

'Come on, let's go now.'

She looks uncertain. 'Really? I haven't got any money.'

I dig around in the back pocket of my jeans and wave my wallet at her. 'I have. Come on.'

There's about twenty quid in there but I don't tell her that. I'm having to improvise.

We walk down the wide pavements to the train station. The houses at this end of town haven't all been cleaned. It's something about this kind of honey-coloured stone that the city of Bath is built with that when it's clean and sunlit it looks golden, but it also sucks in pollution, takes it readily into its pores like a smoker to their lungs so it gets black and sooty. These crouched Georgian buildings in this part of town haven't yet been in the city cleaning programme and they are nearly completely black, decades, centuries of coal smoke and car fumes clogging up their façades. At the station we buy the cheapest ticket possible for the next stop from here on the London train. 'We can hide in the loos when the ticket inspector comes round,' I tell her. 'Then we'll go as far as we want. We'll go all the way to London.'

We sit on a bench, waiting for the train and talking. Around us the darkness encroaches. Bath is such a tiny place really. We're surrounded by fields, by quarries and woods. The countryside is so close; it creeps into the edges of the city. I hear an owl hoot nearby. I catch a musty leaf smell carried on the breeze. Orla is lit by moonlight, her thin arms blue with it, and it makes me realise, we must have been sitting for hours, the two of us, talking.

I heard an old wives' tale once that stayed with me as if it was information that would be needed at a later date. If there's a pot of frogs in boiling water and one tries to escape and crawl out, the others will not allow it to; they will pull it back down to die alongside the rest of them. That's what we are now: we are three frogs in the cauldron.

'Listen . . .' I say, and she turns her head.

'What?' she asks, her eyes dull, her arms crossed across her chest. She asks the question as if she needs me to tell her something, anything that would be a last-ditch attempt to save her.

'No, I mean *listen*. There's a train coming.' It's far away, on the breeze. I stand and walk to the edge of the platform and she follows behind.

'It's coming,' I say. 'It's coming.'

Beside me I feel the flurry of her. She is all at once alive, electric. Something passes through her, an energy, a thought. I see it out of the corner of my eye. It blurs her edges as if she's moving, but then I realise it's because she *is* moving, kicking up her legs, her hair and arms swinging as she lifts off the platform and onto the tracks where she stands in a petrified second in the moonlight before the train hits her.

Afterwards, after they've taken her body and they've talked to me, I go back home and find Mum asleep in the chair. I shake her awake by her shoulder and lift her up in my arms and carry her to bed. I take in a plastic cup of water and help her brush her teeth, then I peel back the covers and help her climb in. Only then do I allow myself to ask, *What was that? What just happened?*

Don't be a stupid soft bitch, I tell myself. You know exactly what happened. Don't for one fucking second forget that or try and tell yourself otherwise. You understand completely.

# 46

# Phoebe

*No, no, no, no, no, no, no, no.*

I'm to see pussy-cat face again. The news has sent me reeling. The worst of it is that it's just at the point when I started to feel better, when I sensed I'd begun to tie everything up like a Christmas pudding bandaged neatly in snowy white cotton, ready to be lowered into the pot to steam. When I started to feel it might be possible to contain it all.

Now, every night until the appointment is dread. Guts writhe. Horror seeps through my brain. I am sick with it all.

On the Sunday beforehand we have a roast and the sight of *the knife* sticking into the beef, squelching in the blood and sinew and then rising up, red and dripping, sends me running from the table. I hang over the toilet and dry-heave. The rest of the day is spent in bed, curled and miserable, with pain tightening around my head in a cap.

Mum comes into my room. 'Don't think you won't have to go,' she says to my hunched body under the sheets. 'That appointment is happening if I have to march you up the stairs myself.'

And that is what happens. She drives me to pussy-cat face's office, which, like our school, is in a building that used to be a house. There are boarded-up fireplaces in every room. Everything is covered in a pristine layer of thick white paint and carpets the colour of pale wood cover the floors, giving it all a neutral, medical air that is supposed to be calming. There is a receptionist at a heavy wooden desk in the first room on the ground floor. She speaks in a low voice as if not to disturb all the discussions being held above her head, the great mass of confusions and longings and fears that are being released up there from hour upon hour of appointments. It's surprising there's not a cloud, as black as a swarm of stormy bees, above the roof.

We have to wait, sitting side by side on the leather sofa in front of the receptionist, who has to pretend that our four eyes are not watching everything she does and our four ears not listening to what she says on the phone.

As we wait the old feeling comes back, but worse, the sense that pussy-cat face is actually able to see right through me. That she is my hunter and I am her little mouse and she will pursue me until I am half dead with exhaustion, until my tiny heart is about to expire from going like the clappers so long, until I know for certain it's better to give up than to go on with the chase. Then I will have to roll over and lie on the dusty floorboards surrounded by my own little droppings and admit defeat. I'll have to let her chew me up alive.

I look at the clock above the receptionist's head and imagine it an hour on and me looking at it then and what will have happened in between. Who knows? Who knows? I can rub at my mouth or tap the back of my hand or dash at my eyes with my fingers or any of the hundred little tricks that I use to keep myself on track, but I never know whether they'll work or not.

I hear her tread upon the stair.

She puts her head around the door. She has a striped blouse that I haven't seen before but otherwise she looks just the same; if anything, the curve of her top lip and her slanting eyes are more catlike than ever.

'Phoebe, how lovely to see you. It's been, how long . . .?'

Is she seriously expecting me to answer in here with these two looking on?

'Well, anyway, come on up. You know the way.' The last bit is said playfully, lightheartedly, as if we are old friends and we're going to her bedroom to try on some fucking shoes or something. Mum waits on the sofa, reading an interior design magazine.

Upstairs I take my place on the sofa.

'You have a new clock,' I say.

She turns and smiles. 'Yes, what a good memory you have. The old one stopped. It just one day refused to tick any more.'

By the way she's smiling she seems to think this is funny. I don't. I think it's sad and terrible.

'Bit like your patients then.'

She ignores this. 'Tell me a little about what's been happening since I last saw you.'

'Well, we're moving.'

'Where?'

'To York. My sister will be furious.'

'Why?'

'Because that's where she goes to uni. Now my mother's following her and we'll all be camped on her doorstep and she'll think she can never get away.'

The announcement of the move was sudden, unexpected. Dad was moving to new chambers and Mum giving up her job to keep an eye on me. A prospect that filled me with such awful dread it felt like it was choking me. When they told me, I remembered his blue eyes on me that day he picked mu up from school – shrewd and kind, knowing – and I guessed we were running away. All I could think of, though, was that I'd have to dig up all Lucas's stuff and smuggle it up with me and get rid of it again. It being down there never left my mind. Sometimes I thought I'd forgotten to switch the phones off and I could hear them ringing beneath the ground.

Was the move because of Dad's suspicions? In the end I had to do a police interview and he was there, present and watching me carefully. It was weird, I didn't feel nervous that time; I was sleepy. I had to keep forcing my eyes open because I truly thought I was going to fall asleep on the disgusting ripped chair mended with gaffer tape.

'Now then.' Pussy-cat's serious face comes down like a shutter. 'Would you like to tell me what's brought you back here?'

'I think you probably know already.'

'Perhaps. But I want you to tell me what you think it is.'

Oh, the charade of it all.

'I suppose.' My throat tightens. 'I suppose it's because my mother has told you there's a recurrence of the old behaviours.'

I remember her saying that perhaps my mum had some sort of personality disorder and truly these days I'm wondering if I'm getting one too. I'd like to confide in pussy-cat face about it but I'm too scared that she'll go down and tell Mum what I've just said, even though I know she can't do that with ethics or whatever. It doesn't take the fear away.

'Phoebe, I'd like to hear it in your words.'

*Don't make me,* I think. Mum looked at me one day and said, 'You're at it again, aren't you? I can tell by the look in your eyes.' The cut was in such a secret place I thought no one would ever know. So foolish of me. Nothing can be kept private. Every inch of me is monitored and inspected. I stay resolutely silent. If I don't speak, perhaps the hour will go without the cat and mouse. Perhaps I will be able to leave before it gets to the bit where I am torn apart.

'Phoebe?'

I tilt my head back against the sofa and curl my legs beneath me. I'm falling. Something inside my chest is trying to get out and the pain is unbearable.

'Phoebe, dear. Are you all right?'

She's never called me 'dear' before and somehow the word sets up such a welter of longing and pain it nearly kills me.

'Phoebe, please. Tell me what's wrong.'

I close my eyes. 'I think I'm responsible for someone having died.'

I want to tell her how hard it is sometimes to be a girl. That we are drawn by forces that are mysterious to us. We are alone, set apart. When we stop being sweet little girls and our bodies grow hot and difficult, our feelings become too raw and dangerous. Our friendships are too driven by desire. Our menstruation begins and our interiors leak onto the outside. We find it hard to know what's real. How can I explain to her that I've dreamed of flying, of sorcery, of having that flashing power in my fingertips, my eyes turned into hard diamonds. At certain times I feel I really am capable of sailing in a sieve, like the witches of *Macbeth* say. Other days I have a soft and dreamy longing for a cocoon. It's only yesterday I remembered with a shock that when Rapunzel pulled up her plait, the witch was dangling on the other end. Rapunzel didn't have the power. She got it all wrong and it was the other way round and the witch got into the tower easily. It's a kind of birth and if it goes badly, if the midwives and doctors are negligent or worse, all sorts of terrible things can happen. All sorts of terrible things *have* happened and go on happening.

Pussy-cat face clears her throat. 'Well, I'm sure that's not the case but let's examine what you mean by that. What was that person's name?'

'Orla,' I manage to say. 'Her name was Orla Connor.'

It's not him, not Lucas that breaks my core. It's my beautiful Orla. My girl. I fought it all the way through when I knew she loved me. I let myself get bothered by him and now they are both dead.

'Her name was Orla Connor,' I say. 'And I loved her.'

Later, I take my coat from the cupboard at home and slip out. I won't even tell Mum and Dad where I'm going. We've got beyond all that, the three of us. The cold wind lashes at my cheeks and tosses my hair about. I head down the hill into the slanted park set on a hill. I look at the tree where Orla and I had our kiss, and I jump when I see Grace walking up the path, each boot step thumped onto the asphalt, her head down, mowing like a bullet. I think of fleeing but she's seen me, fixes me with her eye, and even at this distance there seems no option but to meet her. Is it luck or bad fortune that we move towards each other and end up underneath *the* tree when we join up?

'How are you doing?' she asks, and it's then I know she's checking up on me. Orla told me she did the same with her, 'testing out the defences' as she put it.

'I'm OK,' I say carefully, then start crying.

'We must stay safe,' she says. 'I'm counting on you. If ever you feel weak, you must remember about my mother and you must think what would happen to her if anything happened to me, and you must come straight to me to talk it over. Are you listening, Phoebe?'

I nod but I can't stop crying and a bubble blows out of my nose. I wipe it on my sleeve like a three-year-old. 'What's happened is so awful, though, Grace,' I whisper. 'It's unbearable.'

And then she says this thing that damn near finishes me. It makes me sink to my knees the force of it's so great, and I always thought she wasn't listening, never taking anything in – certainly nothing from that cancerous, murderous, hellish play – but she must have been because she turns to me and quotes those terrible words:

*What's done cannot be undone.*

# 47

# Grace

Wipe that smile off your face, you stupid bitch.

Except I can't.

He needs to sleep. His tiny eyelids came down in a second, making two pods of his eyes. His cheeks have turned sleepy pink from the warmth of the cot. I know he needs to sleep yet I cannot quite draw my fingers away from stroking his soft hair and feeling the hard nut of his skull beneath. And I still haven't wiped the silly-bitch smile from my face. It comes unbidden, stretching my cheeks.

I wind up the mobile above his cot. Not to soothe him, because he is deep and fast asleep now, but for the pleasure of seeing the constellations of stars and planets whir around the room and across his face. The music it plays is such a soft tinkle it barely stirs him. There are carrots and potatoes on the breadboard downstairs, chopped ready for tonight when Daniel will be home. There are sheets flapping on the line in our tiny garden. What a good little housewife I've turned out to be. I grin some more and twirl the mobile with my finger. In our tight compact new build it's easy, really easy, to keep everything clean. It comes naturally to me, caring for a baby. I'm always mindful. On the coffee table downstairs are the accountancy books I will study once Sam is asleep, then at the first sign of his cry I will mark my place in the book and go to pick him up. For the moment, though, I linger, smiling and stirring the mobile.

Then, reluctantly, I quietly gather the dirty laundry from the floor and bundle it under my arm. I hesitate when pulling the door to and end up leaving it ajar, not wanting to be cut off completely from his sleeping form.

I'm still smiling on my way downstairs to the kitchen, the babygros for the laundry packed under my arm.

In this house I have known such moments of perfect joy that I didn't think were possible. The baby tucked into the crook of Daniel's arm at the breakfast table, steam from the coffee fogging them over slightly, is an image for me that no masterpiece of Italian art, no piece of music or chunk of carved marble could ever even get near.

All this love, but what was that . . .?

A chill descends the back of my neck. I stop halfway down the stairs with my foot poised in mid-air. It's the love that over the years has made me like a hunter. It was either that or to feel everything I cared about could be hunted down and slain without a thought. I had to turn the tables to survive, so now I strain my ears. That's how it's got me through the years. The hyper-alertness. A bird pecking on the window will have me suddenly sitting straight up, the trill of the phone sends a bolt of electricity through me, my hands tremble as they open any letters that look official. I'm always thinking I've heard something when it's just the wind or the house settling in on its foundations or a shouted greeting two streets away. Since Sam was born it's got more acute to the point where sometimes I actually put up my head and sniff the air. I do this now and finally the stupid grin gets wiped off my face in an instant.

What alerted me? Had it been an imperceptible cough from the kitchen? I can't be sure but I know my skin is crawling.

I run my hand over my scalp, over the short and bristling hair.

'Who's there?'

It may be my imagination but it's like something has gone stiff and silent. I drop the baby things and clatter down the rest of the stairs.

I recognise Phoebe straight away. She's aged more than you'd expect in the two decades since I've seen her but I know who it is, sitting at my kitchen table.

I look at the open window, the soft breeze blowing through, and I don't bother asking how she got in. I imagine her scissoring her way in one long leg at a time while I was upstairs folding the blankets over Sam, and it makes me think of the snake coming into the Garden of Eden. Did I sense something upstairs? A momentary darkness shivering over me, or am I only thinking now that I did?

I sit opposite her. 'Can I make you some coffee?' I ask, like she is a normal visitor.

Her long fingers flutter at her eyes for a second. 'No thank you.' Then, 'You don't look very pleased to see me.'

I force a smile back onto my face.

For years I kept some hemlock in a plastic bag wedged behind the boiler, ready for just this eventuality. I'd foraged it myself and dried it out. Those were the years of fear that could sometimes overtake me and having it seemed like some witch talisman against her; the thought I could give it to her to drink if she ever turned up again somehow soothed me. Then Sam came along and it worried me having it in the house and I threw it away. Would I have really done anything with it anyway? I doubt it. When it was gone I was left with addled fantasies, the kind you have just before sleep, which curdle and break apart, that I could possess a special gun meant just for witches, for Phoebe, and she would disappear in a puff of smoke when I shot her. That perhaps she was dead already and lying rotting under the ground.

There's silence. We examine each other's faces, with our hands on the table. It reminds me of prison visits I've seen on the television. She's lost her beauty, that's the first thing that strikes me. It's become pinched and unlovely. The undertow of fear has left a mark on her face and sharpened all the lines. Her baggy stylishness has gone too, the days when she could simply throw on an old man's long coat and look beautiful and dashing. Now, it looks sloppy and unkempt. Her dark curls have become fizzy and worn, cut shorter so they slump on her shoulders.

I ask her, 'Where do you live now?'

She shrugs. 'Still in York. Dad left – he's living in Hong Kong now but Mum's still around. I'm her carer, like you used to be for your mother, Grace.'

So, her mother got her in the end then. It doesn't surprise me.

'What about your mum?'

'She died. It was fine, it was peaceful.' It's true – she died as she lived, I guess, surrounded by people and by love. Grateful to the end. Gracious, like the name she gave me.

'When *my* mum dies I'll have the house,' she says in such a flat way that I can tell this is a mere echo, a reflex desire that's dwindled over the years to become almost meaningless.

390

I want to know, why now? Why has she chosen to come here now? I need to get in there gently.

'And you, how have things been for you?' I ask softly.

She shrugs. 'I have the same dreams but they don't bother me any more.'

I force myself not to glance upwards, towards the bedroom where Sam is sleeping.

'What dreams?'

She shoves her hands in the pockets of her baggy black blazer. 'It's always in Bath.' She stops, then starts again. 'I'm out and I realise that people are covered in blood. Not loads of it, though, more like it's a sweat on them, a kind of sheen. But gradually it starts coming from everywhere, gushing out of the downpipes on the houses, swirling across the streets, running down the walls. It comes down the sluice that fills the Great Bath up until it is full, one sticky glistening mass of it, and I know I have to go and swim in it and it terrifies me.'

No guesses for what that's about then, I want to joke, but I don't.

She shrugs again.

Then I see it. In a way, she doesn't care any more. She's so full up with horror that it barely registers. She's come to the end of something. That's why she's here.

She shakes her head and then stops; she has caught sight of Sam's bottle, half hidden by the teapot on the dresser.

'You have a baby? Grace, really? Do you really have a baby?'

I'm thinking of lying but her eyes are clicking all over the room, taking in tiny bits of evidence: the blue plastic spoon with the rabbit handle on the dresser; the jar of puréed food

391

by the kettle; even the special sensitive soap powder on the floor by the washing machine.

She leans forward. For the first time she looks awake. 'Where is it?'

I dry-swallow. 'Out. Being looked after by a friend.'

I cannot let on that Sam is sleeping upstairs – not with her here and her hands touching her face in some sort of pattern every few seconds. With the dead look in her eyes. If Daniel came back, who knows how things might spill over. It's not only that thought that makes me want to get her out of the house. She stinks of the night; there is a darkness about her. I don't want that smell travelling upstairs and filling Sam's nostrils.

I pray that he doesn't wake and start crying.

The thing I remember about Phoebe is that if you don't agree with her she can go wild, thrashing, unpredictable, like the time she wouldn't give Orla the coat and I had to slap her. I have to coax her.

'Let's go for a walk,' I say.

She looks up. 'Where?'

I widen my eyes at her.

'What? Really – there?'

'I go all the time.' That's a lie, of course. I haven't been anywhere near the Spinney since that day.

She thinks it over. 'Perhaps,' she says. 'It's time.'

We leave the house, leaving Sam asleep upstairs, and I try not to think of that invisible thread between Sam and me getting thinner and thinner and running out. It reminds me of Mum and when I sneaked out of the flat and thought of her as a little breathing insect she was so far away. I think of a pair of scissors and chop the thread between us.

Our footsteps fall in line with each other. My house is on the edge of town and closer to the Spinney than when we lived in the tower block, so it's not long before we're on the path by the river. There's a sharpness to the day that pricks at my face. The vegetation next to the river stirs.

We reach the fields that lead to the Spinney and I want to cry out. The tall grass and the crops ripple and moan, and the lines of the horizon cut into the sky in a way that is both dreadful and familiar. Phoebe turns into the path that leads to the Spinney. She looks like an ancient scarecrow in this landscape.

'We can't go in there,' I cry out.

She turns sharply and I can see I'm on the point of giving myself away.

'Why not?'

'They've mended the hole and put barbed wire on top of the wall.' I'm lying, of course. I can't bear going near that stinking place with all its dirty magic still hanging in the air. If I breathe it in it could finish me.

She frowns. 'I thought you said you come here all the time.'

'I do.' I nod over to a stand of trees fringing the top of the ridge where the field slopes upwards in a gentle hill. 'I go up there and look. It's peaceful. Come on.'

I turn and start walking and hope that she'll follow without an argument. After a few minutes I hear her footsteps behind mine.

It's a fair way to the trees and uphill so by the time we reach them we're both a little out of breath. We stand on the bare brown earth and look out across the fields towards the river and to the other trees that border it.

Over there, I think, among those trees we murdered a man.

I think of the years since, how many times the leaves have wept to the ground and the grasses crumbled and rotted away and then sprung up again in the next year, over and over.

'It wasn't you,' Phoebe says softly, and I can't help it – I startle.

'What do you mean?'

'I'm not sure if it was you. I find it hard to remember now. For a long time I thought it was Orla, but now when I think of it sometimes I see the knife in my hand. It's all so difficult.'

'Let's sit,' I say, and we do, on the cold earth.

'Do you remember us talking about the three of us being buried side by side?' Her eyes are on my face.

I don't but I nod anyway, to humour her, but also because there is a kind of sense in it too. The three of us are locked in such a way that maybe we will lie in our graves side by side, our flesh gradually conjoining because of what binds us. But there is Daniel and there is Sam, and that's why our flesh cannot meet just yet.

She speaks quietly of how she longs for it sometimes. When she tells me she has actually bought the two plots next to Orla, a bone-deep dread takes hold of me that almost causes me to gag.

I breathe my way through it and let her speak.

And then we lie down and I let my voice join with hers. I roll onto my side and look into her face as she tells me about a tree in her garden, one with seeds so poisonous that eating just one or two is enough to kill you.

I remember how our minds are magic lanterns and we can see what we want or what we're most afraid of, even if it doesn't exist. How things can be pushed in there, just like the weird sisters did with Macbeth. I ask her to describe those seeds and how they feel to the fingers and what they'd look like on the tongue. She tells me in a way that is shot through with longing.

The sun is high in the sky by the time she leaves. I come back to myself with a start. I'd even forgotten Sam, lying there all this time, probably screaming blue in the face by now, so intent I was. I didn't let on once or tell her how I know it's those with other people to protect who fight the hardest to survive. That's how I've done it all these years.

I see her leaving, her figure getting smaller and smaller as she walks away into the landscape.

I know how it'll be and what will happen now when those thoughts start creeping back to her late at night. I know what I've just done. She came back for some kind of resolution, for us to finish this together, but I knew I'd have to weave a kind of magic to survive. And after all, she forgot.

I was a witch once too.

# Acknowledgements

A heartfelt thanks to my inspired and inspiring editor – the brilliant Louisa Joyner. Also thanks to the very lovely and very talented Alice Lutyens – you are one in a million, Alice. A huge thank you to Faber publicist Sophie Portas for her sheer energy and dedication – you are a total joy to work with. Melissa Pimentel, deep gratitude for your outstanding work in foreign rights at Curtis Brown. To the sales team at Faber & Faber – who traverse the country, combining phenomenally hard work with enthusiasm and good humour – a huge shouted-out thanks!!! Libby Marshall, thank you for your wonderful reading of the manuscript and help with all things practical. Luke Bird, whose cover design captures the book so creatively and boldly – a big thank you. Thanks to Tamsin Shelton for her impeccable and elegant copy editing. Anne Owen for seeing the book safely through to press with such care and professionalism, and to Ruth O'Loughlin who applied the same care and kindness with paperback editions – thank you! To the brilliant proofreader Lisa Morris – I am extremely grateful for your assiduous and creative work. And to all my fellow writers who, when startled out of writing burrows to meet at literary events, are unfailingly generous and great fun to share a stage with. I feel ridiculously lucky to be part of this community – thank you. Also very special thanks to my Mum, who sowed the seeds at a very early age for a lifetime love of books and reading.